Praise for

'A stylish and entertaining debut in which a coven of lesbians use every means at their disposal – community, witchcraft, art and love to preserve their women-only paradise from men. The dialogue absolutely sparkles. *A Circle Outside* is funny and full of heart – but also wise in its resistance to easy conclusions about whether the sexes can or can't share a planet and a history in harmony'
Polly Clark, author of *Ocean*

'*A Circle Outside* will instantly transport you to the dusky beauty of California's redwood groves and the heady liberation politics of lesbian community in the 1980s. Rosewood has written a wild, witchy and whimsical book with engrossing and complex characters. This novel is nearly impossible to put down'
Irene Reti, author of *Out in the Redwoods*

'With enthusiasm, good humour and fellowship, the women of *A Circle Outside* break new ground. The fresh growth on this farm is joyfully rampant, in so many ways'
Roger Swain, presenter of *The Victory Garden*

'Witches, lesbians, psychedelic trips and political activism set among the redwood groves of 1980s California is a bubbling cauldron of interpersonal strife, love affairs and feminism – all dished up with a side order of wisdom and humour. *A Circle Outside* is a cracking read which is sure to appeal to anyone who ever had a misspent youth or an ideal or two'
Sally North, Holythorn Press

Linda Rosewood writes about lesbian culture, politics and history. She is a Californian now living in Ireland. *A Circle Outside* is her debut novel.

A Circle Outside

Linda Rosewood

Published in 2025
by Lightning
Imprint of Eye Books Ltd
29A Barrow Street
Much Wenlock
Shropshire
TF13 6EN

www.eye-books.com

ISBN: 9781785634284

Copyright © Linda Rosewood 2025

Cover design by Nell Wood
Sappho translation on p5 by Mary Barnard
'Sleeping Beauty' by Olga Broumas on pp92-3 by kind permission of Yale University Press
Typeset in Adobe Caslon Pro and Caflisch Script Web Pro

The moral right of the author has been asserted. All rights reserved. No part of this publication may be reproduced, stored in a retrieval system, or transmitted, in any form or by any means without the prior written permission of the publisher, nor be otherwise circulated in any form of binding or cover other than that in which it is published and without a similar condition being imposed on the subsequent purchaser.

British Library Cataloguing in Publication Data
A catalogue record for this book is available from the British Library.

Our authorised representative in the EU for product safety is:
Logos Europe, 9 rue Nicolas Poussin, 17000, La Rochelle, France
contact@logoseurope.eu

We shall enjoy it.
As for him who finds fault,
may silliness and sorrow take him!
Sappho

At the continent's edge, deep waters rise frigid and flush with food. When chilled vapours meet hot exhalations from the long inland valley, they condense and shroud ocean-facing ridges. Under the fog, life thrives in a churn of kelp and crab, raptors and salmon, cougars and carrion. Towering over this bounty is the tallest thing alive, the California coastal redwood.

Redwoods once lived in many forests, on all continents. Now, *Sequoia sempervirens* grows only at the edge of California, on long mountains beside the sea, surrounded by lands too hot or too cold, like a secret island.

California: so named by men far from home who remembered a story about an island; an island of women, living alone without men.

I

Casting the Circle

One

The lesbian witches intended to fix their own shit, not the whole wide world and everybody in it. They were practical that way.

'The circle is open, but never unbroken,' affirmed a witch, wearing a white robe covered in feathers.

'*Merry meet, and merry part, and merry meet again,*' sang another in a black robe and a mask of flame.

Then the witches – they were a coven of eight – tossed up their hands and took off their masks, laughing and wiping the sweat from their faces. They had visited the Land of the Dead and returned safely. They were back in Santa Cruz, on the last day of October, 1983.

They left the candles burning on the messy altar in the living room and crowded into the kitchen. They pulled dinner from the fridge and oven and sat down. The seven housemates and one guest fitted perfectly around the table, and Wren happened to sit next to the guest, Robin, Nikki's cousin. Wren noted Robin brought tabouli.

A witch in a satiny, rainbow-hued robe and a stereotypical pointed black hat called over the commotion. 'Hey, Robin, what's the difference between parsley and pussy?' This was Lupe, who often soothed social awkwardness with a joke.

Robin looked shocked. 'I don't kn—'

'EVERYBODY EATS PUSSY,' the coven shouted, Lupe conducting the chorus with her chopsticks.

Robin shook her head, smiling. 'Ah, lesbians.'

'We sure are,' said Lupe. 'Aren't you?'

'Let's say I like parsley also,' Robin replied drily, in a voice like Jodie Foster.

Wren filled her plate and took more tabouli than anyone else. She liked ritual magic, but loved the feast afterward more. She hadn't eaten parsley for a long time. She kept silent for most of the meal, as her housemates complimented Lupe on getting the harvest in just before the rain, Hazel on her succotash, and Ginny on her elaborate salad. The women explicitly avoided discussing the ritual they had just completed, or their impending eviction. That would come later.

Wren half-listened and slowly buttered a roll. She used it to push tabouli onto her fork. The ritual had left her disappointed and she wanted to figure out why. They had begun as always, with each witch swearing to enter the circle 'in perfect love and perfect trust'. They had raised a cone of power, grounded the energy, then entered a trance. Together, they had imagined walking into a cave, crossing a dark lake on a magical boat and meeting ancestors on an island.

But when the other women began murmuring and communing with ancestors, Wren had just stood there, wordless. In her imagination, an old lady approached, crowned with yellow hair in a beehive. Her pear-shaped body swam in a purple paisley shift. More middle-aged fat ladies in loud dresses appeared. They led Wren in a circle-dance she had learned as a child, but gave her no messages from beyond the grave.

She should have expected this feeling of dissatisfaction. The coven held Halloween rituals on the night 'when the veil between the worlds is thin', they said. Her coven sisters sought advice from their ancestors, learning family secrets, and speaking again with loved ones they actually knew. For these witches, Halloween wasn't macabre. But Wren was adopted. She wished rituals could help her understand her mother, but ancestor rituals engendered a curiosity about blood-relatives that conflicted with a shameful disloyalty to the single parent who had raised her.

Wren avoided further contemplation of her mother-damage and helped stack up plates. Everyone else was avoiding talking about The Eviction.

Kelsey had pushed her mask up onto her head. Now she looked like her hair was on fire. She was teaching Robin to pronounce Samhain, *sah-win,* and said it was an Irish word.

From Wren's other side Lupe was shrieking, 'I vant to saak yoour blaad,' baring her teeth on Hazel's neck. Her witch's hat fell onto the table and Wren saw it was covered in plastic spiders. Hazel laughed and squawked. Hazel's pointed hat was a straw cornucopia, tied under her chin with green ribbon. It looked sillier than she probably intended. Her shirt and robes and jewellery were all oranges and yellows. Hazel never dressed up like an identifiable goddess – only the pure essence. Wren loved how her coven sisters interpreted the symbols of their Dianic wiccan tradition by doing whatever they wanted. Across the table, Ginny was still wearing small horns, visible among her dark curls. She always dressed like an animal at their rituals. Wren assumed they were meant to invoke a goat, not the devil. Nikki had worn her usual plastic child's mask, this one featuring the huge teeth of a beaver.

Suddenly, Wren heard Robin's voice in her ear, asking who she had been dressed as.

'Persephone.' Wren adjusted the black bodice of her gown and wondered how much Greek mythology Robin knew. 'Do you know her?'

'I've met her.' Robin answered as if the goddess were someone who worked at the Food Bin, and not Persephone, Queen of the Underworld, Daughter of Demeter All-Giver.

Gloria had overheard. She leaned forward, pushing back the sleeves of her white-feathered owl robe. Wren assumed it had something to do with Gloria's favourite goddess, Athena. Gloria could dress like a bird and never look ridiculous. She asked expectantly, 'Did you speak with Persephone tonight?'

'I didn't speak to anyone.'

The witches around the table fell quiet.

Robin looked at the faces of her intensely curious new friends. 'I saw what I always see.'

Wren felt an instant affinity. Robin also had a mediocre ritual. She noticed that Robin was still wearing one of the coven's black choir robes from the Bargain Barn. During the ritual, she covered half her face in a black velvet mask rimmed with orange sequins. Wren wondered what that costume meant.

'I've heard of the Land of the Dead, but it's not that,' Robin was saying. 'I'm cold. A circle of stones surrounds me. Outside the circle is nothing but open prairie, with lights far away, like campfires.'

Gloria put down her wine. 'You're all alone without your ancestors?'

'When I die, I don't meet anybody,' said Robin. 'I'm stuck

in that stone circle and must live again, remembering every life that came before. The future is my afterlife.'

Gloria wanted more detail, but Kelsey interrupted.

'It's getting late. Robin, if you don't mind, we have some household business to deal with.' She looked significantly at Gloria.

'We've all read the letter,' Gloria said. 'He's kicking us out. We only have thirty days.'

'That *fucker*!' Lupe spoke for all of them.

'I don't want to move again,' moaned Hazel. 'Last summer's garden had the highest yield yet.'

Lupe put an arm around her. They had been best friends since high school, and they were so often together that people assumed they were lovers. They weren't any more.

'If we move, maybe I can get a dog,' Ginny said. For her, the worst part of being a renter was the prohibition of animal companions. Ginny had put on Nikki's silly mask, and Nikki was wearing Ginny's horns. Above Nikki's heavy eyebrows and wide grin, they absolutely looked devilish.

'Can't you do something, Nikki?' asked Gloria, pointedly. Nikki and Robin were related to most of the old Italian families of the county, including their landlord.

'I can talk to him,' Nikki said reluctantly, 'but that family connection isn't what it used to be since I came out.'

'They had to have known,' said Lupe. 'It's not how she looks…'

Nikki completed the joke. '…It's how she looks back.'

Their chuckles died, and the certainty of impending eviction settled around the table. Wren felt the warmth of Robin's shoulder against her own, then caught Nikki nodding at Robin. The cousins shared a familial resemblance, but Robin's delicate features contrasted with Nikki's burliness.

The corners of Robin's mouth turned down when closed, a sad expression that Wren found perversely attractive.

Robin cleared her throat. 'Nikki wants me to tell you I bought a property up in Bonny Doon. It needs some work, but maybe you'd like to move there.'

'Robin bought Nana Nicola's old apple ranch,' Nikki explained with a wicked chuckle. 'The uncles were counting on inheriting it.'

The dejected women exploded with excitement. Robin and Nikki described a large old house surrounded by acres of redwoods, with an orchard and vegetable garden. As Robin tried to answer Lupe's questions about apples and Hazel's about southern exposure, the other women wanted to know about the number of bedrooms and how much the rent would be.

Robin shrank back and pretended to duck under her own arms. 'Maybe you should just come up and see.'

A quick survey of work schedules resulted in everyone looking at Wren.

'I was going to paint in the Pogonip, but—'

'We all like your landscapes,' Gloria said, not even hiding her manoeuvre, 'but your coven needs you.'

Wren glanced over at Robin, who gave her an inviting smile. Wren could not resist returning it. She agreed to visit Robin's land the next morning. The dread of eviction seemed magicked away.

Two

Early the next morning, Wren heard Robin's truck and ran down the driveway. She felt confident in that blue shirt-dress she made last summer.

She opened the door of the red Toyota pickup and climbed in. Robin hadn't stopped for coffee, but the cab was delightfully warm. They headed up Bay Street, past the open fields of the university, and into the mountains. Santa Cruz was known for its beaches, but redwood forests surrounded the city.

'Sorry about the bouncy truck,' Robin said, twisting a dial on the dashboard. 'But the heater works.'

'I don't mind.' Wren pulled her legs under herself and leaned against the door. 'I like old trucks.'

Robin had the soft-butch look, hair like Jackson Browne, dark eyes, that serious mouth, and a decisive hand on the gearshift. Wren suppressed a desire to caress her worn suede coat. That, and the lack of coffee, ended conversation for a while.

They wound through redwoods on Empire Grade, the road following the ridge of a long mountain called Bonny Doon. After fifteen minutes of watching the growing winter light on the passing redwoods, Wren was able to ask, 'Did you grow up in this house?'

Robin answered after a moment, as if she had been half-asleep too. 'No. I visited Nana in summer. Nikki, me, and the other kids used to run wild over her ranch. Old buildings to explore and rusted equipment to play on. We camped in the meadow, caught turtles in the pond. We climbed trees so high we could see forever.'

'When you're a kid, you think summer will never end.'

'That's right. But suddenly you become a girl.'

'Puberty?' Wren rolled her eyes. 'I wasn't a tomboy like you, but I wouldn't live through that again for all the tofu in hippie town.'

'Besides breasts and periods and the end of roughhousing, I also started having past-life memories.'

'Puberty *and* past-life memories? What a nightmare.' Wren had never had a past-life memory.

'Before I figure it out, growing up *is* a waking nightmare. My memories speak to me from trees and hillsides, pictures and foreign languages. Stuff like that. Memories sing in my head.'

'Your memories sing to you,' Wren repeated politely.

Robin smiled at her. 'I don't care if you believe it. It's true for me.'

Wren had already experienced some pretty weird shit with her coven. 'I'd like to know more. Our coven doesn't question our gnostic revelations.'

'Is that why your rituals include talking to dead people?'

'We use the altered states of ritual to bring back wisdom.'

'I thought you used rituals as an excuse for a party after.' Robin winked.

Wren winked back. 'We don't need an excuse. We live together. But that's why we need to find a new place. It took a long time to find the right housemates who don't argue about chores or meat-eating.' Wren looked out of the window at the passing trees. They had worked so hard to get to where they were, and now it could all fall apart. 'My housemates are my true family. I'm adopted and don't know my birth mother.'

Robin didn't make that mewing sound that most people did, so Wren continued.

'My mom lives in San Francisco. She's really cool. She was a Beatnik before the hippies.'

Robin slowed through a tight curve. They'd gone further up Empire Grade than Wren had ever been.

'She's been taking care of my grandmother, who had a stroke. That's why I dressed like Persephone last night. I've been thinking about mothers and daughters and how they love each other, even when separated by death.' Wren patted that soft suede sleeve. 'Sorry, I don't mean to get heavy. We don't need to talk about it.'

'It's okay,' Robin assured her. 'But this is our road.'

They had reached the top of the ridge. A smaller road to the right led down to Boulder Creek, but Robin eased into the one-lane gravel road on the left. They crossed a narrow bridge over a creek, then up the other side to a muddy clearing in the forest. Robin stopped in a large open area in front of a boxy Yankee farmhouse, with deep Mexican porches ringing both storeys. Narrow dormers studded an attic. A long time ago, someone had painted it white, and most of the windows still had their faded red shutters.

'This is the place,' Robin said. She tossed the keys on the dash and jumped out. She gestured to the left. 'Over there is the barn. Beyond it is the orchard. The creek we crossed is our water supply.' She pointed to a rutted road on the right. 'Up there is an old garden, and beyond it, a meadow. We can call this clearing in the forest "the plaza", but mostly it's a parking lot.'

Wren slipped down from the truck, grabbed her bag and settled the strap over her shoulder to calm herself. Her tummy fluttered. She walked toward the house curiously, aware this could be her first moment of walking on their own women's land. She heard quail calling from the edge of the forest.

Robin called to her from the porch, playing tour guide. Wren ran across *the plaza*.

'Wren…' Robin's sad mouth broke into that friendly smile that showed her teeth. 'Wren,' she said again, as if she was admiring it. 'Is that the name your mother gave you?'

'She named me Brenda. But "Bren" becomes "Ren", so I spell it with a W. The name I chose fits me better, don't you think?'

'Much better.'

'I tell people my last name is Kildare, but it's not my family name. It's the place where Bridget's fire burned in Ireland.' Wren didn't understand why she was talking so fast. 'Did your mother give you your name?'

'Yes. She said I liked to watch the birds out the window.'

Robin was staring at her. Was it the blue dress? 'Are those axes on your belt?' she asked.

'Labryses. Nikki made a die in a metalworking class and I stamped the belt.' Wren didn't say that Nikki helped her make the belt when they were lovers. She didn't want to think of her ex-lover at that moment. She was contemplating a next-lover.

'From Crete.' Robin knew and wasn't asking.

'It's a symbol for lesbians now. Gloria taught us about labryses from a book. It has a labrys on the cover. Gloria will probably tell you to read it.

'I think I already did. Let's go inside.'

Wren stumped up three sagging steps. Scrap lumber, bed frames, a doorless refrigerator, most of a motorcycle and an erupting couch occupied the porch.

'All this shit was here. I didn't want to hassle Nana, so I bought it as is.'

The front door opened to a room as wide as the house. To each side, an empty fireplace. A cot with a tidy sleeping bag stood near the fireplace on the right. Under it, a phone, phonebook and answering machine. Otherwise, the room was empty.

Wren spun around the centre, arms wide. Then she stopped, noting a dark doorway near the right-hand fireplace.

Robin noticed. 'That's the kitchen through there and that...' she pointed to a door in the other corner '...is so full of junk, I don't know what it is.'

'Is there a bathroom?'

'Not really. Also, no inside stairs. The stairs are outside, around the back.' Robin looked embarrassed.

They picked their way through the kitchen, and Wren felt sad because there was no chance of coffee. She followed Robin to the back porch. Across a narrow yard were a few sheds, decomposing into the forest behind them.

Robin pointed up a stairway to the upper veranda. It didn't seem to be attached at the top. 'The stairs are broken, but I remember a lot of bedrooms up there.'

'How do you know you can live with us?'

'I don't. But I bought this place because women could live here. Nikki told me about your coven. You have worked out the usual problems. I can see that already.'

'You can?'

'Most women's groups last between six and eighteen months, just like relationships.'

Wren silently counted how long it took her to figure out Nikki was sleeping with the Introduction to Women's Spirituality teacher. 'I've noticed that when idealistic groups get together, the love that grows between them opens them to feel old hurts, but they can't name them. They call each other names instead.'

Wren finished counting. 'I thought they break up when they sleep with each other's girlfriends,' she said sarcastically, then regretted it. She felt something in her heart opening up and hoped the answer to her next question wouldn't slam it shut. 'Do you have a girlfriend?'

Robin shook her head as she prodded a rusted pipe with her boot. 'I've had thousands of lovers. This lifetime I'm more interested in what women do in groups, not couples. I like your coven, and you have your spiritual tradition already. But the other groups I've met…'

'Fight too much?'

'They break each other's hearts over one internalised oppression or another. Or one woman takes over and drives everyone else away.'

'We know about power-over stuff. Gloria wants to be high priestess, but we don't let her. We had drama a few years ago, and some women left. We're settled now.'

Wren looked back inside toward the dark kitchen, taking in what Robin might have meant by 'thousands of lovers'.

Behind her, Robin wandered around the junk-strewn yard, still talking about group dynamics. '...They splinter into smaller circles of in-crowd and out-crowd and ever more elaborate ways of signalling the difference. Everyone feels like shit because they know they've hurt their friends. They tell themselves the ex-friends *deserve* to be treated like shit.'

Wren turned back to the yard. She didn't understand what Robin had just said. 'Women hurt each other, then justify it?'

'It's human nature.'

It was all too philosophical for Wren. 'Speaking of nature, I need to pee.'

Robin apologised. 'The outhouse is a disaster. Just pee anywhere.'

Wren walked behind a shed and found a place to squat among broken apple boxes and beer bottles.

If she can't be one of Robin's thousand lovers, she'll be her funny friend. 'Oh great mother, here I squat again,' Wren shouted in a ritual voice. 'Accept this offering of ni-tro-gen.' She pulled up her underpants and rejoined Robin.

'Is that a ritual your coven does every time they pee?'

'No. But Hazel taught us about nitrogen during a ritual.'

They opened the door to a shed filled with junk, smelling of mould and animal poop.

'Gross.'

'Sorry.' Robin looked embarrassed again. 'Let me show you something amazing.'

She led Wren from the back of the house and along the line of trees ringing the plaza. 'In here,' she invited, then pushed through the low branches and disappeared.

'Where are you?' Wren flapped her hands against branches until she found the hidden opening. 'Ow! A branch hit me.'

'Careful.'

'But I made my nitrogen offering.'

The soft branches of younger redwoods closed off the edge of the forest like a prim skirt. Inside, the older trees had lost their limbs, and the two women walked through them easily. Robin strode up a gentle hill, her hips rolling confidently like a backpacker's. Wren's cowgirl boots slipped on the carpet of decaying red-brown needles everyone called 'duff'. She often hiked through the redwoods, but never without a trail. Robin knew where she was going.

Robin stopped at the base of a redwood stump twice her height and just as wide. Reddish-brown bark rolled and buckled its surface. She clambered around it, and Wren followed. When she reached the other side, she saw the stump was a sister to the giant that had once stood in the centre of this redwood circle. The clearing in the forest opened twice as big as their own living room. More than a dozen redwoods spired ten storeys above them. When Wren tipped her head back, she saw morning sun lighting up the crowns.

'This is amazing.'

'I told you.' Robin entered the circle and lay down in the centre, next to rotted knobs, remnants of an ancient tree.

Wren put her hand down to feel if it was dry, then looked back at the interior of the stump on the edge of the circle. 'Wow! It doesn't get more obvious than that.' Where the outer side of the stump was covered in impenetrable bark, a fire had hollowed the side facing the circle, leaving behind a black triangular cave.

'I will crawl inside that *yoni* and experience a vision quest,' Wren vowed. She glanced again at the sun and oriented herself in the circle, noting that the stump was on its southwestern edge. She imagined her coven sisters building altars at the Four Directions and a fire in the middle.

Wren sat herself down next to Robin. She wanted to do magic with Robin. She wanted to never leave this circle of trees. 'This could be our sacred grove.'

'A redwood circle is perfect for us, because it *is* us.'

'Us, like you and me?' Wren was already thinking people would make fun of them as friends with two bird names. She felt relieved her name wasn't Raven. Every coven had a Raven in it.

'Us lesbians. This wasn't always a forest. Not that long ago, this entire mountain was an industrial wasteland. They logged it and built San Francisco.'

'I thought redwood trees were thousands of years old.'

'These trees are the daughters of a tree they cut down a hundred years ago.'

'And those trees are like us?'

'When women grow tall, Patriarchy cuts us down, and our daughters grow up around us. But they don't grow back the same. As beautiful as this redwood circle is, it's a scar. Redwoods don't grow in a circle until they're cut down. But the stumps don't die; they become circles.'

Robin lay on her back and stretched out her long legs. Wren took a deep breath and lay beside her.

Robin said, 'The local Indian word for these trees sounds like "hope".'

Still looking up at the ring of tree limbs above them, Wren asked, 'Do you have hope? If you can remember all your lives, then you'll live forever.'

'I will, but I don't want to keep living in Patriarchy. Women finally have a chance to leave Patriarchy, heal ourselves, and show everyone else how to do it before Patriarchy destroys the world.'

'With nuclear winter?'

'Maybe. Or acid rain. Or outlawing feminism again.'

Wren thought she was kidding. Wren hated Patriarchy, but she had no patience with 'smashing' it. Her first lover taught her never to fight men, just ignore them.

Robin raised her voice and seemed to be speaking to the branches stretching above them. 'We have our moment now to end men's cruelty. We can create a world that is better for everyone.'

Wren took another deep breath and made a mental snapshot of those branches so she could paint them later.

'I want to live with women in a circle like these redwood trees,' Robin said more conversationally. 'Even with our scars.' Robin sat up. 'Lesbian witches like your coven have always existed.'

'You met witches in a past life?'

'There have always been women who disregarded men and created space for themselves. But men always stop us.' She paused and listened to the ak-ak-ak of a woodpecker. 'Sometimes other women try to stop us from escaping.'

'Stick with us; we're not like that.'

'I know. That's why I want you to live with me here. You're not like other women's groups I've met. I can't express it. Maybe you can. You're an artist.'

An owl hooted in the forest outside the redwood circle.

Wren grabbed Robin's hand. 'Did you hear that?'

'She's wondering *whooooo* will liberate women.' Robin pulled her hand away and pointed at the slender limbs reaching across the circle above them like a cathedral window.

'Do you see the dust in the sunlight?'

Wren focused midway down the trunks. 'Yes,' she whispered.

'I have loved and lost so many friends and lovers, daughters and mothers. As many as you can see floating there in the sun. Each one of those women is a person I loved and will never see again.'

Wren wondered again how many women Robin had loved.

'Most of the time, I push those memories away. But when I come here to this circle, I remember them – and all the times I failed.'

Wren promised herself to help Robin not fail again.

While they watched the sunlight play in the dust motes, the owl flew through the centre of the circle and toward the ocean. If they hadn't been looking, they would have missed her, for she made no sound, only flashing through the circle of light and disappearing into the darkness beyond it, leaving the light swirling.

Wren focused on the shining dust floating down on them like a blessing. She composed it all into memory. She pressed her hand flat to her chest and wished her coven sisters were with her. She brought them each into this circle, as if she were squeezing out colours across a palette: organised Gloria, comforting Kelsey, comical Lupe, practical Hazel, skilled Nikki, whimsical Ginny.

Her love for them rose up her body from her womb to her face and was almost too much to bear. She needed to hold these feelings in her heart. She rolled over and pressed her face into the duff. She smelled the decay, and because she was a witch, she smelled the release of the dead into the gathering of the living. Under the duff, she imagined the roots of the trees entwined with each other, sisters growing tall around the body of their mother. She imagined the trees reaching into the sky, a temple emerging from a horrific wound.

She remembered her mother and her ailing grandmother. Some day, all her friends would be dead, and herself with them. Even her art would decay. The unalterable finality of their lives rang her body like a bell, and she shuddered. Why does death intrude every time she feels most alive? Time to change the energy.

∞

'Let's climb the stump.'

Robin looked surprised, then smiled that smile again. 'Sure. I was getting morose.'

The stump's inner side was too steep. Outside the circle, the burls and deep grooves in the bark gave them plenty of handholds. Wren took off her boots, clambering up in her socks. At the top, the stump was deeply pitted and bristling with ferns.

They found a banana slug and a pink mushroom, but after admiring the redwood circle from this new perspective, Wren didn't know what else to do. Getting down would be hard. She looked over the inner edge. It wasn't too far.

'Let's jump.' Wren didn't know why she said that.

'You're crazy.'

'It will be fun.' Wren sometimes did reckless things when she liked someone.

'You first.'

Wren crossed her heart again. 'I would never leave you behind.'

'I'm not chicken.'

Wren lost her nerve. 'I'm too afraid to go down that way.' She turned away from the edge and carefully scooted down. She looked to see if Robin was following, just in time to see her disappear.

Wren shrieked. She looked over. Robin wasn't where she should have been.

'Robin? Robin!'

Wren crouched on the edge of the stump and jumped. Her legs buckled and absorbed most of the fall, and the duff was soft and accepting. As she rolled to her feet, she felt Robin's hands steady her, and their faces were suddenly very close. Wren pulled away and noticed again the intriguing hollow in the giant stump.

This is reckless. She tugged at Robin's hand and Robin followed to sit beside her inside.

'Let's try something. Do you know how? I'll show you.' Wren wrapped her legs around Robin's waist and her arms around her neck. She showed Robin how to fold her legs under so Wren could sit on them. They relaxed into a comfortable, but not-at-all-sexual embrace. They sat that way for a long time, resting their heads on each other's shoulders until they were breathing together.

'This feels good,' Robin said. Wren nodded her cheek against Robin's jacket. 'I'm rarely this comfortable in my body.'

'Our magic can help with that.' Wren squeezed her legs and held Robin even closer. 'I don't want this moment to end and be a memory.' Wren couldn't stop her heart filling up and melting open. She felt the heat of Robin's body surrounding her and melting into her own.

Robin shifted her legs. 'Would you like coffee now?'

'Coffee?'

Robin untangled herself and soon returned with a duffel bag. They sat at the mouth of the stump as Robin produced a flat stone from the duffel. The stone served as an altar for a backpacking stove she re-articulated in some skilful way, inserted a can of gas, and then crack! Blue flame!

She reached into the duffel again and extracted a tiny espresso pot, a canteen of water, and a bag of coffee that smelled like a million mornings. While the coffee heated, Robin produced six croissants, a wax paper bundle of butter, a small thermos of cream and a stack of espresso cups. Wren watched this conjuration without a word. Soon, Robin opened the espresso pot's lid, and they marvelled as the coffee bubbled out and down the sides of the centre spout.

'I hoped more of you would come today, so there's plenty.'

'You thought of everything.'

'I wanted to welcome you properly.'

Robin manifested multiple cups of espresso and they ate most of the croissants. Wren knew Robin wouldn't discard her like Nikki. But Robin didn't want another lover. 'Can I draw you?' Wren asked, retreating into art as she often did to console herself.

'Sure. Remember, every revolution needs artists.'

'I'm no revolutionary. I just want to capture this moment. I do that sometimes.'

Wren pulled her sketch pad out of her bag and moved away from Robin until she composed the apex of the stump's opening over Robin's head like a frame. A ray of sun touched her cheek.

Wren sketched for a while. After a few minutes, she looked up from her drawing. 'How old are you? Right now, I mean. If you don't mind me asking. I'm twenty-three,' she added, to be polite.

Robin tossed her bangs from her eyes. 'I don't mind. I was born thirty-three years ago. I'm as old as Jesus.'

'You're *older* than Jesus. He's only nineteen-hundred and

eighty-three.' Wren returned to her drawing.

Robin leaned back against the stump and let her bangs fall over her eyes. 'Will you help me explain to the others what we can do here?' She sounded less confident than before.

'I promise.'

Wren sketched for many silent minutes. In childhood, she had to console herself every day.

After she closed her sketchbook, she and Robin packed up the remains of breakfast and walked back through the forest. She planned to keep that sketch for the rest of her life.

But she kept her promise for less than twelve hours.

Three

'Hi, this is Wren. I hope I'm not waking you up. My mom called and I need to go to the city to be with her. My grandmother is bad and…this might be it. She'll kill me if I don't come. You don't know how she gets.'

Wren hated herself right now as she left her message.

'Robin, you're wonderful; your place is perfect for us.'

She almost said, 'I already love you.'

'Kelsey and Ginny are going to visit you in the morning. I told them everything. You don't need me to draw a picture. Ha ha. Bye.'

∞

Wren flaked out, so Kelsey had to do it. The sun wasn't yet up as Kelsey and Ginny drove to Robin's ranch.

'Wow, did you know Empire Grade went this far?' Ginny asked again.

Ginny was a morning person. Kelsey was not. 'Nope. Are

you wearing your horns?'

'Why not? We're headed to wimmin's land, aren't we?'

'So I hear.' Kelsey glanced at the gas gauge. 'This must be the turn.'

She wondered if the wooden bridge would support something as modern as her ancient VW. She blew out a sigh when they reached the other side. Ginny's head was out of the window; she was oblivious to Kelsey's caution. Downshifting, Kelsey drove up and into a clearing ringed with redwoods.

A two-storey house faced them, the kind Kelsey knew Lucy would love. Between themselves and the house was garbage. Men's garbage. Machine parts, noxious fluids, mildewed scrap wood, engines. The entire clearing was saturated in garbage, and at the centre, a hill of garbage. True to her nature, Wren hadn't mentioned the garbage.

Kelsey glared at the gauge one more time before switching off the engine. She could get to the station if she coasted.

Robin welcomed them with a smile as she strode toward them, stepping around the junk. As Kelsey often did when she was getting to know someone new, she wondered what Lucy would think of her.

'Robin! Robin!' Ginny leaped from the car, all legs and elbows, slamming the door behind her. It bounced open unnoticed. 'Sorry we're early. Have to go to work later.' She took one look at the house and threw her hands over her head like Nadia Comăneci at the Olympics. 'I love it!' She ran over to Robin and gave her a hug before the other woman was ready for it. 'Can I walk around by myself?'

'Go ahead,' Robin urged. 'Check out the garden. It's up that road.' She pointed to a rutted opening in the trees to the right.

'See ya!' Ginny scurried away.

'Be careful,' Kelsey called out, and unfolded herself from the driver's seat. She was a woman built for comfort, not speed. She reached into the back and retrieved a paper bag and her backpack. Ignoring the trash, she raised her eyes, admiring the morning light on slender redwood spires.

Robin didn't hug her, which Kelsey appreciated. 'I'm sorry about Wren's grandmother,' Robin said. 'Is she okay?'

'No. Her grandma is dying; she's grieving her and what they never had together.'

'She lived far away?' Robin walked toward the house and Kelsey followed.

'No. Wren's mom kept them apart. Wren's family is fucked up.'

Robin opened her arms toward the house, then turned around to face Kelsey. 'I'm afraid she's missing out on everyone's first impressions.'

Kelsey could see Robin's disappointment, a Wren-related feeling she knew well.

'Well…' Kelsey shrugged and nodded toward the pile of garbage. After a moment of awkward silence, they both laughed, and Robin said they already had something in common.

Robin pointed out the broken step as they walked inside. Kelsey placed the paper bag on it.

'What's in the bag?'

'Housewarming gift. For later.' Kelsey stepped into Robin's living room and immediately felt at home. 'Two fireplaces? Nice.' She reached in and prodded the handle of the damper.

'I'm sad about Wren's grandmother. They used to be close but her mother got jealous and fucked that up.' Kelsey stepped toward the kitchen. She poked the worn threshold with her foot and reached around for the switch.

'That light doesn't work.'

Ever the good girl scout, Kelsey pulled a serious flashlight from her backpack. It flashed on the metal sink under a grimy window and a huge range next to it.

'It's an O'Keefe and Merritt,' Robin said proudly. 'Old, but good quality.'

'I know. No relation though.' Kelsey explained the non sequitur. 'My last name is O'Keefe, but I spell it o-a-k-leaf now.'

Robin chuckled. 'That's good.'

'Not all puns are painful.' Kelsey opened and quickly shut both oven doors. 'I hope we can get it working.' She swung the flashlight to the left. The kitchen stored a rolled carpet, bits of plumbing, rusted tools, never-washed plates, a pile of hunting magazines and three chairs with busted cane bottoms.

'What's in that garbage can? It seems like people here didn't believe in garbage cans.'

'That's just *my* garbage,' Robin admitted. 'I've been camping here for a month.'

'I wonder if Nikki could build a kitchen table for us – you.' She stuttered, as if they were moving in. 'Where does that door go?'

'A pantry.'

Some day, the narrow room and its shelves would be perfect for storing the dry goods of a large household. Right now, it contained rows of rusted cans with their labels chewed off.

'Can you live here?' Robin asked anxiously.

Kelsey wordlessly retreated from the smell and began opening cabinets under the filthy counters. This place would take a mountain of work, but she tried to be hopeful. 'We have to live somewhere big enough for the seven of us.' When she got to the cabinet under the sink, her heart jumped and she slammed the door shut. She held her voice calm. 'There's a snake in there.'

'Can't be.' Robin rushed over.

'I'm not imagining.' Kelsey opened the cupboard again. 'There's a *snake* in your *house*.'

Robin peered in. 'Looks like it just ate something.' She tried to explain, as if Kelsey knew nothing about rattlesnakes. 'She's sleeping it off. Snakes are everywhere in the Santa Cruz mountains. It's more afraid of you than you are of it.'

Kelsey pressed down a rising red emotion. 'Somebody could get bit.'

'Snake bites are actually pretty rare.'

Only sarcasm could calm her now. 'Snakes are rare in kitchens and yet…' She gestured to the closed cabinet door like Vanna White, and lost her sense of humour. 'I'm getting the fuck out of here. Where does that go?' She strode out of the back door.

She sat on the step of the deep porch, head in hands. 'Why do I have to be the responsible one? I should be more like Wren.'

Robin squatted close but didn't touch her. 'It's more afraid of you than you are of it,' she said delicately.

'You said that.'

'Nobody is going to get bit.'

'How do you know?'

'I'm trying to help.'

Kelsey lifted her head and looked around. The yard smelled of old metal and fresh mould. A steep, dank, forested hill rose behind two wrecked cabins.

'Your place creeps me out.'

'I'm sorry. But we could make it a home.'

'I don't mind funky houses, but I won't risk my life reaching for a frying pan.'

'You won't. I'll fetch your pots and pans for you.'

Robin was doing her best. Kelsey gave her an indulgent smile and came back to herself. 'I'm sorry I freaked out.' She looked past the cabins at the trees behind them. 'I need to take a walk.'

'There's a path through there. It switchbacks right up to the orchard.'

'An orchard? That's what I need.'

Since her childhood, Kelsey had felt safe under trees. The old path rose steeply, covered in fallen limbs and thick duff. She loved feeling the thump of her heart under her breasts. At the top, she pushed away low branches and emerged into a meadow – no, not a meadow, a clearing in the redwoods – planted with apple trees.

Finding the snake had startled her, but something else had enraged her. The forest enclosed the orchard, and beyond them, the ocean, miles away. As Kelsey's heart steadied, her knees shook. She held onto the slender trunk of an apple tree not much taller than herself. A jay complained from a fir. She sat in the damp weeds and felt Lucy arriving.

She stretched out her legs so they wouldn't cramp and carefully laid her right hand over her left in her lap. 'Light of my life,' she whispered, and held in her mind the image of a flame, with Lucy's eyes beyond it, looking into her own. She breathed consciously, taking a slow breath in, holding it, then breathing out, and waiting a few beats before the next inhale.

'Hello, Kelsey.'

'Hello, Lucy.'

In Kelsey's imagination, a girl of about sixteen with high cheekbones and long dark hair rested a few yards away against her own apple tree. This time she wore a black leather jacket and the soles of her Doc Martens looked worn. *How can a ghost wear out her boots?*

'There are snakes in the house.'

'They won't be there long with the racket you guys make.'

'True.'

'Why did you run off up here?'

Kelsey opened her eyes. Sitting on the ground, she couldn't see the ocean any more, only these scraggly trees hanging on to last summer's ugly apples. Lucy looked cute, as always. She'd never know how archaic that turquoise choker was. 'When I walked into that kitchen, I already felt home. I feel I could live and die here.'

'What about the snake?'

'I got fucking *territorial* and could have ripped it in half. That kitchen feels like mine already. It's my destiny.'

'You know destiny is bullshit. What's the real problem?'

'I'm not like Wren. I'm poor; my parents are poor. This place is so far from work, I don't know if I can afford it even with free rent. It takes two extra hours to get to work and there's no bus. But I want to live here so bad.'

'Being poor doesn't matter. You have me.'

'I'll always have you, Lucy.' A golden light rose between them, a living woman and the memory of a dead girl. Lucy soothed Kelsey's anger, as always. 'Maybe I could work for Robin?'

'She seems like a controlling know-it-all.'

'Maybe someone in Bonny Doon needs a home health

aide?'

'You hate private clients.'

Kelsey shifted. Her butt was cold. 'If they move up here, I can't follow them.'

'Easy come, easy go. Everything you love can be gone in a moment.'

'You always say that.'

∞

Kelsey returned from the orchard to find Robin and Ginny devouring the last of the granola bars in the brown paper bag.

'There's stables up there, and a big meadow!' Ginny said. 'And Robin says we can get goats.'

Robin nodded at a thermos of milk and an empty mug.

'No, thanks.' Kelsey needed the oblivion of an eight-hour shift right now. She noticed that Ginny was sitting awkwardly on the wooden step. 'Are you okay sitting there, Ginny?'

'She means my littler leg,' Ginny explained to Robin. 'I had polio.'

Robin patted the leg affectionately. Somehow, they had become friends already. 'Hasn't slowed you any.'

'Never again.' Ginny crunched through a granola bar. 'Thanks for making these, Kelsey.' She caught the crumbs in her palm. 'When Kelsey's not working, she cooks. She says it keeps her sane in a man's world.'

'I haven't had home-cooked food in a long time,' Robin said. 'I could get used to this.'

Kelsey tensed up. 'Ginny, we need to get—'

'Okay, I'll go.' Ginny steadied herself on Robin's shoulder as she stood up. 'But Robin wants me to tell you I saw a snake, too. I'm not sure what it means. Does it mean something about reincarnation? Maybe it means something about Robin and this land? Or maybe it means something about my sexual energy and *kundalini* awakening.'

Kelsey stared at Ginny until she could recover from that tangle of symbols. 'Does it mean that Robin has snakes?' She looked at Robin, hoping she would laugh.

But Robin looked chagrined. 'I saw it too,' she admitted. 'It was only warming itself in the sun.'

'Since it was near the garbage pile, maybe it means' – and Ginny sang – *'all that dies shall be reborn.'*

'Maybe it means you won't move in,' Robin said softly.

'Maybe I will get a dog,' Ginny responded, but didn't explain because Gloria had arrived in her battered Volvo.

Kelsey had to agree with most people: Gloria Arriola was gorgeous. But Kelsey wasn't attracted. Women tended to admire those soft dark curls that framed Gloria's face, as well as her romantic eyes occasionally accentuated with natural makeup that she pretended didn't look like makeup. People also said Gloria 'took up a lot of space'. She wasn't demure; she was big-boned and wore low-cut tops that showed off her clavicles. Kelsey was only a little envious that she was an x-ray tech and could support herself working part-time.

Gloria joined them at the steps. 'Sorry I'm late; tell me everything.'

Ginny didn't disappoint. 'Me and Kelsey saw snakes. And there's a garden.'

'Oh. My. GODDESS!' Gloria shouted, and pretended to look for one in the clutter on the porch.

'You might want to keep your voice down,' said Kelsey.

'Snakes are deaf,' said Robin.

'Good to know, Encyclopedia Brown,' said Gloria. She

laughed to cover the insult. 'What's the plan for getting rid of them? Let's call the exterminator.'

'We don't need to call anyone,' Robin reassured her. 'The snakes will go away once we start living here.'

Gloria imagined the worst. 'Could someone be bringing the snakes here to scare you off? Nikki said her uncles wanted this land.'

'I don't think so,' said Robin. 'It makes more sense that the snakes were already here.'

'Don't be paranoid, Glow,' Kelsey said. Sometimes people called Gloria that, but she didn't like it. Kelsey tugged Ginny's hand. 'We need to get to work. I'm in Aptos today. Drop me off and you can drive yourself to Watsonville.' She tossed Ginny the keys. 'We'll come back another day and find out what the snake means.'

When they were back in the VW, Robin rested on the passenger window. 'Does the snake mean you won't move in?'

Kelsey wished she wouldn't keep asking that. 'My parents – goddess bless them – meant well, but I spent my childhood in a cold house with every kind of vermin.' She didn't want to answer. 'You're right about snakes being part of nature.'

'They are.'

'Let's see how everyone else feels. I have some concerns.'

'I hope you move in.'

Kelsey looked at Robin's earnest face and thought maybe she saw there just a hint of a spark. *Never sleep with a housemate.* Robin didn't pull back from the window.

'Are you two going to keep talking without saying anything?' Ginny turned the key and blew Robin a kiss. 'Say goodbye, Kelsey.'

Kelsey patted Robin's arm. 'Thanks for inviting us. You have a nice orchard.'

Four

Whether or not she moved in with Robin, Kelsey was leaving her kitchen. After work, she started packing it up, and when Gloria came home from Robin's land, she convinced her to help.

Gloria started by sorting the better leftover containers while Kelsey divided plates, bowls, and cutlery into 'needed this month' and 'potlucks and storage'.

'First of all,' Gloria began, 'I went to our *sacred grove.*'

'Ours?'

'Robin said even if we don't move in, we can use her redwood circle for rituals. She took me through the trees; it was really far going in and took no time to get back. Like another dimension. There was no path, but she knew the way. I could feel the energy signatures…'

Kelsey withheld comment with difficulty.

'…until she said, "We're here." The redwood circle is huge, bigger than the living room and dining room. At one side, a huge burned-out stump looks just like a *yoni.*'

'How appropriate.' Kelsey started in on the drawer of spatulas and ladles.

'It. Is. Perfect.' Gloria clapped her hands at each word to make sure Kelsey understood. 'First thing I did was lay hands on every tree in the circle. They revealed to me they are dryads. We could make a fire pit in the centre and build altars in the four directions.'

'Could you go through those towels and rags?' Kelsey said, annoyed. Wren would have pitched in without being asked. 'She wouldn't mind?'

'No. She gave it to us. We can drum all night, go sky-clad; all of it.'

'I'd like never to have to haul blankets and cauldrons in the dark for miles.'

'I *know*. So I did some magic. I lit sage and smudged the redwoods around the circle.' Gloria stood and re-enacted what Robin must have seen. '*Mighty and Formidable Athena: I invoke thee, and vow to keep this circle sacred, to protect this circle from those who would profane it, and dedicate my life to teaching your wisdom and ending Patriarchy.*' She sat down again and folded more dish towels.

'What did Robin say to that?'

'She said something about lifetime vows lasting longer than you want them to. She looked sort of freaked, like what happens in the presence of real magic.'

'She didn't look freaked at the Samhain, and that was real magic.' Kelsey remembered Robin looked sad, like Wren did. She needed to ask Wren about it. If she ever came home. 'Does she know much about…what we do?'

'Very little. When I said I dressed like an owl at Samhain because I aspected Athena, she thought Athena was someone in the coven she hadn't met!'

'Well, there *are* a lot of us.'

'She's been to Dianic rituals on wimmin's land, but was never initiated.'

'We're not initiated.'

'That's because you wouldn't let me.'

'It's Patriarchal.'

Gloria waved her hand to dismiss an old argument. She had finished the towels, but didn't start on anything new. 'I said I'm writing a book like Z Budapest, but Robin doesn't know her. When I asked if she knew her horoscope, she only knows she's Capricorn.' Gloria paused with a finger on her cheek. 'So maybe she *is* good with money.'

'If you think she's good with money, did you ask her about how we could afford to live way up there?'

'Of course.'

Good old Glow. She could be depended on to ask the hard questions no one else would. Kelsey dug through the recycling, looking for a box she might tape together.

'She can't expect us to move up there and work on her land for free. I won't do it, anyway. I told her all these women's collectives fail because they have to share money. Women need their own money, and to be paid for their work. I said just because I *like* to teach witchcraft doesn't mean people shouldn't pay me for it.'

'What did she say?'

'She asked me how we should do it.'

Kelsey handed her the box and a roll of tape. 'Please make this into a box again and fill it with cookbooks.' Gloria accepted this new assignment, maybe a little chagrined. Kelsey didn't rub it in. 'She didn't already have a plan?'

'No, she doesn't have a plan. She just wants us to move up there and live together. I told her I won't move in unless we figure out how to do money.'

'How does she expect us to live all the way up there, work on her land and still make money?' Kelsey shouted over her shoulder. 'I am barely making it as it is. Ginny makes even less than I do.'

'I know, Kelsey. You don't need to keep saying it. I'm going to do some aspecting work with Athena on Friday. Did you know she's the goddess of accounting? She'll know what to do.'

Kelsey was relieved that, as irritating as Gloria could be sometimes, she had talked to Robin about the money. Most lesbian feminists pretended money was the one part of Patriarchy that wasn't real.

Kelsey returned from the pantry with a paper bag of wax candle ends and drippings. 'Should we keep these?'

'Absolutely, there's still magic in them.'

'Okay. What does she do for a living?'

'I didn't ask her. She doesn't seem to have a job. Maybe a trust fund?'

'I don't think she and Nikki are a trust-fund sort of family.' Kelsey felt a spark of hope. Maybe Gloria would come up with something. But if they moved in with Robin…. 'I'm not sure I want to be in a coven with the landlord.'

'She's a natural. She has to join.' Gloria's enthusiasm was a surprise; usually hers was the strongest voice against new coven sisters. 'Think of it, Kelsey. If she can remember past lives, she would teach us how to do it. It would be our coven's Secret Teaching.'

Kelsey decided it was time to sit down and have a cup of tea before making dinner. 'We don't need secrets.'

'I told her Dianic witchcraft is not all incense and head-dresses. We do intimate things. Dark things. I told her

Dianic witchcraft is why we're still together.'

Kelsey had to agree. 'What did she say to that?'

'She's so focused on how separatism will change the world, she doesn't know how living with us will change her.'

This was another old argument between them. 'Gloria, I'm a separatist.'

'No, you're not. You work in a rest home full of men.'

'That's not what I mean.'

'She has a separatist rule: no men on the land.'

Kelsey lit the stove under the kettle and chuckled. 'What's the problem with that?'

'Rules aren't feminist.'

'*I'm* a feminist and I like that rule, although inconvenient.'

Gloria looked at Kelsey before visibly deciding not to argue. 'I don't mind separatism; I just don't think it is necessary. It's run its course.'

'Is that so? Women live free of men's oppression now?'

'We don't need to separate from men, because we are witches. We're empowered.'

Gloria couldn't see Kelsey roll her eyes because Kelsey was searching for the box of Almond Sunset tea. She found it, empty. 'What did she say to that?'

'She thinks all we need to do to defeat Patriarchy is live separately from men. As if that hasn't been tried before.'

'Has it?'

'What hasn't been tried before?' came a voice from the back porch. 'Sign me up.' Lupe came in, tearing off her boots and dirty rainbow socks. They could hear Hazel on the porch, starting the shower.

'We're talking about Robin.'

'I haven't tried her yet,' Lupe said salaciously. 'But Hazel and me are going up tomorrow afternoon.'

Kelsey served soup from the freezer for dinner. Before retreating to her room, she left another message for Wren on her mom's phone. Maybe Gloria and Athena would figure out the money. Maybe she wouldn't have to be left behind when they moved to a feminist utopia without her.

⊗

The Poet and Patriot was an Irish pub, pouring its warm Guinness in welcome to locals and immigrants and outcasts of all kinds. Santa Cruz didn't have a lesbian bar, and many dykes preferred the Poet's quiet tables to the Blue Lagoon's disco around the corner. The Poet had a unique odour that had taken root under the carpet and never gone away.

Kelsey sat opposite Ginny at a corner table. Something was stuck in her hair – no, Ginny apparently felt comfortable enough to wear goat ears in public. Kelsey loved that hand-knitted sweater, the one with a flock of goats gambolling across her chest and shoulders. Actually, Ginny looked normal, but was speaking nonsense.

'...Alabaster, Ringo, Lady...'

'What did you say?'

'I'm trying out names. Robin said I could get a dog.'

Kelsey looked up as Lupe and Hazel entered from the door on the alley. Lupe paused to theatrically inhale the Poet's aroma; Hazel waved and grabbed the two pints Kelsey had ordered for them.

Lupe was only twenty-five, and often tried to look like the tough girl – denim jackets and eye-liner on dress occasions – but had a lightness in her manner and made friends easily. She melted when she met a new mushroom. 'All mushrooms are magical,' she would insist if asked about some common toadstool. She didn't speak Spanish and didn't give a shit. 'My people owned all the land from the Blue Mountains west to Los Banos,' she sometimes said, but never elaborated on these Californio ancestors.

The Blue Mountains rose east of the Pajaro, the rich agricultural valley south of Santa Cruz where Lupe and Hazel had grown up. Relative to Lupe's, Hazel's family were new to California; her grandparents were Japanese immigrants who provided the labour and innovation for the 'salad bowl of the world'. Her face was wide, her thick legs ended in big feet, her muscled arms in small, strong hands. She kept her hair in a braid down her broad back. Where Lupe owed her garden centre success to her love of talking to strangers, Hazel had mastered the forklift and botanical Latin. People in town greeted her awkwardly because they knew her, but couldn't remember how. Mostly likely, she had converted them to her mulch religion.

Lupe sat next to Ginny, Hazel at Kelsey's side. Lupe toasted, 'To new horizons!' and at the same time Kelsey said, as always, 'Fires of Freedom!'

They drank and Hazel asked where Gloria was.

'She's doing a ritual with Athena tonight. We already know she wants us to move to Robin's land. What do you two think?'

'I like Robin,' Lupe said. 'But the first thing she wanted to know is if we'd heard from Wren – we haven't, of course. She thinks she needs Wren to convince us to move in.' Lupe tried to keep a straight face.

Nikki finally arrived, with a fresh barbershop haircut, wearing her shiny shirt and leather pants. She drank Anchor Steam, not Guinness. She pulled a stool over to their table. 'I can't stay. I don't have time for a lot of processing.' She kept her eyes on both doors, obviously waiting for someone. Kelsey asked her if there was anything about Robin they should know about.

'I'm glad she bought it, and not the uncles. It's perfect for us, and closer to my work up in the Valley.'

Kelsey tried to introduce her biggest worry. 'Why is she doing this free rent thing?'

Nikki didn't answer, distracted. 'She'll need me to restore it. I took a day off and made her a kitchen table. We're starting on the stairway next week, but you'll have to deal with your own rooms.'

Ginny returned to naming her dog. '...Arthur! Brodie! Pippin!'

Hazel leaned forward and asked mischievously, 'Since you can't spare your precious time, just tell us the worst thing about her.'

'I guess...I like her.' Nikki turned toward the table and gave them her attention. 'I have *always* liked her. In fact, she was my first crush.' Kelsey couldn't tell from Nikki's tone if this was a happy or sad memory. 'Then she grew up and left town. She abandoned me.' She put a dramatic hand to her forehead without messing up her hair. 'But I don't mind now.'

Hazel snapped her fingers. 'So that's why you have never had a long-term relationship!'

'No doubt— My friend is here. Gotta go.' Nikki got up and greeted a woman who looked like one of her kitchen remodel customers – and straight. They raised their eyebrows at each other, but said nothing. Nikki was Nikki.

'Moving on,' said Lupe. 'There are two cabins behind the main house. If no one objects, we want to fix them up and live in them.'

'And we found the old outhouse disgusting.'

Kelsey realised something. 'I didn't see a bathroom. Or even a toilet.'

Lupe and Hazel reached the same conclusion. Ginny stopped reciting dog names.

'I once built an outhouse with my dad,' said Kelsey. 'We can build our own. Make it nice.'

'Your back-to-the-land childhood will come in handy, Kelsey,' said Hazel with admiration. 'Robin showed me the old garden. It's about a half acre. Grown over with berries, but better than starting new like I had to do at Walnut.'

Kelsey knew Hazel already mourned her garden. The house would become offices, Hazel's garden a parking lot.

'Robin says she's been a farmer in her past lives.'

'Jeez, do you believe that past life story?' Kelsey scoffed.

Hazel shrugged. 'I told her we could convert one shed up there into a greenhouse. Robin accused me of being an optimist, and I said that's because I'm a gardener.'

'So, as an optimist, you don't have concerns?'

'Not really. And we connected on something else. She knows how, during the war, Japanese families like mine lost their farms. She says just because women and lesbians have rights now doesn't mean they always will.'

'Pessimists!' Ginny declared.

'You can joke, but my family never got their land back, and that's why every time I bring my parents homegrown tomatoes, they take it as an existential threat. I have a good feeling about her. She knows Scout Godfree.'

Kelsey brightened. She knew Scout from the herbalist conference last year. The only women's gathering she could afford.

'Robin met her last year when she was travelling. Robin knew Scout's limerick about the Vagetarian from Butte.'

Kelsey wished she could know Scout better. Maybe she should move to Oregon, where it was cheaper. 'Lupe, what did you talk to Robin about?'

'I told her about the tripping.'

'How did that come up?'

'She said Gloria told her Dianic witchcraft would change her, so I explained our ritual use of psychedelics.'

'And?'

'She said I could grow mushrooms on the land even if we didn't move in.'

'To sell?'

'You know I won't sell sacred elixirs. But she's cool with growing them. She asked if she could have some for her birthday.'

'Did you talk to that restaurant about gourmet mushrooms?' Hazel asked Lupe.

'Yup, already on it. Remember you laid me off already?'

Hazel needlessly apologised and gave Lupe a side hug. Hazel laid Lupe off every winter.

Everyone wanted to move up to Robin's property, but nobody was thinking about money. Too patriarchal, no doubt. Kelsey turned to Ginny. 'Have you thought about how you can afford to live so far away from work?'

Ginny looked at Kelsey like she was the crazy one. 'We'll figure it out,' she said confidently. 'Gloria has a *sliding scale*.' She made a motion with her hands as if it was an actual device. 'She is working with Athena on it.'

'Yeah, I heard.' Kelsey looked around the table at the excited faces of her friends. Robin's place seemed a perfect solution to the eviction. Free rent, big house, room to grow vegetables and mushrooms.

She glanced around for Nikki, but she was absorbed in

seducing her new friend.

Ginny had returned to trying out names: 'Luna! Shasta! Otter!'

Hazel and Lupe were talking about soil dynamics and mushroom compost. No one else was thinking about how to afford it, and how hard they would have to work. Kelsey tried to sound more enthusiastic than she felt. 'It sounds like everyone wants to move up there.'

'Gloria said we should have a meal at the house before we decide,' Ginny said, looking at Kelsey, because Kelsey would cook it.

They decided to gather at Robin's on Sunday, and initiate the kitchen table Nikki built.

'I'll leave another message on Wren's mom's phone,' Ginny offered.

'I won't cook a meal in that kitchen until it is cleaned,' Kelsey declared, and when no one responded, said, 'I guess I'll spend my day off cleaning Robin's kitchen.'

'You will love spending a day with her,' Ginny said.

'Why would you say that? I hardly know her.' But she did owe Robin an explanation if she wasn't going to move in. Just because you want something doesn't mean you can get it. Even if you get it, being poor can take it all away.

Hazel and Lupe finished their pints and decided to go to a movie at the Nickelodeon. Kelsey and Ginny said they were too tired, but really, they had just spent all their money.

'Pepper! I will name my dog Pepper!'

Five

With her work hours, Kelsey always woke up early. She didn't care if Robin wasn't up when she got there. For ten miles up the mountain, she rehearsed her speech, not noticing she took the curves too fast. She parked near the pile of garbage and walked into Robin's house without knocking.

Robin sat on a couch that wasn't there last week, warming herself by a fire, flipping through the *Express*. Kelsey held up a small foil package. 'Coffee cake? It's still warm.'

Robin nodded and sipped her coffee. Maybe she wasn't a morning person either. Kelsey walked past Robin and entered the dingy kitchen. It smelled like sawdust. Nikki's new table and benches filled the space across from the sink. Someone – probably Nikki – had fixed the overhead light. Now that she could clearly see the condition of the stove, Kelsey avoided opening the oven. The floor was swept, but the linoleum was torn and stained. A new refrigerator hummed in the pantry. It contained only beer and milk. Rust and rat shit remained on empty shelves.

She stood in the doorway to the living room. 'It's worse with the lights on.'

'I noticed,' Robin replied without looking up. Kelsey didn't feel ignored, but comfortable, like they were already housemates.

'Where's the coffee?'

'Help yourself.' Robin pointed at the blue camping stove that featured in Wren's story about the grove, and the white Roasting Company bag next to it.

'Couldn't face those burners, huh?'

'Maybe when I'm older.'

Kelsey set up the espresso pot and lit the stove. 'Coward. And yet I hear you plan to end Patriarchy simply by ignoring men,' she gently taunted.

Robin chuckled.

'Did you know we invited ourselves to dinner tomorrow?'

'Gloria told me. I'm looking forward to it now that we have a table. But the kitchen—'

'Let's clean that big O'Keefe and Merritt first – work up to the hard stuff later.'

'But you haven't decided to move in.'

This was the moment to fill the silence with all her rehearsed reasons, but the phone rang.

Robin straightened off the couch with a sigh and reached under her cot for the phone. Kelsey heard Wren's voice before Robin said anything. 'Robin, I just found out that everyone has been trying to call me.'

Robin held the phone so they both could listen. 'Hello?' she said.

'I'm so sorry.' The tempo and volume of Wren's voice exploded the quiet companionship between Robin and

Kelsey. 'My mom erased all the messages. She thought they were a wrong number.'

Robin responded tenderly. 'How is your mother?'

Wren heard Robin's compassion and calmed down. 'She's crying all the time but gets mad if I cry. The funeral was yesterday. I need to leave.'

'Everyone is coming up tomorrow for a meeting.'

Wren's tone got anxious again. 'I know. I just found out. I woke up Gloria.'

'Why are you calling so early?'

'Because I just found out that you were trying to call me.'

'Did you just say that?'

'Did I wake you up?'

Robin winked at Kelsey. 'Not yet.'

'Can you pick me up from the train in San Jose? There's no Highway 17 bus on Sundays.'

'Sure. We need to talk anyway.'

They arranged when and where. Robin hung up, and her face darkened. 'I'm trying not to feel abandoned.'

'We know that feeling. When her mother calls, she obeys.'

'She doesn't realise how much you need her.'

We do? 'Can you say that again?'

Robin misunderstood. 'I will, when I pick her up tomorrow.'

Kelsey wondered what Wren offered that was so needed. She helped out with cooking, was a reliable dishwasher, but a sort of unreliable friend. Kelsey appreciated her costumes and decorations and other witchy crafts – when she finished them.

She needed to tell Robin she might not move in, and that would be easier without eye contact. 'Let's clean up enough so I can cook tomorrow. Hungry dykes do bad things at meetings.'

The espresso gave them a delightful buzz. Kelsey scrubbed the sink and submerged the oven racks. Robin started in on the pantry shelves. Then Robin asked that question that lesbians always ask each other, the one that always broke Kelsey's heart a little.

'When did you come out?'

'I was young. Lucky me.'

'How did your parents react?'

Kelsey appreciated satisfying conversations, but she avoided telling her serious stories until she knew you better. Her friends had heard about her parents, two feckless back-to-the-land hippies who raised her in a home-made house in the forest outside Willits. So instead of telling her coming-out story – or confessing that she wasn't moving in – she gave Robin the one about the glass pyramids that sharpened razors, and the zucchini bread bakery disaster.

'...So yet another failure for the commie hippie entrepreneurs.'

Robin took a break and filled a glass from the faucet. 'Thanks for cleaning the sink, but I think I'll get a new one.'

'Let's get one of those new sprayer things too.' Kelsey paused. She was acting like this was her kitchen. 'If you want to.' She pulled off the oven knobs and dropped them in soapy water. She didn't want to talk about being too poor to accept free rent. 'Are you vegetarian?'

'No.'

'We're not either. Hazel works miracles in her garden, but it's never enough until it's too much. You can't feed this many women without a supermarket.'

'Most women's communities are vegetarian.'

'I know, but we're not like them. I don't apologise for liking meat. Or fish! I'll cook vegetarian, but how can people live this close to the ocean and not eat crab?'

'No one wants you to.' Robin returned to scrubbing shelves. 'If subsistence farming was a feminist revolution, women would rule the world.'

'I don't think feminism is about women ruling the world,' Kelsey countered. When Robin said nothing, she added, 'Hope that doesn't offend you.'

'Not at all. You know, there's an old-fashioned word for the indispensable woman like you.'

'Really? Housewife?'

'You're the *châtelaine*. It means woman in charge of the castle, especially the locked pantries.'

'I thought a *châtelaine* was a kind of bracelet.'

Robin stepped out of the pantry. 'The *châtelaine* carried the keys to the castle's storerooms and treasure chests on chains attached to her belt. Eventually, people used her title to refer to her bundle of keys.'

'And I thought you knew a lot about snakes!' Kelsey teased. She looked over at Robin, who shrugged and went back to the pantry.

Kelsey wiped the cleanser off the stove, stuck the knobs on and stood back to admire the shiny range. She started opening cupboards.

Robin heard. 'It's gone,' she offered.

'I know. Nothing but rat shit and a space for us.'

'So…it feels like home?' Robin winked.

Kelsey forced herself to say it. 'Everyone wants to move in, but I don't see how I can.'

'What? I need each of you.'

'I know I'm *needed*, but I don't see how I can work and live way up here.'

'Oh, if that's—'

'Let me finish, please.' Robin relaxed against the counter and assumed an expression that Gloria would call active listening. Kelsey sat across from her on the new bench. 'If I live up here, I'll spend more than an hour each way going to work. That's a lot of gas on minimum wage. Ginny's in the same boat, and Lupe doesn't have a job at all.'

'I didn't know.'

Kelsey felt encouraged by Robin's tone of surprised concern. 'Yes, because no one told you. Everyone is so excited, they don't realise you need women to fix this place up. But who? You want this to be women-only land. Nikki can't do it all. Are we supposed to help you? We already have jobs.' Kelsey stood up, opened the oven, glanced at the rust, grease and charcoal, and slammed its door. She hated being poor. 'It's overwhelming. No one else sees beyond the free rent and a redwood circle we can get naked in.'

To Kelsey's surprise, Robin agreed. 'I know they aren't thinking about how hard this will be.'

Now Kelsey felt embarrassed for getting overheated. As usual. She had no control over her temper.

Then Robin ruined it. 'One thing I've learned over my lifetimes is that problems that can be solved with money aren't hard problems.'

Magical thinking bullshit. 'Maybe your past-life memories give you a perspective on women's lives that we mere mortals can't see.'

'Kelsey, thanks for telling me. I'll figure something out. Or Gloria will.'

'You're willing to let Gloria figure out the money?'

Robin surprised her again. 'Sure, if it's a good idea.'

Gloria was a pain in the ass sometimes, but she was excellent at organising the incomprehensible. If Robin also saw the good in Gloria, maybe that alone would be worth sticking around for.

'If we can resolve your concern about money and jobs, would you move in?'

Kelsey remembered the excited faces of her friends at the Poet last night. Gloria's confidence. Wren's exhilaration last week when she first returned from Robin's land. She wanted to feel that, too.

Robin was still talking. '...Because a group like us needs an artist doing art.'

'Art?'

They heard a car outside. Lupe's van, by the chatter of it. Robin and Kelsey walked out to the porch, but Ginny had arrived, not Lupe.

With a black and white border collie. 'Say hello to Pepper!' Ginny shouted. 'Our new housemate!'

six

Wren stood in the vestibule all the way to San Jose, even though she knew it annoyed people. She was too exhausted and exhilarated to sit down. The week with her mother had fried every emotional conduit. She had stewed in turmoil, obsessing about Robin but never picking up the phone. She feared rejection. She feared judgement for her desire. Only yesterday did she discover that Robin had been leaving messages. Robin might be angry, but she had driven over the hill to meet Wren's train. Maybe she liked her?

The doors slid open and Wren ran down the subway to the station. Robin definitely liked her. For the millionth time, she remembered Robin asking her about her name, lying down together in the grove, the owl, the coffee. She wanted a lifetime of memories like that. Wren calmed herself and smoothed her hair as she crossed the station to the traffic circle.

She touched the handle, made a wish, and opened the

door of the truck. Warmth and Pat Benatar billowed out.

Robin turned down the music and didn't look angry. 'Good trip?'

'Thanks for getting me.' Wren put her backpack behind the seat and slid in next to her. 'Sometimes I wish I had a car, but living in the city, I never learned to drive very well.'

'I don't mind. I wanted to talk to you anyway. I'm sorry about your grandmother.'

'Thank you. She's been sick so I sort of already lost her.' Wren didn't want to explain old arguments about spending too much time at Grandma's house.

Robin seemed to sense that. 'How's your mom?' Robin was so sweet.

'She feels lost without her mother, and expects me to feel the same. By the end of the week it was like being sixteen again. She threw a tantrum when I left. She doesn't get it, that I need a separate life. She wants me to move in with her now. Thinks I abandoned her.'

Robin made a noise of concern.

'Don't worry; she always does that. I'm good at handling her. I'll call her; apologise. We'll be fine.' Wren didn't want to talk about her mother now that she was with Robin. 'I want to know what's happening. Do they like it? Are we moving in?'

'Well, Gloria—'

Shit, she doesn't like Gloria. 'You probably think she's bossy. You'll get used to her, and see she uses her powers for good.' Then Wren regretted interrupting.

'Everyone likes the place. Even Kelsey, who says some of you can't afford to live so far from work. Gloria might love it too much. Everyone is willing to come live on the land and turn it into a home for us.'

Robin took an exit off Highway 17.

'Why are we turning here? I thought we were going to Santa Cruz.'

'Bear Creek road goes to Boulder Creek. It's the back way to Bonny Doon. You might like it.'

Wren did. The dark wet road twisted above the lake then plunged through the redwoods. These woods were indeed her true home. As she lost herself in the trees flashing past, exhaustion seeped into her core. She stared out of the window for so long Robin probably thought she was being rude. 'How have you been? Have you been there alone this whole time?'

'Gloria spent the night doing some kind of ritual in the redwood grove.'

'Aspecting Athena?'

'If you say so. Lupe and Hazel camped out in the living room with me one night. We smoked a bunch of Lupe's pot and had a great conversation I can't remember. Nikki built me a kitchen table. Ginny stopped by and we went for a long walk in the redwoods. She's delightful and weird. Kelsey says she can't afford to move in, but she spent her day off yesterday getting the kitchen ready for today.'

Wren really regretted not calling Robin sooner.

'Why didn't you call while you were away?'

Robin could even read her mind. 'I told you – my mom deleted your messages.'

'But didn't you want to talk to me?'

Robin wants and needs me. Wren had been focused on the fantasy memory of that day in the grove and was afraid to spoil it with reality. Mother's obsessions and complaints and insults always disconnected her from her real life.

This life, real life, next to Robin in her pickup truck,

forever. 'Let's talk now.' She kept her mouth shut, and silence grew between them as they wound around the mountain, higher and higher.

Finally, Robin explained herself. 'I picked you up because I want to propose something. Everyone is excited about moving in. But already I see small fractures that will lead to the group splitting apart.'

'You barely know us. We'll be okay.'

'The worse fracture is that Gloria doesn't want the land to be women-only.'

'She's probably thinking about her brother. She's very close to him – more devoted to family than most of us.'

'Kelsey is already talking about leaving because she can't afford it.'

'She always feels that way.'

'Lupe got laid off and may need to move somewhere else to get work.'

'What? No!'

'Hazel helps other people grow food and flowers and barely has time for her own garden.'

'She always found time before.'

'Nikki isn't giving up her contracting business. We can't depend on her to repair the house. And Ginny – Ginny is just nuts, but she works long hours and it's hard on her body. She's not as well as she pretends to be.'

'Yes, but we all want the same thing. We want to be living on women's land, outside Patriarchy.'

'I sense that's what you all want. But how will we get there? You might think there is one true way to live, and Gloria – or someone else – will think it best to go another direction.'

Robin didn't have anything to worry about. 'We know how to deal with Gloria. You don't know us. Besides, our differences make us stronger. We know how to work out conflicts. We're not new to this.' Wren turned down the heater.

'That's why I invited you and not the other women's collectives I've met.'

Wren hadn't considered that Robin might choose some other group. She turned the heater back up.

'I have an idea of how to fix most of those fractures, but I can't do it all. When you took off like that, you missed experiencing these first crucial early days.'

'It's no big deal; I was only gone for a week.'

'You have a unique contribution, Wren. You're the artist.' Robin stuttered a bit, trying to find the words. 'We will need our land to be filled with art that embodies – expresses – and challenges what we are doing.' Robin paused again and glanced at Wren. 'This is hard for me.' Wren put her hand on Robin's arm. 'We need art that connects us to deep truths about ourselves doing something women have never done. Art that will last, that touches us as time goes by.'

Wren understood why Robin had a hard time expressing this. 'I get it. I know what art is.'

'I knew you would. We need you to be there, to see, listen, feel what we do. To use one of Mary Daly's words, we will be living in the Background. Outside Patriarchy. We will be doing what has been impossible, living on our own land, unsupervised by men.'

'Right on!' Wren exclaimed, sort of as a joke, then realised she meant it.

'But we may lose our way in this new Cunt-try.' Robin said the word with emphasis, as one does when thinking like Mary Daly, and they both laughed. 'We will face challenges and, without meaning to, solve them with expediencies we don't know are dangerous. We could adopt beliefs we think are harmless and kind, but pull us away from each other as lesbians.'

'Oh, I doubt—'

'I'm pretty sure it will happen, because I've seen it happen before. Women exercise Power Over and tell themselves they have no choice. We can leave Patriarchy, but wherever we go, we will bring it with us.'

'That's definitely true. Our coven does lots of rituals about internalised Patriarchy.'

'I know. That's why I think we have a chance. Even if we live together for years and years, we will forget what it was like at the beginning. Everything we do now will become memories. When you're in your sixties, your twenties feel like another lifetime.'

'Sixties! I hope I live that long.'

'Me too, because you will create art that captures what we are doing and why. Art that will sustain us and challenge us, expressing without words what we want, even if we are fighting about how to get there.'

'So you need me to make some sort of Important Sacred Art Thing?'

'I guess so.'

'Sure, I can do that. I do art for the coven already. You haven't seen my paintings, or the little sculptures. My mom always encouraged me to create art for the people, not myself. She commissioned paintings – so to speak – since I was a little girl. I can do that; no problem.'

'You're sure?'

'I'm already getting ideas. I'll make your "magical statue". Something life-size. Like the Nike in the Louvre, or a garden Buddha, or a statue of the Virgin Mary.'

'Magical statue. I like that.'

'I don't mean *magical* in that it will hear prayers, like in a church, but because it changes us and changes with us.'

'You get it.'

'Robin, this will be easy.' Wren could see it clearly. In her mind, Wren posed a procession of goddesses striding through redwoods: Demeter, Kali, Innana. She would make whatever it was that Robin wanted. As they created this work of art that Robin said they needed, they would fall in love.

Robin said something about Wren's mother.

'What did you say about my mom?'

'Last week I wondered – because you took off like that – if you've come out to her yet.'

Wren wondered why Robin cared to ask. 'Not yet. But she must know.'

'No doubt.'

Robin didn't understand anything about Wren's mother. She didn't get how Mom must be appeased and evaded. Someday she would understand, like Wren's friends did eventually. 'I'm sorry I missed the first week, but you're right. If we have a magical statue or whatever, it will be easier to know what we're all doing together.' Wren actually felt good to apologise already. She felt closer to Robin. 'I'll start on the art thing right away.'

Robin smiled, lifting the corners of her mouth, filling the truck with light.

Seven

Wren leaned back against the wall and soaked up this kitchen's energy. She tried to be present to every detail of the current moment, just like Robin wanted. The kitchen felt like paradise after a week in Mom's Bernal Heights kitchen, lighting her cigarettes and mixing bourbon-and-sodas. If only Robin were here, too. When they arrived, Robin had dropped Wren off in the plaza, then turned around to do an errand in town.

Wren sat at a table that filled up most of the room. She thought the bare walls could use a mural.

Kelsey deftly lifted a bag of potatoes and dumped them in the sink, with a grunt and a splash, her wire-straight dark ponytail swinging. She was so tall and strong, like a big-titted kitchen goddess.

Gloria sat on another bench, surrounded by notebooks and stacks of papers, wearing one of Ginny's old knitted sweaters.

Gloria was saying something scary. '…too late. If we don't live here, we'll have to break up.'

'We *can't* break up!' Wren wailed. 'We solved the Chore Chart!'

'Settle down, Wren.' Kelsey left the potatoes to soak and pulled a garlic bulb from the braid that Wren recognised from their own kitchen. 'I have *concerns*.'

'What concerns? Two words: Free rent.'

'It's more complicated than that, and you know it,' Kelsey retorted. Wren wilted. 'For one thing…'

Gloria straightened her back and threw her hands in the air as if making a benediction. 'The Land embodies the Goddess. The Land acts through Robin and—'

'Gloria, your *goddess* doesn't offer gas money.' Kelsey smacked the flat of her knife on the clove. 'Even with free rent, I can't afford to live way up here. I've already talked to Robin about it.'

'She talked to me about it too. It's not like we don't have employment.'

'Gloria, we don't make as much as you…'

Wren suddenly felt worse. 'That reminds me. My supervisor at the Roasting Company gave all my shifts away.'

'You lost your job again?'

'Not my *job*, just the shifts.'

'That means you're fired, dear. But I'm not like you. You can make withdrawals from Bank of Mommy.'

Wren groaned. 'I can't depend on her any more. Because I have no career and no boyfriend, she wants me to live with her.' Both Kelsey and Gloria laughed. Wren couldn't help defending her mother. They didn't understand her relationship with her mother. 'Give her a break. Her own mother just died.'

'May I remind you of the time you dropped out of art school because Grandma had a stroke and the nursing home smelled bad?'

'I learned a lot in that one year.' Wren pulled her sketchbook from her bag and drew a cartoon of two small women holding hands between towering redwoods.

'Wren, you're a free Amazon. I'm sure your mom's met lesbians before. Did you come out to her yet?'

'Robin asked me the same thing.' The fact that Wren's mother was well acquainted with lesbians was exactly why Wren couldn't come out to her.

'Robin too? I like that woman more every day,' Kelsey said airily.

Everyone liked Robin. But Wren liked her first. Robin and Kelsey were both wrong. 'I can't destroy my mother's fantasy of me as the wife of a land developer,' Wren asserted. Encouraging her mother's romantic fantasies conveniently obscured her own carnal realities.

Gloria tried to find a compromise. 'Nikki could be your husband. She builds houses.'

'That bridge burned.'

'How about Robin?' said Kelsey, sounding sincere. 'She's your type.'

Wren ignored that suggestion and returned to her drawing, adding texture to the trunks.

Gloria noticed Wren's non-response and changed the subject. 'How are you feeling now that your abuela joined your ancestors?'

Gloria always forgot Wren was adopted. 'I'm not as torn up as my mom. Grandma taught me how to sew, but Mom gave away the sewing machine I was supposed to inherit. I don't understand why she did that.'

'Because your mother is a jealous bitch and a little creepy.' Kelsey scraped the pile of minced garlic off the cutting board.

'Some day, when she gets old and sick, she can hire a home health aide. I've worked for dozens of wicked mothers who drove their children away.' Kelsey rolled three large onions onto the table. 'Maybe we could work for Robin?'

'I don't want to *work* for Robin,' Wren said.

'What *do* you want from Robin?' Gloria teased.

Panicked, instead of answering, Wren told them about San Francisco. 'Did I tell you the Mission is a lesbian Castro now? I ate at a new women's café called Artemis. And I went to Amelia's a few nights.'

'My favourite is Maud's.' Kelsey looked lost in a memory.

Wren wondered who Kelsey was thinking of. She had had lots of lovers, but never anyone long term. 'I took the streetcar to Maud's one night and talked to a woman from the Richmond, but she didn't ask for my number.'

'Our new phone number is Robin's number,' Gloria said sharply. 'Did you memorise it?'

'Of course.' Wren felt her cheeks warm. *Dammit*. Wren had imagined kissing Robin in Maud's backyard. 'I met a woman at Amelia's who belongs to a wheat-paste collective.'

'What's wheat-paste?' asked Kelsey. 'Toast-Art?' She never missed a chance to point out artistic pretension.

Wren didn't mind. 'It's very cool. They make art on a collectively owned Xerox machine and paste it up all over the city.'

'I'd like to have my own Xerox machine.' Gloria straightened a stack of papers.

'One night after my mom passed out, I went to the women's bathhouse. You should see the tattoos! Maybe I could learn how to tattoo?'

'We definitely need a bathtub here,' said Kelsey.

Remembering the women's community at the bathhouse

lifted Wren's spirits, and she recalled the best part of the week. 'After the funeral mass, I heard drumming at the park. There was a women's drum circle at the park and I danced for the rest of the day, and sweated through the black dress my mother bought me.' Wren started a new cartoon, women dancing and drumming on the slope of Dolores Park, the city skyline behind them.

Kelsey gestured to Wren. 'Can you get started on the potatoes, please?' She knew better than to ask Gloria. 'I'll finish the onions.'

Wren closed her sketchbook and stood up. 'Mom didn't want the funeral at our little parish, but at the big Mission church.' Wren focused on deftly peeling the first potato while telling her story. 'I lit a candle to St Anne and Mary. It's the only statue of a girl you'll see in a Catholic church.'

'We know who St Anne is, Wren.' Gloria stood up to leave the kitchen. 'We may be witches, but the three of us are recovering Catholics.' She put her stacks of handouts in a box. 'While you were doing all those city things like dancing in women's bars and appreciating ecclesiastical art, we've been packing up the old house and getting ready for the yard sale. We have to *move*, Wren, and we don't even know where we're moving to.' Gloria must have noticed how harsh that sounded. 'I missed you, darling. We had to take your paintings off the walls without you.'

That hurt. 'Gloria, my mom needed me. Her mother *died*,' Wren whined, but guilt overpowered her righteousness. She looked around the kitchen, scrubbed and painted. 'I'm sorry. I should have helped. Look!' Wren pointed to the little pile of potatoes.

'I see you and offer my gratitude,' Gloria said, and would have made prayer hands, but she held up a notebook instead.

She had elaborately lettered the cover: *CtCA & CtCP.*

'What does that spell?' asked Wren.

'I'll share my dark moon revelation at the meeting. If Athena convinces Robin, we *can* afford to live here. Athena wants me to teach my class full-time.'

'Can I help you with the class?' offered Wren. 'I need a job.'

'Sure, but I can't afford to pay you yet. I need a seven-colour drawing of the chakras.'

'I'll do it,' Wren agreed. Maybe the magical statue would have something to do with the rainbow of energy centres that ran up their spines.

'Gloria, did you tell Wren about Juggling the Spheres?'

Wren looked confused. 'What spheres?'

'If we move here,' Kelsey explained, 'we need to make this dump liveable.'

'In the revelation, I saw each of us in a Sphere. Hazel will focus on the garden. Lupe will help her, but has her mushrooms and The Grow. Nikki will do construction.'

'What does Robin do?' asked Wren. It was obvious what Kelsey's and Gloria's Spheres would be.

Gloria rolled her eyes. 'I have no idea what her Sphere is.'

'I know what my Sphere is,' said Wren.

Kelsey and Gloria looked at her in shock.

'Robin told me on the way here. She wants me to be the artist-in-residence.'

Gloria said it would be nice to have more decorations. Kelsey didn't say anything, but Wren felt her disapproval. Kelsey would assume that organising – if not doing – all the housework would fall on her.

Gloria couldn't think beyond Wren's crafts. 'So you'll paint those cupboards like you did at Walnut?'

'I'll do that. But that's not what Robin says we need. She said we need art that expresses our common vision.'

'She's right,' Gloria said. 'We need a record for future generations of how we built our women's land. Cameras intrude and film is toxic.'

'You sound like Ginny,' said Kelsey, packing the compost bin with Wren's pile of potato skins. 'That reminds me of another problem.' She turned back to the stove. 'Robin doesn't have enough propane. Those little five-gallon tanks are too small for a household like ours, but the foundation under the big propane tank is washed out. *And* because of Robin's rule about men on the land, we can't get it fixed anyway. So we're – she's – fucked.'

Wren and Gloria smiled at each other behind Kelsey's back. Kelsey's rants were legendary. They watched her deftly strike a match on the same flat rock she kept by the stove at the other house and light the burner under her frying pan. She might as well have moved in already.

'Maybe they have women drivers,' offered Gloria.

'If we move in,' Kelsey was getting loud. 'We need propane delivery.'

'Let's not argue,' Wren pleaded. She wanted this first meal to be a happy one, and not get derailed by stupid fights about men. She sliced two wafers off the end of a potato and offered them to her friends. 'Body of Spud. Take and eat.'

'Amen,' Kelsey agreed, and stuck out her tongue for the bit of potato. So did Gloria, who crossed herself and chewed hers impiously.

Kelsey reached into a drawer. 'God dammit!'

Wren jumped. 'A snake?'

'No clean towels. Robin needs a washing machine.'

Eight

Kelsey shouted, 'Dinner!' from the front door and returned to the kitchen. 'If we stay, we'll need a dinner bell – Wren, will you set the table? I brought that stuff from the house.'

Wren pulled paper plates and plastic silverware from the potluck box.

Hazel pulled off her belt and red-handled pruning shears as she and Lupe clumped in. 'Early Girl might do well up there,' she was saying. They pulled out the bench and sat down at the new table, like they had done it all their lives. Ginny and Pepper came in, but Ginny sent Pepper out to the living room. Gloria appeared in the doorway, dressed in the shiny green gown she usually wore at Spring Equinox. Robin and Nikki followed with the wine. Kelsey set down her two largest frying pans, heaped with fried potatoes, onions and cheese.

'That's the best dinner I could make with what she had,' Kelsey said, looking pointedly at Robin before dropping into a chair nearest the stove. 'Thanks for your help, Wren.' The eight of them fitted comfortably: three on each bench, with Robin opposite Kelsey.

Gloria picked up the spatula like a wand and announced, 'We begin our first meal together on the land. We should do a blessing.'

Nikki reached for the spatula. 'I'm too hungry to bless anybody right now.' Black goddesses danced across her chest under a month of moons. Wren had always loved how Nikki wore that shirt differently from any other lesbian.

Ginny was wearing her horns again. 'Let's offer our gratitude to people who lived here. Our land ancestors, not our blood ancestors.'

'I know what you mean.' Robin filled a jam jar with wine. 'I'll start.' She raised the jar ceremoniously. 'To our Italian ancestors who lived at this ranch. You were immigrants, feared by your neighbours, but they loved your brandy. We forgive you for cutting down all the redwood trees.' She took a sip and passed the jar to Nikki.

Nikki put down her fork. It looked like she was growing her hair out. 'Thank you for building this house and its solid bones. Thanks to Kelsey for spuds 'n' onions. Amen.' She passed the jar to Hazel.

'I raise this glass to whoever broke the land and grew food in this forest. May we never hunger.'

Lupe took the jar. 'I give thanks to this land, for lessons we will learn, and… *pehhhh-shhhhew*.' She waved the jar in an arc over her head. Like many stoners, Lupe often substituted sound effects for words. She handed the jar to Kelsey and refilled her plate. 'Do we have any salsa?'

Kelsey got up and returned with a bottle of Tabasco, then raised the jar. 'To any woman or man who ever cooked in this kitchen.' She toasted the stove and handed the jar to Ginny.

Everyone passed the hot sauce around enthusiastically while Ginny turned the jar in her fingers. She took her sip and handed it to Wren. 'I gave thanks without language.'

Wren wanted to say she was thankful for all butches throughout all time, but instead proclaimed, 'I give thanks to my grandmother for dying, so I didn't have to work last week.' It was always better to go for the laugh at these occasions.

Robin laughed too, and then said, 'Don't worry Wren, I'll force you to make up for it.'

Wren liked having a secret joke with Robin.

Gloria concluded the blessing with a long prayer to Hestia, goddess of the Hearth Fire. She stood, flicked wine on the stove, and left the kitchen to pour libations into the fireplaces. No one followed her. Gloria sometimes preferred doing elaborate witchy stuff by herself.

They devoured the spuds 'n' onions and were pouring out the last of the wine when Robin got everyone's attention. 'I want to talk about money.'

'You said we wouldn't have to pay rent,' Gloria, back from her fireplace ritual, reminded everybody for no reason.

'That's right—'

'Robin, if you permit me, I want to share what Athena revealed to me last week. In addition to organising our contributions in the Juggling the Spheres house meeting, I was shown a path toward resolving the inherent classism that we brought with us from Patriarchy.'

'Sure.' Robin leaned back against the wall. 'Let's hear it.'

Gloria placed both her palms on the decorated notebook. 'Some of us earn more, and can therefore contribute more to the household. But we need to record those contributions, right? If we're working on Robin's land, we'll need to record the value of working contributions, and Robin will need to pay us for it.' She looked over at Robin tentatively, who nodded.

Gloria picked up the notebook with the CtCA & CtCP on the cover. Wren wished Gloria had asked her to letter it. Gloria didn't have great handwriting.

But she did have lots of ideas. 'There's so much we need to do, right? If we quit our jobs, we could work here full-time. But we need to be compensated for our contributions. I know I would. And Wren, you lost your shifts.'

Ginny gasped. 'You did? No more free coffee?'

Wren mouthed, 'I'm sorry.'

'Some contributions, like this beautiful table that Nikki built, are a contribution to the *community*. It doesn't enhance the value of Robin's property, but gives us something valuable that we all share. So the time and materials that Nikki put into this table would be recorded in the book as a Contribution to Community *Assets*. C-t-C-A.' Gloria opened that notebook. 'This is the ledger book I set up for us.'

Ledger book. That's what you call it, Wren realised. A sketchbook for number artists.

'But what if we rebuild those old cabins back there?' She glanced at Lupe and Hazel. 'That's a contribution to the *actual value* of Robin's property, so your time and materials would be added to Contribution to Community *Property*. C-t-C-P.'

Robin looked like she understood Gloria more than Wren did. 'Gloria, are you saying everyone will quit your jobs and I will pay you for your work here?'

'Yes, if you can afford to pay us what we're worth,' Gloria said, as if beginning negotiations.

'I've been thinking of something like that—'

'Perfect. Let me finish. You haven't said yet, but we should value CtCA at around ten dollars an hour. CtCP needs to be more like twenty-five dollars per hour, because eventually this place will be worth a lot. What do you think of that, Robin?'

Wren worked out that Gloria wanted to be paid double what she made taking X-rays.

'Let me tell you my idea; then you can decide which is better.' Robin leaned back even further and pulled something out of her pocket. 'We can live like women never have. We can own our land in a country at peace, free of fathers, husbands and priests. It won't be easy. We will face problems we don't even have words for. But some problems have known solutions.' She sat forward. 'Kelsey told me that even with free rent, some of you can't afford to live here. Gloria, you told me everyone needs money of her own.'

'That's right; I did.'

'How much money does a woman need? In my experience, if you make four times your rent, you feel safe – unless you have kids or bad habits. Back at your old house, you were each paying about $100 to rent your rooms—'

'We paid a sliding scale,' Ginny clarified, and moved her hands up and down.

Robin opened her hand and set a thick stack of bills on the table. 'I propose giving each of you $400 a month. If you need more, let me know.'

'And we pay rent out of this?' asked Gloria.

Robin dealt out four new hundred-dollar bills to each woman.

'No. Nobody pays rent.'

Gloria was speechless. Wren felt relief that she wouldn't have to write numbers in a ledger book.

'This will definitely help me with cash flow.' Nikki picked up her stack. 'No strings?'

'No strings,' agreed Robin. 'If you want to work off the land, you can do that. Otherwise, just live here on our women's land. Let's see what happens.'

Gloria held her hands palms up with the bills across them. 'Thank you, Robin, and thanks to Athena. This is exactly the solution She would arrange.' Gloria seemed to have forgotten CtC…whatever. Wren gave Athena thanks for that.

'I also will buy our common food and household supplies,' Robin said, looking at Kelsey.

'I've never seen this much cash in one place before.' Kelsey's eyes filled up.

'I have,' Lupe said mysteriously. 'I'll take it.'

Hazel's eyes fluttered but she didn't cry as she stared at the stack of bills in front of her. 'I can have my own garden.'

'And if you need materials for the property or whatever…' Robin gestured at the ledger book. 'You can charge it to my account at Scarborough Lumber.'

'Well, sisters,' Gloria said, assuming her usual role of meeting facilitator. 'I propose we move to Robin's ranch by Thanksgiving. Anyone have concerns?'

'I do,' said Nikki, surprising everyone. 'Those back stairs will murder someone.'

'But you'll help me rebuild them?' Robin asked, assuming she would.

Nikki told Robin she'd be back early in the morning with a load of lumber, and expected coffee and lunch.

'Any other concerns?' Gloria asked sincerely.

'I have a concern,' Kelsey said, and she sounded sort of afraid of what the answer might be. 'Where does your money come from, Robin?'

Robin didn't appear to mind the question. 'Remember how I told you that I can remember my past lives?'

'Lots of people have past-life experiences,' Kelsey challenged. 'But they don't go around with hundreds in their pockets.'

'I didn't always. I was poor for a thousand years. Then I lived with rich people. They invented financial accounting before alphabets. I learned how families hang on to fortunes over generations. Eventually, I figured out how to give it to myself over and over.'

Gloria looked satisfied that Robin's secret could be explained both financially and supernaturally. 'I forget women couldn't own property in olden times.'

'We are the first generation of women who can live on our own land without men,' Robin said. 'I won't let a lack of money be why we fail.'

Kelsey wasn't satisfied. 'But how *do* you make money?'

'Same way the Queen of England does. Commercial real estate.'

Kelsey looked like she understood Robin's answer. She examined the bills in her hand, and noticed Robin was staring at her. Wren could tell Robin was pleading with her to stay. Wren squeezed her bills under the table and sent the same wish.

'Are there any more concerns?' Gloria asked.

Wren waited anxiously through the four seconds Gloria allowed. Kelsey said nothing. 'It's decided. We will leave Walnut Street and move to Robin's land.'

'So mote it be,' the women said together, as if Gloria had cast a spell.

'We need to find the name of our land,' Ginny said.

Kelsey muttered something as she rose from the table and

lit the fire in the living room. Lupe and Ginny started on the dishes. Nikki expertly opened another bottle.

Wren refolded her four bills and pressed them into her sock. Robin saw the bills disappearing down her leg and winked at her. Now Wren could afford to focus on her Sphere and create the magical statue – whatever it would be. She would make it, and Robin would like it, would take her in her arms, and kiss her, and they would be lovers.

Nine

On her last morning at the Walnut house, Kelsey rose early. She quietly made herself tea. She looked around the kitchen. Their kitchen. Her kitchen. Every evening she cheerily cooked dinner for everyone, but she ate breakfast on her own. She put her teapot, milk and one last granola bar in her wicker basket and carried it back to her room.

After she finished, she watched her room fill with light. She put her empty mug in the basket, leaned against the wall and laid her right hand over her left. She imagined a candle flame and breathed deep and slow.

'Light of my life,' she whispered.

'Hello, Kelsey,' said a muffled voice. Kelsey loved that voice.

Lucy was in the bed with her, snuggled under Kelsey's quilt, with only her smooth black hair exposed to the chilly room.

'I don't need to work any more.'

'I know. But you'll work harder than ever.'

'No more landlords or bosses.'

'Robin is still in charge. She might not like you if she finds out what a bitch you are.'

'Don't be negative. Maybe now I can afford to tell my secrets.'

'It's not a secret, honey.'

'I want to savour this. No more dawn drives to Aptos and a twelve-hour shift.'

'But will you have time for me?'

Kelsey scooted down without breaking her trance. She felt Lucy, warm and naked beside her, just like that time when her parents went away. That one time when they stayed in bed all weekend. Kelsey remembered it. She remembered every moment.

⊙⊙

The day after Nikki and Robin finished the back stairs, Wren and Gloria loaded the Volvo and drove up to Bonny Doon. For this first load, Wren had packed her essentials: brushes, pens, paint boxes, easel. Paper stash, fabric stash, sewing machine.

Gloria pulled into the plaza and parked next to the garbage pile. She said someone needed to go to the dump, which gave Wren an idea to mull as she unloaded. Gloria left to inspect the stairs.

'Wren!' Gloria called from upstairs. 'Can you bring up the pendulum? It's in the purple bag behind my seat.'

Gloria had also packed treasures, including a rose quartz crystal on a silver chain, the coven's pendulum. She kept it rolled in a circle of velvety deerskin the size of a dinner plate. Last year, at Gloria's request, Wren had painted a moon glyph in the centre with the secret sigils of each coven member around the circumference.

At the top of the new stairs, Gloria and Robin stood in front of an open door. Wren handed the bag to Gloria, who informed her that Robin had asked her to choose everyone's bedroom.

'Cool,' Wren said, and hugged Robin like it was no big deal. Wren didn't care which bedroom she had, as long as it was near Robin.

Gloria led around to the front and laid the deerskin in the threshold of the first door. She squatted, dropping into a trance and holding the crystal over the centre of the painting. Wren stood next to Robin and wondered if she knew what Gloria was doing. The pendulum quivered, and soon it was swinging directly over one sigil in particular.

'This will be Kelsey's room,' Gloria proclaimed.

She walked to the middle room and repeated the divination. The pendulum swung over another sigil.

'This is Wren's room.' The room was smaller than the one Gloria had chosen for herself, but Wren knew she would like its morning sun.

Gloria laid the painting at the third door. The pendulum swung immediately over a sigil set apart from the others. Gloria declared this one Robin's room. Wren silently gave thanks to Gloria's skill with a pendulum.

'How do you know it's mine? Am I in that...' Robin gestured to the painting, '...oracle?'

As Gloria walked away toward the back of the house, Wren explained. 'The painting contains a sigil for each of us, plus *the un-looked-for*. That's where the pendulum went.' Wren wondered if someday she and Robin would do the ritual to create her own sigil.

From the back of the veranda, they heard Gloria call, 'Ginny!'

Robin looked uneasy. 'I want to live in one of the cabins out back, but Nikki says I should live in the house.'

'Nikki's right. Don't separate yourself from us. Take the room the oracle chose for you, facing the sunrise.'

Robin opened her door and peered into its darkness. 'I guess you're right. Who am I to argue with a pink rock?'

Wren offered to help Robin clean out her room, but Robin said she would finish cleaning out the cabins with Lupe and Hazel first.

So Wren spent the rest of the afternoon with Gloria, emptying their new bedrooms, tossing other people's garbage off the veranda and onto the pile.

'This is fun,' Gloria said. 'From now on, every day is Saturday.'

'You never had to work Saturdays.'

∞

Robin said Wren needed a studio and gave her the mysterious room in the corner between the living room and kitchen. It was hers if she emptied it of its accumulated garbage.

For hours Wren loaded Hazel's wheelbarrow with newspapers, magazines, bottles and beer cans and tossed them all on the garbage pile. Soon she and Robin would go to the dump. The Santa Cruz dump was in a valley at the end of a narrow country road, the most beautiful dump in the world. As you tossed your garbage out of the truck, beyond the acres of other people's garbage, you beheld the vast ocean stretching out to infinity. Wren felt dump runs were the most romantic of all household chores.

It took her an hour to clear a path to the far wall. When she got there, she pried open a window. From the backyard she heard Lupe say, 'I will work with men, but they are sometimes too much of a good thing, and most of the time, no good at all.' Then everyone laughed.

They must be talking about separatism again. Women got so political about it. Why think about men when you're on women's land? Then she smelled Lupe's homegrown and decided Robin might need a break from politics.

Wren washed her hands in the kitchen sink and walked out of the back door. The air was wet and cold with the promise of winter rains.

'Wren!' Lupe passed the joint to Robin. 'Where have you been?'

Robin passed it to Hazel without smoking.

'Preparing my studio so I can work on my Sphere.'

Hazel took a hit and declared, 'We will live like the Three Sisters.'

Robin tried to puzzle out Hazel's reference. All her references involved plants. 'I've heard Three Sisters refer to corn, beans, and squash.'

'Yes! Yes!' Hazel confirmed, with cannabis enthusiasm. 'Eros is the energy of plants reaching for the sun and growing fruit. We're no different. Lesbian community grows from eros and eros grows from community. A community needs all of us individually. We put down roots, reach for the light, repel predators, grow seeds.' She looked at the joint and said, 'I swear this one makes people psychic,' not remembering that Robin wasn't smoking any.

Hazel's baroque description sparked an image in Wren's mind. *The magical statue needs to be about the eros of sisterhood.*

'Wren,' Robin said, breaking into Wren's imagination. 'Hazel was telling us how you cured jealousy.'

Before she could respond, Hazel inhaled briefly and handed the joint to Wren. 'Robin, you say it like you don't believe in magic.'

Wren glanced at Robin and handed the joint back to Lupe.

'You remember?' Lupe waved the joint to encourage Wren to tell the story. 'The jealousy ritual?'

'Wren was The Other Woman,' Hazel explained.

Wren didn't mind people telling her stories, but she wished Hazel wasn't telling that one to Robin right now.

'And Gloria was hung up on a DTM,' said Lupe.

'Dark, Troubled, and Moody,' Hazel translated. 'You know the type.'

'I slept with her one time,' Robin quipped.

'We all did,' Lupe said dismissively. 'But don't say the lesbian community is incestuous.'

'I didn't.' Robin sounded defensive, and Wren wished Lupe weren't so harsh sometimes.

'Sorry, but people do,' Lupe said. 'There's nothing wrong with women coming together and acting on their lust.'

Robin didn't seem insulted. 'Can you stop jealousy with a ritual?'

'A ritual doesn't stop feelings,' countered Hazel. 'Rituals give a channel for emotions to flow, one after another.'

'Huh,' Robin said, with pleasure, as she did when learning something new. 'But how do your girlfriends feel about eros in the coven?'

'Girlfriends who don't get it don't last long,' Lupe said. She paused. 'That can be a bummer.'

Wren laughed along with everyone, reassured she knew

more about eros than Robin did.

Hazel handed the roach to Lupe, who tore it apart and scattered it from her fingers. She grew enough pot that she didn't need to conserve the roaches.

Lupe pulled on her gloves. 'Let's get back to work. I don't mind your slumber parties, Robin, but I will need a private room by the time everyone gets here for Thanksgiving, if you know what I mean.'

Wren returned to clearing out her studio. It took her the rest of the day, and she relished the solitude. She swept up the last of the rat shit and mopped the floor. She appreciated the texture of the wide yellow floor planks, that looked as beautiful as furniture. Red light from the winter sunset filled the sky above the ridge beyond her freshly washed windows. She imagined walls lined with shelves of paper and paint, fabric and yarn, her sewing machine in the corner. In this studio, she would create the art Robin said the household needed to stay together. Maybe the household would never need it, but for sure it would bring Robin into her bed.

The Revelation of the Snakes happened after the night they slept together in the living room in a slumber party. Wren woke up next to Ginny, wishing she didn't want Robin so bad.

At breakfast, Lupe said she was taking a break from cabin restoration to start the mushroom spawn. Everyone said they wanted to learn mushroom spawning too, except Gloria, who planned to organise her bedroom, and Nikki, who had a remodel in Ben Lomond.

Wren wondered if Lupe's mushrooms could reveal the big

idea she needed if she was to get started on Robin's magical statue. They threw on coats and walked up to the garden. Wren always loved the bright winter mornings and the smells that only came out in cold weather.

Lupe and Hazel led the way, Lupe explaining something about spores and substrate. Wren couldn't hear and didn't care. Robin and Kelsey followed Lupe and Hazel. Wren amused herself watching Robin's stride, and loved that everyone was already Robin's friend too. Ginny took Wren's hand as they walked.

When Lupe and Hazel reached the top of the hill, Hazel shouted, and Wren and Ginny ran forward. The women formed a cautious circle around a big rattlesnake, sunning on a piece of broken concrete in front of a shed. Everyone was enraptured.

'It's odd to see snakes this late in the year,' Hazel said.

'You know what that means,' Ginny said to Robin.

Robin didn't have a clue.

'All that dies shall be reborn.'

'I thought you said it had something to do with your – what was it? "rising *kundalini*"?'

'That too.'

The door to what Lupe called the shroom shed was still broken, so she and Robin lifted it off. 'I've been wanting to start the spawn since I hauled up these supplies,' Lupe said, as she walked in. 'Shit-goddammit-piss-fuck-cock!'

Wren and the rest of them crowded the door. Lupe dragged a bag of rice off a stack as tall as her waist. Grains poured onto the floor.

'I can't see anything,' Robin said.

'Stand back and let the light in,' Lupe said testily. She bent and inspected her rice supply. 'I don't get it. There is a hole in every one. Rats!'

Hazel chortled. 'Are you feeling okay? The Lupe I know has a bigger vocabulary.'

Lupe turned on Robin. 'We have rats.'

'No,' said Hazel, pointing her finger at Lupe. '*You* have rats. You left out this rice, and *you* caused the rats.'

Wren didn't quite get it. Kelsey helped Lupe re-stack the rice.

Hazel seemed upset and raised her voice. 'Has anyone put it together that the rats caused the snakes?'

'Oh, yeah,' said Robin. 'Let's get out of here; it stinks.'

They backed out of the shed, silently passed the sleeping snake, and stood on the other side of the road near what Hazel called the Greenhouse. Wren thought it smelled like a garage, and the roof was caved in.

Hazel was suddenly yelling at Robin. '*You* piled up garbage since before we got here. *Then* we added all the *shit* from the house, *plus* food waste. Garbage doesn't *go away*. That's Patriarchal thinking. You feed the prey animals, predators will feed on them.'

That made sense to Wren, but she didn't know why Hazel was angry at Robin. Robin didn't seem to mind. She had that look of wonder again, like when she learned something new.

Then Robin held her arm out toward Wren. 'This is why we need Wren to make that art thing. When we make mistakes like this, the ideals in art will help us see what we're doing wrong – and maybe even forgive each other.'

'That's putting a lot of pressure on a statue,' Wren tried to joke.

'Maybe snakes should be part of it, to remind us that we can't throw things away,' Robin suggested.

'Just don't invoke snakes in the kitchen,' said Kelsey.

'That's a great idea,' Wren said, but regretted it. Snakes symbolised potent meanings, but Wren never made art that challenged anyone. She thought living as a lesbian witch was enough.

From that day forward, the women securely composted food waste. Later, Ginny found a snakeskin in the garden, and she brought it to the fireplace mantel. The exquisite relic reminded the coven that they lived in a forest, among wild nature and its terpsichorean patterns.

Wren mulled over the idea of a snake motif for the magical statue. The snake skin reminded her of how many times she went to the dump with Robin, falling ever deeper in love.

Ten

'*City centre, mid-traffic, I wake to your public kiss….*'

They had spent the day painting Robin's ceiling indigo blue. Now, at the end of that sparkling day of work and friendship, Wren read Olga Broumas' poetry to Robin.

'*Your name, is Judith. Your kiss a sign…*' She paused and looked at Robin lying beside her, handsome and kissable. '*Your kiss a sign to the shocked pedestrians gathered beneath the light that means stop.*' Wren laid the book on her chest. 'I remember kissing a woman in public for the first time.'

'What happened?'

'Nothing.' Wren laughed. 'And everything.' Robin laughed too, like she knew what Wren meant.

Wren picked up the book again. '*…means stop in our culture, where red is a warning and men threaten each other with final violence: I will drink your blood.*' Wren wished red didn't mean stop. For her, red had something to do with the feeling of reading poetry next to Robin.

'*Your kiss is for them a sign of betrayal, your red lips suspect, unspeakable liberties as we cross the street, kissing against the light, singing, "This is the woman I woke from sleep, the woman that woke me sleeping."'*

Wren put the book down and kissed Robin playfully on the cheek. How could Robin live with lesbians but not be one herself?

Robin responded to the poem, not the kiss. 'Women kiss each other awake all the time. That's a marvellous power, wielding those unspeakable liberties. When our bodies are free, there's no stopping us.'

Our bodies. A tide of ache rose through Wren. She let it crest and then pass through, like her witchcraft taught her. 'Did you know me in a past life?'

'Probably not. A long time ago I would have. Families lived in one village for two or three hundred years and I would recognise old women I knew when young.'

'When I met Gloria, I felt I had known her in a past life. Like she was always my teacher.'

'Women like her; you want to follow them.'

'We don't follow her,' Wren protested. 'We have no hierarchy.'

'She guides you. And she wants more.'

'That's why she teaches women outside the coven. She was initiated into another coven before ours. She taught us a lot.' Wren patted around for the rest of that joint but couldn't find it. 'I wish I remembered my past lives. Maybe I would be a better artist.'

'You're already good enough.' Robin turned toward her. 'I need to tell you something.'

Wren turned on her side too. She soaked in the warmth and a scent coming from Robin's body. *What was happening?*

'I'm afraid all the time. Afraid we won't stay together long enough. Long enough to figure out what we need to.'

That again. 'Don't worry. I'm going to make the magical statue, like you asked for.'

Robin smiled, but indulgently, and it didn't feel good this time.

'Trust me. Trust us. The only thing *I'm* afraid of is coming out to my mother.' Wren had intended this to be a joke, but Robin took it seriously.

'You should call her and come out.'

'I don't want to tell her I'm lesbian.'

'And yet you read lesbian poetry so well.'

That's not the only lesbian stuff I do well. Wren considered a future where her mother knew she loved women, women wielding unspeakable liberties. 'Now that I'm here' – Wren waved her hand to include Robin's room, Robin's house and Robin's money – 'maybe she can't ruin the things I love.'

'How does she ruin what you love?'

'She likes them too much.'

'How about sending her a letter? It's traditional.'

Wren leaned over Robin's body, appreciating the chance to bring their breasts closer, and grabbed the other joint and matches.

'I'll think about it,' she said, lying back. Talking about her mother with Robin felt like picking a scab, and she was sorry now that she had started it. 'Is there anything you want to get better at? What haven't you done?'

'I would love to go to space, but I'm scared of heights and already too old. Maybe in my next life.'

Her next life. Someday, Robin would be alive and Wren would be long dead. Robin was either the most interesting woman in the world, or unabridged bat-shit crazy.

⚭

Thanksgiving weekend, the plaza filled with Toyota pickups, the Lesbian National Vehicle. Years ago, when Kelsey left home after high school, she started a Thanksgiving tradition wherever she lived, welcoming any woman who avoided family on that fraught holiday.

This year, the long weekend doubled as a four-day housewarming. Kelsey supervised the roasting of the turkey, the baking of the tofu, the preparation of traditional vegetables, casseroles and pies. Wren noticed that Kelsey cooked all day but still had time for a fling.

On the long weekend's Sunday afternoon, Wren ran into Kelsey in the plaza. She had just kissed Her Fling goodbye. Wren couldn't remember her name, but she was a friend of Hazel's.

'Will you see her again?' Wren asked, trying to smile and not smirk.

'She knows lots of dirty limericks.' Kelsey was definitely smirking. 'But she lives way up in Ashland.'

'So, just a fling?'

'Nothing wrong with a fling.'

They entered the warm front room, now empty, quiet and feeling like home. Wren flopped on the couch. Kelsey dropped two logs on the fire and sat down at the other end. 'Speaking of flings, what's up with you and Robin?'

'She's not a fling; she's my housemate.'

'I thought you were sleeping together?'

'Sleeping. Her room is warmer, and Lupe's friends from Hollister needed my room. Robin and me just talk and sleep. Don't get excited.' *She's so exciting.*

'I'm not excited. Did you hear we're giving her the birthday massage tomorrow night?'

The massage! 'Just the massage? Not the trance?'

'I explained it to her, and she wants the massage. She's not ready for the trance.'

'She's going to love it.' Wren looked forward to Robin's birthday back rub because she'd been sleeping with Robin for three nights in a row and not touching her with anything but pure sisterhood.

⚭

There was an altar, and there would be a woman lying on it, but the altar was just the massage table covered in a sheet, and Robin was no virgin. Still, white-robed witches, room lit by candles, air scented by pungent oil – the whole scene might remind an outsider of a satanic horror movie.

Wren wondered if Robin still felt like an outsider. She hadn't done any rituals with the group since Halloween. They had built the fire up, backed the couch to the middle of the room, and stood in a semi-circle around the 'altar'.

Gloria began the ritual, explaining everything for Robin's benefit.

'In this rite, our hands will touch you intimately. Open to our touch, or choose your boundary. Your body is sovereign. Do you understand?'

Robin nodded, and said, 'I'll let you know if I don't like it.'

Wren appreciated Robin's boundaries, but knew she'd love this. If only Gloria would get on with it.

'We are grown in our mother's body, into the hands of women,' Gloria continued, raising her arms over her head. 'Women care for us when we die, and they return our body to the Mother.'

'You will lie on an altar, Robin, but you are not a sacrifice. Each birth is a unique gift in this world, a gift to ourselves. Each one of us is a living goddess, experiencing every facet of creation. As She says, "I counted you my own in the womb of your grandmother."'

The witches passed a kiss from one to the other, and then drew secret symbols on each other's foreheads with oil, saying 'Blessed Be.'

'The circle is cast,' Gloria affirmed, 'setting apart the inside from the outside, the sacred from profane.' Then Gloria explained that they would raise a Cone of Power.

'We don't chant "om"; we chant the opposite: "ma" like the Great Mother. We call up life force from our wombs, through our lungs, and out our lips into this circle.'

The witches sang 'maaa' in one note, then harmonically, then discordantly. The coven's voices sounded louder and louder, separated into other tones, low and scary, and then high-pitched ululations that caromed off the ceiling. Higher and higher rose their voices. With these sounds, a ring of energy rose around them, swirling and physically perceptible, rising up to a point above their heads. Each witch seemed absorbed in her own cries, but in a single moment, they stopped with a shout and flung their arms skyward.

Then they knelt, setting their hands flat to the carpet, letting silence overcome the reverberations. They each perceived the earth under the floorboards. In their imaginations they pushed deeper, and the stony heart of the planet accepted their offering and returned the sensation the witches called Grounding.

They rose silently, and everyone looked at Robin. Robin eased herself onto the altar and lay on her stomach. Nikki asked if she was warm enough.

Wren thought Robin looked scared and brave. While the birthday massage wasn't like sex, Wren had been looking forward to touching her all over and giving her pleasure, while the ritual structure protected her from awkwardness and rejection.

Robin lay with her head in the face cradle, breathing evenly. The witches surrounded her, placing their hands on her back and legs. Gloria asked if she needed a pillow under her breasts, and Robin said no, her voice faint.

'As Mary Daly taught us, Patriarchy forbids women to touch each other like this without constraint, restraint, or observation. But on the day of our birth, we leave the first embrace of our mother's womb, and with our first breath, enter the waiting arms of midwives. Midwives, an old word that means "with women". Our touch tonight connects you with your birth and your body. As we touch, we will sing, and at the end, we will sing you a new name. You need not take it, but it is our gift to you.'

The witches passed urns of oil from hand to hand, warmed it in their palms, and began the massage: head, arms, back, all at once.

But Wren stepped away. A few minutes ago, she had wanted to touch Robin. But now, in the ritual, it felt wrong. She wanted her first time touching Robin to be as lovers, not the birthday back rub. Before the ritual, Gloria had asked Wren to create an in-the-moment drawing of Robin's massage. Gloria knew sketching the ritual would be what Wren needed. *She does take care of us, even though she's a pain in the ass.* So Wren sat on the couch and sketched the coven as they bent and swirled, poured and sang.

Their hands stroked Robin's skin, shiny and warm. They sang about The Lady, and they sang about the Ones Who

Love Her. They sang about the waxing and the waning moon. They sang about seasons, following each other in rhythm. They sang Her names in many languages. They sang about endings and beginnings and poetic mysteries that informed their creed, such as it was.

They sang on and lifted Robin's arms and gently tugged. They kneaded her arches, pressed her skin, sought out knots and tightnesses, rubbed away old hurts.

Wren turned the page and started a new drawing, thankful she could still look forward to her first caresses with Robin, their first kiss. With a shock of embarrassment and shame, she remembered the first time she kissed a woman. Switching from the blue to the orange pencil, recording curves and strokes, the scene alive with movement, she let those feelings rise and make vivid the memories, without judgment. She was fifteen, and had been persuaded by her best friend to meet up with two boys from their school in Golden Gate Park. The others wanted to play kissing games. She reluctantly kissed a boy she barely knew, and plucked at the pine needles in her socks when the other two took their turn. But then her boy urged Wren to kiss her friend. Wren wanted to kiss her at any cost, so she did, flushing in embarrassment and desire as the boys watched.

Now, under the spell of this ritual, she remembered her boy more clearly, and realised that he was gay too, and didn't want to kiss her either. As her puberty progressed, she expected to eventually like boys, especially the artists. The boys won the prizes. But they ignored her and ridiculed her art. For her first year of college, her mother took her to Paris. There she met Esther.

A song ended. Gloria whispered to Robin, and she sat up. Nikki offered her a chalice of water. Wren put more logs on the fire. Robin lay on her back and again the witches drenched her in oil. Now they sang the sounds in Robin's name, finding harmonies and discordances in the growling 'arrrr', singing 'ooo', 'beee', and the humming of 'ennn'.

Wren moved to the kitchen door to capture the ritual from another angle. Gloria stood at Robin's head, sending her fingers through her hair, pulling gently and firmly. Robin gasped. The women sang rhymes and rhythms of Robin's name, and bird calls.

As Gloria said, this massage was unrestrained, every inch of Robin's body an erogenous zone. It was erotic, but not like sex between lovers.

Wren sat back on the couch and turned to a new page. She remembered her first real lover. Her art teacher in Paris. She never mentioned her to anyone. She told her friends she had had lovers before she moved to Santa Cruz, but never gave details. Details lead to disclosures. Disclosures to judgements. Judgements to condemnation. She kept Esther a secret, and called her 'art school'.

Wren watched the witches' faces and sketched their expressions. Nikki's concentration – the same as when she textured drywall. Gloria's focus on Robin's jaw. Wren knew she had learned the cranium-something method from a book. Lupe and Hazel swirled around Robin's breasts, moving the muscles under the softness, then making their way toward Robin's nipples, focused on each other, keeping in sync. Wren remembered her own massage last winter. *So that's how they do it.*

Esther tried to talk her out of it, saying 'impossible'. Wren was too young to know why. One afternoon, she brought Esther's turpentine-scented fingers to her mouth and kissed them. Later they drank cognac in bed from one breast-shaped glass. She surprised herself at how easy it was to become someone's lover.

Ginny and Kelsey stood at Robin's legs and feet, squeezing firmly and never tickling. Maybe Robin would want a foot rub some time?

Her first kiss in the park was embarrassing, but knew she would be a lover of women. Being torn from Esther's arms taught her to never let her mother know.

She looked up from her drawing. The ritual was coming to an end. The witches sang Robin's new name to her over and over, in harmony and syncopation.

Esther taught her about art and about lesbians. But Wren left art school because her mother knew she loved it. She was nearly nineteen, but everyone agreed Wren was too young to stay in Paris on her own. When she left Esther's studio for the last time, she thought her body was split in half. In their last moments together, Esther asked only one thing: Wren's promise that she would never seek or expect the accolades of men.

So when she returned to San Francisco, she went looking for the lesbians. She slipped away from her mother's social connections. In a way, Wren left the Patriarchy then. But she remained stuck between the demands of her mother and her desire to support herself. Thus, she created beautiful things for her friends, but could never explore the infinite dimensions of her creativity. Sometimes, in ritual moments, she knew this about herself.

As she listened to her coven sing Robin's coven name into being, she felt Robin being adopted into the coven. Robin was one of them now; not the landlord; not an outsider.

Wren flipped back through the pages of her sketches. This is what Robin wants her to do. To record this vision: where women touch each other, where women like Robin – who conceive of their souls as disembodied – find love and power. Men never understood what women do together, alone. The 'magical statue' – whatever form it takes – will be about the embodiment of women with each other, alone.

Wren tore a page from her notebook and folded it into the tiniest square possible. She joined the witches as they stood in a semicircle around Robin's supine body. They had already wrapped her tightly in a sheet, like a newborn. The coven laid small gifts of rose quartz, malachite, turquoise and garnet along her chest. Wren added the scrap of paper. They spoke Robin's new name three times and ended the ritual.

The ritual circle opened and instead of wine they drank cognac, at Robin's suggestion. Wren felt more like the young woman who made love to Esther, and less like the girl who left her behind in Paris.

After the coven folded away the massage table and tidied up, Nikki, Lupe, Hazel and Ginny went out to Nikki's loft in the barn to smoke pot and listen to music. Robin and Kelsey settled in front of the fire, and Wren stepped toward the couch to join them.

Gloria slipped her arm around Wren's waist and whispered in her ear. 'I think they need to talk about something. Let's go up to your room.'

Eleven

After the birthday massage, the women scattered to their cabins and bedrooms, but Kelsey and Robin stayed at the fire, the house dark and quiet around them.

Kelsey brought both of them a cup of tea. She pulled the band from her hair with a sigh and pulled her fingers through it.

Robin added a log and watched the sparks. Then she broke the comfortable silence. 'Patriarchy has no idea what magic is.'

'Nope.'

'Birthdays used to mean my body felt less a part of me. Tonight, I feel like this body *is* me.'

'You're not the first woman to tell me that after her first birthday massage.'

'My childhoods are unique, but once I remember my past lives, I'm always me: same personality, the same woman-loving woman. Now that I've found you and your coven, this life might be different.'

Kelsey wanted to tell Robin about her childhood and how it shaped her. 'I need to tell you something.'

Robin turned on the couch. 'After tonight, I'm ready for anything.'

Kelsey remained still, watching the flames. Not yet. 'First, thank you for giving us money so we don't have to work. I think I like it.'

Robin might have been expecting her to say something else. She returned to watch the flames. 'You work hard.'

'I know. But now I can't afford to leave.'

'Why would you want to?'

She intended to tell Robin about Lucy, but couldn't imagine a future where that secret was told. 'The other women know something about me.'

'What do they know?'

Not a secret, but Kelsey felt the words jamming her throat, demanding to get out, but embarrassed they had to. 'I have a terrible temper. It scares people. I might drive you away.'

'That would be impossible.'

'Would it? We've done rituals about anger, but you weren't part of them. We trust each other now.'

'It takes more than a raised voice to scare me.'

'I suppose that's true, if you're a thousand years old.'

Robin chuckled. 'You don't believe I remember past lives.'

'No offence, but does it even matter? Look at that flame – there. Is it now the *past flame* of that new one?' In the firelight, she saw Robin's mouth slowly lift in a smile. 'Beauty and heat and light, becoming and then going. That's a lifetime. What will you do with that kind of magic?'

'How did you get so wise?'

'I had a good girlfriend in high school. Since her, I've met no one I can love like that.' That was as much as she would reveal.

Robin reached her hand over and laid it on Kelsey's thigh. 'And you never will.'

Kelsey picked up Robin's hand, still soft from the massage oil. She remembered the coven's hands passing – rushing – pressing – Robin's skin. She dropped the fingers in mock anger. 'Pessimist! I *am* trying.'

'I'm sorry. I said that wrong.' Robin quickly squeezed Kelsey's hand again before sitting back. 'I mean, you won't be sixteen again, and no one loves like a sixteen-year-old woman. I've been there so many times.'

That was enough about her own past. 'About your past-life memories.' Kelsey swallowed. 'I can't live my life *now* as if it is some future woman's *past* life.' Kelsey looked over to catch Robin's reaction. 'I don't want to offend you.'

'You can't. I'm glad to know that you have a temper. It makes me like you even more.'

'Really? I'm trying to get rid of it. Most women get scared around anger – for good reason.'

'That's for sure. But your anger won't frighten me.'

'Even little irritating things like dealing with the fucking propane. Inside me they get tangled up with every horrible injustice in the world.'

'Who's saying they aren't?'

'You're saying I'm justified in being a bitch?'

'It *is* unjust that women can't drive propane trucks. Does your temper interfere with your friendships?'

'Not much since I've been aware of it. Witchcraft helps.'

'What should I be afraid of?'

Robin was looking at her, but the flames had quieted and Kelsey couldn't read her face. 'Absolutely nothing.' Kelsey stood and stretched. 'Now that I got that off my chest, I'm tired. See you tomorrow?' She lifted her fingers to her nose. 'I love how we smell like sacred oil after a ritual.'

'Me too. Hey, can I ask you something?'

'Of course.'

'I want to know how witchcraft helped you with anger.'

'Gloria is a better teacher for stuff like that.'

Kelsey wasn't sure if Robin was disappointed or intrigued, but she sat back, her eyes to the fire. 'Sweet dreams, Kelsey.'

'Happy birthday, Robin. I'm glad you were born.'

Kelsey used her flashlight to make her way up the backstairs. She couldn't remember if she had heard Robin say her name before. She liked the sound of it in Robin's mouth, and it worried her.

⌘

When they got to Wren's room, they undressed, shivering, still singing a massage chant, *rising, rising, rise and fly*. Wren still felt altered from the ritual.

They snuggled together under one of Wren's quilts, Gloria warming up Wren's backside with her front. It was nice to be in her own bed, and cuddling with Gloria truly felt like being with a sister, and without the one-sided sexual draw she felt toward Robin. Wren felt herself drifting into the half-sleep where sometimes she found her best ideas. She had filled two sketchbooks with ideas for the magical statue, and maybe tonight, after Robin's massage, she would dream the final design.

But Gloria wanted to talk. 'Birthday massages are the best ritual idea I ever had. Do you love the new amber oil blend?' Gloria put her fingers to Wren's nose and cuddled closer.

Gloria stopped talking long enough for Wren to begin drifting again, then said, 'Robin amazes me.'

'Do you "like her" like her?' Wren asked, fully awake now with adrenaline of dread.

'I think we're all a little bit in love with her, don't you?'

Wren relaxed. 'You like her. I saw you popping a truffle in her mouth.'

'She told Nikki she's not really into sex.' Gloria thrust an arm from the quilts and pinched out the candle flame in that witchy way Wren never could. 'How is Robin's Moon Money working out for you?'

Wren gave in to Gloria's desire for conversation. 'She said she'd buy my art supplies, too.'

'She will? It can't last the way she's spending it. I bet she needs someone to manage her money.'

Not that Wren used any of her new art supplies. She had been sketching, thinking about a tarot deck, but nothing had gelled.

'She thinks she fixed all our problems with her money, but it would be more feminist if we managed it together, like a collective, rather than her giving us whatever she feels like.'

Wren knew Gloria still loved those ledger books.

'If she *can* manage money,' Gloria chattered on, 'then she should teach us, so we learn.'

'Sounds like something to bring up at a house meeting. Go to sleep, Gloria.'

'Maybe I will.' Then, out of nowhere, Gloria said, 'I heard you're finally going to come out to your mother.'

Startled, Wren wondered who had told her that. Robin wouldn't. Kelsey? 'No one knows what my mother is capable of. I'm right to be afraid of her.'

'You might be surprised. She's like Demeter and she needs

you, little Persephone.' Gloria wrapped her arms around Wren and held her close. 'She's your mother and will never abandon you, no matter what. That's what being a mother is.'

'You forget my mother isn't Demeter. I'm not afraid of abandonment; I'm afraid of a corporate takeover. Whenever I like something, she takes it away from me. Being a lesbian is the one thing she hasn't ruined.'

Gloria sighed, sounding more annoyed than sympathetic, but said, 'She can't ruin your life any more. We won't let her. Sisterhood is powerful.'

Now that they lived on their own land, platitudes about sisterhood might just be true. And Robin and Gloria agreeing on something? Maybe it was time for Wren to come out.

In those many trips to the dump after the Snake revelation, Wren sketched her housemates tossing the debris of generations into the pit. Over the darkening weeks of December, she sketched Lupe and Ginny pruning the apples, Hazel and Nikki roofing the greenhouse with recycled windows, and the eight of them, wrapped in cloaks, singing their hearts out around a fire in the redwood grove.

As Yule approached, Wren was well settled in the studio, art supplies stored neatly. She sat at her worktable with one of those new infrared heaters at her knees.

Dear Mom,
    It's weird to be writing you a Christmas card, but I want to tell you I love you, and I am grateful to you.

Because you loved me, you made it possible for me to know that I love women. I'm a lesbian. Is that a surprise to you? Kelsey says it won't be, and she's usually right. If you knew I was a lesbian already, I'm sorry that I didn't tell you earlier. Now that I'm living on this women's land, everything seems so clear. (No, Kelsey is just a friend.)

I know you wanted me to move back after Grandma died. Please forgive me. Because you are the BEST MOM, you raised me to be independent and strong.

I've been working on an important art project. Since I was a little girl, you have encouraged me. I think I will do amazing things.

Merry Christmas and Happy Yule.

With all my love,

Your daughter, Brenda

Wren decorated the letter with a star, a sun, and their phone number. She then put her fingers flat on the sealed envelope, and a blessing poured out of them, surrounding her letter with love and light and hope. As she did this small act of ordinary magic, the vision shifted and she saw the letter on her mother's kitchen table, a cigarette burn in its centre.

Wren jumped as Gloria came into the studio.

'Is that gold leaf?'

'It is. I can afford it now. You like the haloes?'

Gloria was wearing the baggy green velour top that showed off a jade goddess resting on her chest. She always looked so clean and put together, unlike the rest of them, with men's shirts from the thrift store and overalls.

Gloria took the card and tilted it in the light. 'You are so talented. It's just like the St Anne and Mary window in our church in Hanford. Can you put gold leaf on anything?'

'Like what?'

'I've always wanted to add gold leaf to my tarot cards. Will you teach me?'

'It's easy, but I can't now; I need to get this out.' If she didn't mail the card today, she never would, and Kelsey would make fun of her forever.

'No rush. It's something we can work on together someday.' Gloria looked around the room, art materials neatly stacked and stored. 'What did I come in here for? Oh yeah – coloured pencils. Do you have some?'

Wren gave her a pencil box and then ran across the living room. She borrowed Robin's suede coat off its hook and walked up to the main road. Maybe after she comes out, she can be the kind of artist Robin thinks she is.

The rain had stopped, and the redwoods dripped in winter's early twilight. Since that first day in the grove with Robin, she regarded redwoods as venerable daughters growing tall from the bodies of their mothers. As she walked up their road to the mailbox, she felt like they were cheering her on.

Raising the flag on the mailbox, she imagined a future where she told her mother everything without fear. She saw herself talking to a headstone.

She walked back to the house, and the sight of their home took her breath away. The six windows glowed orange in the winter gloom. Both chimneys cheerily poured smoke into a pink sky. Her own bedroom on the veranda, with Robin on one side and Kelsey on the other. Even if her mother showed up braless in a purple tee-shirt, beating the door down with a labrys, her coven would protect her. She ran up the steps and threw open the door, shouting, 'I'm no longer the girl who never came out to her mother!'

Lupe, Hazel, Robin and Ginny were composing feminist

carols by the kitchen-side fireplace. Kelsey and Nikki were stretched out at either end of the long couch at the other fire, reading their lesbian mysteries. Everyone seemed to be drinking pungent cinnamon tea.

'Congratulations!'

'I knew you could!'

'Is that my jacket?'

Twelve

On winter solstice, the witches watched the sunset from Bonny Doon beach, then ran back and forth through the waves, splashing each other and calling it a blessing. Then they drove up the mountain, warmed themselves around the fire and passed a wishing glass. After that they ate a ham, a chicken, green-bean casserole and candied yams. Everyone tried to stay up, to keep vigil so the sun returned. Only Robin and Lupe made it until dawn. They roused whom they could, and a bleary gaggle of women stumbled up to the orchard to witness the sun's rebirth.

The Solstice ritual itself wasn't as significant as the long twelve nights of Yule afterward, when friends arrived from Santa Cruz, the Bay Area and even Oregon and Washington. The Lesbian Nation might not appear on a map, but its citizens occupied every corner of the world.

One highly regarded woman arrived in mid-December. She had been travelling from one women's land to another. Her name was Diane, but everyone called her Cayenne. Not just because she had red hair, but because her energy was intense and a little bit dangerous. As Nikki and two carpenter friends were building a bathhouse in the back, Cayenne volunteered to help Wren decorate it with mermaids. She said she loved mermaids because they made their home in a different world, just like the women who created wimmin's lands.

By Christmas Day, the bathhouse was nearly done. The Yule fire had burned for three days, warming the house up to the attic. Anyone who couldn't use a skill saw was playing music in the living room or had retreated to a room for private celebrations.

At first Wren thought she didn't need a helper, but she was painting the mural on two plywood sheets. As she sat hour after hour, her tongue in her teeth, painting scales, she thoroughly appreciated Cayenne's meticulous contribution. Right now, Cayenne was singing to herself as she filled in kelp fronds.

'Are you singing *Gloria in excelsis deo*?'

Cayenne laughed. '*In excelsis dea*. Kelsey was teasing Gloria about it yesterday, and I got it stuck in my head. Do you sing?'

'Not well, but I don't let that stop me.'

Wren sang one of their own songs:

Dark is retreating, the light grows stronger every day. We witches will rise and greet the dawn.

'I like that.' Cayenne sang it back until Wren had taught her all the words. She worked out the melody, despite Wren's inability to carry it herself.

Wren wondered if Cayenne liked her. The other woman praised Wren's art specifically, not just the usual 'wow-you're-good'. Cayenne made Wren's mermaids better.

The household phone had ended up in Wren's studio because it was the quietest room, with a loveseat perfect for private conversations. Wren and Cayenne had been working all morning for hours when it rang. They both yelped and laughed at themselves. Wren got up to answer.

'Good afternoon, Wicked Ranch! How may I bewitch you?'

'May I speak to Brenda?'

Oh shit. 'Mom! How are you?'

'How do you think? Meet me at that place you always took me.'

'Are you in Santa Cruz?'

'Yes, on your Mission Street.'

'At The O'mei?'

'The place with the ice cream.'

'Saturn Cafe?'

'Yes, that one. But they're closed, so I'm just sitting here by myself. Don't bring any of your friends.' She hung up.

Wren fell into the loveseat and sat there until the phone in her hand complained. She couldn't face her mother alone. Then she heard Robin come in.

'How's it going, Cayenne? Oh – hi Wren. These mermaids are beautiful.'

Wren's feet did an involuntary dance on the floor. 'Cayenne and I inspire each other.'

Robin was on the bathhouse construction crew. Her lips were chapped and she had hat hair. Stunning. 'This is amazing, Cayenne. Wren could use a partner. Did you see the poppy meadow on the cupboards?'

'She's amazing,' Cayenne agreed, pretending Wren wasn't right there. Then she thanked Robin for opening her land to travelling women like herself, and they started talking about the many women's lands they had visited.

'Robin, what are you doing this afternoon?' broke in Wren.

'I'm the plumbers' assistant.'

'My mom got my coming-out letter and called. She wants me to meet her at the Saturn.'

'The Saturn is closed on Christmas.'

'I know. But it's the only place she knows in Santa Cruz. I assume she will want to see the ranch. She said to come alone, but…'

'She wants you alone? I'm definitely coming with.'

Wren's heart leapt. 'Cayenne, do you mind staying here and working without me?' Cayenne might have looked like she minded, but Wren was already out the door.

'I'll warm up the truck,' she shouted to Robin.

Wren ran down the steps, propelled by a wave of dread and a thin stream of thrill. She knew what to expect, but Robin would be there.

Wren slid over when Robin got behind the wheel.

'What did she say exactly?' Robin asked.

'That she wanted to meet me at the Saturn. Hey, is anyone sleeping with you tonight? Whatever happens, I'll want to talk it over with you.'

'You can sleep with me any time. I got some poems by a local dyke called *To Live with the Weeds*.'

'It is about gardening?'

'It's about living with women who don't serve men. You'll like it.'

∞

Robin negotiated the last curves through the redwoods, then the trees opened and the dark mountains and majesty of the Monterey Bay appeared. Empire Grade ended at Bay, where

Robin turned right toward Mission. Wren always felt they entered enemy territory at that intersection. She couldn't wait to bring her mom back to the comfort of their home. Would she like Robin? Would she want to smoke inside?

Robin interrupted Wren's meandering obsessions. 'Are you sure you want to sleep with me tonight?'

Wren's stomach dropped. *Doesn't she?*

'I was wondering if something was happening between you and Cayenne.'

'Cayenne? Hardly.'

'She seems to like you.'

'Does she?'

'I know Cayenne from Oregon women's land. I think you might be good together.'

'Me and Cayenne?' *Me and Cayenne?*

'Kelsey told me you've been in a dry spell since last summer.'

'That's right. That was before I met you, though.'

'That's my point. It's been a while. Don't you think one of our guests…?'

'I have enough to deal with my mom.'

'Maybe. Anyway, Gloria told me she thinks Cayenne likes you too.'

'Are we in high school now?'

'You know what I mean.'

'I know what you mean.' *And wish I didn't.* 'I'm uptight about my mom.'

'Did she ever do this before?'

'Show up? Unannounced? No. I've tried to make my life in Santa Cruz uninteresting. But that means I need to visit her a lot.'

'Did she answer your coming-out letter?'

'No. But if she was angry about it, then she wouldn't be here now.'

The Saturn Cafe's parking lot was bleak on a good day, contrasting with the whimsical welcome inside. The vegetarian restaurant occupied a sixties-era pizza parlour anchoring a dingy strip mall. A Baskin-Robbins across the parking lot couldn't compete with the outrageous desserts the Saturn concocted, but the tourists didn't know better. The Saturn was locals-only.

'That's her car.'

Robin pulled in next to an old Mercedes.

'Wish me luck.'

'I'll be right here.'

Wren ran around to her mother's car. Her mother got out. She was taller than Wren, hair still blonde, today feathered and sprayed. She cinched her camel coat tight to her waist. Wren put on her best smile and thought they might hug, but her mother twisted away and opened the rear door.

'This won't take long,' her mother warned. Wren froze, her arms stuck out like a robot. Her mother pulled a flat brown paper-wrapped package almost as tall as herself from the back seat. The edge of it hit the ground, and Wren heard it crack. 'This is yours now. You'll get nothing more from me. Have yourself a Merry Little Christmas, you ungrateful brat.'

Wren steadied her hand as she reached for it. 'Mom, I don't need—'

'Your needs? Isn't it always about your needs?' Wren's mother's voice got loud, and Wren felt a familiar ice in her brain. 'I *needed* you, Brenda!'

'Is this because I'm a lesbian?'

'Lesbian?'

Surprising mother was always a mistake.

'I knew this was just like Paris. Those women took you from me. *Dykes.*' Wren's mother's face twisted in disgust with a memory, then reddened with rage. 'Did it ever enter your head to think about how *I feel*? I needed you after Mother died.'

Her eyes began to tear up, and Wren knew that meant she'd get more dangerous. She opted for retreat and rested the thin package against the grill of the car. Her mother stepped forward, pushed her purse back on her arm, and restarted the assault.

'Just try to live without me.'

'I have my life here.'

'Your life!' *Here it comes.* 'Your life is mine. Don't forget I adopted you out of that place. I should have given you back.'

'Mom, I know you don't mean it. Please stop.'

'You have always been selfish.'

Wren took another step back. Robin was getting out of the truck.

Her mother looked confused and surprised. *Another mistake.* 'Who's this?'

Wren glanced over. Robin was leaning against the hood of her truck with her hands folded across her stomach.

'I told you to come alone.' Wren's mother turned to get into her car.

Wren followed, caught the top edge of the door, but snatched her hand away when it slammed.

'You won't defy me again.'

'Mom! You almost hurt me!'

Her mother rolled down the window and lit a cigarette. Wren froze, waiting for it.

'Never call or write to me again.'

Wren held her fingers to her mouth. She heard a moan

from inside. *I'm going down.*

Robin caught her before she fell, standing behind her. Her mother reversed, and the package slapped on the pavement. As the car disappeared up Mission Street, Wren actually felt her heart break.

'Robin!' Wren sobbed into Robin's neck. 'Oh, Robin!'

'What did she say?'

Wren gripped Robin's arms and shook them. 'We have to go after her.'

'What did she bring you?' Robin pried Wren off, picked up the package and opened the wrapping. A wide gilt frame surrounded a portrait of Wren's mother: younger, nude, posed in front of a window overlooking the Bay and distant Oakland hills.

Wren knew the painting. It had hung in her mother's bedroom since Wren was in high school. In Wren's childhood, her mother often volunteered to be her model. Early on, Wren loved to play The Artist. Her mother let her use the good paints and new brushes for these special portraits. But by the time she painted this last one, she was sixteen, and she dreaded the nights when her mother switched off the TV and demanded a 'life drawing session'.

'That's the last one I painted.'

'That's…that's fucked up, Wren.'

'I know. I'm sure in some families it's perfectly normal to paint nudes of your mother, but I feel sick right now.'

'I get it. Let me tell you, speaking from experience, it was wrong for your mom to do this to you.'

'You're right. It seemed normal to me, like most kids feel with the weird shit their parents do.' A wave rose through Wren's body, a fluttering and roaring that started behind her knees. It tugged at her stomach and crushed her lungs tight.

'We have to go after her.'

Robin grabbed Wren's hand and led her over to the passenger side of the pickup. 'No.'

'We do. Please.' Wren looked down at Robin's fingers holding her own. 'I need to explain. She's so hurt.'

'You don't need to explain.' Robin guided Wren's head as she sat on the edge of the seat, then lifted her legs and shut the door.

As Robin turned over the engine, Wren asked if they could go to the city. 'I need to talk with her.'

'She can't be trusted.' Robin turned the heater up. 'Remember how she deleted my messages?'

'I can fix this.'

Robin warmed her hands on the vent.

Wren tried again. 'She might get in an accident.'

'She might. What did she say?'

Wren sat back and stared through the windshield at their reflection in the dark restaurant window. So many memories of the Saturn – first dates, after-game parties, tomato soup with rice. Every one now blighted by this scene with her mother. Like everything else she loved. 'She said…' Wren tried to repeat what her ears had heard, but instead something was leaking in her brain, covering all the words. She was leaning on Robin's shoulder now. The heater blew warm on her cold cheeks. She smelled Robin's jacket under her nose and she was getting snot on it.

'I'm sorry.' Wren pulled away. 'I'm getting…'

'Here.' Robin handed her a bandana that smelled like pipe dope and Robin.

Wren leaned against the door and blew her nose, returning a sense of solidity. 'I don't know what I would have done without you.'

Robin put the truck in reverse and backed up. 'I'm here. What did she say?' Robin stopped before turning onto Mission.

'She didn't mean it.'

'What did she tell you?

'Mothers don't…'

'You came out to her. Ended the lies and her power over you.' An element in Robin's voice dried up the remaining mess in Wren's brain.

'I came out to her, and she didn't care.'

'You began to live truthfully when you decided to move in with us instead of staying in San Francisco.'

'But I didn't know it. Living on our land is why I could write that letter. I came out for myself, not her.'

'So what did she say that upset you?'

'She told me never to speak to her again – but she says stuff when she's angry. She doesn't mean it. Can you take me home? I need to explain.'

'I'm taking you home.' Robin turned left across the empty thoroughfare.

'That's not what I meant!' Wren cried. Robin was going in the wrong direction. 'Please, Robin!'

'When someone like that tells you to' – Robin's voice rose screechy and theatrical – 'NEVER SPEAK TO ME AGAIN, you need to do what they say. People like her will burn the relationship to the ground rather than lose control. I've seen it happen more times than even I can remember.'

Wren lay her head in Robin's lap and cried some more as they drove through town, but by the time they reached the redwoods, she was breathing normally.

'When I sent the coming-out-letter to my mom, I made her a Christmas card. I drew the Blessed Mother and St Anne.'

'Herself and Her Mother?'

'Yeah. The big church down from Dolores Park is my mom's favourite.' Wren sat up and blew her nose again. It felt better with her head on Robin's shoulder, so she leaned back into her. 'When I was about twelve, I ran away from home.'

'How far did you get?'

'Down Dolores to that church. I wanted to talk to Mary about her mom.'

'You thought she'd understand you.'

'I did. I went in by myself, which I had never done. I felt grown-up when I blessed myself and genuflected to the altar. I approached Mary and St Anne and knelt at their feet. They didn't say anything, but after a while I felt better. I was ready to walk home.

'When I got to Dolores Park, I met a group of older girls there. This was the early Seventies; they seemed like fairies to me, with their flowered skirts, blue eyeshadow and red lips. They didn't have boyfriends with them. It was just women. They had a radio and were singing that Carpenters song about singing loud, singing strong.'

'And you didn't worry if it was good enough.'

'Exactly, because I couldn't sing then either.' They both laughed. That felt good. To laugh with Robin.

'They were probably high, but I was too young to know about getting high. I only knew about grown-ups getting drunk. So anyway, I danced with them, and they must have thought it was cute and they picked up my hands and danced in a circle, and then later one of them dumped out her purse and made up my face with long, cat-eye mascara and her reddest lipstick.'

'You must have felt beautiful.'

'I did! I didn't recognise myself in her little mirror.' Wren pulled herself away from Robin and leaned against the door. She remembered the rest of it now.

'Anyway, while she knelt in front of me and put on the eyeliner, I remember her cleavage so close to my face. I just stared at her boobs. I didn't want her to finish because then I'd have to stop looking at her breasts.'

'And, in a way, you never have.'

They laughed again. *Robin doesn't judge. Just like the Blessed Mother at Mission Dolores, Robin understands her.* Wren moved back closer. 'I wanted to keep looking at that fullness. But she finished my eyes, and I danced with them in their summer dresses.'

'How idyllic.'

'Then my mom showed up. She had been driving all over, looking for me. I know she was terrified, but she could only act angry. The girls apologised, but they were so stoned they started laughing, and that pissed her off even more. She threw me in the back seat and, the next week, installed locks. I didn't get free until art school.' Wren blew her nose again. 'I remembered this when she opened the car door just now. The same as then – leather and smoke and perfume.'

Wren stopped talking, drained. As Robin turned down their road and they crossed the bridge, she knew the magical statue had to include what those girls in the park showed her.

Wren pressed her boots into the mud of the plaza and started walking slowly toward the house.

Robin came up behind her and steered her toward the back. 'Maybe you should lie down for a while. I can tell them what happened.'

Wren reached across for Robin's hand at her waist, her chest aching and exhausted.

'I'll tell them your mother ruined Christmas.'

'Won't be the first time.'

'But definitely the last.'

Robin always said the right thing.

Thirteen

Wren sought sanctuary in her room, colder inside than outside. She kept the light off. She could see a square grey paperback on her bed. The poems about weeds that Robin wanted her to read. She stepped around to Robin's room, crawled into Robin's bed and switched on Robin's reading light. The poems in the book weren't about gardening, but about living with the women who men disregard. The kind of women Wren's mother warned her about.

Wren read the first poem aloud to herself before she fell asleep. She awoke an hour later, hearing her mother's voice: *Dykes! Dykes! Dykes!* How like her mother to see exactly who Wren was – and criticise her for it. She tried to shove her mother's voice away – like always – but tonight, succeeded. Her mother's tantrum today broke her spell. For the first time, Wren felt out of her mother's psychic reach.

She heard music and voices downstairs. She felt hungry and ready for company. She slipped on her clogs, savoured the chill night air as she walked around to the back stairs. She opened the kitchen door to light, warmth and sisterhood.

Alix and Julz, Nikki's contractor friends, were finishing the dishes. On the table were leftover mac-and-cheese, sweet potatoes, green beans, olives, nuts, cranberries, all styles of potato and the carcasses of a few turkeys. Scout from Oregon – Kelsey's fling at Thanksgiving – was sitting at the table eating a pecan pie directly out of the tin. Wren's mother would hate that.

Alix greeted Wren with a hug and a kiss. 'We heard what happened. So sorry.'

'Thank you,' Wren said, relieved she wouldn't have to explain. She tore a hunk off a turkey breast and stepped into the living room.

The living room blazed with candles: tapers in multi-armed holders, square pillars on plates, votives in smoky jars and lanterns hanging from the beams of the ceiling. Someone had burned tangy myrrh and sweet frankincense again. Tonight, the musicians convened across the room at the other fireplace. Straight ahead, around the fire, dykes flopped on the long couch, perched on the red chair and squeezed onto the leather sofa. Many feet rested in someone else's lap and heads rested on bosoms. Bottles and ashtrays and trays of fudge and baklava filled the low tables between the furniture and the fires. Wren looked for Robin.

Cayenne patted the couch next to herself. Wren squeezed in.

'I'm sorry that happened today – oh, your hands are cold, let me warm them.'

Wren let Cayenne fuss over her. Robin was sitting across on the little couch with Lupe, their heads together.

Wren chewed the turkey, but it was dry. Kelsey leaned

over Cayenne and squeezed Wren's knee. 'I told you, she's a creepy bitch. She's not right.'

'Is there any wine left?'

Cayenne filled her own glass and offered it to Wren.

She drank a few sips and tuned into the conversation.

'I have been a priestess many times,' Gloria was recounting. 'I remembered my past lives when I was a girl and first read Greek myths.'

'I remember my past lives.' Ginny was knitting something complicated with lots of little needles. 'Since I met you, Robin, I listen to myself. "What would I have done in a past life?" And the answer comes.'

Robin brightened. 'That's what it is like for me.'

Wren looked over and waved. Robin winked back. They would sleep together tonight.

Gloria leaned forward. Wren noticed she was wearing the big obsidian stone she found in Nevada last year. It swung delightfully between her breasts. 'Robin, can I ask you more about your reincarnations? Do you remember being born?'

'I don't, but I remember being dead. After I die, I come to that circle of stones – I told you about it at Halloween – and outside the stones I see many campfires. Each of them is a pregnant woman. The first few times, I ran out to the nearest one, but after a while I learned I could endure the cold and search among them. I can choose someone I recognise. Then everything changed after I chose the daughter of the landlord and was rich for the first time.'

'Are you always a woman?' Gloria asked, like she knew the answer. Wren wished she wouldn't use that tone of voice.

'I have lived as a man, but when I am born male, I never get the memories. On the other hand, when I live as a man, I can make money, and travel.'

'You would have a sympathy for men, since you've been one,' Gloria probed.

'That's why I want to end Patriarchy, Gloria. We're all suffering.'

'I've been a man in a past life, too,' Hazel said. 'Men were different before Patriarchy.'

'They were,' Ginny said with atypical authority. 'We had personalities like animals do, not gender roles. We've lost what human maleness really is. And femaleness.'

'I doubt that,' said Cayenne, playfully patting Kelsey's breasts.

'Me too.' Kelsey grabbed Cayenne's fingers and kissed them.

What the hell? Something must have sparked up between them that afternoon. Wren felt that lovely emotion, the opposite of jealousy. And relief. Cayenne was sweet, but Wren wanted Robin.

'I've played all the gender roles,' Robin continued. 'Every role is just another form of domination. The end of gender roles is the end of Patriarchy.'

'I'll drink to that.' Nikki opened another bottle.

'Did you ever live as a man and get discovered?' asked Hazel.

'Of course.' Robin asked Nikki for a refill. 'Now, that's where it gets dangerous. They don't like it when you trick them. When they caught me, at first I never survived it. But I got better at killing people, so if someone learned my secret, I had to kill him before he killed me.'

The circle of peaceful, loving women sat unusually silent for many long minutes, until Hazel said, 'So. You've killed people.'

'Sure, but not often.' Robin didn't seem to know what to

say next.

'I need to say something,' Kelsey said, like an announcement. 'Robin knows this, so nobody get defensive on her behalf. I don't believe in past lives. I'm afraid of fire, but I came by that honestly because my dad is a bad electrician.'

Wren laughed along with everyone and said, 'I don't know if past lives are real, but I'd like them to be.'

'You use past lives in your art,' said Gloria. 'Didn't you tell me your new tarot deck is inspired by a past life?'

Everyone burst into a chorus of 'How cool', 'Please!' and 'I want one!'

Wren had wondered if the Sacred Art Thing was their own private tarot deck. She designated herself as the Fool, Gloria as the Priestess, Kelsey as the Goddess and Robin as The World. But the prospect of inventing dozens and dozens of images for a tarot deck overwhelmed then bored her. Everyone's enthusiasm felt slightly embarrassing. 'Quiet down, everyone,' she said. 'I got stuck on the Dire Fives.'

The women groaned.

Wren felt worse, so reluctantly told the past-life story Gloria wanted.

'I was turning over cards from the Motherpeace deck and had a memory of reading cards in a round room overlooking a bay, like I was in a castle tower. The memory made me feel that reading the tarot was wrong.'

'You were doing something right, probably,' snorted Scout. 'I was a witch in a past life and they burned me for it.'

Gloria reminded everyone that 'a lot of us were burned'. That was a real buzz kill. At least no one was asking about the tarot deck any more. Wren hated for Robin to see that failure.

Lupe rolled a joint and lit it. The flame caught everyone's

attention, and they silently watched the glowing cherry in the semi-darkness. Most of the candles had gone out. Wren noticed that quite a few women had gone to bed, and caught Robin's eye. Maybe they could go upstairs now too.

Robin smiled as if she knew that, but said, 'Since it's Yule, I'll tell a ghost story.'

Kelsey put another log on and disappeared into the kitchen. Cayenne announced she was going to the biffy.

Wren lay down in the warmth that Cayenne's butt had left and pulled a blanket around her. If Robin felt like telling a ghost story, she could wait. She would do whatever Robin wanted if it meant they would be together.

⊕

'About a hundred years ago, I lived in San Francisco and worked as a medium – people paid me to give them messages from their beloved dead. I can do a good cold read. Being a medium also allowed me to travel.

'One night, I was working in someone's home, and the host had brought in some neighbours and friends for the seance. The host and his wife were true believers, the kind of people who would be New Age-y if they lived today.

'They had invited a guy who ran a school, who considered himself a man of science and a sceptic of Spiritualism. There was a minister and his wife who weren't sure if this was godly, but they wanted to speak to their dead relatives. Then there was this rich widow, and the hosts were angling to get an inheritance from her. They were very obsequious, giving her the best chair, serving her tea – all that. She took their hospitality as if she deserved it.

'As I watched her getting settled, I saw that she had been

beautiful. She wore East Coast clothes, but from forty years earlier. But as soon as she spoke, memories of who she was came flooding back.

'The host turned down the gas until the room was dark except for the candle in the centre of the table. I put the black veil over my hair and did my thing. They expected a medium would fall asleep like this.' Robin sat back with her chin on her chest.

'And then I stiffened up, like this.' She sat up straight and opened her eyes wide at the ceiling.

'SPIRITS!' Robin shouted so loud that everyone jumped, and Hazel and Ginny spilled wine on each other. They laughed and started to get towels to wipe up, but Gloria shushed them.

'Never mind. Keep going, Robin.'

'SPIRITS OF THE DEAD. I WOULD THAT YOU SPEAK! COME FROM YOUR DISTANT DARKNESS AND SPEAK! SPEAK IF YOU CAN!'

'And again I would pretend to fall asleep. Then I would wake up like this. "Sister? Sister, is it you?" Because everyone had a brother or sister who had died. That always worked. Then someone said, "Is it you, Anthony?"

'And I would say, "Yes, it is I, Anthony, I have something to tell you."

'"Oh Anthony, I've missed you so much," she would say, and then I would take it from there.

'I did a few of those, but I was waiting to come around to the widow. Finally I said, "Mother? It is I, your daughter Beryl, who died so long ago."

'This had the right effect because none of the ghosts so far had given their name before someone had offered it. The Professor leaned forward.

'The widow's eyes filled with tears. "Beryl? How can this be?"

'"Mother, I forgive you." The widow burst into tears, which was satisfaction right there, but I kept on. "I forgive you for giving me to that man. I forgive you."

'The widow said, "You need not forgive me, my darling. He loved you! You were so lovely on your wedding day!"

'In my anger, I revealed her dark secret. "Beautiful on my wedding day? I was. What happened then? I burned in a terrible fire the next day, didn't I? Someone opened all the windows so the flames would race through the house faster than hope."

'The widow cried and grabbed my hands, but I pulled away. She said, "My darling girl, a cruel accident cut short your life. Truly, God needed another angel."

'I leaned forward and yelled at her. "It was no accident you married me to that old man. You calculated every dollar. All my life, you wanted a doll, a perfect projection of your self-absorption. I was a baby when you bought me from the orphanage. God was too merciful to give you your own children."

'The widow regarded her circle of neighbours, who sat embarrassed but fascinated, wondering what the medium would say next. The widow said, "God gave me two strong boys – and you. It doesn't matter where God found them. We were loving parents."

'I stopped yelling and told the rest of the story without emotion. "My childhood was a living hell. I didn't know better. Then I grew up. I rebelled. You didn't like that, did you? I was too clever. I couldn't go to school like my brothers. I refused to attend the meat-market cotillions, but you sold me to an old man anyway."

'The widow looked at the hosts. "Make her stop!"

'The Professor said, "Let her speak," but the host got up and shook my shoulder. "Wake up, wake up! Stop this minute!"

'I continued to feign my trance. I listed everything I remembered: the beatings, the incarcerations in the attic, the forced feedings, every humiliation. I was never good enough. Any little thing I loved, she took away.

'On and on I went, pretending to be insensible to my host's attempts to stop me. I worked myself up into a rage again. "I will rest when you're barking in hell," I screamed into her face, "which can't come soon enough, you festering boil!"

'The widow ran from the room, screaming. She ran down the street, terrified by her own past.'

Robin stopped talking. Sometime during the telling, Wren had sat up, knees to her chest. She unfolded herself and poured another glass of wine. 'Pass the ginger snaps, please.'

Gloria handed her the bowl. 'The widow was your mother in a past life?'

'I didn't remember until I heard her voice.'

'Whoa.' Lupe summed up everyone's feelings. 'Brutal.'

Brutal. That described Wren's childhood. Robin sure knew how to be a friend.

With Robin's story over, tête-à-tête conversations started again. More women left for bed. Wren pulled the blanket around herself, waved at Kelsey and Cayenne at the kitchen table finishing a pie, and went upstairs. She knew Robin would follow.

∞

Wren picked up *To Live with the Weeds* and had read up to

the poem observing that the existence of unicorns enjoyed more cultural proof than lesbians.

Robin entered the room. Without saying a word, she undressed and spooned in, careful not to freeze Wren's feet with her own. Wren switched off the light. Robin pushed her warm backside into Wren's stomach.

Wren pulled her closer and soaked in Robin's warmth. She stroked her friend's forearm and sensed the strength there. Maybe, at the end of this horrible day, because of what Robin's story meant, this would be the time – their first time.

'Thanks for the story, Robin.'

'You're welcome. Sweet dreams, Wren.'

'You too,' Wren said. 'I love you.'

'Love you too. I'm so sleepy.'

Wren stayed awake for a long time.

A terrible dream woke Wren in the morning, a replay of the scene at the Saturn, this time her mother screaming, '*I alone* adopted you. No one else cares for you.'

Wren let the soft morning light and breakfast noises from the kitchen wash away the remnants of the nightmare. Robin slept beside her. She felt grateful Robin brought her home instead of chasing after her mother. Wren came out and survived. Her mother removed *herself* from Wren's life. She had never imagined that possibility.

'Good morning,' Robin whispered, and got out to use the chamber pot. 'You were talking in your sleep.'

Wren took her turn at the pot and returned to bed. 'Last night you told that story for me, right?'

'I thought you could relate. Sometimes I weary of all this mother goddess adulation.'

'My mother is the Helmet-Haired Harridan of Bernal Heights.' Wren imagined her mother as a living statue striding into their plaza, fighting a labrys-wielding sorority, while redwood trees pulled off their long limbs and threw them like spears. 'What if she tries to come here?'

'If she does, I'll give her a *piece* of my *mind*.' Robin lifted her arm from the blankets and shook her fist, dissolving Wren's bizarre vision.

'No one understood why I never came out to her. It was too dangerous.'

'She can't hurt you here. I won't let her.'

'You mean you'll enforce boundaries? I've been told women like me don't know what boundaries are.' Wren wanted to blur the boundaries with Robin.

'Wren, I was so lonely before. I love living with you.'

Wren took a breath and held it.

'Do you also know how great it is to sleep with another woman – just sleep?'

'Not really.'

Robin chuckled. She thought Wren was kidding. 'I never knew a group who were so free with how they touch. And it's not weird.'

'It's not weird, but it can be...' Wren buried her face in Robin's hair and whispered, '...so frustrating.'

'And your coven! When women understand how to work with erotic energy like you do – well, I don't know what will happen. That's the mystery I want to explore.'

Wren hoped Robin would do something else. But she didn't. Wren knew she should go downstairs and eat breakfast. But she felt a temptation and inner strength. Perhaps it was this new freedom. Why wait? Why not ask for what she wants? 'Robin, it's so hard not to make love to you right now.'

'I know.' She didn't sigh; she wasn't annoyed. Robin turned around and pressed her forehead to Wren's. 'You would be a delightful lover.' She brushed Wren's hair away from her face. 'I know it. But I'm not that woman for you.'

'Don't you want to have sex?'

'Those desires don't come to me any more. We're not going to be lovers, Wren.'

'But I only promised to make your magical statue so we could be lovers.'

'I know.'

She knew. Wren twisted onto her back and away from Robin's unkissable mouth. She glared at the familiar blue ceiling, and its specks of white, like stars. They had never finished painting it and had grown fond of the imperfections.

'I can't wait to see what you create now.'

Wren gasped in exasperation. 'I can't make your big art thing. I don't even *want* to. It will just remind me of what I can't have. I lied and now I must pay the price.'

'Nothing is changed.'

'We can't sleep together any more.'

'Of course we can still sleep together. Come here.'

Wren could not resist. She embraced Robin, and the desire to kiss her even faded a little. Being rejected could do that. She listened to Robin's steady breath. Again, she felt a reckless temptation. They might not be lovers, but she couldn't stop loving. 'I won't be in love with anyone else but you, Robin.'

'That's not true.'

Robin was probably right, but she said, 'It's true for me now.' She *would not* give up her devotion. Her creative soul, where good art came from, told her that if she kept loving Robin, she'd find that Big Important Art Thing. With the sourness of Robin's rejection seething around her, she needed to – just like Robin said – make art to heal the Patriarchy they carried with them.

'I might have other lovers someday, but I'll never love anyone like I love you. You will be my best friend, better than lovers that come and go. I will be *emotionally* monogamous with you.'

Robin raised an eyebrow. 'I can't tell you what to do, Wren, but I counsel against that path.'

Wren pulled back and sat up. 'Really? With your ginormous wisdom of a thousand years? I happen to think that if you want me to create the art that will keep us together and represent our highest ideals and solve all our problems – I happen to think that the way to create it is to follow my feelings. That's the kind of artist I am.' Wren lay back down and stared at the ceiling again. 'And I love you.'

Robin lay down beside her. 'You're setting yourself up for heartache, but you will love me as you love me.'

Robin understood her. She didn't judge. They could both have what they wanted. Wren felt Robin's spare body touching her all along her own: legs, hips, shoulders.

She repeated her vow the rest of the day, and all through that winter: *She is to me what no lover can be; she's the best friend that I'll ever know.*

II

Raising Energy

One

First of May! First of May!
Outdoor fucking begins today!
(Traditional)

Kelsey switched out the propane canister, sat down on the porch step and lit a joint. The first hot day. The forest didn't smell of wood smoke any more. What was that sweet summer flower in the air? Lupe was so funny last night. They did mushrooms. So warm today. Maybe go swimming? Oh jeez, here comes Gloria.

The witches celebrated their holidays to fit northern California seasons, which was why they celebrated the first day of summer with Beltane on May 1. As she often did, Gloria prepared the coven for this year's ritual and found Kelsey first.

Kelsey looked at her through a puff of smoke. 'That's a cute outfit.'

'I bought it with my Moon Money.'

'Silk becomes you.' She held out the pipe. 'Join me?'

'I smell gas.'

'It's fine. I just changed the propane tank.'

'Maybe later.' Gloria offered a small leather bag. 'Pick your Element?'

'Sure feels like the first day of summer, doesn't it?' Kelsey reached in and pulled out an orange stone with swirls of yellow.

'Lucky you!' Gloria congratulated without envy.

'I could use it, for sure.' Kelsey put the stone in her pocket. 'I'm going for a swim. Do you want to?'

'I need to organise Beltane.' Gloria reached out to ring the bell.

'Don't do that,' Kelsey warned.

'Why not? Everyone needs to pick our Elements before tomorrow.'

'We decided the bell is only for meals.'

'Did we? I thought that was something Robin suggested.'

'We decided. You used to be better at remembering our decisions.'

Gloria pressed her lips together, then smiled. 'I'll just have to wander the land and find everyone.'

'That sounds fun.' Kelsey offered the pipe as she stood up. 'I'll come with.'

As they left the house, Kelsey unconsciously hopped over the broken front step, then noticed that Nikki had finally fixed it. They found Nikki herself in the barn, unpacking dusty boxes.

'Would you like to choose your Element for tomorrow?' Gloria said, offering the bag.

Nikki drew a blue stone and tucked it in her coin pocket. 'Cool.' She gestured to a pint jar, empty but for a few dried cannabis flowers. 'Look what I found. The one that gave good orgasms.'

Gloria said she'd never forget it, and Kelsey said she thought her head was coming off.

Nikki returned it to a neat row of pint jars lining a new shelf. 'Lupe says she can finally start a breeding programme.'

She told them that Lupe, Hazel and Ginny were in the orchard, so Kelsey and Gloria walked up there next. As they crested the hill, they could just see Lupe and Hazel at the top of slender ladders, thinning apples. Ginny was weeding in a row of small green shoots between the apple trees. Everyone wore broad hats, their bare backs strong and brown under the sun.

'I have the Elemental stones!' Gloria called out. Pepper trotted up to Gloria for her ear rubs.

Hazel climbed down her ladder and crossed the orchard toward Gloria and her leather bag. She chose a black stone. Lupe got the other blue one. Then it was Ginny's turn.

Ginny stared at the orangey-red one in her hand. 'I am Fire?'

'Me too,' Kelsey said.

Ginny sighed. 'Can I try again?' She tossed the stone in the air and caught it again. 'It's easier for me if I'm Earth or Water.'

'Trade you?' Lupe offered.

'No, don't!' Gloria pushed Lupe's hand away.

Ginny considered for a minute. 'I will heed the fates.'

'I will let you get back to work,' Gloria said.

Kelsey had an unkind thought. But somebody had to organise rituals, otherwise the holiday came and went. The magic wasn't the same if you didn't perform it on the actual day. 'Where are Wren and Robin?'

'Up at the garden, getting the goat shed ready,' said Ginny.

'We are blessed you're a Fire woman this year,' Gloria told Ginny before leaving. 'You'll bring back something important, I'm sure.'

Ginny beamed and returned to her weeding.

The gentle heat felt delicious. From the brush, a quail chirped his warning. Bees foraged the mountain lilacs. When they reached the garden, Wren and Robin were lifting a tall sliding door onto a small barn next to the shroom shed.

'Come help us!' Wren called, and together they dropped the door solidly on its track. Robin slid it open and closed, testing it.

Wren beckoned. 'Look at what we did!' Inside, they had built low enclosures. 'The goats will love it.'

Gloria approached, holding out the bag. 'I have the Elemental stones.'

Wren turned to Robin. 'What do you know about Beltane, Robin?'

She drew a green one.

'You said this was different from a birthday back rub.' Robin chose a black. 'This means Earth?'

'Which can represent memory, so that's appropriate for you,' said Gloria. She shook the last stone into her hand. 'That leaves Water for me, like you, Wren.'

'Who are the Fire women this year?' Wren asked, sounding disappointed.

'Kelsey and Ginny.'

'We're going to massage Kelsey?' Robin asked. 'And Ginny?'

Wren explained that at the end of the ritual the Fire Women would give a prophecy. 'Maybe I'll get a message about the magical statue.'

Kelsey didn't laugh, because Wren was so sincere about this statue she thought Robin wanted. But it was amusing. Wren had been saying all winter that if she didn't create this one thing, someday the coven would break up in a tragic meltdown. At Imbolc she made a pregnant goddess out of clay, but it blew up in the kiln. Wren couldn't bring herself to make it again, and hadn't even taken a picture. Then at Spring Equinox she had finished that big painting that now hung in the living room. Kelsey liked the dancing naked fat ladies, but Wren felt it wasn't good enough.

While Kelsey knew full well how a symbol could unify diverse women into a cohesive group, she didn't mind a bit of healthy conflict. She put her faith in a healthy meal around the table, followed by vigorous debate.

Anyway, the Moon Money solved most of their problems. Now that she had enough – more than ever – Kelsey believed that lack of money was the root of all evil.

Kelsey helped Wren and Robin put away the tools. She pondered Robin's interest in who got the massage at the ritual. Kelsey wouldn't sleep with a housemate. Wren and Robin had built a friendship out of the wreckage of Wren's obsession last winter. Robin would understand if Kelsey had to say Let's Be Friends.

The Fire Women smudged the coven with smouldering sage as they entered the living room from the front porch. The colours they wore evoked the Elements. Kelsey and Ginny, the Fire Women, wore scarves and saris of orange and yellow. Lupe and Nikki wore blue, and decided together to decorate their eyes, because they brought Air energy and wanted to appear all-knowing.

'Wren, look.'

Wren turned to Lupe, who slowly shut her eyes. She had painted black eyes on her eyelids so they looked open, even when closed. 'Trippy?'

'Trippy,' Wren agreed, delighted to be entering into a heightened state with the coven. She hoped to experience a gnostic revelation, giving her a hint of what Robin's magical statue might be. Because as the days had lengthened, her failed attempts last winter might make her doubt her resolve that the path to The Big Art Thing ran through loving Robin in an emotionally monogamous way.

Gloria fastened a jewelled belt that Wren had made years ago around the waist of Wren's green sari, exactly like her own. Wren looked over her shoulder; Robin and Hazel looked handsome in the black choir robes.

The coven spent too much time anointing each other with sacred oil. Finally, they settled down on to the futons and pillows in the centre of the room, the two Fire Women naked in the centre. The Elements encircled them, singing a song about how a woman's sex is the source of her creativity, and a woman's sex is a mystery, and a woman's sex is her healing. The last verse of the song affirmed the wisdom found in their bodies, if they only listened.

One of the Earth Women started the cassette of Kay Gardner's *A Rainbow Path*. The Elements passed a bottle of oil around and began the massage of the Fire Women. Their massage started at the hands, feet and heads, but each of the Elements freely massaged their Fire woman, never avoiding her breasts and vulva as massages did in Patriarchy. Her entire body was the talisman that would channel the prophecy.

After the first movement, 'Processional', both Fire Women changed the pattern of their breath. The second movement had a travelling rhythm. Each Fire Woman breathed deep through her mouth, as if through a straw. Then exhaled long and slow. When her lungs emptied, she inhaled again without pausing.

This was a magical breath. They had learned it from different teachers over the years. A breath that induced a trance. The coven didn't know why it worked. They only knew when they breathed like this, their bodies would tingle, and a pleasurable sensation rose from their pelvis, to their heart, to their throat and out of the crown of their heads. The sensation connected their body, mind and spirit. They rode out to the edges of the universe and brought back messages.

By the time they reached the fourth movement of the *Rainbow Path*, the Fire Women breathed slowly, deep in trance. Hands danced over their bodies. More oil poured over fingers. Singing, swaying, chanting. No giggles.

After the fourth movement, they paused for an Earth Woman to turn the cassette over. The Fire Women opened their eyes, sat up and took a break from the labouring of their trance. Water Women held chalices to their mouths.

Wren felt buzzed. Since her vow to be emotionally monogamous with Robin last winter, she had craved any erotic touch. She heard the water in Ginny's throat as she swallowed. Wren refilled the dark blue chalice, with a pretty pattern in its glaze, like waves under clouds. She glanced over at Kelsey, drinking deep from an identical chalice. Robin and Lupe sat on either side of her, like cat temple guardians.

Ginny lay down and resumed trance breathing. Wren couldn't help one more look toward Robin, who was massaging Kelsey's feet.

When Hazel rejoined them after dealing with the tape, Wren offered her the chalice. Hazel was always so intense and serious during ritual, but just now gargled her water. Wren giggled, and Nikki shushed them. The music started.

Wren loved 'Castle In The Mist' best. Elements sang along in wordless tones through the sixth and seventh movements, which were less melodic. The *Rainbow Path* reached its climax with the eighth movement. Both Fire Women breathed ecstatically, pulling the living earth up and through their bodies, up to heaven and down to the ground. The Elements caressed with oiled hands, pulling and pushing as each Fire Woman flew her consciousness along the music and her body's ever-rising desire.

As the music faded, both Fire Women took three deep breaths and then held the air inside, stiffening every muscle. This holding, at the end of the breath-induced trace, the witches called The Bearing In. The Fire Women lay with their legs clutched to their chests, holding and silent for long, long minutes. The other Elements sat back on their heels and waited for the magic.

As they waited, Wren perceived that the magical statue needed to represent this Bearing In. A woman in a state that looked scary – if you didn't know what it was.

When the Fire Women released with a roar and a moan and a long inhale, they felt the ecstasy of the Bearing In, a wave of light and pleasure and connection.

A Fire Woman spoke slowly, pulling the revelation from her fast-fading trance: 'We cultivated the weeds. We plucked seeds from the squash. We wiped the table clean. We grew new trees in old orchards.'

The other Fire Woman answered this with her own prophecy: 'We live where women speak without bounds. The name of this place is Ove, a circle outside.'

The Elements cuddled their warm and oily bodies and pondered the revelation of the Fire Women.

Gloria closed the ritual by intoning, 'So mote it be.'

'So mote it be,' everyone affirmed. They lay together in silence until someone got a cramp, someone else had to pee, and the magic circle reshaped into the sacred ground of their ordinary living room.

'Now let's eat.' Kelsey moved to get up.

'No, you *don't*,' said Robin, pressing her hand down on Kelsey's chest. 'I was told the Earth Women bring the feast.'

Robin and Hazel untangled themselves and disappeared into the kitchen. Everyone heard the refrigerator open and shut many times, drawers open, dishes clank. The rest of the coven adjusted themselves, cuddling closer.

Wren drowsed in the warmth and softness. When she was first a witch, she easily replaced her Blessed Mother and Saints with a god-less religion without intercession or forgiveness. In this cosy pile of sister witches, Wren felt Aphrodite, a familiar, loving presence who made everything better. Gloria had taught her that the name 'Aphrodite' was an ancient word for orgasm. This seemed sensible to Wren. For the first time in months, she didn't feel sexually deprived. She felt aroused, satisfied and joyful.

The Earth Women returned with trays heaped with cheese, fruit, bread and honey. Robin set hers on the blanket, disappeared, and came back with a basket of glasses and three bottles of wine. The witches passed around a loaf of bread and a cup, blessing each other with 'May you never hunger' and 'May you never thirst'. Then they devoured the feast.

The first topic was Ginny's name for their home.

The witches pursed their mouths to taste the word and then closed their lips in a moan and a hum: Oooooove.

'Oveland.'

'Ovia.'

'Ovish.'

When they had exhausted the permutations, they discussed Kelsey's revelation, weeds and seeds as a metaphor, and then turned to their horticultural hopes for the summer. They were deep into the blocks of cheese, bowls of strawberries and loaves of bread when Wren heard Robin talking quietly with Gloria.

'This was amazing. Did you invent this?'

'I don't know. We learn things from all over.'

'Do other covens do this?'

'I doubt it. Some women do breathwork, but they never touch each other *below the waist* – you know what I mean.'

'The rituals I've done with you so far were about healing yourself. But this tapped into something else.'

Gloria was doing her favourite thing: teaching witchcraft. 'We believe that these sexually charged altered states connect us with the Goddess, and she sends us messages about our community energy and purpose. It was a Beltane ritual that led us to find our last house on Walnut Street, for instance.'

'I was glad I didn't get the orange stone, but now that I've seen it, I want to try it.'

'I can teach you.'

Robin looked up and across the circle. 'I think I'd like to learn from the Fire Women.'

Gloria looked surprised, but smiled indulgently at Robin's apparent effort to work out the correspondences. 'If they want to.' She raised her voice above the chatter. 'Hey, Kelsey! Ginny! Robin wants you to teach her how to be a Fire

Woman.'

Kelsey glanced at Ginny, then turned to Robin. 'You think this is just a shiny new technology, don't you?'

'Can I help being myself?'

As Wren watched that exchange, she could nearly see the spark between Robin and Kelsey, and a vile bubble roiled her stomach. She knew this feeling.

Wren looked around for her green sari. She couldn't be *jealous*. She knew how Robin felt about her. They were best friends. Ginny was lying on her sari, so Wren wrapped herself in Hazel's black robe instead. She didn't feel sexy any more. She felt like running out of a room that felt small and smelled too strongly of something to avoid. Her hands picked through the remains of brunch, filling a basket with strawberry tops and cheese rinds.

'We're not done eating yet,' Hazel complained.

'I'm just cleaning up.' Wren rose to her knees with the basket of trash and grabbed the ritual chalices between the fingers of her free hand. 'I ate too much cheese,' she joked. She stood, but lost her balance halfway up and fell backward onto Hazel.

'I got ya.'

But Wren's arm flew out, and the chalices smashed against the floor.

Wren screamed and grabbed at the ruined cups. Hazel took the pieces resolutely from her hands. Wren wrenched herself free of Hazel's arms and clutched her stomach. She felt like she'd swallowed a whole potato covered in acid. Everyone was looking at her.

Wren heard Gloria say, 'They are just things, honey. No need for tears.' Wren felt Gloria's hand pressed reassuringly between her shoulder blades, right above her heart. 'Deb and

Marla will make us a new set.'

Lupe leaned close to Wren's face, her painted-on eyes smeary and dark and seeing nothing. 'Get a grip. You're a witch. You know everything dies.'

Then everyone laughed, and the women tidied up the feast together.

'I'm sorry I broke our ritual chalices,' Wren said, which was the honest truth. 'I don't know why I'm crying,' she kept saying, and her effort to repeat this lie erased the memory of a Goddess, her face an ugly grimace of ecstasy and power.

Two

Kelsey welcomed the coolness of her room. On these May afternoons, the fog cleared early. She put a redwood cone from the grove on her altar. She opened her window, fluffed up her pillows and sat on her bed, putting her right hand in her left. She imagined a candle flame and whispered, 'Light of my life.' Lucy sat cross-legged just beyond Kelsey's feet, wearing her dad's flannel shirt, bell bottoms, and a wide black leather belt.

'Your dad used to get so mad when you borrowed his clothes.'

'Borrowed? I'm dead. He's never getting this back.' Lucy opened the shirt slightly, showing it wasn't buttoned. 'Kelsey, you fool yourself with those acts of service, helping women find their own sexual power, but the Kelsey *I knew* couldn't keep her hands off me.'

'We had sex every day, and twice on Sundays.'

'They never worked out why we liked sleepovers more than the other girls.'

Kelsey remained in trance, one hand inside the other. She could hear someone in the kitchen, music on the stereo. She brought her attention inward again.

'Robin told me she never let her lovers give her orgasms.'

'She's getting intimate with you.'

'That's what friendship is. She said the grove always reminds her of how many lovers she's lost.'

'Grief is grief.'

'That's what the counsellor told us. Told me, I mean. Back then, it was hard to remember that you're not real.'

'Tell me these aren't real.' Lucy sat up and opened her shirt.

'I miss you.'

Lucy lay back and crossed her arms over her chest. 'So. Robin. What just happened?'

'She resisted when we started. I think it surprised her when she felt the energy rising. By the end, she got into it, and let it move her body in a way she didn't expect.'

'She didn't expect that message, either.'

'The vision gives women what they need. She needed to hear that *you are your body*. It's a cliché, but she pretends she's the Undying Wandering Lesbian Soul.'

'She must have her reasons.'

'I reminded her again that we have great power in the present moment.'

'Did she get it?'

'She lives in the past, or in a distant future beyond Patriarchy.' Kelsey stopped. She couldn't help smiling. 'I have to admit I loved it when the yearning arrived and I urged her to reach for it. And when to Bear In.'

'Graceful.'

Kelsey remembered Robin's sounds.

'Then what happened?'

'I came back here because she wanted to be alone.'

'I'm afraid you'll be lovers with her.'

Kelsey nearly fell out of the trance. 'You know the point of breathwork is that it's not about lovers – it's about helping a woman know her own body, becoming—'

'*Be Friending, Be Witching, Be Coming.*' Lucy said it with the capital letters and a teenage sarcasm that Kelsey was starting to get sick of. Lucy scooted up the bed, propped her head on her hand and let her shirt open.

Kelsey smelled patchouli. 'Robin said she wants more practice. I want her to not pull back and be alone.'

'You've been alone.'

'But not lonely. I have enough friends – and flings.'

'Flings are good. You don't want what we had.'

'Robin says I can't, anyway. I'm not sixteen.'

'I'm not either.'

'Now that I have everything I've ever wanted, I won't screw it up by fucking the landlord and getting evicted. Anyway, she's not my type.'

Lucy pressed her nose against Kelsey's. Kelsey could not feel her breath as she said, 'She will never be me, but you're getting turned on remembering what just happened.'

'I can't keep anything from you.'

'I am you.'

Kelsey opened her eyes. Ginny was shouting in the plaza. Something about goats.

The goats could wait.

∞

'Everybody! The goats are home!'

Wren ran out of the front door, but didn't see the goats. She saw Robin emerging from the grove, clumsily carrying an armload of blankets. She dropped them to let Pepper jump into her arms like a prize at the fair.

Wren immediately resumed an argument with herself. Since Beltane last week, she'd been struggling to win both sides of it. *She's letting Pepper kiss her on the mouth!*

She ignored Robin and Pepper wrestling in the dust and spoke to Ginny. 'Where are the goats?'

Pepper rushed over to give a thousand kisses to Wren. *If dogs are emotionally non-monogamous, why not me?*

'How many did you get?'

'Five. They're up in their barn already.'

Robin walked up, her hair sticking up in the back and oily.

'Where have you been?' Ginny asked her with great curiosity. 'You look…altered.'

'Kelsey is teaching me Beltane breathwork.'

Wren whipped around to take in Robin's face, still flushed. 'I thought Ginny was doing it with you.'

'I was supposed to,' Ginny said. 'But the farmer changed the plan this morning, and Robin and Kelsey told me they could do it themselves.'

'Why didn't you ask me to help?' Wren hated something in the tone of her voice.

Robin tilted her head and squeezed Wren's hand. Wren smelled the oil and maybe something else. 'You know why. Because I was afraid you'd feel like you do right now.'

Ginny obviously sussed out what was happening with Wren. 'They don't have names yet.'

'You know how I feel right now?'

Robin grimaced, and also ignored Wren. 'Do goats need names?'

Wren didn't want to fight either. But suddenly she was in a black-and-white war movie and couldn't stop herself, even though she crossed her arms. 'You should have asked, instead of predicting how I would feel.' Somewhere just under where she hugged herself, Wren felt something strong and wicked.

'Let's go see the goats instead of arguing,' Robin said brightly.

'First you have to agree you don't know how I feel unless I tell you.' Wren wished Robin would hug her. She needed a hug. 'I hate this feeling.'

'We all do,' Ginny observed.

Robin reached out her hand, but didn't touch Wren. 'You can't tell yourself not to feel something—'

'I. Know. That,' spat Wren, that thing in her chest whipsawing her from pain to fury.

'The goats await us in the palace you built them,' Ginny announced, like a mistress of ceremonies.

Wren had started crying. 'I just want to love you as I love you.'

'And I love you. You need to find yourself a real girlfriend. You need sex with love.'

Wren wiped her eyes, making herself even more pissed as she told these lies. 'You're my best friend. Friends are better than lovers.'

Robin reached for Wren's hand again, which was infuriating.

'You may be ten thousand years old, but you don't know me.' Wren didn't need to say she wanted to be more than friends. Even Ginny would hope nobody ever said *that* again.

'Wren, you keep inviting me to do things I can't. It hurts both of us to tell you *no* all the time.'

'Jealousy is a hungry mask,' Ginny interjected.

'I'm not jealous, I'm—'

Ginny grabbed Wren's hand and shook it like she would shake the neck of a naughty dog. 'Stop talking. Meet the goats.' She turned away and strode toward the barns.

Wren felt the fight drain out of her. She couldn't look at Robin, but heard her as they both jogged and caught up. Wren thought she could speak honestly, now they were all facing the same direction. 'I thought you'd be doing that ritual with Ginny, too.'

'Why does that matter?' Ginny asked. 'They weren't having sex.'

'Wren, believe me,' Robin pleaded, then sounded pedantic. 'I'm only trying to help when I ask this: what do you non-monogamous women do when you are jealous?'

Wren kept her eyes straight ahead. 'Don't make fun of me.'

'I'm not. I want to know.'

'We say being jealous means I'm not getting my needs met,' Wren recited, as if from the lesbian non-monogamy manual.

'You see? That's true. How can I help you meet your needs?'

'I know!' Ginny exclaimed, raising her hand like in school. 'I've been at lots of lover drama meetings.' She pointed at Robin. 'You're the one person who can't help her.'

Robin considered for a moment. 'Shit.'

They reached the wide spot between the sheds and greenhouse. 'This is why we cultivate friends in the garden.' Ginny ran over to the first row of eggplants. 'Every day they grow three inches!'

Wren imagined friendships growing three inches every day, and some colour returned to the world.

'Why can't we be friends like you and Nikki are friends?' Robin was suddenly standing too close.

Wren walked to the goat barn, but Robin followed. She didn't know how many sketchbooks Wren had to burn before she could be Nikki's friend. 'Robin, maybe you can meet the goats later?'

'Yeah. Sure.' Robin turned to leave. 'I left all the blankets and stuff down there in the dirt.'

As Robin walked away, Wren took no pleasure in watching that familiar gait, and felt both relieved and angry that Robin understood her better than she knew herself. Just like a best friend.

∞

Wren followed Ginny into the barn where five young goats boldly approached her. She rubbed a thumb between each pair of tiny horns. 'What are their names?'

'They haven't told me yet. Let's show them the pasture.' Ginny opened the pens, and she and Pepper guided the little herd up the road, under the redwoods and up to the bright open meadow not far beyond. The goats raced ahead, then stopped to graze in the sunshine.

Wren and Ginny sat down and Pepper sat between them, panting. Wren inhaled the warm dry smells of the meadow. The flowers had faded already to muted pastels, the grass dried to straw. Pepper pawed Wren's leg and Wren pulled the dog into her lap. Then she started bawling again. She could always cry when she was with Ginny.

'I *want* Robin to learn breathwork. I liked that you *and* Kelsey were teaching her. But when I saw Robin with those blankets – she'd been alone with Kelsey…'

Pepper put her forepaws around Wren's neck and Ginny rubbed Wren's back. 'Your next girlfriend won't be like

Robin,' she said.

Wren felt embarrassed that Ginny was thinking of her next girlfriend when Ginny herself hadn't had any yet.

'When a woman loves you, it doesn't mean she wants to be your girlfriend. When you get obsessed with a woman, you think she will give you everything. But that's for children.'

Annoyed, Wren plucked a strand of tall grass and tore apart the seed head. 'I'm looking for a better mother? Like Demeter All-Giver?'

'Maybe? What happened to The Girl Who Hadn't Come Out to Her Mother?'

'I got rid of her.' When did that happen? Early spring. When she was here in the meadow, painting, every wildflower wet and blooming. Now they were finished, except for one.

'Did Robin tell you about that rose?' Wren pointed to a vine of tiny pink roses covering a diminutive madrone tree. 'She said a woman planted that rose a hundred years ago.'

'I heard that after you painted it.' Ginny grabbed a handful of dead weeds and pressed them against Wren's chest, scratching her a little. 'Something is stuck in there.'

Wren looked down at Ginny's hand and took it in her own. 'Remember when we met? I only painted outdoors.'

'I do. You trespassed on the Pogonip.'

'I called them *Outlaw Landscapes*.' Wren remembered painting the hills and meadows surrounding Santa Cruz. So different from the cities where she learned to paint portraits. 'I wish I could have stayed in art school longer. But my mom needed me.'

'You're in art school now.'

Ginny was right. 'I need to do an art thing.'

Wren ran down to the barn, even though she knew Ginny

couldn't keep up with her. She was tossing things around when Ginny arrived.

'Where's that painting of my mom?' she shouted.

Ginny pointed to the loft opposite Nikki's room. 'Someone leaned ladders against it, so I moved it up there.'

Wren dragged the heavy-framed portrait by one corner to the middle of the plaza. Then she found Nikki's Emergencies Only gas can. Nikki was always making disaster plans.

Robin called down from the veranda. 'With gasoline, a little goes a long way.' Robin and Kelsey stood outside their bedrooms – together.

Wren hesitated before opening the gas can. 'I need to see it burn.'

Ginny tore off the paper wrapping. She scrutinised the figure from head to toe before laying it on the dirt in the centre of the plaza. 'She would be pretty if she weren't made of viciousness.'

'Stand back.' Wren splashed a little gas out. The blonde coif dissolved a little, in a satisfactory way. She didn't look any lower. She tasted toxic-sweet fumes in her mouth. She splashed more.

'That's enough!' Robin called.

'I'll take this far away.' Ginny lugged the can back to the barn.

Wren patted her pockets, but didn't find what she wanted. She loped over to Kelsey's VW and rummaged under the hood.

'Stand back everybody,' she warned.

Robin and Kelsey didn't move, but Ginny and Pepper jogged to the porch.

Wren stepped back twenty feet and scratched the rough end of a highway flare. It lit like a giant match, rasping and glowing red. 'I banish thee, old mother of mine…' she whispered, '…and with this flame I do unbind.'

She flung the flare in a high arc. Before it hit the painting, its sparkling end ignited the vapours with a satisfying FUH-womp! Instantly the painting was alight, flames invisible in the sunshine, and very, very warm.

Wren stepped as close as she dared to get a good look. She heard Robin and Kelsey running down the back stairs. Ginny and Pepper ran up behind her a few seconds later with the hose, but it couldn't reach. Wren and Ginny, Robin and Kelsey watched the painting burn. The sad little fire wasn't a threat to anything but itself.

Uncovered by this act of magic, she felt the sources of her jealousy drying up like mud on a May morning. *That ridiculous vow to unrequited love.* She laughed at herself and gave thanks for Robin's indulgence.

For weeks afterwards, Wren made a point of scuffing across the scorch. One day in June, she couldn't find it, and remembered the grey winter afternoon when the girl who had never come out to her mother crossed the plaza to mail a letter. That girl was well and truly gone. Wren could remember her mother's relentless assaults. She could remember her survival strategies. But from now on, that girl had nothing to do with her. She had left that past life behind. She didn't have to imagine a future free of her mother-damage; she was already living it.

This summer she would finish Robin's magical statue, free of complicating her creativity with a childish plea for attention. This summer would be the best ever.

Three

Mushroom Hot Dish
INGREDIENTS

½ cup uncooked wild rice blend. Cook as instructed.

1½ teaspoon peanut oil

1 medium onion, chopped

1 large celery stalk diced to ½ cup

3 cloves, garlic, diced

4 cups coarsely cut mushrooms: shiitake, black trumpets, enoki, king oyster, white beech – whatever is available. Use plain old brown or white mushrooms from Safeway if that's all you have, but they aren't as good.

1 teaspoon lemon zest

1 can mushroom soup. Or your own mushroom soup concentrate.

2 tablespoons lemon juice

½ cup sour cream

2 tablespoons more fried onions

METHOD

Cook rice. Separately, dry sauté mushrooms until liquid releases and boils away. Continue to sauté in butter until mushrooms brown. Add and sauté onion, garlic, celery until onion is soft. Add zest.

Season with salt and pepper.

Stir in soup and lemon juice. Remove from heat.

Stir in rice, sour cream.

Spoon into baking dish and top with fried onions. Bake at 350° for 25-30 minutes or until golden brown and bubbling. Excellent for pot lucks.

⊕

On a warm early summer evening, the Ovem – as they called themselves now – hung out on the porch, digesting the hot dish Kelsey had cooked with Lupe's enoki and king oyster mushrooms. A nutritious meal like that made the pan of baklava necessary.

Wren sat next to Gloria with a second piece already in her mouth. She looked up from her sticky fingers and admired Robin ambling up from the bridge. Wren poked a place in her heart and felt a solid crust of scab.

She looked over at Kelsey and Nikki on the other couch, where they also nibbled their baklava. Kelsey said something to make Nikki smile. Nikki looked tired. She'd been working all week to improve garden irrigation. There was a problem with a pump or something.

While Wren contemplated the butches of her life, Gloria worked on *Emerging Athenic Wicca*. Wren had been working too. Since burning the portrait, she had tried approaching the magical statue project obliquely, returning to what she used to do for the coven: decorations. She sewed heavy drapes for everyone's bedrooms to keep them warm next winter. She used up the rest of the clay on a Diana of Ephesus for the garden. Today she was sketching a mural for the living room.

Robin nimbly stepped between Lupe and Ginny, who sat on the steps close to the baklava. She handed Kelsey a thick blue envelope from a stack of boring business mail. 'That's from Cayenne, isn't it?'

Kelsey repeated 'Cayenne' with a warmth in her voice. She opened the envelope and extracted thin blue sheets. 'So sweet of her to write.' She flipped through the pages. 'She's been travelling again. This is her news from the women's lands.'

Wren wanted to know all of it. 'Will you read it to us?'

'Why don't you read it, Wren?'

'Sure,' Wren said, sucking her fingers and reaching for the letter.

'I'll read it later,' Robin said, her mind obviously on something that had come in the mail, and went upstairs. Wren wished she would stay.

The outside of the envelope was illustrated with 'Haircuts of Wimmin's Land' cartoons, and Cayenne had added nipples to the 'Bonny Doon' of their address.

Wren looked at the letter's illustrations before reading it. 'Look at the sketch of the Moonvale motherhouse. Remember when we went there?'

'Yes. Magical,' Lupe said, but didn't mean it. Wren glanced at page four, where Cayenne had drawn two women making love. She covered it with page one.

Gloria looked up from her notebook. 'At Moonvale I thought, this is why Open Women's Lands don't last. If you let anyone in, everyone fights.'

'Remember that one woman?' Kelsey imitated outrage:

'She touched my drum!'

Gloria laughed wickedly.

Lupe stood up, saying she would get Hazel.

'Hear that?' said Kelsey, pointing up. 'She's listening to *Shadows on a Dime* again.' She reached for the baklava. 'Wren, read the letter.'

Inside the envelope, Wren found an 'I Saw You Naked at Michigan' bumper sticker and a dried oak leaf, which she handed to Kelsey. 'First is a wellbeing report. They had scabies at Dirt Circle and pinworms at Raven Mountain. What are scabies?'

Ginny knew this one. 'Like tiny crabs. The goats have been teaching me about parasites. Why don't we get scabies?'

'Robin bought us a washing machine and dryer,' explained Kelsey.

'...and shigella at Lunaloom,' Wren continued. 'In good news, Dirt finished their kitchen. Raven started bees.'

'BEES!' shrieked Ginny. 'We should keep bees!'

Lupe and Hazel returned with a teapot and mugs.

'Some people might say it's bee slavery,' advised Gloria.

'We've been through this!' said Ginny, instantly exasperated. 'We wrote down in the book that the keeping of small traditional farm animals was okay without further discussion.'

'I was just testing our process.'

'Don't scare me like that.'

Wren read on. '...she visited a group in Ohio called Dykelandia, who created a secret hand gesture. They use it to greet women when they return to the land.'

Ginny looked thoughtful. 'I'm home when I can smell it.'

'That's why we have the bathhouse,' teased Kelsey.

Wren remembered Cayenne's pretty voice. 'Every woman wears a hat they take off if they leave the land. And they put a symbol on their tools because they were walking off.'

'That's a good idea, actually,' said Gloria.

'I already do it.' Nikki had her legs stretched out in front of her, resting on the porch rail, her hands on her belly. Such long legs.

'But with *your* mark,' Gloria corrected her. 'We need one for stuff we own collectively.'

'...Star Dance added two more women, so it looks like they will pay off their loan.'

'We are so lucky we don't have a mortgage.' Gloria wasn't pretending to work on her book any more. 'Remember the women who sold their land to men and bought a house in Provincetown?'

'Lesbians are usually poor,' said Kelsey. 'And the poor dykes do all the hard labour as a work exchange. Rich dykes don't share.'

'Robin is rich; she shares,' said Wren.

'That's because she was poor for thousands of years,' said Kelsey.

'I give thanks for prosperity,' said Gloria.

'Prosperity is luck,' said Lupe.

'You make your own luck,' said Kelsey.

Wren wanted to keep reading the letter. If she had created the magical statue already, she could point to it at moments like these. 'Don't argue. You're both right.'

'Do you ever wonder what will happen to Ove when we are old and Robin dies?' asked Gloria, as if she had never wondered this before.

'I assumed she'd give it to whoever is left alive,' said Wren, and started to read.

'But *is* that her plan?' Gloria interrupted. Lupe suggested they talk about it at a meeting.

'I bet her plan is to give it to herself in her next life.' Gloria looked around. 'Are we concerned that Robin owns the land and controls the money?'

'She doesn't control *my* money,' said Nikki.

Wren hated it every time Gloria brought this up. She never did when Robin was around. Wren wordlessly waved the blue letter at Gloria.

Gloria ignored her. 'She could sell or tell us to leave or whatever she wanted at any time.'

'Gloria and Robin want the same thing,' said Ginny. 'Wren, keep reading.'

'I'm saying the land ownership will be a problem, eventually. We should own it together.'

'So that when one of us wants to leave, we can have a huge fight?' Kelsey lifted her mug toward Lupe, who filled it.

'We should be on Robin's trust.'

'Gloria, paperwork doesn't protect you if someone powerful wants your land,' said Hazel.

Wren decided to do what Ginny told her. 'Cayenne met someone who painted her own tarot.'

'How is your deck coming along, Wren?' asked Gloria. 'Are you still stuck on the Fives?'

At least she wasn't talking about Robin's money. The tarot deck was another Art Thing To Save Us failure. 'I am,' Wren admitted. 'The Fives are such a downer.'

'If you want, I can help you with them.'

Wren realised Gloria probably *could* help her finish the tarot deck. 'Uh oh, Cayenne had an affair. That's why she had to leave.'

'Which one?'

'She doesn't say, but she's at Star Dance now.'

'She left because she slept with the wrong woman?' scoffed

Nikki. 'Typical.'

'Kicking someone off the land is Power Over,' said Gloria.

'…and they have a menstrual hut.'

'I was thinking,' said Ginny. 'Maybe it's gross, but what if, once our goats give us wool, what if we made moon pads out of it?'

Nikki and Lupe volunteered to try the prototypes.

'There was a Land Dyke conference in the Midwest. Women are planning retirement homes for dykes.'

'Like I was saying,' said Gloria. 'What happens when we're old?'

Wren had reached the fourth page and its sketch of two women, one lying back, a leg drawn up. Her lover, who looked a lot like Cayenne, cradled her and buried her other hand inside. Wow. Beautiful. Wren showed the drawing around. 'See? Cayenne met someone.'

Cayenne's drawing caused an enlivening envy in everyone. While she had been emotionally monogamous with Robin, Wren hadn't had sex for more than a year.

Ginny interrupted her pity party. 'It's late, but see how much light?' The women stopped talking and admired their redwoods, golden crowned.

'We should invite women from the lands and show what we've done so far,' Ginny said. 'While the days are still getting longer.'

'Should we ask Robin first?' asked Gloria.

'I'm sure she'll love it,' said Kelsey.

The Ovem planned how to get the land ready for visitors. Wren imagined herself having a fling. If she's to be the great lesbian artist Robin thinks she is, that means having sex with women. And drawing her own pictures of naked lesbians in love.

∞

Kelsey's Baklava
INGREDIENTS
Syrup:
2 cups sugar or 1 cup honey
1½ cups water
2 tablespoons light corn syrup
½ teaspoon ground cardamom
1 tablespoon orange blossom water
Filling:
1 pound chopped pistachios and walnuts (about 4 cups)
¼ cup sugar
1 to 2 teaspoons ground cinnamon
¼ teaspoon cardamom
1 pound (about 24 sheets) filo dough
1 cup melted butter

METHOD
Make syrup: Stir the sugar or honey, water, and corn syrup over low heat until the sugar dissolves, about 5 minutes. Stop stirring, increase the heat to medium, and cook until the mixture is slightly syrupy, about 5 minutes. Let cool and add orange blossom water.

Combine nuts, sugar, cinnamon, cardamom.

Preheat the oven to 350°F. Grease a flat pan.

Place a sheet of filo in the pan and lightly brush with butter. Repeat with eight more sheets. Spread with half of the filling. Top with six more sheets, brushing each with butter. Spread with the remaining nut mixture and top with eight sheets, each with their butter.

Using a sharp knife, cut through the top layer of pastry,

making stripes, then diagonal cuts to form diamond shapes.

Bake for 20 minutes. Reduce the heat to 300° and bake until golden brown, about 15 additional minutes.

Cut through the scored lines. Drizzle the cooled syrup slowly over the hot baklava. Try to let cool before anyone eats it. Don't burn your tongue.

⊗

The 'While the Days Are Still Getting Longer' party aroused the Lesbian Nation. All over California, up to Eugene and Portland, even from Minnesota and Arkansas, women loaded their cars and pickups with tents, bags, drums, dogs and beer. Some packed skirts, some packed leather. Nobody packed a swimsuit.

Friday morning, Wren and Gloria finished the living room preparation and filled both fireplaces with Hazel's calla lilies. Wren stood in the middle of the room, under the India prints that someone had tacked to the ceiling, for a final check. Gloria had talked someone into permanently loaning them the piano. Wren didn't play, but she liked it when Hazel did. The multi-coloured velveteen pillows she had made satisfied her, but maybe there weren't enough.

Gloria stood beside Wren. 'I'm glad we can show off your vulva plates.'

'I'd be embarrassed if Judy Chicago ever came to visit.'

'She would be delighted with them, like I am.'

Wren checked to see if Gloria was teasing. She wasn't.

Above the southern fireplace hung her big painting of eight naked fat women, an homage to Matisse's *La Danse*. It was one of her many failed Big Important Art Things. Her Pre-Raphaelite *Sappho* was another, glowering from over the other fireplace like the dark and moody poet Sappho no doubt was. But Wren had made those before she burned the portrait. Since then, new pillows lined the couches, new muslin curtains framed the windows. She was halfway done adding a frieze of vines and poppies to the walls just under the ceiling.

'Do you like the mural so far?' Wren asked Gloria.

'I love it. I love everything you do.'

Wren's home decorating, though hardly enduring symbols of radical feminism, felt well-connected to her emotions, as if burning the portrait two weeks ago had unblocked her. At today's gathering, she had a feeling she'd find that idea for the magical statue – and maybe something else.

'Do you have an intention for today?' Gloria asked, and immediately answered for herself. 'I hope to meet women curious about Athena.'

'You must be psychic. I was just thinking about how I hope to get inspiration for Robin's magical statue.'

'I thought you were being like Kelsey and looking for a fling.'

Wren walked out of the door so Gloria couldn't see her face. 'Only if she's an artist who will help me in my Sphere.'

'So mote it be,' Gloria called after her, as if casting a spell.

Four

By Friday afternoon most of the campers had arrived and tents ringed the pasture where women played hacky sack and frisbee. The fog burned off and the forest warmed. Some women swam in the pond while others lay in the sun. Robin's stereo kept women dancing on the veranda. No one wore more clothes than were comfortable.

Wren wandered the party, collecting sketches. She was in the goat shed when Ginny introduced the goats to two little girls, both named Sierra, because 'Sierra' had been a popular name ten years earlier.

'That one is Artemis,' Ginny said. 'He's a ram. That one is Oscar the Un-wild because he's neutered, and so is Jeff. The other two are Amalthea and Caprotina.'

One Sierra said, 'Amalthea spoke to me with her eyes!'

The mother of the other Sierra said, 'I love bringing our daughter to a party where we don't have to worry.'

Ginny told her the girls needed to be careful. 'Farms can be dangerous.'

The mother laughed. 'I'd rather take her to the ER for a rusty nail than because she was attacked by a drunk uncle.'

Wren labelled the drawing 'Haven' and walked to the shroom shed. A huddle of women studied shelf upon shelf of canning jars filled with something white.

'What kind of mushrooms are you growing?' asked a Famous Poet.

'The sacred kind,' Lupe said. She opened a basket and shared around a handful of dried mushrooms with small round caps. 'Here's some of the first crop.' All three of Poet's friends tucked the slender-stalked fungi into their shirt pockets.

Wren labelled the drawing 'Visions'.

The inside of the greenhouse was moist and bright, its roof and the upper half of the walls a messy mosaic of recycled windows. Hazel was herding a group of women out of the door. She could tolerate women standing around and admiring plants for only a few minutes. 'The best manure is the gardener's shadow,' she told them, and soon they were weeding the onions. The furrows filled with a line of women on their knees, straw hats tilting under the sun. Wren labelled the drawing 'Manure'.

Up in the orchard, tiny fruits swelled on the apple tree. Kelsey, Robin and a group of visitors picnicked at the top, admiring the view.

'Are those what I think they are?' asked a woman from Boulder Creek. 'I thought gardeners didn't like weeds.' Everyone laughed.

'Wren, you're burning. Put on this sunscreen.' Kelsey tossed Wren the tube and returned to the conversation. 'In fact, we're experimenting with a new technique from Big Sur where you kill the males.'

'Is *that* what we do now?'

'Without males around, the flowers get juicy and wear purple, just like lesbians,' said Kelsey. 'Wren, let me get your back.'

Wren labelled the drawing 'Weeds without Seeds'.

∞

Throughout that long day, Nikki and Robin's new two-seater biffy was over-used, and women took more outdoor showers than necessary. A couple from San Francisco broke up, one blazing off on her motorcycle and empty sidecar, and the other retreating to Kelsey's room. 'I comforted her,' Kelsey confirmed later, without details. Everyone liked Cayenne's new girlfriend, who had travelled with her all the way from Arkansas.

The party quietened down at twilight, and Nikki lit the fire in the redwood grove, the trees welcoming the visitors. Women gathered, eager to learn more about the land and its women. Wren folded a blanket under her and flipped through her sketchbook. She felt she had captured what women do when they are alone together. She wanted to show them to Robin, but right now, Robin was the centre of everyone's attention.

'Robin, do you own all this land or what?' asked a woman from Mendocino.

Women always wanted to know about who owned the land. They didn't know Robin like Wren did. Robin said she owned the land. 'But we live together as a collective.'

'I love coming here,' declared Scout, one of Kelsey's intimate friends. She wore a faded Oregon Herbalist Conference tee-shirt, a fresh dyke haircut and two earrings from each lobe. 'I hope you can stay together forever.'

Mendocino wasn't sold on collective living. Maybe she had had some bad experiences. Wren knew most women had. 'I heard you share everything, but that's not possible.'

'We share our feelings – and our weed,' Lupe answered, and lit the first of many joints. 'But not our dolphin dildos.'

'Gross! Penetration is no joke,' said a woman from Oakland. Wren started a cartoon of Nikki with dildos in a tool belt.

Gloria passed around thermoses of tea. The other Ovem had dressed for the occasion in cotton dresses and shiny party shirts, but Gloria stood out in her vintage hibiscus-print bathing costume with built-in bra and a modest bottom half that showed off her curves. 'We share all the work, but we each have a Sphere.'

'Did you see that chore chart in the kitchen? I couldn't handle it,' said Oakland. 'Doing the dishes is the death of any women's community.'

'Or the lacto-ovo vegetarians versus the vegetarians who eat nothing with eyes,' said an older woman sitting next to Nikki.

'And exes,' Oakland said, as if no one ever thought that.

'Aren't Wren and Nikki ex-lovers?' said Nikki's friend.

'Nikki is everyone's ex-lover,' said Wren.

'Not mine,' said someone from LA, wearing a pastel-green polo shirt with a popped collar. Wren didn't understand why women found them attractive.

'Not yet?' suggested a woman from San Luis. Wren recognised her as the witch who had cursed Diablo Canyon and reversed the construction blueprints.

Nikki casually put her arm around the Older Woman. 'Men wish they could be butch, but they don't wear the clothes right.'

'I like girls who look like girls,' said a witch from Monterey, the first woman to turn Wren's head all day. Slim, shoulder-length dark hair, crisp indigo work shirt. Wren had to laugh at herself. The woman looked a lot like Robin. Wren turned the sketchbook to a new page.

'I like women who don't look like girls,' said Older Woman.

'And breasts. I like breasts,' added Lupe.

'There you go, objectifying,' teased Kelsey.

'I won't apologise. I love boobs.'

'That will be my next art project,' announced Monterey. 'Boobs of women's land.'

So, she's an artist too. Wren filled the new page with boobs.

'Speaking of wimmin's lands, here comes Cayenne,' said Kelsey. Cayenne wiggled in between Robin and Kelsey. Her girlfriend sat across from her and they flirted relentlessly.

'We started out talking about women's land collectives,' Kelsey explained, 'but as usual, now we're talking about breasts.'

'And pussies,' said Lupe.

'Don't say pussy; that's vulgar,' said LA.

'Cunt?' offered Cayenne.

Oakland made a face. 'I hate that word.'

'I love it,' Cayenne's girlfriend said, and then she sang it. '*I love cunt. I love cunt.*'

'Can you not say that word again?'

'Cunt, cunt, cunt,' Cayenne shouted, jumping up and dancing around the fire pit, lifting her skirt and flashing her bush. Wren looked on, both shocked and admiring.

'Rock on, Amazon!' sang Kelsey. Robin laughed so hard she fell off the log and Kelsey had to pull her back.

'I thought we were talking about women's land.' Oakland

had lost her sense of humour.

'And how they always fall apart?' scoffed LA.

'They don't always fall apart,' said Kelsey. 'Cayenne visited a dozen women's lands last year.'

Gloria passed around the thermoses again. 'We won't fall apart because we were already coven when we moved here.'

'Covens fall apart all the time,' said LA. 'Not that I know. I've never joined one.'

'Why hasn't yours fallen apart?' asked Oakland.

'Because we do what Glow tells us to do,' said Kelsey, sticking her tongue out at Gloria. Wren sketched her quickly, maybe to finish later.

'Really?' said Mendocino.

'No,' Robin reassured her. 'But she's a good organiser.'

Gloria smiled like she always did when Robin acknowledged her. 'As a coven and land sisters, we share magic and the mundane.'

'And by that she means we already satisfied our sexual curiosity about each other,' said Lupe.

'You more than satisfied my curiosity.' Hazel crossed the circle and, although women made room for her, she sat on Lupe's lap, put her arms around her, and gave her a kiss on the lips. 'It's hard to remember how into you I was.'

'I'll never forget, not as long as I live,' and Lupe rested her head on Hazel's chest.

'Get a tent,' said Kelsey.

'Don't worry – we're not lovers any more,' Lupe assured her.

'Because you live together. Everyone knows you stop having sex when you move in together,' said LA's Friend.

'Don't tell me that,' Mendocino said with mock despair. 'My girlfriend is moving from Vermont to live with me.'

'We used to have long meetings where we processed stuff,' Gloria continued. 'Now we heal our internal Patriarchy with magic.'

'We're too tired for long meetings,' Lupe added.

'That doesn't stop most collectives,' said Oakland.

'I heard something about your coven. I hope you don't mind me asking,' asked Monterey.

Wren didn't mind one bit. She must have heard the gossip.

'Do you women do orgies together?'

'I heard how you get all Beltane-y on May day,' said Cayenne, winking across the circle to her girlfriend.

Wren's stomach turned with the memory of her jealousy at Beltane. For a moment she feared someone would mention it.

But the comedy team of Lupe and Hazel saved her.

'We banished the ol' Chalice and Blade,' said Hazel, grabbing at Lupe's crotch before sliding off her lap and squeezing in beside her.

'All chalice, all the time,' said Lupe.

'We are a Dianic wiccan coven, but I teach Athenic wicca. It's not separatist,' Gloria explained defensively.

'Athena sounds powerful,' said Monterey.

'If you're interested, I'm teaching a class in Athenic wicca this fall.' Gloria tilted her head toward Wren. 'Wren is a talented artist. She's helping me visualise the more esoteric elements which speak to the unconscious mind.'

'I am?' Wren asked, but Gloria didn't hear her. Wren never liked Athena. On the other hand, if Monterey connected with Gloria's favourite goddess, she might visit Ove again.

'In Athenic wicca, we work with the emblems of owl, panther – or as we know it here, the mountain lion – and snake.'

'That's very cool,' said Monterey, which Wren found very cool in a different way.

'Since Robin joined us, we have access to an ancient magical tradition, stretching back to the land of the Amazons.'

Robin looked surprised to hear her name mentioned. She reached for the joint. 'This coven does something I've never seen with other women's groups,' she said, glancing at Gloria. 'We touch each other.'

'Women are naturally affectionate,' said San Luis.

'Not like this coven. They taught me a ritual that helped me understand how to receive touch in a magical, not a sexual, way.'

That's true, Wren thought, remembering all the birthday massages they had done since Robin's last year. It's not the sex that builds a women's community, it's the affection. How to put that in a magical statue?

'We don't talk about our rituals outside the circle, though,' Gloria added, with a tone of warning Wren knew well.

'I've heard you're all non-monogamous,' said LA. 'It's an ideal, but it just leads to drama.'

'I tried it with a lover last year,' said Older Woman. 'I didn't know I could feel so much *hate* toward another woman.'

'What happened?' asked Herbalist.

'She and my ex are together.'

Robin sat forward. 'Lesbians want to make love with lesbians. That's our nature. When lesbians work hard together, it's normal and we need to expect it. But it's not the sex we want…'

'Speak for yourself, old lady,' said Wren, under her breath, sketching Robin, leaning forward with her arms on her knees, imparting wisdom.

'I mean, we *want* sex, but passion lasts a month, maybe a

year, and then fades.'

'Lesbian bed death, you mean,' said LA. The circle of women tittered because they knew all about it.

'That's what I mean. Let's not shame ourselves. A sexless long-term relationship is no better than being single.'

Nikki perked up. 'We should never be ashamed of wanting sex – or *not* wanting sex.'

'Shame can keep you from doing stupid things,' Oakland said with a bitter laugh.

'The second time,' said Lupe.

'No. Shame is *always* bad for women.' Nikki said it so emphatically, no one joked again about shame. She stood, added another log and adjusted the embers. Sparks rose through the redwoods' thin branches and onward to the darkening sky. The fog was coming in.

The woman from LA took that moment to observe that 'the lesbian community is *so incestuous*'.

'No,' Robin said sharply. 'Lesbians loving each other and having sex together isn't incest.'

Lupe smiled like a proud teacher.

Hazel didn't agree with LA either. 'Men invented monogamy to serve themselves.'

'That's it,' Robin said, getting uncharacteristically animated. 'This coven taught me. Look, lesbians have sex. That's what we do. The gay guys have sex with each other regularly, and they don't call that incest.'

'They call it a gay pride parade,' admitted LA's friend.

'They touch each other. They see each other's naked bodies,' continued Robin.

'Lots of covens do that,' said Herbalist.

'Like Z Budapest's ritual, where you stand in front of a mirror,' said Monterey. 'So powerful. Especially for straight women.' Wren smiled at Monterey and Monterey looked back. Wren set her sketchbook on the ground.

'There's a great magic in women touching each other. That's all I'm saying,' continued Robin.

'What about survivors?' asked Ginny's friend.

'No one has more memories of abuse than I have,' said Robin.

Oakland looked at LA to see if she knew what that meant.

'But you're not everyone,' said LA.

'I'm just answering the question. Our coven and our women's land are doing well because we aren't afraid to touch,' said Robin.

Wren loved Robin so much in that moment. Sure, sometimes when they slept together, she still wished they would make love. But the friendship filled her heart. Robin was so brave. Her ideals should have inspired Wren to make something worthy by now.

'If I don't want to hug one of my coven sisters, it's because something isn't right,' said Ginny. 'Like when we enter the circle and say "perfect love and perfect trust".' She held her hands over her heart and left them there. 'If trust is there, I hear it in my chest.'

'If you hear it in your chest, then I touch it in our voices,' said Hazel, her tone mirthful.

'I've been visiting the women's lands,' said Cayenne, her tone serious in contrast to her earlier frolicking. 'I don't know if Robin's right. Seems like internal Patriarchy gets worse the longer women live secluded together.'

Cayenne's girlfriend crossed the circle and sat next to her. Wren couldn't remember what her name was; it was the name of a colour. 'Cayenne and I saw how every woman's land has the same problems as women in Patriarchy – and worse because we don't expect it.'

'We're not perfect,' said Gloria. 'In fact, every year we do a summer solstice ritual about killing the Patriarchy inside us.'

'So – are you taking new members?' asked Mendocino.

'No, not now,' Gloria answered, and started to talk about the Athenic wicca class again.

Suddenly Scout raised her hand and said, 'Excuse me!' Through this long conversation, she had sat silently with eyes shut. Now she stood up and announced, 'I have composed a limerick in tribute to our sisters, the Ovem of Ove.'

She cleared her throat theatrically and recited:
I met dykes who call themselves Ovem
Who slipped away from the macho implosion.
They argue and fight,
Then make love all night.
It's Revolting and utterly Wholesome.

Scout took a bow, and the women begged her to say it again. So she did, and the serious talk was over.

The Witch from Monterey murmured, 'I'm getting cold.' Wren handed her the blanket she'd been sitting on, Monterey wrapped it around her shoulders, and they ended the evening in Wren's room. Wren forgot she'd left her sketchbook in the grove.

Five

The next morning, Robin opened Wren's door and stuck her head in.

'Oops, sorry,' she said, withdrawing. 'Can I bring you two coffee?'

'No!' shouted Wren. 'We're busy.'

'Later? Kelsey and Scout are making biscuits.'

'Forget it. Come in.'

Robin stepped inside and greeted the Witch from Monterey with a warm hello.

Wren and Monterey sat against the headboard, blankets to their chins.

'This is Willow. She's a photographer.'

'Oh, a sister artist. Hi, Willow.' Robin stood by the door and beamed at Wren. She did not wink, but Wren felt a wink.

'I don't drink coffee,' said Willow.

'Tea?'

'Thanks, I can get my own tea.' Willow looked confused by Robin's apparent servitude.

'She doesn't mind,' Wren reassured Willow. She put her arm around her lover's shoulders. That's when Robin winked. 'When those biscuits are ready, we'd love some, and a pot of tea.'

'Coming right up.' Robin bowed and shut the door behind her.

Willow rolled over and picked her camera off the floor. 'Let's take a picture of us.'

'With a timer?' Wren knew some cameras had timers.

Willow held the camera over their heads and pointed the lens down.

'How do you know we're in the picture?'

'The camera knows. Say cheese!'

'Ch…' Wren tried, but pulled the blanket over her face. 'I don't want my picture taken.'

'I'm sorry. My camera is a part of me.' Willow returned it to the floor. She twisted around and put her lips close to Wren's mouth without kissing her. 'How do you see the world?'

'With my hands.'

Winter solstice is the birth of light in all its metaphors, so at summer solstice something has to die. In their tradition, the Ovem celebrated the death of Patriarchy, inside and out. They gathered at noon wearing nothing but sweet pea crowns and the shawls they wore against the breezes reaching up from the ocean.

Nikki and Ginny led the coven to Lupe's chamomile circle in the orchard. The carpet of herbs released a euphoric scent as the coven entered the sacred precinct.

The High Priestesses blessed them with water from the pond, then traced pentacles on each witch's forehead with oil consecrated on a dark moon. Ginny held a long knife and traced a circle on the ground just outside the circle, singing names of the Goddess:

'Demeter, Persephone, Hecate, Isis.

Deborah, Innana, Al-Lat.

Artemis, Melusine, Cerridwen, Aphrodite.

Bridget, Arianrhod, Anna Marie.'

Nikki approached the witches in turn.

'How do you enter the circle?'

Each witch replied with magic words: 'In perfect love and perfect trust.'

The witches raised their cone of power, singing *She Changes Everything She Touches* and *Hoof and Horn, Hoof and Horn, All That Dies Will Be Reborn*. The chants broke into rounds, harmonised, then became a wordless cry. The coven's voices rose discordantly. Louder and louder. One of them cried so loud it was kind of terrifying. They made low and scary sounds for a while, then high ululations. The witches danced, catching their hair in their teeth, falling into each other, shrieking.

Higher and higher rose their voices, faster and faster they circled the covered cauldron in the centre. At the proper moment, they shouted in unison, flinging their arms skyward, and sending the energy into the sky above the orchard. Then they kneeled and grounded the energy into the circle Ginny had cast.

A warm wind lifted their scarves. As they unbent their backs, they held hands and met each other's shining eyes.

Nikki uncovered a cauldron of coals and added applewood until the fire leaped up, visible even in the sunshine.

They sang their summer solstice song:
Fire and smoke.
Smoke and fire.
Rule of men dies on this pyre.
Smoke and fire
Fire and smoke.
Now is the time of Womenfolk.

When the coven was new, they had celebrated summer solstice as the death of Patriarchy. But this year they gave attention to internalised woman-hating.

They performed their acts of magic in order of age. Before Robin joined the coven, Gloria always went first. Today, Robin stepped forward to declare what she was burning out of herself.

'I must not hold myself apart. When I invited you to live here, I forgot I couldn't predict how you would change me.' Everyone laughed, but the ritual mood remained intact. 'I burn up my reticence.'

Like a prayer and a promise, the witches chanted, *So Mote It Be.*

Gloria stepped forward. 'I burn up my bossiness. I don't have all the answers. I will trust to the Goddess to speak to women in their own time.'

So Mote It Be.

Before adding her stick, Nikki asked them not to laugh. 'I'm burning away my lust. I need to make room for love before I let my clit make my decisions.' The coven respected Nikki's vulnerability at that moment and recited *So Mote It Be* again.

Lupe approached the cauldron. 'I've been smoking too much. No more pot until two full moons have passed.'

So Mote It Be.

Kelsey dropped her sticks on the fire. 'I'm burning up my anger. I vow to not get so angry any more. I'm so done with anger.' The coven looked at each other, wondering where this came from.

So Mote It Be.

Hazel held her stick over the fire. 'I'm burning up my guilt about not honouring my parents.'

She dropped her stick on the flames.

So Mote It Be.

In the week since meeting Willow, Wren had been swimming in love like an otter in kelp, tossed and lifted high and pulled, rushing down in tidal forces. Like how she felt during the Beltane ritual – before that meltdown over Robin and Kelsey – she felt aroused, satisfied and joyful every day. And Willow wanted to work on the magical statue with her.

She stepped forward. 'I'm burning up the last of my mother damage. Aphrodite has healed me.'

So Mote It Be.

Ginny stepped toward the centre. 'I cast into the fire my need to be alone all the time. I will never find a lover until I can be a good friend.'

So Mote It Be.

Wren smiled at the lugubrious faces of her coven sisters. These vows… She tried to imagine an acquiescent Gloria, a repressed Nikki, sober Lupe, complacent Kelsey, filial Hazel and gregarious Ginny.

Robin watched the fire, her eyes far away, as they often were.

Nikki stirred the fire to burn up the last of the bad stuff. Ginny filled eight cups with mead, and they drank to the death of the sun and the end of Patriarchy in their lifetimes. They lay on the chamomile and inhaled palliative oils. Wren felt that by this time next year, she would have finished the magical statue. They would still be together, and not broken up like Robin feared.

But it was Robin herself who brought Patriarchy onto Ove that summer. And no art could have stopped her.

six

Kelsey thought about Robin when she washed the cucumbers. She thought about Robin as she sliced them. She thought about Robin again as she packed the spears and spices into canning jars. Then she thought about Robin as they boiled.

She had been thinking about Robin. Last week, after their third breathwork session, she told Robin she didn't need more sessions – not with herself anyway. Since then, they hadn't spent any time together alone. Robin was up early every day helping Lupe, Hazel and Ginny in their Spheres. Kelsey liked to sleep in, take walks, smoke pot and do nothing for most of the day until it was time to cook dinner. Maybe she was avoiding Robin.

Kelsey's lovers came into her life like a scent on a breeze. Robin wasn't any kind of air at all. She was earthy and dark like a stone, where Kelsey felt like the fire in the centre of those stones.

That sort of poetry wasn't like her. Kelsey checked her

watch. That batch of pickles was boiled.

Wren bounced in with cucumbers. 'This is the last of them, Hazel says.'

That girl has energy. Kelsey told Wren to put them in the sink and then help her lift the canning rack from the pot. Kelsey submerged another rack into the bubbling cauldron.

'Let's have tea.' Kelsey fetched the jug of sun tea from the fridge and poured them both tall glasses. They sat on the front porch, the coolest part of the house on this August afternoon.

'I heard Nikki Craft is leaving town,' Wren said, uncharacteristically aware of current events.

'I saw that in the *Sentinel*. Pretending to be ridden out of town on a rail.'

Like many feminists in Santa Cruz, Kelsey had been uplifted by Nikki Craft's artistic, satirical and poignant activism, all of which demonstrated how men tolerate their violence against women. Craft organised groups of women to enter liquor stores and tear up pornographic magazines, because 'pornography is the theory, rape is the practice'. She spent a night in jail for writing in chalk on the sidewalk 'Violence in the media = Violence in society'. Nikki Craft was Kelsey's hero.

'Who will take her place? Maybe your art thing should be an action, like what Nikki Craft does.'

'I never make art that scares people. Willow does feminist art, but it doesn't scare people. She's going to help with the magical statue.' Wren hugged her knees. 'I'm so proud of her. She sold a photo to the Monterey *Herald*.'

'She seems like a great person. I'd like to know her better.'

'Kelsey, I already love her so much, but it's hard for her. We have to sleep in the living room because she can't deal with the stairs.' Wren grabbed her pen from her bag and twisted it in her fingers. 'She's so different than other women I've been with.'

'You can say that again.'

'She asks me about myself, and when I answer, she wants to hear more. She pushes me to dig deeper. If she's nervous, she says she's nervous. She can talk about her own feelings – like she can see them.'

'She sounds emotionally available and sort of grown-up.' Kelsey looked at her watch and stood up. Until she met Robin, an emotionally available grown-up was the kind of woman Kelsey avoided. Those women expected intimacy and commitment.

Wren followed Kelsey. 'Yes, she's "emotionally available",' she said, as if learning a phrase in a foreign language.

The pot wasn't boiling, and the flame was out. Kelsey went around to the side of the house and picked up a can, then another. All four were empty.

'Shit, we're out of propane. I still need to bake the lasagne for after the Juggling meeting.'

Kelsey drove alone to Boulder Creek to buy fuel. She thought about Robin all the way down that twisted road, curve after curve. She didn't know what she wanted, but she knew one thing for sure: she wasn't going to ask Lucy about it.

∞

Kelsey had returned with the propane in time to throw the lasagne in the oven. By the time Juggling the Spheres started, the aroma made everyone hungry, so Kelsey put out Ritz crackers and cream cheese.

Wren felt anxious about her agenda item and couldn't snack. She'd eat later if she got what she wanted from the meeting.

'Who's first?' Gloria asked, looking around the table. Gloria always went last.

Hazel said because of the heat, the tomatoes, beans and cucumbers were ripening together and she needed extra help. 'The hornworms found us.'

'I'll kill them for you,' Ginny said enthusiastically.

'Thanks, Gin. While you do that, I'll get the rest of the cukes in.'

'You said no more,' Kelsey groused. 'I swear I will compost the next cucumber I see.'

Hazel apologised but didn't mean it. Neither did Kelsey.

'I also need help with double-digging another row. As I've said before, the soil here is actually quite poor.'

'I'll do it,' offered Lupe. 'I'll have more shroom compost next week.'

'Why is our soil poor?' Gloria asked.

Hazel explained patiently. 'A redwood forest creates the soil that it prefers, and nothing but ferns and mushrooms grow under the redwoods. When we expand the garden, we transform the soil.'

Gloria looked significantly at Wren, but Wren didn't write anything because everyone knew that.

'Do you want to go next, Ginny?'

'I have some good news.' Ginny folded her delicate fingers together in front of her on the table. Like a confession, she said, 'I'm afraid I've fallen in love… with cashmere.'

There were a few groans, and Wren drew a picture of a naked woman running towards a spinning wheel surrounded in hearts. Wren lifted the notebook and showed Ginny the cartoon. 'Wren, you get me!' and everyone else wanted to see it, too. Wren knew interruptions like that annoyed Gloria, but she couldn't help it.

Gloria moved the meeting along. 'Nikki, what are you working on?'

'Kelsey ran out of propane today.'

'I told you when we moved in, little cans don't work,' Kelsey said.

'Why can't we have an electric stove?' asked Gloria.

'*You* cook on a fucking electric stove. I won't.'

'You know best.'

Kelsey slapped the table. 'We. Need. A. Propane. Tank.'

Nikki said, 'I'll get to it.'

'You've been saying that for months.' Everyone stared at Kelsey. She lowered her voice. 'Thank you again for the bathhouse, but I thought the propane tank was part of that deal.'

Nikki sighed and sounded uncharacteristically hesitant. 'I don't know what to work on first. Hazel needs irrigation. Kelsey wants a propane tank. And I need to re-insulate my own room. Even with the stove, I was too cold last winter.'

Wren sketched the barn against a night sky, with labryses rising from Nikki's skylight.

'Nik-keeey,' Gloria teased. 'Don't you also need to prioritise sleepovers with your baby dyke – what was her name?

'Since visiting Ove, she changed her name to Madrone,' Nikki explained. 'But she's not a baby dyke. She's nearly as old as Robin – no offence.'

'No one is as old as me,' Robin said with mock pride.

Lupe didn't like Madrone for some reason. 'She found that lesbian haircut in a Sears catalogue.'

'Don't be mean,' said Nikki. Lupe apologised.

Gloria tried facilitating again. 'How can we help Nikki

prioritise?'

Nikki turned to her cousin. 'Rob, you know I want this place to be women-only, but most women don't have the skills—' She put her hands up to defend herself from everyone's protests. 'I know why! I'm saying it's too much for me and I need help.'

'Do you want to hire skilled *people*, regardless?' suggested Gloria.

'I don't want to hire men, but I need skilled *people* to do the skilled work. I don't know how to do that without hiring the guys I know who can do it.'

'Nikki, it's your Sphere,' said Gloria. 'If you need to prioritise or hire *people*, do it.'

Nikki glanced over at Robin, but Robin was tipped back in her chair, eyes closed. 'I won't bring men on the land,' Nikki said. 'I need women-only space as much as anyone.' She closed her eyes for a moment to collect herself. 'Wren, write down that my two top projects are more water in the garden and replacing the old propane tank.'

Wren wrote 'Nikki: water & propane' on a fresh page in the notebook.

Kelsey harrumphed.

'Kelsey,' Nikki said. 'My jobs will take longer. If you can think of a better way, tell us now.'

'I'm sorry,' Kelsey said. 'If I do I'll let you know. I don't want men on the land either.'

'Are we done?' Lupe waited only a moment. 'My turn. We smoked most of last year's weed, but the girls in the orchard grow fast up here above the fog. Mushrooms – I'll be harvesting enoki again next week, and that's where the compost will come from, Hazel.'

Robin offered to help with compost, and Lupe continued

down her list. 'Some early apples are ripe, so I'm going to ferment the juice and distil it.'

Gloria attempted to tease Lupe. 'So you're a moonshiner now, as well as a drug dealer?'

'I'm not a drug dealer,' Lupe said without laughing, and closed her notebook. 'I think it's Wren's turn.'

Finally. Wren pressed her hands to her thighs and sat up straight. 'When Willow visits, she can't climb the stairs, and she's not our only friend who's differently abled.'

'Like me,' said Ginny.

'Exactly. Not all our guests climb the ladder to the attic. And sometimes women need privacy.' She then proposed in a formal tone, 'Ovem, we need a cabin for differently abled women.'

Kelsey said, 'I'd say a new propane tank is a higher priority.'

Nikki agreed.

Wren had planned for this. 'Nikki, can you prioritise teaching me to build it?'

While Nikki visibly tried to avoid unkindly expressing her doubts, Wren made her move. 'Maybe Robin could help me.'

Wren had never manipulated a Juggling discussion like this before, but she was desperate. Willow hated making love in the living room underneath Robin's bedroom.

Robin probably knew that. 'Actually, Nikki, if I were a better carpenter, that would help with our lack of skilled labour.'

'She's right, Nik,' Wren said. 'And Robin, I don't know if you've noticed, but I'm not getting anywhere with your—'

'Don't worry about—'

'But I *want* to make the magical statue.' She caught Kelsey rolling her eyes. She would ignore that. 'While we build this cabin for Willow, and other women' – Wren caught Ginny's supportive smile – 'we can talk more about what you want. You explained it so well last winter – about art that reminds us of our ideals and stuff. I need to hear that again.'

'I'm always happy to talk about art and politics with you, Wren.'

Wren didn't wait for Kelsey or anyone else to offer *concerns*. No one could be against a plan to help disabled women. Under the previous note, she wrote: 'Robin/Nikki/Wren: cabin.' By the time she looked up, it was Robin's turn.

'I want to announce something, but don't worry about it. I'm being sued.'

'The uncles?' Nikki guessed, with a venom that told everyone exactly who they were.

'Our uncles. If you see any sign of trespassers, just tell me.'

'If I see the uncles on the land, I'm going to do more than gossip about it.'

Robin nodded. 'But after you've buried the bodies, let me know, so I can do the legal stuff.'

Everyone laughed, and Gloria opened her binder. She announced she had finished the first draft of *Emerging Athenic Wicca*. She said the book's three sections were named Owl, Mountain Lion and Snake, which are animals who lived with them at Ove. While she prattled on, Wren reached for a cracker and covered it in a thick layer of cream cheese. She stuffed it into her mouth, examined each woman around the table and drew their breasts from memory. This sketch could be a contribution to Willow's *Boobs of Wimmin's Land* project. She loved being in love with another artist.

'…Three women signed up for the class, and Willow is one of them. If you finish the guest house by then, we can use it for workshops. Maybe the cabin is your magical statue, Wren.'

No, it's not. Worse, Willow hadn't mentioned signing up for Gloria's class. Wren didn't like the idea of her sitting at Gloria's feet and learning about owls and lions and snakes. She returned to her breast sketches. Willow was entitled to her own explorations of witchcraft. Besides, Gloria's classes would bring Will to Ove more often.

Gloria must have finished, because everyone was getting up to clear and set the table. Gloria reached for the Ove book.

'These are your notes?' Gloria's eyes narrowed as she flipped through the cartoons. 'It must be nice to have a girlfriend.' Gloria came to the row of breasts. 'Which ones are mine?'

'Those.' Wren printed 'GLORIA' under them.

Gloria put her arm around Wren's waist and pulled her close. 'You are so talented.'

Gloria had been saying things like that a lot since the party, and Wren didn't mind it. After that Juggling meeting, she felt like she had the talent to solve all her problems.

⚭

Robin got Wren excited about the octagon cottages women built in Santa Cruz a long time ago. Nikki swore a lot while calculating the angles, but agreed it was a perfect shape for a woman's home.

Wren copied Nikki's construction drawing and kept it on her altar. The octagon would have a ramp and a porch big enough for a couch and wheelchair. The single room was twelve feet across, with two triangular closets. A sturdy ladder would rise to a loft. Nikki found a sweet little wood stove. Wren imagined her and Willow making love there, and from the love they made would come great art.

She called Willow nightly.

'…And we should finish framing the walls tomorrow and start the roof. Can you come up to see it this weekend?'

'I'm doing a photoshoot Saturday. Joanie and Barb and a bunch of us are recreating the *Triumph of Venus* down at Lover's Point. Get it?'

'By Boucher? What about the flying putti?' Wren knew Willow would invite her to join them.

'With balloons I think. And a kite. Joanie has costumes from her theatre club. Do you have costumes we could borrow?'

When Wren didn't say anything, Willow added, 'We'll be there at two-thirty for low tide. Are you coming?'

'You know I don't like having my picture taken.'

'But this is different. We're pretending. You love costumes!'

'I've tried to tell you…' Wren hated refusing Willow, but this was the only thing they ever argued about.

'I'm sorry. I won't ask again.'

Willow always meant it when she apologised. Wren felt the warmth of Will's love flowing through the phone line. 'Can you catch a ride to Santa Cruz with Barb afterward? Robin and I can pick you up downtown.'

'I'd love that.'

Wren felt safe enough to apologise too. 'I'm sorry I got testy. You have fun with your friends and I'll see you after.'

Wren hung up and joined Kelsey to help with dinner. Kelsey seemed like she needed cheering up, but Wren couldn't figure out why.

Seven

Wren and Robin built the octagon together on long, hot afternoons. Soon enough, Wren wasn't afraid of the nail gun or the chop-saw.

'Kelsey said Sonia Johnson is coming to town next week.' Wren climbed down the ladder to get more roof shingles. 'I might vote for a president this time, since I can vote for a lesbian.'

Robin chuckled from above her. 'Did you know Susan B. Anthony visited Santa Cruz?' She was on the roof, despite her fear of heights. They wanted to finish the roof today. 'She travelled here in support of a local woman who tried to vote. The case went to court, but she lost. We had to wait forty more years before men let us vote. Like Sonia says, fighting them just makes them stronger.'

'I should have known you were a suffragette.'

'That's where I found the lesbians.' Robin winked. 'One thing the suffragists had was great visual propaganda. Golden banners and sashes. Very pretty.'

'Is that your sly way to remind me about the Art Thing?'

'I'm only curious. Take your time.'

'Willow and I have been tossing around ideas.' Willow had initiated a few brainstorm sessions, but nothing sparked Wren's imagination. She was starting to wonder if she did her best work alone.

Wren lifted half a stack of tiles to her shoulder and had just put her foot on the bottom rung when it shook under her free hand. 'Quit it,' she yelled, because she thought, improbably, that Robin was messing around, shaking the ladder with her on it.

But Robin wasn't messing around. Robin's frightened face loomed toward her and Wren fell backwards, the heavy shingles dragging her off-balance.

It was 'just a little shake'; not an earthquake anyone would remember, but it caught Robin as she leaned over to steady the ladder. She lost her balance and slid forward. She tried to catch herself, but could only twist her body enough that she didn't fall on her head. She landed off-kilter, feet first, amid the wood scraps and nails.

She yelled, then started swearing. 'Don't touch it!' she barked as Wren crawled over on her hands and knees.

Wren's shoulder was wrenched, but she ignored it. 'Help,' she yelled. 'Kelsey! Somebody! Help!'

Wren sounded terrified of something. Kelsey rang the bell and met Nikki running out of the barn. When they got to the octagon, Wren looked helpless, and Robin was swearing and crying.

'Calm yourself, honey.' Kelsey sat behind Robin and she

relaxed into the cradle of Kelsey's body. Nikki started clearing away construction trash, and Wren looked relieved to have something to do. 'Wren, hand me the water.'

Robin took a sip, then threw it up.

Gloria appeared and dealt with the emergency by taking charge. 'She needs to get to the hospital.' She ran back to the house to call the ambulance.

'I think your leg is broken,' said Kelsey softly into Robin's ear. 'Puking is a clear sign.'

'I felt it go.'

Wren and Nikki sat next to them; there was nothing to do and no need to panic. Gloria ran up. 'The ambulance won't get here for at least twenty minutes.' She handed Kelsey a blanket. 'They said to keep her warm.'

'I *am* warm.'

Ginny appeared and gently patted Robin's other leg. Pepper smelled the broken one and shook her head.

'Don't touch my ankle,' Robin shouted in a pitch that Kelsey hadn't heard before.

'Is anything else hurt?' Ginny asked. 'You've scraped your hands.'

'Just my ankle,' Robin grunted.

Robin tried to wiggle out of Kelsey's arms. 'Stay put till they get here.' Kelsey squeezed Robin tighter.

'No men on the land,' said Robin.

'You're delirious,' said Gloria. 'You need to get to the hospital.'

'Get your van!' Robin told Lupe.

'The ambulance is quicker,' said Hazel.

'Stay still,' said Kelsey. 'If your leg is jiggered, you might never walk again.'

'It's only a broken leg. They heal.'

Lupe warmed up the van. Kelsey knew she should weigh in on this Van vs Men's Ambulance controversy, but she couldn't participate in a group discussion right now because Robin was alive and she could have been dead.

'Absolutely not,' said Gloria. 'The ambulance is on its way.'

'I'm with Gloria on this one,' said Wren, looking terrified. Was she afraid to argue with Robin?

Hazel had another idea. 'What if we adjust the no-men rule for medical emergencies?'

'No,' said Robin. 'No men. You all promised.'

'Your life is at stake,' Wren pleaded.

'No men. Anyway, my life isn't at stake.'

The other women said nothing, but Kelsey knew they wanted her to say something. She didn't want to argue with Robin either. The no-men rule was important; she understood why. She also understood medical emergencies.

'Maybe there will be female EMTs?' offered Ginny.

Kelsey knew there was zero chance of that.

'No men on the land,' said Robin. She turned her head and snuggled closer in Kelsey's arms. Kelsey pulled the blanket tighter.

'Forgive me for using this word, Robin, but you're being hysterical,' Gloria said.

Robin chuckled, then groaned. Kelsey hoped that they could just let the EMTs arrive; they could just let it happen, regardless of what Robin wanted. If nobody said anything right now, they could get Robin to the hospital and argue about it later.

Gloria bent down and declared, 'The ambulance is coming and you're going to the hospital.'

Kelsey tried to say 'shut up, you idiot' with her eyes.

Lupe pulled up in her van, jumped out and opened the

sliding door. 'Good thing I never put the seats back!' she shouted, shifting empty produce boxes off the floor. 'Get blankets!'

'She can't ride on the floor!' Wren wailed.

'Nikki!' Robin found Nikki's face in the circle of panicked women. 'Please, Nikki, help me get into the van.'

Nikki obviously hated being in the middle. 'I dunno, Rob. Ambulances are pretty comfortable. They'll give you something for the pain.'

'It doesn't hurt that much.'

'It will by the time you get to Dominican ER,' said Gloria.

Ginny said she heard the siren.

'No men on the land,' Robin repeated, like she was practising her Last Words.

For once, Kelsey had a genius idea. 'Let's put Robin into Lupe's van and drive her to the road. No men on the land, and Robin will get her ambulance ride.'

Once they established the alternative, they picked Robin up, carried her to the van and tucked her back into Kelsey's arms. Wren steadied Robin's leg as Lupe drove slowly across the bridge and up to Empire Grade. Robin cried with every jolt, and Wren and Kelsey wept with her. Their beautiful friend, suffering because of her ridiculous separatism.

They waited there in silence until the ambulance arrived. Two EMTs competently extracted Robin from the van and lifted her into the rig. Finally, she was safely on her way. Everyone piled into the van and bounced down the mountain to the hospital, uncomfortable and crowded on the floor, but together.

They got home just after dawn, all eight Ovem in the van. Robin appreciated the velcro boot instead of the cast she had expected, but mostly she liked the pain pills. Nikki and Lupe pulled Robin's mattress down from her room, and Kelsey made up a bed for her in front of the fireplace.

The next day, Gloria went to Horsnyder's for crutches and a wheelchair. She said she would help Wren with the octagon while Robin recuperated. Everything got back to normal, but Kelsey knew her friendship with Robin would never be the same.

∞

A week later, Kelsey was shelling fava beans with Robin. 'And that was the price we paid to be solar electricity pioneers.' She loved fresh fava beans, but jeez, they were a lot of work. She didn't mind it though, on these long, lazy summer afternoons. Too hot for shirts, and she relished their privacy.

'Where did you live after the house burned down?'

'The church found an RV for us, and then Dad built a dome home.'

'It leaked, right?'

Kelsey chuckled. 'They all do.' She flicked shells off her apron and into the chicken bucket. 'Cripes, I'll be glad when that hammering is done.'

Across the plaza, Wren and Gloria were meticulously blind-nailing siding to the octagon.

'It feels good to see Gloria working on something in the physical realm,' Kelsey said. She wished she could describe other good feelings. She wanted to get closer to Robin, but didn't want complications.

Which would be inevitable if she let it go further. Unlike Wren, Kelsey accepted Robin's disinterest in sexually romantic relationships. Robin was definitely a lesbian; she loved women and put them first. Having sex with women didn't make you a lesbian. Kelsey had had sex with enough straight women to learn that lesson.

'What will we do when we're done?' Robin pulled over the last full basket of long bean pods.

'I'm afraid I have to go to town to get more propane.' Kelsey kept her mouth firm, her tone serious.

But Robin looked so guilty. 'Kelsey, about what happened at that Juggling meeting…'

Kelsey held her tongue.

'I've been wanting to apologise. I realised later we should have prioritised the propane tank, but Wren looked so cute and in love and she wanted her lover to be able to be comfortable… I'm sorry.'

Kelsey had meant to simply poke fun at Robin, but this was a serious apology. Kelsey shrugged. 'Don't worry about it. That's why we call it Juggling.'

'You weren't okay about it.'

'I was butt hurt for a while, but mostly because I thought you didn't care about me.'

Robin sighed and stopped splitting her bean pod. 'I regret that even more.' She resumed shelling. 'I had a chance to show you how I appreciate you, and I blew it. I know how you care for me. Like when you wanted me to shut up and get in the ambulance, but you found a way to get me to the hospital in a way that respected our women-only space.'

'I'm glad you remember that.'

'I'll never forget it.'

Nikki walked across the plaza from the barn. 'How's the leg, Robin?'

'It only hurts when I do what Kelsey tells me not to.'

Nikki took a seat on the porch railing she had recently repaired. 'Don't you look cute with an apron on?'

'Kelsey says it brings out my eyes.' Robin grabbed the edges of her apron and tossed bean shells at Nikki. 'What have you been up to?'

'I found a tractor behind the barn. I thought I might be able to get it running, but it's been stripped for parts already.'

'That's too bad. I've never worked with a tractor.'

'Most women haven't,' said Nikki.

'I mean, *never*. Thousands of years of oxen, donkeys and my two strong thighs, but never a tractor. And since I've been laid up—'

'The Ovem won't allow a tractor,' said Kelsey.

'Yeah, there's a lot of masculine energy in a tractor,' said Nikki.

Robin seemed fixated on making her point. 'Tractors don't have gender. They have gears and hydraulics.'

'Well, it's dead anyway.' Nikki jumped off the railing. 'Do either of you want a beer?' They did, and Nikki went inside.

Kelsey looked over at Robin. She wished they could return to the conversation about what happened when Robin fell off the roof. From the look of Robin's eyebrows pinched together, Robin was planning something. Kelsey was pretty sure she wouldn't like it.

Eight

A few long summer afternoons later, Wren and Gloria were panelling the insides of the two closets with cedar, loving the scent. Gloria was teaching Wren how to make a cedar essential oil when they heard an alien monster rumbling down their road and crossing the bridge.

Wren and Gloria saw a shiny orange tractor entering the plaza, Robin behind the wheel and Ginny standing on the step next to her.

Wren hated it.

'Isn't she gorgeous!' Ginny exulted.

Robin shut down the engine and called out, 'Kelsey, come see what I bought for us.'

The Ovem gathered around as a cloud of diesel exhaust dissipated. Robin was obviously pleased with her new toy, but Wren assumed the Ovem wouldn't let her keep it.

'The tractor can work for me while I'm laid up. We won't need to postpone the propane project any longer, Kelsey.'

Robin delicately lifted herself down and leaned on one

foot. Lupe and Hazel arrived from the garden. Robin waved them over. 'Look! It can move compost and firewood and all the heavy stuff.'

'Where did you leave your wheelchair?' Kelsey asked. Robin pointed up to the road.

Hazel ran her fingers over a rear wheel, almost as tall as she was. 'My grandfather was part of a Japanese farmer co-op who owned a tractor in the Thirties. He said the tractor meant they could compete with other farmers.'

'For once, a patriarchal tool will help the sisterhood,' said Lupe. Hazel scowled at Lupe.

'Do you even know how to work it?' Kelsey asked.

'Not yet,' Ginny admitted. 'Only the clutch.' She pumped a pedal to prove it. 'It's like having a giant for a friend.'

Robin chuckled, besotted.

Hazel gave the tyre an affectionate slap. 'Thanks, Robin. But we don't need it. A tractor is more trouble than it's worth.'

'I agree,' said Kelsey. 'The propane project can wait while you recover, Robin.'

Wren watched Gloria choose her tone carefully before saying, 'You said no men on the land.'

Robin laughed her off. 'Ginny, what will you name her?'

'Let's name her Penny!' Ginny jumped down to kiss the warm engine housing.

'Penny?' Robin was confused. 'Like a coin?'

'Penny. Short for Penthesilea, the Amazon Queen.'

'Let's get out of here,' Gloria said. 'We can add this to the agenda later.'

They retreated to the octagon. Wren took deep breaths of the cedar scent to clear her head of diesel exhaust. She knew she'd never create a magical statue in the presence of a *man machine*.

◯◯

Wren hated the tractor so much. She hated its roar, the stench of grease, and how it bulged into every space it entered. She detested its orange skin, inappropriately garish. It left marks everywhere: more than once Wren had twisted her ankle in an angular footprint.

Robin accepted that her still-healing tibia couldn't handle the brake, so Lupe and Ginny volunteered to operate the Mechanical Amazon. They left their chores undone and spent hours learning how to turn and back up, attach the bucket to the front and switch out the harrow for the backhoe.

Robin still helped Kelsey with food prep, but read the manual on the kitchen table. She took notes in her monk's handwriting in a small notebook she kept in her shirt pocket. She sent Ginny to the mailbox with a handful of tractor magazine subscription cards. She spent days exploring each oil-access point and hydraulic connection, consulting the schematics on the clipboard she carried everywhere.

Clearly, she was in love.

Robin, Lupe and Ginny wouldn't stop talking about Penny's competency. Penny was skilled at everything. She dragged the old propane tank across the plaza and tucked it near the carcass of the other tractor. She took a bite from the hill behind the house and hauled the extra dirt up to Lupe's compost pile. As she drove up and down the hill, she widened the road, to mixed reviews. Penny graded the platform for the new propane tank. Robin explained that the propane delivery truck could get in easier, too. Nikki inspected the exposed hillside and said something about a retaining wall.

When the new tank and pipes were dropped off at the top of the road, Penny carried it all down in two trips. Then she dug the trench between the tank and the house with her strong arm.

As Penny and friends made progress on bringing Kelsey her propane, day after day Wren and Gloria griped about how awful the tractor was. These conversations left Wren muddled, not righteous. She wanted to be a friend to Robin and love everything Robin loved. Why couldn't she see the good in Robin's tractor like Lupe and Ginny did?

When Wren and Gloria finished the closets, Gloria said Wren would have better dreams if the octagon didn't have electricity. That saved days of work. They finished the insulation and started in on trimming the interior with beautiful mouldings.

Gloria didn't tell Robin's sort of stories, but she could explain why today they were especially clumsy (moon transit through Sagittarius). With a dogged resolve, she practised every skill Nikki taught them. Gloria especially excelled in hiding nails under a sliver of wood, something Nikki called 'blind-nailing'.

Gloria liked learning new words like that. Wren appreciated Gloria being obsessed with something other than Athenic wicca.

When they finished the interior moulding, they celebrated with beers, sitting against the front wall where the porch would be.

Wren looked across the plaza at the house, where they could hear Kelsey banging around in the kitchen. Robin was probably in there too. The two of them spent all their time together now.

'You know, Gloria, I think I'm finally over my Robin-crush. When I think back to how I felt at Beltane... I just needed a real girlfriend.'

'Nothing beats a hand in the bush.' Sometimes Gloria could be so funny. Then she asked, 'Have you been working on your big art thing that Robin wants you to do?'

'Not really. I thought Robin could help me, but…' She raised her bottle in the direction of Robin and Kelsey.

'I have an idea. Athena is a goddess of California. Maybe she would help you figure out what Robin wants.'

Wren tried to smile. 'You know I don't get Athenic wicca.'

'I still need illustrations for my Athenic Wheel of the Year calendar. Since I've been helping you with the octagon, I wonder if you can help me? Maybe Athena would inspire you.'

Gloria was right. Athenic wicca might be a shortcut to some powerful symbol. She wouldn't find it in conversations with Robin as long as Robin was married to the tractor. 'I will try, but you'll have to tell me exactly what you want.'

'You know me; that won't be a problem,' Gloria said with a self-knowing laugh. She really was mellower lately. 'Speaking of Willow…' Gloria took another sip of beer. 'Because she and her friend Barb are taking the class – and maybe another woman from Salinas – they asked if I could teach them down there instead.'

'But you need to teach it here so Willow can visit more.'

Gloria offered giving Willow a ride back after the class, but Wren wasn't listening any more.

When she called Willow that night, she couldn't hide her hurt. 'Gloria said she's teaching her class in Monterey, not at Ove.'

'That just made more sense to us. It's better if we keep the class separate from you and me. Since you're not into it.'

'But I am now. I'm drawing her Athenic calendar. She said you could ride back with her. The octagon is almost done, and we'll have privacy.' She pronounced 'privacy', as if it was a synonym for cunnilingus.

'It's easier to have privacy at my house, but you never visit me. I wonder sometimes if that's about something else.'

'Is *what* about something else?'

'Why you didn't want to do the Rococo Re-Creation?'

'I don't like having my picture taken. Why bring this up again?'

'I get that, but what else?'

Then Willow was silent; she was letting the silence help Wren discover something. Wren saw through her. 'You're trying to get me to say that I don't like having my picture taken because of what my mother did.'

'I don't know,' offered Willow. 'But you seem to have a charge around having your picture taken. Is that why you're withdrawing?'

'Withdrawing? I'm literally building a cabin for us with my bare hands.'

'Can we talk about why we didn't make love last time?'

Not the lesbian bed death conversation already. 'I must not have felt like it.'

'Is there something about me you don't like any more?'

The pathetic drift in Willow's tone infuriated her. Wren tried to answer 'no', but it wasn't true.

Willow went into her Wise Woman aspect, which was worse. 'I only ask because when women get intimate, stuff comes up that needs healing. We've only been together a few weeks. I'm sure stuff about my trauma will come up, and we'll need to deal with it.'

Was she always this self-centred? 'I don't think you respect my boundaries. "Taking a picture." Do you hear how violent it is?' Willow made a noise like she was going to argue, but

Wren talked over her. 'This is why long-distance relationships don't work. Maybe you shouldn't do Gloria's class.'

'Are you breaking up with me?'

Was Willow crying? 'I said maybe you shouldn't do the class. I'm not breaking up with you. Maybe you're the one with abandonment issues, not me.'

'Honey, we all had fucked-up childhoods. Mine is about my accident. Yours is about your mom. How has wicca helped you? It helped me.'

Does Willow think she knows more about the Craft? *I burned up my Mother Damage,* Wren didn't say. Instead, she said she was tired.

Willow agreed it was time to stop talking for a while. 'I might want to send you a letter. Do you mind?'

'Of course not,' Wren said automatically, and then panicked. 'Willow, I don't want to break up.'

'Me neither,' Willow said, but hung up first.

Wren didn't want to sleep alone, so asked to sleep with Gloria, who cheerfully fluffed up the other pillow. Wren had bad dreams anyway.

Nine

Hazel pointedly announced at breakfast that, again, she needed help. On their fog-less mountain, vegetables ripened too fast for her to be able to harvest them all alone. The Pennyphiliacs, as Gloria and Wren secretly called them, pointedly said nothing. So Gloria said she and Wren would help Hazel instead of finishing the octagon. In other words, breakfast was tense.

When they got to the garden, Wren saw the new irrigation thing. Hazel used a word for it that sounded like 'The Sister.' Above the blue can that Nikki called The Pump, a grey plastic cube bigger than a washing machine squatted on a metal platform with spidery legs. Not beautiful like Nikki's usual work. To Wren's imagination, two white-rimmed openings stared out like eyes, and the spigot below them made a sour expression. Hazel used the hose that snaked out beneath it to send water down the rows. The Sister was an ugly but suitable companion who gave them what they needed.

The tractor was unsuitable.

Hazel assigned chores, passed out tools and the women got to work. And gossiped.

'I swear it's a monogamous four-way,' Gloria joked. She was weeding a row of tomatoes and checking for worms. Hazel stood in another row, picking peas. Wren was on her knees, mulching young olallieberry vines with cardboard. She hated jokes about the tractor.

'Did you hear Ginny's song about her?' Gloria asked brightly.

'*It*,' Wren insisted and Gloria apologised. 'I don't understand why they like it so much,' Wren said, tearing apart a cardboard box and arranging the pieces carefully around the base of a vine. Hazel had told her the berries needed to be protected from weed competition in their first year. Wren liked berry pie, and right now she distracted herself from tractor thoughts by tearing the cardboard into precise shapes and arranging them in overlapping patterns.

Gloria asked if she had talked to Robin about it. 'If she respected you, she'd hear you out.'

Wren hadn't said a word to Robin. She tore some red cardboard and tried to ease it under the delicate plastic tube Hazel had put there for some reason. Frustration overcame her, and she shouted '*shit*' so loud that Pepper came over to check it out. Pepper hung out in the garden these days.

Gloria thought they were still talking about Robin. 'Wren, just talk to her about it. You shouldn't be scared of her.'

'I'm not afraid of Robin – Hazel, I have to move this... I'm afraid I'll break the irrigation tube.'

'You won't,' encouraged Hazel. 'That system is tougher than it looks. Anyway, Robin felt guilty she couldn't work. She brought a man-substitute to the land. Not every bright idea is a good one. Every row needs to be weeded, Gloria.'

Gloria threw a grassy clod in Hazel's direction. 'Sometimes she's so selfish. I can't teach with that thing here.'

'How is the class coming?' Hazel asked, but didn't sound interested.

'I might not finish in time because I worked on the octagon, and now you need me in the garden.'

Hazel inspected the row next to her. 'Gloria, do you think we'll have time to get to the eggplant today?' She grew the slender Japanese eggplants, not Mediterranean monsters. 'They all came in at once.'

'Maybe Kelsey will make chutney,' mused Gloria.

'Just ask her.' Wren straightened the edge of another layer and smiled at the result. 'Why isn't Kelsey against the tractor?'

'She wants the propane,' said Gloria. 'I understand why. I had to replace the tank once and *never again*.'

Hazel said Kelsey didn't want to argue with Robin right now.

Wren agreed. She never wanted to argue with Robin either. 'Because Robin is still hurting from her leg?' She tore into a new green box so it would contrast with the red.

'Uh, it might be something else,' Hazel said, and Gloria laughed.

'Somebody needs to tell Robin everything is falling apart.' Wren worried the mulching was taking much longer the way she was doing it. She looked back along the row. But the patterns were so pretty.

'Wren, will you talk to her?' Hazel asked.

'Good idea, Hazel,' Gloria said. 'If Wren convinces Robin, the other two will listen.'

'Gloria, conflict resolution isn't my Sphere. I'm the visionary.'

Speaking of conflict, Willow's *Triumph of Venus At Lover's Point* had arrived the other day, printed on real postcard photo paper. It was a brilliant *tableau vivant*, with Willow's friends posed on kelp-strewn rocks above a low tide, blowing shells, riding inflated pool toys shaped like dolphins, flying kites with billowing red and white tails. Their antics encircled a majestic Venus, bare-titted, round-tummied, resplendent on a blue beach towel. A masterpiece. But Willow spoiled it by writing, 'Join us next time: Gentileschi's *Judith and Holofernes!*'

Wren knew well the Renaissance painting of Judith decapitating a king. Wren didn't make art that scared people.

'But when you avoid conflict,' Hazel was saying, 'we get new quilts.'

'We have enough quilts.' Wren put Venus out of her mind and tore more cardboard.

Gloria dumped her weeds on the compost pile and tried another angle when she returned. 'Wren, at summer solstice you got rid of blaming your mother for your problems.'

Wren stood up. 'My mother? Robin isn't my mother.'

'That's my point. Because of your mom, you're always afraid to confront strong women. Athena will help you change that about yourself.'

'I'm not afraid of Robin.'

'Then talk to her. She needs to respect you and see how selfish she's being.'

Wren bent down between the rows, tearing up and placing cardboard. After a few minutes, the conversation went to when they would see *The Black Cauldron*, the new Disney movie about witchcraft. Wren wondered if she would invite Willow.

Wren carefully covered her cardboard assemblage with

wood chips, then took off her gloves and admired her work. Yes, she had spent too much time, but the vines were well protected, and it didn't look like someone had just thrown around garbage. She walked over to Hazel with a bargain. 'I'll talk to Robin if you two come with me now, before I lose my nerve.'

∞

The women put the tools away and walked down to the house. Gloria and Hazel held Wren's hands. Wren found a little courage there between them.

Someone had parked the tractor, stinking and warm, near the front door. They avoided it and walked around to the back. Wren had only seconds more to figure out how to avoid confrontation. Gloria and Hazel were treating this like something they could fix with talking, but they didn't know Robin like she did. How to confess she didn't like the tractor and not piss Robin off?

She knew Robin wasn't her mom, but Robin did get angry sometimes, like when she fell off the roof and yelled about men on the land. She yelled at Wren that day. Sometimes people lost control when they got angry and you couldn't predict it. Sometimes they got mad about one thing, and it reminded them of worse things you had done. Sometimes it started with yelling, and then they said you were a shitty little brat, and then they slapped your face, and if you couldn't hide in the closet, they'd pull a hairbrush out from their purse and smack you on the bottom to teach you not to get smart with them.

At the back door, Wren froze. Her throat constricted and dried solid. 'I can't.'

Gloria started to console, but Hazel hushed her. Wren slowly bent her knees and crouched on the back step, holding herself. She started to cry, and the tears helped her come back into her body. Robin was not her mother. Gloria and Hazel squatted next to her, letting her cry. They could hear the conversation inside. Wren shivered for some reason. She heard murmuring, a champagne cork popping, then cheers.

The Propane Project was finished and the Pennyphiliacs were celebrating.

Gloria patted Wren's shoulder. 'Lucky you. You don't have to tell Robin you hate the tractor.'

Wren didn't feel lucky. She felt like she had missed out on something important, but couldn't remember what it was.

Hazel handed her a bandana. 'Let's not spoil it,' she said, and followed Gloria inside.

Wren sat on the back step and heard another champagne cork. The afternoon felt warm again. She blew her nose. She stood and walked into the kitchen. It smelled like tomato-sauce heaven. 'What are we having?'

Kelsey looked up from the stove. 'Good. I was about to ring the bell.'

'Drink your champagne!' Robin put a slender glass in her hand. Wren had never seen Robin so happy. 'And then, Nana's spaghetti sauce.' Robin lifted herself out of her wheelchair and onto the bench.

Lupe and Ginny cleared the kitchen table of diagrams and hardware store receipts. Kelsey put a cauldron of sauce on the table. 'One silver lining of Robin's injury: more Italian food.'

'I thought menus were *your* Sphere,' Wren asked, amazed she could speak normally. She had practised this all her life.

'I like new recipes. I've had enough Bloodroot and

Moosewood to last three of Robin's lifetimes.'

Wren tried to laugh but choked instead. Robin looked at her, concerned. *Don't say anything.* Everyone was hungry and about to eat Nana's spaghetti. *Don't spoil it.* She raised her glass to Robin and drank it down. 'So you're finished?'

'Yup, the lines are laid in and sealed. We're ready for propane delivery.'

'That's great.'

Gloria and Hazel came back from washing their hands. Wren hadn't even washed her hands yet, and here she was drinking champagne and talking to Robin like normal.

'The new tank is further from the house than the old one, so the pipe has two ninety-degree bends,' Robin explained, as if Wren cared.

'I tested our plumbing. It's faultless,' Lupe said, setting the noodles on the table.

'Are you really, really done?'

'We are. Kelsey will be so happy.' Robin was radiant, plugged into some underground source of heat and light.

After dinner, Wren felt so good she left a message on Willow's machine.

'Hi. It's me. Thanks for the postcard. I'm glad you're doing art that scares people. I can never do that. Let's get together next week? If you want to.'

Wren wished she hadn't added the last bit, and the machine relentlessly recorded the silence of her regret. She messed up again by saying, 'I'm sorry.'. The apology sounded small compared to the words in their last conversation. She wanted to make it larger, but only silence grew, so she hung up.

Ten

While Wren, Hazel and Gloria worked in the garden the next day, a propane delivery truck entered Ove for the first time. Later, they heard its driver was the gas company's receptionist. Nikki knew the owner from a remodelling job and had paid for the receptionist's hazardous-hauling driving school. The receptionist now made twice as much, and Ove remained women-only.

By dinner time the trench was filled, and the tractor sat like a carbuncle in the plaza. Kelsey cooked her first meal with the new supply: three chickens, mashed potatoes, fresh peas. Robin explained that ancient Romans made water pipes of lead, and that's why it was called 'plumbing', from the Latin word for lead.

In the days that followed, the Ovem returned to their Spheres, and the tractor stayed in the barn. Wren hoped it would become a friendly giant like Ginny said, and she would avoid that confrontation with Robin forever.

In the octagon, as they swept out the sawdust and oiled

the mouldings, Wren asked Gloria why it had been so hard for her to talk to Robin about the tractor. Gloria said it was the Patriarchal messages causing fear of other women. She suggested a ritual where you recorded those internalised messages on cassettes and then smashed them with white rocks. Wren felt she had healed from her Mother Damage, but Gloria was right. She was afraid of Robin sometimes, but didn't know why.

Every night that week, Wren worked on *The Athenic Wicca Calendar of the Year* until she finished it. The final painting was 'Autumn Equinox, the Witches' Thanksgiving'. In the centre presided Athena, surrounded by every vegetable, fruit and fungus the Ovem grew. By the time she finished the calendar, Wren saw that Athena was powerful, and not scary. Maybe Athena *could* help her smash those Patriarchal messages.

The octagon was finished, the calendar was finished, and the more time Wren and Willow spent apart, the more she forgot what they had fought about. The day after finishing the calendar, she went to her studio to call Willow. Through the window, she could see Lupe out back messing around with a big bucket and firewood. That was weird.

Willow picked up this time. 'Wren! I was going to call you!'

'I got your postcard and wanted to tell you that although I don't want to—'

'I get that,' Willow said, sounding a little annoyed.

'No, don't worry. I want to help with costumes…if you need me to.'

Willow took a breath. 'We need help with costumes.' Wren could hear relief in her voice. But something else too.

'The octagon is ready. Can you stay this weekend?'

'I'm sorry, but that's what I wanted to talk to you about.'

223

Wren sat down on the loveseat.

'Barb needs me to help her move to Pacific Grove this weekend.'

'Can't you loan her your truck?'

'She broke up with Heather and needs a friend.'

Another lesbian breakup. More ghosts to avoid at parties. 'That's sad. I thought they were good together.'

'Me too. I need to be her friend right now.'

'You're a good friend, Willow.' Wren smelled something delicious in the kitchen. 'We should get off the phone. Kelsey needs me for dinner. I'm glad I remembered about the costumes. I want to do art with you.'

'Me too,' Willow said before she hung up, and Wren didn't feel afraid.

She found Kelsey frying battered fish fillets, flour everywhere.

'Can I help?'

'Ring the bell and set the table,' Kelsey said, without turning round.

Wren couldn't let Kelsey's grumpiness bug her. She and Willow weren't fighting. They only needed time to get to know each other. After all, they had only been together a month or so.

Kelsey had heard Wren talking to Willow on the phone, but didn't miss her in the kitchen. She wanted to cook alone. Robin had given her what she needed, this vast reservoir of stove gas to cook delicious meals on this lovely stove. But she felt indebted. She traded favours with Nikki, but that was different. The difference with Robin was, she felt sparks with Robin.

When Wren finally came in and asked if she could help, Kelsey told her to set the table. Kelsey hated setting the table.

Just after that, Lupe blew herself up. She said later that she'd followed all safety procedures, like she did with everything that required responsibility. She said that while the juice fermented in the barn, she had wanted to test the distillation. So she had assembled 'the pot' – to Kelsey it looked like a cauldron with a lid – and 'the coil' – which looked like what it said it was.

Afterwards, she reminded everyone that she'd carefully raked the ground around the fire pit. She could have used a camp stove, but she needed authenticity, and fire was fun. She filled the pot and rested it firmly on the grate. Then she lit the match.

Right after Kelsey had sent Wren to ring the bell, she heard a pop and a scream. She ran out of the back door and saw Lupe scrambling backwards, hair smouldering. Wren caught her before she hurt herself on the steps.

Lupe shook her head, patting her face delicately. 'What the fuck?'

Kelsey wasn't sure how to describe it. 'You blew up your cauldron.'

Robin wanted to take her to Doc-in-the-Box, but Lupe decided she was fine. It was mostly just her hair burned off, and she could already hear better. Robin rang the bell three times, which was the new signal for 'emergency-come-home-now'.

The explosion had hurt Lupe worse than she had thought. She had burns on her face, chest and hands. Some were blistering. Everyone gathered in the kitchen, watching Wren and Ginny split aloe spears and cover Lupe's upper body with the jelly, offering opinions.

Hazel stepped in as chief detective. 'What happened?'

Lupe, ever the tough girl, smirked. 'Lesbians ignite?'

Kelsey covered the fish in foil, knowing it would get soggy. 'This is not funny.'

'We have a gas leak.' Gloria had already cracked the case.

Hazel thought it was the moonshine.

'No!' Lupe insisted, no longer joking. 'It wasn't *hot*. There was *nothing* in it but water. It blew up as soon as I lit the match. Go look at it.'

Everyone inspected the wreckage of Lupe's moonshine campfire. Hazel squatted down and sniffed. 'Nik, you already shut the gas off, right?' Nikki nodded.

Hazel asked Lupe if she had smelled gas earlier.

'Now that you mention it, I did. It came and went, so I didn't think it was real.'

Hazel dug with her boot heel at the packed earth over the trench. 'I wonder if there's a leak down here?'

Kelsey tried to deal with her fear, anger and adrenaline by feeding people. 'Nobody likes cold tacos,' she said, but no one moved.

Hazel scanned the yard. 'This could be dangerous.'

Nikki started for the plaza. 'I have shovels in the truck.'

While Hazel and Nikki dug holes, everyone else followed Kelsey inside. As they munched on chips and salsa, Lupe explained her distillation plans. She seemed more animated than usual, and Kelsey wondered if she were in shock. 'Do you need more aloe?'

Lupe waved her off, and Robin told them that witches were known for concocting magical wines since ancient times. She said ancient Babylonian priestesses invented distillation, not Islamic male alchemists. She then told the story of how wine distillation in the Industrial Revolution flooded poor neighbourhoods with cheap hard liquor and destroyed families. Usually Kelsey liked Robin's 'history is a spiral' stories, but it seemed like everyone was talking too loud.

Ten minutes later, Hazel leaned through the back door.

'Everybody, come watch!'

Hazel and Nikki had opened the trench, exposing the gas pipe. Nikki poured a mug of soapy water over a sharp-angled bend. Slow bubbles formed. 'We have a gas leak.'

Nikki's mouth was set with guilt. 'Robin, I should have paid better attention. You didn't know what you were doing.'

Robin looked puzzled. 'We knew what we were doing. It's not complicated.'

'You should have protected the gas pipes with a conduit if you're driving heavy equipment over them.'

'The *tractor* did this!' Robin exclaimed, squatted down, and reached for the pipe. 'Of course.'

'Don't touch it,' Nikki warned, and Robin backed off.

'It's not Penny's fault,' Ginny said defensively.

'It is Penny's fault,' Gloria countered, and Ginny flinched.

'This is why we need inspectors and standards and stuff,' Nikki said. 'I'm sorry I wasn't here.'

'It's okay, Nik. You're right. We should have filled the trench by hand,' Robin said, like a conclusion. She looked pleased, like she did with a tidbit of new knowledge. 'We learned something. Let's eat.'

'Wait, wait, wait!' Hazel shouted, waving her arms.

'Listen to Hazel!' Kelsey shouted, because Robin had ignored her.

'This isn't over,' Hazel said decisively. 'I've been trying to tell you that the tractor doesn't belong here.'

This is why she felt indebted to Robin. It wasn't about propane. Hazel said it so easily.

'Penny lives here already,' said Ginny, looking more bewildered than usual.

'You could have filled the trench by hand,' Hazel continued. 'But you *had* to use the tractor. Lupe got lucky today. I know you love it, but you have to get rid of it.'

Ginny crouched down to hug Pepper, hiding her face. Robin stood with her hand on her forehead, looking sad.

Then Hazel turned on Lupe. 'I *told* you not to use the tractor to move your compost, but you did anyway. You tore up the road and wrecked the soil between the sheds and garden.'

'But if you had bothered to learn to drive it, you'd see how great she is,' said Lupe. 'Not to mention fun.'

'I prefer my fun *with* eyebrows.'

Lupe suppressed a smile. 'Hazel, I get it that you're upset the tractor broke the pipes, but we've all benefitted.'

'I'm upset *because you got burned*,' Hazel said, her mouth firm. 'Your fun could have killed you. Or burned the house down. But you're *so smart*. You know *everything*.' Hazel wiped her eyes.

'Hazel, can we go inside?' Kelsey said. 'You've made your point, and we're all hungry.'

'You're right, Kelsey,' Robin said. 'Hazel, I'm sincerely sorry.'

Inside, Lupe and Ginny made a point of sitting on either side of Hazel, and Robin said opposite her. 'The fact is, I miss working with you,' Hazel said, and sobbed for real. Lupe and Ginny held her, apologising.

Robin looked over at Nikki. 'This feels like shit.'

Nikki grimaced. 'It sucks when your own fun wrecks other people.'

'*This* is that feeling?'

'I'm the expert.'

Kelsey watched while the two cousins ruefully reached an understanding about shame and guilt. Robin loved fucking up and learning a lesson. Clearly, Kelsey had let things get too far with her feelings. Robin was no different than her own father, always 'learning a lesson'. Kelsey had ignored her concerns about the tractor, but worse, she'd ignored why Robin brought it to Ove. They didn't need to replace Robin's contribution to chores. Robin had brought the tractor and the completion of the propane project as a gift to Kelsey. But like the time when Kelsey's dad gave her a biorhythms calculator, Robin was the one who was infatuated with the gadget. She couldn't be depended on, just like Dad.

∞

Penny stayed in the barn until the next Juggling. 'Having a timeout,' as Ginny put it.

At the meeting, Hazel proposed getting rid of the tractor. Gloria and Nikki supported her. Kelsey said nothing. Wren took notes.

Robin started them off. 'Let's address the concerns *and* keep the tractor.'

Ginny asked Wren to write down 'Penny is a strong Amazon'.

Hazel rolled her eyes. 'It's not female. It's smelly and loud.'

'Women are smelly and loud,' said Ginny.

Robin leaned back with her eyes closed, like she did when she was thinking hard. Wren started to sketch her, but scribbled it out and turned to a fresh page.

'You bring diesel onto the land, and that hurts everything organic,' said Hazel.

'She's powerful,' said Lupe. 'She saves our bodies from so much labour.'

Hazel wasn't having it. 'While you drove the tractor, I threw my back out because you weren't around to help. I'd rather do our best with a bunch of sweaty dykes than rely on that monster.'

'She's not a monster,' asserted Ginny.

'That's right,' Gloria said, pretending to agree. 'It's merely diesel-powered Patriarchy.'

Each woman gave her opinion. Wren wrote everything down until she announced that no one was saying anything new.

Hazel counted on her fingers. 'Most of us want to get rid of the tractor.'

'You mean sell Penny into slavery?' Ginny said with a pout.

'Please don't compare selling a machine with human slavery,' Nikki admonished her mildly.

'You're right. Sorry.'

Hazel asked again if anyone had an alternative. Robin, Lupe and Ginny looked at each other with faint hope. No fresh ideas.

'I propose we sell *the tractor*,' said Hazel, 'and ask that if you oppose, you stand aside.' She paused and said formally, 'Should we sell the tractor?'

Everyone said yes. Wren wrote 'sell tractor' in the middle of the page. Now that the tractor was leaving, she could empathise. She added eyes to the letter 'o', a down-turned mouth and tears.

'Does anyone *not* want to sell the tractor?'

Robin, Lupe and Ginny said 'yes' together.

'Do you stand aside?'

'Yes,' they said again.

'We recognise that Robin, Lupe and Ginny voted to sell the tractor, but didn't want to, *and* they stand aside, *and* we will sell the tractor.'

Wren wrote: 'We stood aside: Rob, Lupe, Gin.' Then she started sketching the onions hanging from a corner of the ceiling.

Hazel continued to move the meeting along. It was nice for Wren to have someone else running things instead of expecting Gloria to do it.

'Robin, I know you didn't want to sell the tractor, but will you take the lead on selling it?'

Robin agreed, resigned to accept their process. 'Haze, I'm so sorry I didn't listen to your concerns about the tractor – and I didn't use our group process. This is why we need Wren's art. Conflict resolution needs a common vision. After I broke my leg, I got lost. No one was able to say anything to me—'

'I said something,' Hazel reminded them.

'True, but I couldn't hear you. Last year, when I asked Wren to create art that expressed our vision, I knew it would help us resolve inevitable conflict. I never dreamed I'd cause it.'

Wren started to apologise for not working her Sphere, but Gloria patted her leg under the table and took over instead. 'You're saying that art gives us a language to speak the unspeakable. Is that right, Robin?'

'Exactly. It's not enough to learn from our mistakes. With a common vision, we can help each other choose our actions *before* we cause harm.'

Kelsey gasped, then pounded her chest and coughed. 'I'm fine,' she said, even though her eyes welled up.

'If we had this "magical statue" as Wren calls it, Hazel

could have reached Robin where words couldn't,' Gloria stated, sort of unnecessarily at this point. Then Wren realised where she was going. 'I agree Wren is the one to do it,' Gloria continued. 'She just finished a beautiful calendar that will bring her closer to creating what we need.'

'That's great, Wren,' Robin said, smiling warmly, just like old times. Wren turned to a new sheet and stared at it, wondering which of Athena's emblems best expressed the Ovem way of life.

'It's so weird that I couldn't see my mistake,' Robin said to Hazel.

'That must be so hard for you, professor.' Hazel leaned into Robin for a hug, but winced. 'My back is still tweaked.'

Robin offered to give Hazel a back rub after dinner.

∞

Over the next week, everyone did something nice for Hazel. Daily routines returned. Wren, Hazel and sometimes Gloria worked in the garden and got the harvest back on schedule. Kelsey pitched a fit when someone used soap on a cast-iron frying pan.

At dinner one night, Ginny said, 'The goats aren't as calm as they used to be.'

'Maybe they are having abandonment issues, and don't trust you any more,' said Gloria. 'Just kidding,' she added, seeing Ginny's visible shame.

'I know. I am sorry I lost it over Penny. Now I want to get more goats and let them graze in the meadow. They might attract mountain lions. What I'm saying is, I've heard llamas make good goat protectors.'

Robin perked up. 'How about a mule?'

Eleven

Not long after they sold the tractor, Kelsey sat in her bed with her back against the headboard, legs straight out, right hand over her left. She imagined a candle flame and whispered, 'Light of my life.'

Lucy arrived, sitting cross-legged at the end of the bed and pouting.

'I can explain,' Kelsey started.

'I *told* you not to have sex with Robin,' she shouted, bouncing up and down, but the bed didn't move. 'You're risking the money, your home, your coven.'

'You're not the boss of me.'

Lucy jumped off the bed and walked over to the window. She faced away from Kelsey and touched the redwood cones and white stones there without moving them. 'Then tell me how it happened.'

Kelsey reviewed her life with Robin over the past few months. 'I felt something between us a while back but thought she wasn't into me. Then she got hurt and could have died. I knew she was as important to me as you were. Then we started spending all our time together. When women spend time together, especially when they work for other women, they become intimate; you know that.'

'You know that,' Lucy imitated, without turning around.

'There was a day when she apologised, and I thought we'd be friends, and then—'

Lucy turned and pointed her finger. 'She tried to bribe you with propane.'

'Yeah. That was a mistake.'

'She almost killed Lupe with the tractor.'

'True.'

'Nobody's perfect,' Lucy recited in a sing-song, then her tone got nasty. 'That's your dad talking. He wiggled out from under the aftermath of every fuck-up, saying, 'Everything is a life lesson.'

Kelsey sat with that for a moment, comparing her dad to Robin.

Lucy picked Kelsey's plaid shirt off the floor and put it on. It was too big.

'When she apologised, I saw we had the same picture of what she did. I can relate to why she did it, even though it hurt me. Call me weird, but I could trust her – and that was sexy.'

'She didn't want to be sexy with anyone.'

'Lucy, I've never been lovers with anyone either – not really.' Kelsey felt regret for the woman she had been, and for lovers who might have loved her but lived too far away, or lived closer to their hearts. She was already a different woman today.

'Does she know you don't believe in monogamy?'

'I've told her I've been to a dozen lesbian hand-fastings

but never a tenth anniversary.'

'She'll remember that joke when you've broken her heart.' Lucy sat on the edge of the bed, but not too close. 'How did it start?'

'When she asked, I said yes.'

'So cliché! Put it on a tee-shirt!' Lucy pulled off Kelsey's plaid shirt; now she wore a pink tee-shirt with 'When she asked, I said yes' written in hideous purple glitter across the chest. Dead-girl magic trick.

Kelsey laughed. 'We – I mean all of us Ovem – we've lived together for nearly a year. We don't need to deal with men unless we want to. Because of that, we're changing. The worst has been Patriarchy we brought here ourselves.'

Lucy put her head in Kelsey's lap. She was wearing her blue work shirt from the '70s again. 'Kelsey, I can't change, because I'm dead.'

'You don't have to change.'

'Kelsey, I'm scared for you. You need me. What if you change so much I can't offer you anything? You'll put me in a box and not talk to me.'

Kelsey ran her fingers through Lucy's hair, but felt no warmth from her body. 'I need you now more than ever.'

A voice startled her. Kelsey opened her eyes to see Wren at her window.

'Can I come in?' Wren was in tears.

'Of course.' Kelsey patted the bed beside her.

'I just got a call from Willow.' Wren crawled in and lay her head where Lucy's had been.

'She called you? During the day? I thought she couldn't afford it.'

'She broke up with me,' Wren wailed. 'She said she always walked on eggshells around me.'

'That doesn't sound like you.'

'I thought we were getting back together, but she didn't want to have sex. Or even cuddle.'

Kelsey bit the inside of her cheek, glad Wren couldn't see. 'Sometimes a sexual relationship can't grow beyond itself.'

'She hopes we can be friends.'

'I hope so too. I like Willow.'

'I think she's lovers with Barb now.'

Kelsey assumed Wren needed the comfort. Kelsey wanted tea. And needed to pee. 'Honey, I need to get up.'

Wren lifted herself out of Kelsey's lap and wiped her eyes. Kelsey turned and sat on the edge of the bed. Wren reached over, suddenly concerned. 'Are you okay? Did I interrupt something?'

Kelsey didn't turn around, but stared down at her own crumpled shirt on the carpet. 'I was remembering someone I lost.'

Wren pushed her lover drama away, climbed over Kelsey's bed and kneeled in front of her. 'You keep everything inside.'

Kelsey tried a smile and failed. She stood and pulled Wren to her feet. Normally, she would have returned their attention to Wren's breakup, but she couldn't. So she picked up the shirt and pulled it on.

'Wait.' Wren stood in front of Kelsey and searched her face. 'Something's wrong.'

Kelsey turned away and slipped on her clogs. 'Nothing's wrong. Let's go downstairs.'

'I feel something is wrong.'

Kelsey paused at her door. She wished Wren could hear this from someone else. But she'd done nothing to be ashamed of. 'I don't want to add more problems to your life – maybe you won't mind at this point – but I need to tell you something. This is hard – Robin and I made love yesterday.'

∞

Anger tore through Wren, leaving a wake of shame. She had to escape this place and every reminder of her own delusions. She rushed past Kelsey and around to her own room. Spots in her vision made it hard to identify clean underwear and socks to stuff into a backpack. She opened a drawer and found four twenty-dollar bills. *Robin and Kelsey.* She tucked Bridget's candle from her dusty altar into the front pocket.

'I knew Robin was lying when she said she was celibate,' she shouted, and didn't care if Kelsey heard her. 'I'm not the fool she thinks I am.'

'Where are you going?' Kelsey stepped aside as Wren stomped out of her room.

'Lesbians always do this.' Wren wanted to throw the backpack off the veranda, and herself with it. 'There's no escaping the magical pussy, is there?' She burned with that unique anger arising from a friend's betrayal of a promise they never made. 'Don't you see how selfish you are?'

'I thought you might be happy for us, since Willow.'

Wren ran away from Kelsey to avoid processing non-monogamy's ethics again. Maybe Lupe could give her a ride. Lupe was always going to town on mysterious errands. Where would she be now? Probably the orchard.

Down the steps, out the back, up the path. Push through the trees. A branch snapped her in the face, but she didn't care. Her heart beat in her chest, torn and scorched. *She used me, just like Mom did.*

Wren heard someone breathing heavily up the hill behind her.

'Kelsey, I want to be alone.'

But it was only Gloria. 'I heard.'

'Did you know?'

Gloria looked pained. 'I thought something was happening. We can do a Reconciliation Circle.'

'NO!'

'That's a good start.' Gloria was laughing.

'This is how you support me?'

'Expressing your feelings is good. We've faced things like this before, Wren. You'll feel better if you know what happened – and why.'

'I don't want to feel better. I want to leave.'

'Why?'

'Obviously I can't stay here. You all can live in a women's utopia, but I'm too damaged. I have no control over my jealousy.'

'Where would you go?'

'I can stay with my mom at first.' Wren imagined getting a car to the bus, to the train, to the BART, walking up Cortland, sitting in that kitchen…

'Stay with your mom?' Gloria raised an eyebrow. 'But you haven't talked to her since…the Saturn?'

Everything is fucked. Everything in the world is so fucking fucked. 'You're right, Gloria,' Wren said scornfully, and then regretted it because she needed a favour. 'Can you give me a ride to Alex and Julz's?'

'I'm sort of out of gas, but—'

'Forget it. I'll find Lupe.' Wren marched up the hill.

'Can you wait a day? If you need to leave, leave tomorrow. Come back to the house with me.'

'No!' Wren shouted, without turning round.

'Wren, please.' Gloria firmly held her hand and wasn't

laughing at her.

Whatever happened between Robin and Kelsey – and they could fuck themselves silly – Wren still had friends here.

'Will you come back to your beautiful little octagon cabin we built for you?' Gloria pleaded. 'Can you do that?'

Wren remembered how good the octagon smelled, with its cedar-lined closets, and Robin hadn't fucked anyone in it yet. She took a step toward Gloria, who abruptly turned away and jogged down the hill. Wren had trouble keeping up.

Gloria spoke over her shoulder, now in full crisis mode. 'I'll gather everyone.'

'Now?'

'Now. We know what to do.'

Twelve

Gloria disappeared into the house while Wren waited on the octagon's porch in a fury. Gloria soon emerged with a thermos, a sandwich, Wren's box of coloured pencils and a sketchbook. She tucked Wren into the loft and, by the time she returned a few hours later, Wren had filled many pages with serrated lines.

Gloria called from the porch. 'We're gathering in the grove. There's a fire. I brought you one of Ginny's sweaters.'

Wren and Gloria walked the stone-lined trail to the grove. When they got to the stump, Wren squeezed the shaggy bark. So resistant to every attack. She couldn't leave these trees.

She clambered around the stump and the grove. The grey redwoods stood silent and strong, like true friends. Nikki, Hazel, Lupe and Ginny had taken their places in their elemental corners. Robin and Kelsey, sitting near the fire, stood and greeted Wren. She hated them, because she used to love them.

Gloria turned and stopped Wren from progressing further.

'I offer to stand next to you, as your friend and advocate.' Gloria put her palm flat on Wren's chest. Gloria's strength soothed much of Wren's remaining anger. 'How do you enter the circle?'

Wren tried to recite the ritual response, *In perfect love and perfect trust*, but it wasn't true. 'I can't say it.'

'Can you enter the circle and hear what happened and why?'

That she could do. 'I will.'

'Are you warm enough?'

'I am.' She always felt snug in Ginny's knitting.

'Would you like water?'

Wren took a sip and accepted its clarity.

Gloria asked Robin and Kelsey if they were warm enough, and they both drank from the same cup. They looked so sad.

Then the four of them, Wren and Gloria, Robin and Kelsey, walked across the circle to the north where Nikki stood. Nikki held the priestess staff, but other than that, there was no ritual regalia. No one wore costumes. They were just themselves; women helping women.

'First, we tell each other…' Nikki began in her ritual voice, then spoke normally. 'What the fuck happened?' Her irreverence was a relief. 'Wren, you tell it first.'

'What happened? It's simple. My girlfriend broke up with me. In the same minute, I learned Robin and Kelsey are lovers.'

'What else? No need to explain why – just say what happened.'

Wren took a breath. 'I had a huge crush on Robin since I met her. It went nowhere because Robin doesn't have sex. I accepted that. I had a girlfriend. But now she's having sex with Kelsey.' Wren stopped. 'That is what happened.'

'Robin and Kelsey,' Nikki said. 'Can you repeat what happened from Wren's point of view?'

Robin went first. 'Wren had a crush on me. I knew that. I told her I wanted her friendship, but couldn't be lovers.' Robin looked at Kelsey and they said something with their eyes.

Kelsey spoke after they stopped eye-kissing. 'Wren's lover Willow broke up with her because Wren isn't ready for a relationship.'

'I didn't say that.'

'Is it true?'

Wren had to speak the truth in this sacred circle. 'Yes.'

'We only need to say what happened,' Nikki intoned again, and Wren suppressed nervous laughter. 'Wren, do Robin and Kelsey understand what happened?'

'Obviously, they know what they did to me.' Wren saw that Kelsey looked stricken and just a little bit guilty, which was satisfying. 'Now tell me what the fuck happened?'

Robin and Kelsey stood close to each other, but not holding hands or doing anything romantic. They could afford to be generous and decent. They had each other.

'Robin, what the fuck happened?' Nikki asked it with real curiosity. 'I thought you didn't have sex. I know you call yourself a lesbian, but I thought you were someone who didn't do couple stuff. I understand why Wren is surprised, because I am, too.'

Robin stepped toward Wren. She looked contrite. 'Wren, when I invited you to live here, I dreamed we would do something lesbians could never do before. I wanted to live in a women's world. I didn't know that new world would change me. After I fell off the roof, I was laid-up. I've been hurt before. For the first time in all my lives, I was vulnerable and broken *but safe*. I felt like we already had succeeded.'

Wren snorted. 'Good. Then you don't need me to make your magical—'

But Gloria put her arm around her. 'You don't need to say anything. Just listen.'

'You knew Kelsey and I were doing the breathwork,' Robin unnecessarily reminded her. 'At first you were jealous, but you learned it was related to how your mother treated you, right?'

'Not everything is about our mothers, Dr Freud. Burning that painting was completely separate from this.' How dare Robin presume to know how she felt – again!

Robin apologised. 'After you burned it, how did you feel about Kelsey and me doing breathwork together?'

This ritual's formality helped Wren find words for her feelings. 'I want all women to learn breathwork. We do breathwork all the time. Why did you have to…after you said you didn't?'

'My memories empower me, but they also haunt me. The bad ones, I push away. Kelsey showed me how to make peace with those ghosts. Kelsey lives in the present.'

No argument there.

'Kelsey, can you tell us what the fuck happened?' Nikki loved saying it that way.

Kelsey looked rattled. This must be hard for her.

'I could feel Robin was sparking with me, before she knew it herself. I never have flings with housemates, but I was afraid – I am always afraid – of anything more than a fling.' Kelsey glanced at Robin again, and Wren quickly looked at Nikki so she didn't have to watch them at it again.

Kelsey was still talking. 'Living with you, on our land, day after day, is changing me too. I'm not afraid of the things that keep me from being close to my lovers any more. I was really pissed about Robin bringing the tractor to the land, but then she apologised, and she really gets it why she can't do that again. I feel I can rely on you, Robin. For the first time in my life, I can rely on you like other women rely on me.'

Wren, unfortunately, caught Kelsey looking at Robin. She shut her eyes again, and when she opened them, Kelsey was calmly looking back at her. Kelsey didn't look pained or guilty. She looked mature.

Nikki said, 'Wren, are you ready to move to the next corner?'

'Give me a minute.' Wren shut her eyes and imagined Robin and Kelsey – the shape and movement of their bodies from memory and a perverse need to know. She let herself feel their desire and fear. Wren knew exactly what happened, and why. Indisputably, they loved each other and wanted to be lovers. That was what being a lesbian meant. 'You made love last night while I was sleeping upstairs!'

'We did,' they said at the same time.

Robin and Kelsey were lovers. Bargaining is a stage of grief, right? 'If I stay, I'm taking the octagon for myself. I won't share it.'

Nikki took charge. 'I think we're ready to move to the next corner.'

They followed Hazel to the west, and Hazel took the staff from Nikki's hand. 'Now we know what happened. How do you feel?'

'I'll go first,' said Robin. 'I feel like crap because I hurt Wren.'

'Good.' Wren stared at the duff.

'I do too,' said Kelsey.

'Even better.'

Hazel waited and let Wren take a few long, slow breaths. 'How do you feel, Wren?'

Wren put her arms over her head, and then around her stomach, and then bent over to stretch out her back. From down there, nearly upside down, she was able to say, 'Now that we've said what happened, and why, I don't feel jealous any more. Robin never could have given me what I wanted.' She stood up.

'And is there a feeling growing from that?'

'Everything is alive to you, isn't it?' said Wren, even now lifted by Hazel's perspective. 'I feel something else. I think it's grief.'

Hazel handed the staff to Lupe. The women followed Lupe to the south.

'We have heard what happened, and we have heard how we feel. Now we will describe the harm we caused.' Wren had forgotten how this ritual flowed and was glad she wasn't in charge. 'Robin?'

Robin turned to Wren. 'You're hurt because I told you I didn't make love with other women.'

Wren could only nod.

'My inability to know myself is my own problem. It's not connected to your worth.'

Wren started to argue, and a coil of pain stopped her. She couldn't resist it, so she waited until it relaxed and faded.

Kelsey said, 'Most of the time, when women make love, it spreads out and enhances the world around us. But there's no way Robin and I could have avoided hurting you today. Keeping it a secret would be worse.'

'That's for sure.' Now it was Wren's turn to say how she caused harm, but she didn't think she had hurt anybody. She was the victim here. Because they were in ritual, she knew she could move her body in that sacred space and uncover mysteries. She turned and looked into Gloria's warm dark eyes for a few long moments. Then she stepped over to Nikki, then Hazel, Lupe and Ginny, opening herself to the wisdom of their judgement. She stood in front of Kelsey, then Robin, and saw their pain.

She had seen the same answer in each of her sister witches. 'I see how threatening to leave hurt everyone. If I leave now, it means our coven can't survive when women do normal things, like becoming lovers.'

'It is well,' said Lupe. The witches followed Ginny to the east, and Lupe handed the staff to her.

'We have heard what happened and how we feel. We have named our responsibility. Let's set our intention of what we would do different.'

'I'm not going to leave,' Wren assured herself and her coven. 'If I left now, I will never learn how to fix my shit.' She could laugh again. 'And I'll never figure out how to make the fucking magical statue Robin wants.'

Robin promised to encourage Wren to fix her shit, or make the magical statue, or whatever she wanted. '*Ars longa, vita brevis*,' she said, knowing Wren knew that Latin phrase about the lasting impact of art.

'I won't keep important secrets from my friends,' Kelsey vowed. 'And I'll try to avoid the need for reconciliation rituals,' she added, sealing her promise with the balm of humour.

'So Mote It Fucking Be,' the witches recited.

'Wren.' The ritual was ended, but Nikki was still in charge.

Wren glanced at her and saw an expression there from when Nikki was sleeping with their Women's Spirituality teacher. Back when they believed in non-monogamy because there was nothing more patriarchal than thinking *one* woman was the *only* woman. She survived Nikki, she could survive Robin – whom she had never even kissed.

'I'm so glad you aren't leaving,' said Nikki. 'I can't afford to lose an apprentice carpenter.'

'I was so afraid you were going to leave us, Wren,' said Lupe. 'I can see us circling here under these trees, raising our cone of power and healing the world. We're old ladies. And you're with us, Wren. We'll get through this.'

'Lupe's right,' said Hazel. 'We can't help but bring Patriarchy with us when we leave it. We can't run away, throw it out, or burn it up. Patriarchy twists our innocent desires. Conflict is inevitable. But it need not separate us.'

'I'm so tired of lover drama.' Ginny actually sounded angry. 'I don't get it. Why can't women make love without hurting each other?' She stopped, and everyone waited as she gathered her thoughts. 'It's not just this situation. I'm a lesbian, even though I don't have lovers. People say I haven't found the right woman. But when I see how you suffer, I'm not sure I want to. I like living with you, and I love our magic, but I don't agree that you need to be ex-lovers with someone to know what it's like to be a lesbian. I can live forever without feeling like Wren looked a few minutes ago.'

'Amen, sister,' Wren said. 'I'd hate to leave Ove over something as ordinary as a broken heart.'

Robin said, 'Your heart is not ordinary, Wren.'

Kelsey gestured to her bosom, an invitation and an offering. Wren remembered the Kelsey she knew before Robin, the Kelsey who fed her, loved her and yelled at her. She put herself into Kelsey's arms, and her sister-witches surrounded them. She still felt sad, and she knew she was damaged. But this land and these women, and the magic of her own creativity, would heal her.

The witches sang to Wren until the bitterness in her heart sweetened and their voices rose up the redwoods and met the light of a setting sun.

Peace of the morning dawn to you
Peace of the glowing fire to you
Peace of the gentle rain to you
Peace of the fruitful earth to you
May forever peace descend on you
May forever peace rise to comfort you
Peace, peace, peace, peace.

Afterwards, Gloria helped Wren drag her mattress to the octagon. Wren slept alone and loved it.

She woke up the next morning and admired the slender tree limbs reaching across her skylight. Then she fed the angry pages of yesterday's sketchbook into her own little stove. Her emotions rose and fell with the flames.

Robin and Kelsey. She felt a tingle of that feeling opposite to jealousy, when you feel happy when women you love, love each other. That feeling only lasted until smothered in cold ashes of regret.

Willow. Willow had never seen the real Wren, the woman with all her damage. She added more sheets to the fire and leaned forward to warm her face. Willow was too healthy. Like Kelsey said during the reconciliation, Wren wasn't ready for a relationship. Healing is peeling an onion.

She fed the covers of the sketchbook into the flames and they flared brighter than ever.

Single. She would be single like Ginny.

Single. Since art school, she had lusted for one woman after another. None of them had loved her as much as she loved them.

Single. But not alone. Her coven knew her and loved her despite her damage. The Reconciliation ritual conveyed a grace that recoloured all her relationships, but especially with Robin. Could she make art that expressed the power of the Reconciliation ritual? As she watched the fire consume the last of yesterday's anguish, she felt charged with inspiration to create something that expressed the Ovem's desires and possibilities. It might even be scary.

She closed the stove door and walked out onto her porch. Kelsey was up on the veranda in the morning sun, reading the paper. Someone turned on the radio. She remembered the song the coven sang yesterday: *The peace of the morning…* The household was waking up.

'Helloooo!' From the front door Gloria called across the plaza. She raised the picnic hamper they used for parties. 'I thought we could initiate the octagon.'

Thirteen

Wren waved Gloria over.

'Your first meal,' Gloria declared as she entered the octagon.

'I don't have furniture yet—'

'Up there.' Gloria tipped her head toward the loft.

Breakfast in bed? Wren imagined her mother's bedroom, where she carried trays of coffee, toast and clean ashtrays. *Never again.* She climbed to the loft, straightened the blankets and perched in the corner.

Gloria clambered up and produced warm biscuits, butter, jam, sliced apples, bananas and something unidentified that smelled good.

'I hope there's coffee in that thermos.'

'Of course.'

'What's that? Hot cheese?'

'It's a French thing. I made these biscuits myself.'

'You cooked?'

'Kelsey initiated me into the Breakfast in Bed Church.

What do you think?'

'This is…a sacrament.'

'I agree.' Gloria dragged an apple slice through the melted cheese and popped it into her mouth.

Demolishing breakfast took only fifteen minutes. Wren was on her second cup of coffee before she could talk about anything serious.

Gloria seemed to sense that. 'You look tired. How's your heart?'

'Open.'

'And your tummy?'

'Full.'

'My work is done.'

Wren realised what a good friend Gloria had been over the past twenty-four hours. Maybe Wren could be a better friend.

They heard a car banging over the bridge.

'Who's that?'

'Probably Julz. It's her birthday. Everyone's going to Bonny Doon beach.'

'I like Julz.'

'Me too.' Gloria raised her palm. 'But you're not ready for a party. I propose we stay here today.'

Gloria was right. Wren wanted to be alone. Gloria packed the remains of breakfast into the hamper, then lit a joint. Gloria wasn't ready to leave.

'Did Robin ever tell you about her past lives?' she asked.

'Lots of stories, same as she's told you.' Wren picked the last of the crumbs off the blanket and threw them into the hamper.

'Did she ever say other women could be taught to remember their past lives?'

'I always assumed it was something unique to her.' Wren didn't want to appear ungrateful, but she wished Gloria would leave.

'If Athenic witches had an initiation and afterward could remember their past lives, they would never fear death.'

'Witches don't fear death. Robin is afraid to die again before Patriarchy is defeated.'

'If we were immortal, she wouldn't be alone in her next life.'

Wren knew Robin well enough to know that Robin wanted to recover from her past, not create future friends.

Gloria offered the joint. When Wren shook her head, she asked: 'What are you doing today?'

'I'm feeling blown out after yesterday. I'll hang out here.'

'Let's bless it together.' Gloria looked mischievous. 'Let's do the thing two women do.'

Wren still didn't get it. 'What thing?'

'Let's bless it properly. Like you and Willow would have.'

'But, we're not…'

'Come on, Wren, it's only proper.'

'But we're…'

Gloria pulled a small bottle of massage oil from the hamper. 'Let's start slow.' She wiggled out of her shorts and shirt and patted the blanket next to her. Wren lay down, awkward and a little excited. Being single didn't mean you couldn't have sex with friends, right?

'I want to apologise.' Gloria warmed the oil in her hands and massaged Wren's belly.

'For what?'

'Remember last winter when your mother disowned you? I insisted your mother loved you. I was wrong. I can't apply my family to your experience. I have a great mom.' Gloria moved up, massaging Wren's breasts. She slid her thumbs against Wren's nipples until they responded.

'Thank you.' Gloria, apologising? Gloria has changed so much.

'I didn't understand what you were going through.'

'My mom is unique.'

'Witches honour Mother Earth, and therefore all mothers, but we rarely notice the truly horrible mothers.' Gloria massaged Wren's right arm in long, luxurious strokes.

'I never came out to my mother because she ruined everything I loved. I knew she'd make my lesbianism hers too.'

'Did you know Athena doesn't have a mother?'

Wren sank into sensation. 'I didn't realise how sore my hands are.'

Gloria's mouth made a moue of concern. She spent more time massaging Wren's hands and fingers, then returned to long strokes along her arms.

'Your mother was horrible. You need to find better mothers. I never told you, but when I heard you burned that painting, your witchcraft impressed me. It will take work, but you are well on your way. You're healing. Stuff will come up – turn around so I can do your other arm.'

Wren sat up and swung her legs the other way. Gloria wrapped her arms around her and kissed her cheek from behind. Wren stiffened in surprise and then relaxed. 'Like yesterday?'

'Yesterday was intense. You and Willow were never right for each other. You got together too soon. And Robin? She's nuts. How do you feel now?' Gloria resumed massaging Wren's left forearm.

'Swell.' Both of them knew what she meant. Gloria warmed more oil and returned to massaging Wren's belly in big, strong swirls.

'I love how that feels.'

Gloria swirled her hands to the crease of Wren's thigh, and Wren moved so Gloria could massage in there.

'I know you, Wren.' Gloria's hands were not even coming close to her clit. An absence of touch precisely there began to feel so present. 'Come on.'

'Really?' Wren wasn't against…whatever Gloria wanted, but…so unexpected. Gloria wasn't her type, but Gloria loved her, and she hadn't had sex in a while.

'I'll massage your other leg from here. Don't move.' Gloria leaned over and let her nipples brush Wren's skin.

'I might need a bath.'

'You smell fine.'

'Are you—' Wren stopped. Gloria covered Wren's inner thighs in long, oily strokes, back and forth from one leg to the other, only brushing Wren's vulva as she swirled. Gloria watched and followed her hands. Wren felt seen.

Anyone would say having sex with your housemate is a terrible idea, but this seemed a sacred continuation of yesterday's reconciliation, a final affirmation.

This wasn't like every other First Time. Wren wasn't acting from Patriarchal Messages or Mother Damage. 'Come here,' she whispered.

She looked at Gloria's face one last time as a friend. Gloria kissed her like a lover and not a sister, then laid herself on Wren's body with a comforting weight. A pocket formed deep inside Wren's chest and began to fill. She felt Gloria's desire, and realised Gloria sincerely loved her, and had been saying it for months. Yesterday, she hadn't allowed Wren to ruin her life and leave Ove; she had created the reconciliation. Gloria's leg slid along her own. Wren rippled.

She knew Gloria had witnessed her fears, knew her vulnerabilities and mistakes. Gloria's hips rocked against hers. Gloria pressed harder, and she made a sound Wren had never heard before. Wren kissed her clavicle, and it never felt like friendship again.

'Now,' Gloria said a little while later. 'Will you let me send you on a journey?'

She was so confident. Wren didn't know what to expect from Gloria the lover. 'What should I do?'

'Absolutely nothing.' Gloria glided her hand over Wren's stomach and curved her fingers around her vulva. Wren's pussy reached out. Gloria's hand fell bewitchingly between.

'Let words and images float away. Go into the warm dark.'

Wren yearned for a thing just beyond the limit of their skin, and the yearning was enough, not the arriving. Her pleasure rose, and she silenced the inner voices and fell floating. She felt reckless and immortal.

They blessed Wren's octagon that long August day.

Later, they smoked more pot and got hungry. The breakfast hamper was empty, but they couldn't leave the bed. They remembered home-grown tomatoes and basil, which brought them to how Kelsey made pizza, and eventually they came around to how it would have been better to just let the ambulance drive onto the land, and how awful it was that Robin bought a tractor, which seemed particularly funny right now.

In a lull between that and the next hilarious thought, Gloria said she had called Willow yesterday after the reconciliation.

That caused a bit of a panic, until Gloria explained that she had asked Willow and Barb to take the class when she offered it next year.

'You did? I love you!'

Gloria lit another joint and handed it to Wren. 'There are so few lesbians in this world. We can't excommunicate every woman who breaks our heart.'

'If I can live with Robin and Kelsey—' Wren coughed and returned the joint.

'Let's just see what happens with Robin and Kelsey,' Gloria smirked. She smoked thoughtfully. 'I've been thinking about this art thing Robin wants you to do.'

'I didn't know you understood it until the other day.'

'Robin is quite right. You're a visionary. If radical feminist witches like us don't have art, we will fight about stupid differences and forget how to talk to each other. I just wonder if Athena could help you find what you're looking for.'

There in Gloria's arms, well-loved and very stoned, Wren felt open to Gloria's beloved deity. 'I only made what you told me. I don't know anything about Athena.'

'Would you like to learn?'

'I'm more of a Bridget girl. She's the goddess of creativity…'

'So is Athena!'

'She is? I thought she was a war goddess.'

'That war goddess thing is a patriarchal slur.'

Wren didn't know that. She actually didn't know much about Athena. Gloria might be right, like she was right about so much.

'I'll think about it.'

'Good. That's all I ask.'

'I'm really thirsty and have terrible munchies.' Wren got up, her legs shaky. She didn't want to put on clothes. She was crossing the plaza when Lupe's van arrived.

'Gloria!' she warned, but Gloria followed her down and posed herself on the porch railing, waving like a beauty queen.

'Hi, naked ladies!' Lupe called. A crowd piled out and disappeared toward the bathhouse.

Robin was unloading sandy towels and trash bags from the van. Wren caught her eye, and Robin waved to her before disappearing behind the house. Wren felt around inside her heart. She didn't care what Robin assumed had just happened. She filled a pitcher of water in the kitchen and grabbed a bag of tortilla chips and a jar of salsa. She joined Gloria in her loft and they made love again for hours.

The next morning she sat alone on her porch with a cup of tea and her sketchbook, singing nonsense words to herself and filling page after page with images of female sex and female growth, female choices and female bodies: eyes looking back; lips in song; hands and curves. Inspired, she finally was making progress. Whatever this was, it was hers. She wouldn't call it *Robin's* magical statue again.

The sisterly trees of Ove pulled in the fog. Soon she would lay the fire. She felt free from old patterns. Gloria already loved her. Everyone said her next girlfriend needed to be emotionally available. Maybe leaving Patriarchy was falling in love with your friends? She followed her inspiration for hours, in quiet euphoria of creative flow. She owed all this to Gloria, her old friend and new lover.

III

Making Magic

One

Wren had never been to Athens, but she'd eaten at Vasili's – down the street from the Saturn – so the Athens she imagined looked like a poster in a Greek restaurant. In her imagination, she surveyed the temples and admired marble stairs rising toward the perfect geometry of the Parthenon. A drumbeat held her in trance as she approached her meeting with Athena. Wren wore a white gown and a belt knitted from Ginny's wool. She smelled cedar. She could sense the heat of the huge altar before the temple, heaped with offerings. With a sigh, she snapped her favourite paintbrush in two. She opened her eyes, quickly opened the octagon's wood stove, set her offering on the coals, and returned to her trance. It hurt her heart to make this sacrifice, but Gloria said something precious had to die in the initiation. *Accept this my gift, Athena.*

Wren touched the legendary columns, entered the cool porch and passed through the immense bronze doors to the inner sanctuary.

'Open your eyes, *polítis*! Gaze upon my splendour.' Gloria's voice, but with a deepness in it. *Very cool*.

Wren opened her eyes. Athena stood under the loft, with plaster owl in one hand and a redwood limb resting against her other shoulder like a spear. At her feet lay a ludicrously cute toy mountain lion. The Goddess wore a white peplos gown belted with entwined snakes, and the gorgon Medusa stared out from her chest, showing her teeth like during the Bearing In. Gloria had done a great job with this costume.

Wren kneeled in front of the Goddess.

Athena reached out her hand.

'*Polítis*, rise and gaze upon me. I am Athena, Goddess of this Land, Queen of California, ancient island of wild women.'

The voice definitely wasn't Gloria's, and it shook Wren's chest. Wren called as loud as she could, 'Hail, Athena, Goddess and Queen!'

'Did you hear me when you first came to this Land?'

That is so right. She and Robin *had* heard an owl that first day.

'Yes, Athena, I remember.'

'What is your name?'

'Wren Kildare.'

'Who is your mother?'

Wren knew this was a riddle. She didn't know how to best answer.

'Who is your mother?'

Wren stopped dithering and blurted out, 'I have no mother. She disowned me.'

That must have been the right answer. Athena held her arms over Wren's head, owl in one hand, spear in the other.

'I, Athena, claim you, Wren Kildare, girl without a mother.

I too have no mother, and yet I gave birth to democracy. I claim thee as my own, a free citizen of my people. In this womanist time, women rise, women claim the temples and agora of the patriarchs. Women rise, as I lead them.'

Athena put aside the owl and staff and took up Wren's hands.

'Wren Kildare, you are especially beloved by me. I have blessed you with your talents in fabrics and arts. Dedicate yourself to me, and your art will be seen by all the world, carrying my grace, power and terrible beauty to all peoples. We will restore balance, equality and sisterhood for all.'

A vision came into Wren's imagination when Athena said 'seen by all the world': a flat, white desert stretching to distant, dark mountains.

'Behold my emblems and keep their secrets. Behold the Owl!' Athena held the owl in front of Wren's face, and it appeared to stare back at her with living yellow eyes. 'Inextinguishable knowledge from ancient days!' Athena set the owl on a tripod stool.

Athena leaned down and petted the mountain lion. It seemed to grow larger under her hand. 'Behold the panther, ancient emblem of my strength and protection.' *Panthers, mountain lions: same cat, different forest.*

Athena gestured to her own chest. 'Behold Medusa, snake-headed monster I wear upon my heart, a trophy of my victory over the demons of the past!'

Athena put her hand on Wren's head. Wren felt that Athena wanted her to kneel again.

'Do you vow, *polítis* of Athena, to partake in my rites and to teach my mysteries? Will you widen the circle of women devoted to me?'

'I do so vow.' Wren bowed her head. She meant it too.

'Wren Kildare, I have claimed you and Gloria Arriola as my priests…'

'Priests?'

'I claim you, my priest, because there is no reason to segregate the citizens who serve me. As women rise, there will be no difference between women and men. You, Wren Kildare and Gloria Arriola, are the first priests in a renewed secret sisterhood of Athenic witches.'

Wren lifted her head and saw a small black disc in Athena's fingertips.

'Open your hands.'

Wren held up her palms, and Athena pressed the disc – a coin – into the centre of her right hand, like a communion host. Wren loved it when witches repurposed childhood rites. On one side of the coin, she could make out a striding Athena. On the other, an owl. Very cool. Gloria is very good at this.

'Is this for me to keep?'

'It is my gift to you, but I request a task.'

Wren knew what to say. A quest was traditional. 'As you wish.'

'Seek out and uncover the secret of Robin's reincarnations. I would have this magic among my own.'

Wren loved this ritual: the regalia, the talismans, the syncretism of Athena in California. Until this. She looked up at Athena's serene majesty and found courage there. She asked – more impertinently than she intended – 'Why not ask her yourself?'

Athena's serene expression flickered into anger, then calmed.

'I request it of you.'

Wren pressed her lips together.

'Great Athena, I am not worthy of such a quest, which is better suited to your priest Gloria Arriola. I humbly beg for your help as I create the Important Sacred Art Thing Ove needs to sustain us.'

Wren heard a frustrated exhalation above her as Athena consulted her godlike intellect. 'Very well. Though I am the Goddess of California, men corrupted my icons for their aggrandisement. Create a tarot deck with my emblems. A tarot deck created in my honour will lead you to what you seek. I will reward you with the wisdom of the Athenic tarot.'

'Yes, Athena. I will create your tarot and it will guide me toward my work for Ove.'

Wren felt elated as she made this promise. The grace of her Athenic initiation left her feeling better than ever about *bringing forth* from herself.

⚭

Wren used up all the gold leaf and finished the Athenic tarot by the end of September. Gloria loved it. Every morning that autumn Gloria brought them coffee in bed, they drew a card for the day and afterwards they made love.

Why didn't more friends become lovers? Maybe the friend taboo was too strong. One time Wren asked Lupe, but she seemed embarrassed and they got high instead. When she asked Kelsey, she said, 'Maybe because you know what you're getting into,' but didn't explain. Wren felt it would be rude to ask Ginny.

At times, it seemed Gloria was insecure about Wren's relationships with the other Ovem, but Wren knew why. Gloria was competitive about a lot of things. It made her better at them. The new love Wren felt for her old friend spiralled from deep in her heart, forgiving her for aspects that still needed healing.

One afternoon in late October, Wren came into Gloria's room looking for a sweater. She found Gloria on her bed, surrounded by astrological ephemerides and binders, in the seat of her own power. Wren's tummy fluttered.

She had to ignore those tingles because she needed to get to the kitchen to help Kelsey. She tried a quicker form of intimacy. 'Did you check my aspects today?' She pulled on the sweater.

Gloria's expression soured. 'I thought you didn't like me checking your horoscope.'

'Only that once, before I knew you did it for everyone.' Wren knew how to turn that frown upside-down. 'I like it now.'

'That's good, because I checked our relationship aspects today. Do you know what this hour is good for?'

'Tell me quick, I need to go.'

'Come closer.' Gloria pulled Wren on top of her; books and binders fell on the floor. The sweater came off.

'I need to help Kelsey with dinner.'

'I need you to help me with *this*.'

'*This?*' Wren pulled her hand away. 'Maybe later? I need to—'

Gloria moved under Wren in that way she did. 'Please,' she said between her teeth.

Two

By the time they got downstairs, Kelsey said she didn't need Wren's help. Relieved, Wren doodled, half-listening to Kelsey and Gloria talk about the election and what a disaster it would be if Reagan won again. Her pen stopped when Gloria mentioned Halloween.

'I've been thinking about this year's Samhain ritual.' Gloria was folding the napkins and arranging them carefully under the forks.

'Everyone is.' Kelsey's pot of veggie chilli and cornbread in its cast-iron pan cooled on the table. Wren broke off a bit of crust.

'Wren and I propose an astral journey instead of visiting the ancestors on the Isle of Apples.' Wren liked to sit across from Gloria because she could look at her. Her beautiful hands, and how they smoothed the napkins.

'Astral travel? We haven't done that since Sisterhood of the Goddess kicked us out.' Kelsey took her place at the head of the table. 'Why does every coven need to be clean and sober?'

'I miss singing with them,' said Wren, and sang in her croaky voice, '*She's been waiting, waiting, she's been waiting so long.*'

Kelsey and Gloria joined in and lifted the melody back into place. '*She's been waiting for her children to remember and return.*'

'I miss it too,' said Gloria, when they had finished the song. 'And I miss creating sacred places in our imaginations.'

'That's true, Gloria. But we'll need some of Lupe's potion.' Kelsey drummed her palms on the table. 'I'll ring the bell again.' She got up.

'Lupe won't mind,' Gloria said with a snigger.

Kelsey returned and said, 'I like the idea of showing Robin astral travel. She caught on to the breathwork real fast.' She stopped talking as her cheeks flushed.

Gloria seemed not to notice. 'What if we travelled to that place on the astral where Robin goes when she dies?'

Kelsey chuckled. 'Aren't you afraid we might really die?'

Gloria waved her hand dismissively. 'We know how to travel safely. Aren't you curious how Robin came to live forever?'

'Nope.' Kelsey nibbled on a corner of cornbread. 'I focus on this life, not ghosts. They better get here soon. I'm hungry.' She ladled chilli into her bowl and pulled another slice of cornbread from the pan. 'We don't talk about it. I suppose it's a useful myth.'

'I'm hungry too.' Wren filled her bowl and took a wide slice of the warm bread. 'Robin always seemed like she genuinely believed it.'

'I wouldn't question another witch's gnostic revelation,' Gloria said as she buttered her cornbread delicately. 'But imagine how powerful our coven would be if we remembered like Robin. We wouldn't fear death.'

'I already don't fear death,' said Kelsey.

Wren remembered Her Serene Majesty Pallas Athene and knew what Gloria wanted her to say. 'Let's ask Robin. She could always say no.'

Robin lurched into the kitchen on her walking cast, singing a song with nonsense words. She gave Kelsey's arm a squeeze and sat next to Wren. 'Say no to what?' She reached for the cornbread.

'What were you singing?' Gloria asked, pushing the chilli toward Robin. 'It sounds Native American.'

'It is.'

Gloria put her spoon down. 'Could we do a ritual where you take us to the place you told us about last Samhain?'

'A bleak stone circle in a realm beyond life itself?' Robin said lightly. 'Aren't you afraid we might really die?'

Wren laughed along with everyone else and said confidently, 'Maybe I'll find my magical statue there.'

'I hope you do. Sure, let's do it.'

Wren moved around to sit next to Gloria, who squeezed her hand under the table. Unlike last year, this year's Samhain wouldn't disappoint. She then remembered Robin would need something for the astral.

Kelsey was pretty sure what Gloria was up to with her proposal to visit Robin's stone circle on the astral, but she wouldn't talk to Robin about it. She wanted Robin's experience of an astral journey ritual to be untainted by cynicism.

After dinner she found Nikki by the fire reading *Beebo*

Brinker, one of Robin's lesbian pulp novels.

'Is that any good?'

'It's dated, but I can relate to a woman who looks like a man, working in a man's job. I'll give it to you when I'm done.'

Kelsey nodded, then opened her palm to show Nikki a fat joint. They no longer needed to resort to secret signals of illicit drug use, but Kelsey appreciated their efficiency. 'I need to talk about something and ask a favour,' she said. 'Can we go up to your loft? I haven't been there in months.'

Nikki agreed with enthusiasm and Kelsey followed her to the barn. Since the last time she visited, Nikki had replaced the ladder with a steep staircase. Kelsey went first, appreciating the smooth handrails, just the right size for women's hands. The stairs ended at a narrow landing. A door was framed by a riot of curved and grooved mouldings, many more than normal. Above it was one of those tiny wall lamps where the shade clips to the bulb. The shade had been illustrated by Wren with a goddess Kelsey knew as 'Venus on a Half Shell'.

She stroked the polished dark red surface of the door. 'Is this from our old house?'

'It is. The landlord sold the doors and mouldings to Recycled Lumber. I didn't want to tell you, in case they made you sad.'

'No. I'm happy to see them again.'

Kelsey opened the door into a narrow passage. Shirts and sweaters hung on one side; on the other were shelves neatly stacked with overalls, tee-shirts and long johns.

Nikki flipped a switch behind her and four small wall lamps illuminated a cosy room that might be described as a wooden womb. She had panelled it with more wine-coloured recycled redwood. A low shelf on the right held the stereo, with her record collection above. On the left wall hung a painting by Wren of Sappho reaching for an apple. Directly opposite was a queen bed fitted between three walls of shelves filled with paperbacks. A bed in a library.

Kelsey slipped off her clogs and climbed onto the foot end, Nikki the other. Above them a long rectangular skylight revealed the half moon. They smoked silently, passing the joint back and forth as Kelsey put her thoughts together.

It wasn't until they finished the joint that she knew where to begin. She dropped the spent roach in the ashtray. 'Gloria thinks Robin is going to reveal how she remembers her past lives. She wants a real magical power.'

'That's dumb.'

'Because you don't believe Robin?'

'I *do* believe Robin, but Gloria can't learn what Robin does. Gloria is being dumb.'

Kelsey found Nikki's belief in Robin's magical memory surprising, but she didn't need complete agreement. 'Will you support me if Gloria manipulates the ritual into something dumb?'

Nikki gave a wry smile. 'That doesn't sound like perfect trust to me.' She stretched out and put her hands behind her head. 'You have your problems with Gloria, but I need her.'

'We all do,' Kelsey admitted. 'But I'm afraid she's going to hurt Robin. I wouldn't have asked you if I wasn't afraid.'

Nikki squeezed Kelsey's foot. 'I'll be ready for whatever happens. You can count on me.'

⊗

Two days later, Wren walked up the back stairs, remembering how last year she had longed for something to happen with Robin. On this darkening October afternoon, she only wanted to be her friend.

She knocked, and Robin invited her in. Robin sat in her wingback chair by the window, a book in her lap.

'What are you reading?'

'*Paz*. It's about a lesbian who gets hit by lightning and gains the psychic power to plant desires into other people's minds.'

'Sounds like a book Gloria would love.'

'She loaned it to me.'

'I made something for you.' Wren unfolded the cloak and held it up, dark and heavy.

'I noticed you were sewing something, but assumed it was for Gloria.'

'It's hard to surprise anyone around here. This is the travel cloak you'll need for Samhain. Our bodies get cold when we're on the astral. Back when we went there all the time, I made these. Put up your arms.'

Robin stood, and Wren dropped the cloak over her shoulders. It fell to the floor in black gabardine folds.

'It has a hood!'

'Very witchy. Pockets too, and you can reach them from the outside or the inside.'

Robin turned in front of her mirror. 'I love this.'

'I kinda forgot we had them. They look great in ritual.' Wren remembered the gatherings of many covens, a flock of crows encircling a fire, travelling to a world built with their shared imaginations.

'And it's lined!'

'We used to circle on windy mountain tops. We lost access to those places when they banished us.'

'Kelsey told me about that. She's been teaching me the

songs and breathing that bring you to the astral together.'

Robin looked impressive in that cloak, a natural witch.

'Gloria won't find the magic she wants.' Robin smiled at Wren behind her in the mirror and tried to make a joke of it. 'I wouldn't teach her if I knew.'

Wren didn't want to know that, and wouldn't mention it to Gloria. She stepped in front of Robin and opened the cloak. 'Everyone else has their sigil here,' she said, pointing to another pocket. 'I can add yours.'

'Yes, I'd like my sigil – if you have time.' Robin lifted the hood up and over her face, judging the effect in her mirror.

'If you're not doing it for Gloria, why are you taking us to some scary place?'

'I *am* doing it for Gloria – and for you too. You may find something in my memories you can turn into art.'

'Yes, Gloria thought so too. Maybe Athena—'

'You will find inspiration with Gloria's goddess, but Gloria is only looking out for herself.'

'Everybody says that. She only seems that way.' Wren reached out to lift the cloak off her shoulders. 'Take it off; I'll embroider your sigil.'

Robin stepped away. 'This robe…' She opened her arms, swinging the sleeves. Then she hugged herself. 'It feels like you're cuddling me again. I've missed you and our closeness.'

'Me too. But I'm happy with where we are.'

'Stay a while,' Robin pointed to her chair. She sat on the bed.

Wren settled into Robin's favourite chair and looked out of the window at the trees. Robin's crystals from her first back rub lined up along the sill. 'I got so angry.'

'I know. We almost wrecked Ove. I'm sorry.'

Wren didn't need another apology from Robin. They had

already done that last summer. Since then, she understood why she always fell for women with big personalities. She only needed to find the right one.

Robin pulled the cloak off, messing up her hair and looking cute. 'Would you like some cognac?' She took a half-empty bottle and two shot glasses from her bookshelf.

'I should go downstairs.'

'Kelsey won't mind.'

Robin poured out the cognac. Its flowery billows reminded Wren of Esther in Paris. They were friends now, and anything could happen.

Three

At the head of the procession, Gloria swung her cauldron of smouldering myrrh. The rest of the witches carried their own lanterns, each burning a black candle, except Ginny who brought up the rear with a white glass chalice of well water.

The witches of Ove celebrated Samhain in the redwood grove, creating a place where dreams came true. They built an altar near the north and a fire in the centre. As they entered the grove, they blessed each other with oil and water. Ginny made a bed for Pepper in the stump. Beginning in the east, they invoked the Watchers, made the secret signs and cast their circle. They raised their cone of power, then grounded it.

The witches sang the occult songs that carried them. Black-robed and hooded, they circumambulated the fire, singing a melody that rose and fell, holding them tighter and tighter until they dropped to the ground. They lay with their heads together; their cloaks pressed them into the softness of the grove.

Gloria led them in this trance. They travelled in age order, so they didn't drift apart. Wren lay between Hazel and Ginny, as always. Over many journeys she had come to depend on their interlaced fingers.

As her spirit lightened, Wren sensed Hazel and Ginny's bodies fall away. She heard their voices holding everyone. As they rose through the trees, the circle spun like a wide leaf in a winter wind. Soon the blackness grew lighter and a foggy morning mist surrounded them. Wren oriented to a new gravity and her feet found solidity.

Robin appeared first, and she spoke: 'I am Robin. I am here.'

Wren saw her standing in the grey, dressed in a yellow tunic, cinched with a shimmering belt. She wore high boots and a floppy cap. An ancient Amazon.

'I am Gloria Arriola. I am here.' Gloria also arrived in classical dress, like Athena in her Parthenon.

'I am Nicola. I am here.' On the astral Nikki wore her usual jeans, boots and work shirt, somehow even more handsome.

Then Kelsey arrived. She appeared much like her mundane self, but alert and checking that everyone arrived as planned. She stepped nearer to Robin.

Lupe arrived. Her face looked more delicate, with her hair in braids and wrapped in ribbons of rainbows. Hazel looked somehow taller, but otherwise like she always did, in her plaid shirt and overalls, red-handled snips hanging from her belt.

'I am Wren Kildare. I am here.' Wren looked down at her hands, pomegranate-stained. *I'm Persephone again. Demeter was a terrible mother. Demeter compromised her power to bargain with the god who raped her daughter.* Where did that come from? Wren tried to imagine the stains gone from her hands, but couldn't.

Ginny arrived last, and she looked just like Pepper.

'I'll tend the fire,' Nikki declared, and she stacked logs around a campfire that appeared beside her. Everyone watched sparks fly into the grey sky, which then cleared and revealed uncountable stars in new constellations.

Robin began. 'Let me tell you about this place.' As she spoke, threads of words flew out of her mouth like a pattern emerging from under the weaver's fingers. With every word, her vision grew firmer and more real. 'When I die…'

Wren received a jolt of adrenaline and lifted away from the circle. She calmed herself and fell solidly to the astral ground again.

'When I die, I find myself in the centre of a stone circle.'

Wren had never visited a stone circle, but she knew them from photographs. As Robin spoke, boulders appeared around them, forming a circle as wide across as their redwood grove.

'We are surrounded by stones about my height, roughly formed and weathered. The ring of stones is surrounded by an endless grassland. People live out there, and I see their campfires.'

Wren walked to the nearest stone, taller than herself, and pressed her fingers to the rough granite. It was wider in the middle, tapered at top and bottom. Beyond the stone, she saw campfire lights flickering to the horizon and remembered the orange sequinned mask Robin wore at last year's Samhain. Near her, Nikki was examining a stone, probably trying to figure out how it remained upright.

'My earliest memory is my most precious,' Robin said. As they listened to her story, the witches wandered between the stones and did not leave the circle.

'Our people lived in a garden, like Eden. Wide plains ringed with mountains. Where, I cannot tell you. It doesn't exist any more.' Wren imagined what she knew, the foothills of central California, with high Sierra Nevada beyond.

'We have our dogs and our horses. Some of us hunt with eagles.'

Wren had heard of girls who hunted with eagles. She held out her arm. An eagle landed on it, glared at her, then flew away. She started to fly after the eagle, but Robin's voice brought her back. Wren reminded herself to listen and not get distracted.

'We travel with the seasons as our food ripens, from mountain to plains and again to mountain valleys.'

Wren pulled a berry off a bramble. She knew from stories not to eat it.

'We do not keep herds or flocks; we follow them. We meet other people like us who travel the endless grasslands. We trade furs for golden treasures to make ourselves shine.' A golden circlet appeared on Gloria's forehead, and it looked good on her. Wren put her hand to her own throat and touched a torc. All the witches glittered with new jewellery.

'We are one family, related to the wandering people of these plains, but my family possesses a magic secret, like a technology.'

'Dogs think campfires are magical.' Ginny, still dog-shaped, stopped running around and flopped down next to Nikki's fire.

Nikki lifted her hand toward Ginny. 'I want to pet you.'

Ginny leaned against Nikki, who rubbed her ears.

Robin continued her story. 'Two women lead my family. We have a word that means a woman of wisdom and stories, so I'll call them "sages" in this language.'

Wren saw two women standing next to Robin. One tall and one short, dressed like Robin, in tunics and leggings and tall boots. They had brown skin and tucked most of their sun-bleached hair under tight caps.

'The sages teach us with stories. Where to find water. When to find the sweetest fruit. How to gather the seeds from the marsh grass. Where the mushrooms bloom. Where to follow the path over the mountain. The stories tell us how people get angry, how people fall in love, how people are foolish. The stories tell us when to leave; how things have changed, how they are the same.'

As Robin spoke, more people appeared: women, children, their dogs, horses and tents. Wren thought they looked like the Amazons on the Greek pots she had studied briefly at art school. The witches stepped back toward the edges of the circle as Robin described them.

'Wait a minute' said Gloria. 'Where are the men?'

'They lived nearby, but they did not live with us. We gathered for big parties once a year.'

'Like Rainbow Gathering?' Gloria asked.

'Something like that. Annual gatherings are culturally universal.'

Gloria didn't look satisfied. 'The sages are like you? Remembering?'

Wren wished she would just let Robin tell the story.

'Like I do now, as the sages enter womanhood, they remember. A sage remains with us for a few lifetimes. Before she loses her love of living and remembering she goes into the stone.'

In the centre a black boulder appeared, different from the grey stones surrounding them.

'We said the stone came from heaven.'

'It was a meteorite?' asked Hazel.

'Probably.'

Robin took Kelsey's hand. Wren saw orange flame pour from Kelsey to Robin, and Robin took deep, long breaths until her chest glowed.

'When I was born, my family named me Sunny because I was a quiet child, content to sit in the sun and watch the bustle of the camp around me. It was a name you give a girl before she names herself. One of our sages wanted to go into the stone. I knew her by a name that means Night Bird, so I'll call her Lilith.'

The Ovem laughed and filled their astral air with shimmering recognition. They knew a feminist story about how Lilith and Eve became friends over the wall around Garden of Eden.

'She told us she would go into the stone.'

Wren saw the taller woman step toward the black boulder.

'We call the other sage Honey, because she has a knack for finding bee hives. Honey chose me to become the next sage. I felt lucky. Honey explains that after Lilith goes into the stone, I will become her daughter. On the night she goes into the stone, Lilith and I eat a stew of grain, game and mushrooms. The magic is in the mushrooms. Everyone sings a song like the one that brought us to the astral tonight. The mushroom gives visions. They lay Lilith and me in a hole lined with stones and cover us in soft wool. I am sleepy, and behind my closed eyes, stars spin in spirals and an infinite heaven fills with faces singing with me. Lilith takes my hand. She helps me to stand up, and we are here.'

For the first time since starting her story, Robin's voice broke, but she swallowed and composed herself.

'The stones of the grave have grown huge. Far away, we hear our family singing. Lilith tells me to look to the west, and we see the low sun across a red plain. The familiar land of my home.'

Wren looked to the west, now illuminated by a deep red sunset over distant hills, like coming home over Pacheco Pass.

'She turns me away from the sun and shows me the boulder.'

The Ovem watched as Lilith and a young woman approached the black stone.

Sunny is dressed the same as the others, striped trousers under a tunic. Her shoulders are narrow, elbows larger than her arms. Her body has barely left girlhood. In wonder and excitement, Sunny touches the stone and a kaleidoscope of rainbows swirl under her finger.

'The stone is taller than me, but shorter than Lilith. It is both black and iridescent – like shimmering oil. Lilith climbs on top of the black stone and pulls me after her. It's flat on top, wide enough for the two of us. We lose ourselves in the song. Night falls. We watch the rainbow stars. Lilith says, "After I leave, find Honey's campfire through that door." I sit up and follow her pointing finger. On the eastern edge are two stones, taller and narrower than the rest.

'The gate stones shine with their own light. Between them is a darkness. That darkness is the door.

'"Where is Honey's campfire?" I ask her.

'"Hers is nearest."

'We hear the singing of our people. I am lost in the music. My girlish voice rises high. Lilith and the stones sing in low grandmother tones. The stars spin. Lilith and the stone sing together like old friends. Adding my song enriches theirs and changes it. I sing with the stone. I become the song.

'Lilith disappears like smoke in the wind. The voices fall silent. I am alone. The stars cease to spin, and the rainbows fade. I climb down from the black stone, shaking with cold.'

Robin stopped speaking. The black boulder stood empty and dead.

'I look to the eastern gate.'

Wren saw two circles of light and a dark void where they overlapped, pointed at the top and bottom. 'Gloria, what do you call that shape?'

'It's *vesica piscis* in Latin.'

'That's it.' Wren wanted to anchor this vision in her memory. This might be what she'd been looking for. She made circles of her thumbs and forefingers and brought them to her eyes like binoculars to capture the *vesica piscis* like a photograph. When her hands touched the bridge of her nose, she interlocked her fingers over the dark spot in the gate. 'Check this out,' she called. 'Hold your fingers like this.'

The witches held up their hands and linked their fingers and thumbs, making the shape of the *vesica piscis*. The sadness of Robin's story faded as they made these silly finger shapes and soon they – even Gloria – were standing in a semi-circle around the black stone, their fingers interlocked.

Ginny raised her hands, and the rest followed. 'Behold,' she called. 'The sign of the Ove!'

Four

Gloria dropped her hands first. 'What's outside the gate?'

Robin continued her story. 'Campfires.'

Wren released Hazel and Ginny's hands, but kept her own fingers linked in this new gesture so she wouldn't forget.

'I approach the nearest. Across from me, the warm firelight dancing on her face, I recognise Honey. She holds out her arms and pulls me in. But I will never meet her again.'

'Why not?' Gloria sounded annoyed.

'Honey would have taught me who I was. She would have taught me songs about water and the wheel of the seasons, the paths over distant mountains. All the rest. I would have served my people. Eventually Honey would have gone into the stone, and I would teach the next woman.'

'Like you teach us?' said Gloria.

'Something like that. But we lived in a time of chaos, and great civilisations perished. When that world of ziggurats, golden swords and purple robes ended, so did ours.'

'I know about that time,' said Gloria. 'You're talking about the dark ages of ancient Greece.'

'Yes, you're right.' Robin turned toward Gloria. Threads of connection reached across the circle between them. Wren had seen that sort of thing on the astral, and it reassured her. 'I don't know what happened, but I suspect we met up with people who took advantage of our hospitality. Our little band of women didn't survive them.

'When my memories returned in my next life, Honey, my family and our stories appeared in my mind like a recurring dream. I was enslaved in a city of stone, not a person, but definitely treated like a woman.'

'And you come here when you die?' Gloria asked.

'I do. I don't go to that Isle of Apples you went to last Halloween. My ancestors don't greet me. I wake up alone, surrounded by this circle, next to the black stone. I wish the stone would enliven and sing. Sometimes, if I have died while tripping – I have done that, in my desperation – the stones shimmer in their iridescence. But I never heard the song again.'

Wren shivered. They had been here quite a while already, and it was getting cold. She was glad they were near a fire, wrapped in their cloaks. She imagined warming herself and started to float upwards. She bent and grounded to the astral again, hearing the distant, even breaths of the coven around her.

'What happens if you don't leave?' Kelsey pointed toward the two bright stones as if she didn't like them very much.

'I have tried. But this circle is timeless. Nothing changes. I don't sleep, I just get colder and colder. Bleak doesn't describe it. I go through the gate because there's nothing else.' Robin stopped speaking. Wren thought this was the end of her story.

Gloria pressed on with her agenda. 'You never tried to make the mushroom stew and take another woman to the black stone?'

'No. How could I? Wren…'

Wren started at her name in Robin's voice.

'…You're adopted and don't know your birth mother. For lifetimes, I've been adopted and fostered, raised by loving mothers and cruel mothers. But my real mother never could tell me what to do with these memories.'

Wren realised for all her anguish about mother damage, she had never asked Robin about her own. For an artist, she had a lot of blind spots.

'I might have seen her one time, long after, when Christianity was new. When it started, Christianity attracted women exploring consciousness, like we do now, but they described it as travelling to heaven and speaking with angels. Older religions offered this too, but by that time they had lost their monopoly over ecstatic mushroom rituals.'

'Religions used mushrooms?' asked Lupe.

'Religions usually have a psychedelic secret at their heart—'

'That's amazing,' said Hazel. 'Buddhism has a psychedelic secret?'

'Especially Buddhism.'

Hazel chuckled. 'I wouldn't know. My parents were Methodists.'

'Christianity started out offering a sacred meal and union with its god,' Robin continued. 'It was attractive to poor people like me who couldn't afford to pilgrimage to famous shrines. Women presided over their rituals, mixing the wine.'

'Like I mix the tea?' said Lupe.

'Like you—' Robin began, but Gloria interrupted.

'How did you recognise her?'

'I didn't recognise her face, I recognised her…power. Everyone knew her her name.'

'I need to know something.' Gloria spoke in a voice so sharp, thin filaments flew from her mouth and lightly bounced off Robin's chest. She ticked off Robin's failings on her fingers. 'You *don't* know the song. You *don't* know which mushroom. You *don't* know how to teach someone else to live forever.'

'That's true; I don't.' Robin leaned toward Kelsey, but Kelsey was trying to get Nikki's attention for some reason. Robin continued. 'You asked me to show you this circle, so I did. I kept it secret, but I don't need to any more. Kelsey doesn't live as if she is someone else's past life – I don't want to either.'

'That secret handshake Wren found is the only good thing here,' Nikki said.

Wren wanted more. A stone appeared in her hands a little bigger than her fist. Its surface formed itself into a female face…Eros…snakes…scary but not scary…

Gloria intruded on Wren's concentration. 'I want to create sages.'

Kelsey's reply came out copper-coloured and sour. 'Glow, you're forgetting the part of Robin's story where they killed children in a weird psychedelic death ritual.'

The stone face in Wren's fingers became sand and poured to the ground.

'Imagine what we could do as an immortal coven who didn't fear death!'

Wren held her hands together, trying to conjure the shape that had nearly formed there. It was the image that would reconcile Gloria's Athena with Robin's vision. But as her friends argued, Wren lost it.

'Women sacrificing themselves for eternal life?' Kelsey scoffed. 'Where have we heard that before? That's not the magic we do.'

'But a coven of immortal witches could destroy Patriarchy!'

'We're already destroying Patriarchy,' said Robin. 'All we have to do is keep doing what we do. I'm sure of this. Common lesbians living our common lives, just like Judy Grahn said.'

Gloria wasn't having any of that lesbian poetry stuff. Her hands formed fists at her sides and Wren felt their heat. 'We will die without real power. Reagan is going to be re-elected.'

Wren saw dark shapes forming just outside the stones. 'Gloria, you're attracting scary things. Quick, everyone, make the sign of the Ove with me.'

Wren linked her fingers with Ginny, who linked with Robin and Gloria, and the rest joined in. Their mood lightened. This time Wren felt the energy of the coven spin up between them. In previous journeys, this moment would be when the coven bent their will and created change in the mundane world. This was the magical moment.

'Fuck this,' said Gloria, then disappeared from the circle. She had ended her trance and left their shared vision.

'She knows better than to drop out like that,' Nikki said, with real anger.

The witches stepped toward each other, filling the gap Gloria had left, putting their arms around each other's waists and holding themselves together. Wren dipped her head left and right to smell Hazel and Ginny's ritual oil.

The witches imagined themselves rising into the black sky above the ring of stones, which disappeared under grey mist. They were again a coven of witches, flying through the dark. They pressed their heads to the centre. Moments later, they floated down through the redwood grove, black robes flapping, legs spinning out like a tattered pinwheel. The fire beckoned with its warmth. Wren felt the ground beneath her, Hazel on one side, Ginny on the other. Pepper barked in surprise as they arrived.

Everyone stood up, wrapped their cloaks around themselves, and gathered at the fire. Wren smelled myrrh. Pepper wouldn't stop licking Ginny's face. Hazel passed around the thermoses. As Wren warmed her hands around her mug, she saw Gloria crouched on her own by the fire, her face in her palms, sobbing.

Nikki saw her too. 'What the fuck, Gloria?'

'I couldn't be there any more.'

Approaching her, Nikki pointed a finger in Gloria's face. 'You *don't* do that. You can't just leave the astral. We go up and down together.'

'I know. I'm sorry.' Gloria wiped her eyes with her sleeve.

Wren couldn't be angry. She looked so hurt and scared. Wren bought Gloria a mug. 'It's okay, sweetheart. Tell us what happened.'

Gloria didn't answer, only pulled Wren's arm tighter around herself.

Wren looked across at Robin, who was staring at the fire, most of her face hidden by her hood. She didn't want Robin's first experience on the astral to end in a fight.

She looked around at everyone else. They were back, whole, but not inspired. Wren's vision of…that face in her hands, scary but not scary…had evaporated. No one said anything. After a while, Hazel passed the thermoses around again, and Gloria spoke.

'I'm sorry, everyone. But when Robin said she didn't

remember the songs and there was a lost secret mushroom, I realised that it's just a story.'

'A story that explains my life.'

'I thought you had a magic that we could use to help us live forever, like you. But you're more deluded than anyone I've ever met.'

Robin didn't appear offended. 'I'm sorry, Gloria.'

'You don't have anything to be sorry for,' Kelsey said. 'Gloria, you're angry because you thought Robin would give you the secret that enticed women to your classes.'

'There's nothing wrong with what Gloria wanted,' Robin said. 'Spiritual leaders always have a cool secret. But I don't have one. You teach real magic, and we are lucky to learn from you.'

Gloria lifted her head and wiped her eyes with her sleeve. Robin crossed the circle, Gloria stood up, and they hugged until Wren felt the energy of the circle reposition. If only Gloria hadn't wrenched them out of it like she did. Wren's body still ached. Gloria sat down again.

'Robin, you're intimate with everything awful,' Ginny said. Pepper put her paw in Robin's lap.

Robin rubbed Pepper's ears before speaking. 'Through my lifetimes, I tried to help women escape abuse. But no matter which mother I chose, or how much money I had, we couldn't stop men from controlling us – even the best of them. Until now. This time, in this life, this coven of witches…' Robin looked around, mischievous. 'You chose me. You took a chance with me and you taught me your magic, how to love my body and find wisdom in pleasure. Again and again I have survived. Now I can thrive.'

'Speaking of thriving,' said Kelsey, 'let's eat. I have stew in the crock pot back at the house.'

⊙

'If you hold me any tighter, I'll be behind you.'

Wren knew Gloria didn't mean it affectionately. Robin had predicted Gloria wouldn't get what she wanted from the astral journey. But Wren still felt confused by Gloria's tantrum and apology. Sometimes she didn't know how to handle Gloria's emotions.

She would start with admiration. 'Athenic wicca doesn't need anything from Robin.'

'I should have known she was a fraud.'

Wren felt Gloria getting angrier, but she wasn't afraid. Thanks to her mother, this felt normal.

'Robin's story is just a metaphor for women's herstory,' Gloria said. 'She thinks our ancestral mothers abandoned us to suffer in Patriarchy. She has a mother problem. That's why she gives her money to people who aren't her real family.'

'But families abandon women all the time.'

'Mine didn't. Some people fight Patriarchy *because* their culture doesn't abandon them.'

Wren wanted to believe this, but it didn't seem right. Was there any culture where women were free of Patriarchy? 'I thought your parents helped your brother when he was kicked out of the navy, but didn't help you go to medical school?'

'He wasn't kicked out. The navy wasn't right for him and he resigned his commission.'

'Right. I remember now.' Wren put Pan-Cultural Familial Patriarchy on the list of topics unsafe to discuss. Maybe Gloria would want to help her find the vision she had lost. 'Remember back when I saw things on the astral, and then made them for real in the mundane? I saw something tonight.'

'Like when we met Sappho?'

'Like that. I want to do that again. I need to find—'

'You should. We need to make Athena's temple really cool.'

Athena's temple – the octagon – was something she could work on, and Gloria wasn't angry any more. 'Did I tell you that Athena reminded me she and Diana are sisters? I was thinking of painting Diana and Athena together, supporting each other.'

'We'll have to see what Athena thinks about that.'

'What would Athena think of this?' She slid her hand between Gloria's thighs. Athena approved.

In the morning, they made love again, just like they used to. 'Making love on a holiday is a special blessing,' Gloria purred and everything got back to normal.

Five

In December the house at Ove filled with dykes and their friends. On the twenty-first, they drove two crowded vans down to Bonny Doon beach to watch the sunset. They then returned to light the Yule fires on the coals of the previous year, celebrate a feast and attempt an all-night vigil.

Kelsey didn't make it. She woke from a dream in a panic. The house felt dark and quiet. The dream was about Robin. 'What time is it?'

'Dawn is hours away,' Robin said, and leaned forward to poke the fire. Robin could easily stay awake all night: another weird skill.

Kelsey rubbed her eyes, searched for Robin's fingers and squeezed them. 'I don't want to miss the sunrise like last year.'

Nothing was wrong. Robin was alive. Kelsey needed tea. She stretched her arms over her head and twisted to look behind their couch. Across the room, the other fire – also ringed by couches – glowed low. Above both fires, on crowded mantels, candles flickered at the bottom of smoky jars. She smelled frankincense.

'How are you doing, sweetheart?' Robin had that expression she always had when remembering...the things she remembered.

'I'm awake.' How alluring to fall asleep again in Robin's lap. 'How long?'

'At least two more hours.'

'I might make some chai and take a bath. Do you want some?'

'No thanks, but you enjoy it.'

Kelsey bent over and kissed Robin's sweet mouth. She had never wanted this. Had never known it – this sleeping together every night. This Long Term Living Together Relationship. It never worked out. But here they were, the only two women still awake. Was that a good sign or a bad sign?

Robin smiled, sat back, and her eyes found the fire again.

Kelsey took an unsteady step toward the woodpile and threw on two logs. Need to ask someone to bring in more wood tomorrow. It had to burn for eleven more nights. The last was Kelsey's birthday. She walked across the front room and found two women sleeping at opposite ends of the couch. Nikki was one, the other a woman she didn't know. She looked older than Robin. Kelsey poked that fire and added more logs.

Without turning on the kitchen light, she lit the fire under the kettle, grabbed her coat off the hook and stepped into the chilly yard behind the house. Low lights were still on in Lupe and Hazel's cabins, and she heard women's voices. So she and Robin weren't the only ones awake. Lupe with Letty; Hazel with Ronnie.

Kelsey walked softly past the cabins to the bathhouse, where Wren and Cayenne's mermaids watched her from their shell palace. She hummed a chant from last night about how nothing lasts forever and, as the wheel turns, time changes you. She switched on the water heater. Time for chai.

Back in the kitchen, blue flames cast a soft shadow across the table covered in the remains of last night's feast: meat pies, a ham, a turkey, cheesy cauliflower, green-bean casserole, mashed yams, Brussels sprouts, baked potatoes, meat and meatless gravies, pumpkin pie, pecan pie, a bûche de Noël and an empty pink tin of Almond Roca. Gold wrappers everywhere caught the light from the stove. Someone had twisted them into a circle. Kelsey put it on her head like a crown. Her birthday seemed far away from tonight. Everyone would be partied out. They always were. But she'd get her birthday massage and feel happy to be born.

In the pantry she found the jar of chai by feel, with its tight latch. She and Gloria had invented this mix for the coven's first Yule. She lifted the jar to her nose: sharp, sweet, bitter, all at once. During the ritual when they first made it, Gloria read out the passage in Audre Lorde's *Zami* where she ground the spices, redefining the erotic as power. A sacred text in sacred space. It was also Gloria's idea to crush the cardamom and cinnamon between two stones – otherwise used for corn. Gloria's relatively recent behaviour at Samhain had been shocking and rude, but Kelsey appreciated her contributions to their witchcraft. She packed a tea ball with lapsang souchong, the strongest tea she knew. Before the kettle whistled, she switched off the burner.

She filled the tea pot with steaming water, then added the tea ball. Gloria was less controlling since her freakout at Halloween. Whatever had happened to Gloria's class? Wren and Gloria were still together, but she didn't know why. She couldn't ask. She stirred in the spices, their redolence rising over the scent of the smoky tea. That tarot deck Wren painted for her. Not Wren's best work – rushed – and the symbols had a sort of heterosexuality to them – to Kelsey's sensibilities, anyway. Nothing like Wren's smouldering Sappho over the fireplace. She filled a small jar with milk, screwed on the lid, put it and her mug in her coat pocket. Poor Wren; like so many lesbians, she gave herself to her lover's passions. She used to be so excited about that big art thing Robin wanted her to do. Kelsey dressed the teapot in one of Ginny's knitted cosies.

Outside, her breath came out in clouds and now she felt strong against sleep. The stars were diamonds tonight, like in a poem. Yesterday evening, the coven and their girlfriends had watched the weakest sun of the year sliding into the sea at Bonny Doon. The witches said that if no one kept the vigil on winter solstice, it would lose its way and not come back in the morning. Kelsey knew enough about astronomy to know that wasn't true, but she liked the story.

She grabbed a towel from the laundry and entered the bathhouse. Tea on the shelf. Two candles lit. Turn the taps.

Her head jerked. She'd fallen asleep on the bench. The tub was full, which meant the hot water was gone. She stripped off her clothes and got right in. The heater made one bathtub at a time. Nikki said more was a waste. Kelsey loved having an engineer as a friend.

She poured her chai, added milk, and sipped it, now cool enough and not too strong. Perfect. She placed one hand on the other and rested them on her belly. She whispered, 'Light of my life.'

Lucy sat on the bench.

'You were dreaming about Robin.' Lucy wore the vest Kelsey's mother had crocheted for her the last Christmas. Kelsey had forgotten about it until now.

'She *is* my girlfriend.'

Lucy put her finger in the water and flicked it at Kelsey's face.

'Stay awake. I'm here now. You haven't talked to me in so long.'

'I don't know why.'

Lucy pouted in a way that Kelsey didn't recognise. 'You don't need me any more.'

'I will always need you. You're part of me.'

'It's going to be your birthday.'

'I just keep getting older. It's been more than ten years since you died.'

Lucy ignored Kelsey's reckoning. 'What will you get me for Christmas?'

'Socks?'

'Do better. I got you the Olivia Newton-John album, because I honestly love you.'

Kelsey hadn't thought of that song in years, but now she couldn't think of anything else. 'But have you ever been mellow?'

Lucy pouted again. 'What would you want, if you could have anything?'

'I only want this life I live. Who knew tearing down Patriarchy would be more fun than we could possibly imagine?'

'That's what I would have wanted.' Lucy lifted her arms and shouted, 'Dip me in honey and throw me to the lesbians!'

That made Kelsey sad. 'I wish you could have been here.'

'I am here.'

'You know what I mean. I used to feel guilty that I got to be a lesbian.'

'And I never got to have a threesome.'

'They aren't as great as you think.'

'Still.'

Kelsey remembered her dream. Robin doesn't talk when she makes love. She listens with her whole body. She recalled Robin's eyes, wide and surprised; fascinated.

This wasn't a fling. Kelsey would be twenty-eight next month. Nearly thirty. How did *that* happen? Robin seemed so much older, whatever the truth of her stories. Kelsey felt they were a couple unlike the other lesbians they knew. She didn't feel as desperate as coupled women looked.

'That's because she's not your everything.' Lucy had gotten into the tub with Kelsey. She didn't displace any water, but Kelsey felt Lucy's legs sliding around her own as she sank in up to her neck, her breasts floating, the ends of her hair swirling like the mermaids.

'She's not. I have you. Robin told me she wants to know everything about me. Is there anything sexier than that?' Kelsey blushed, remembering. Robin, curling up and pulling away, then open.

Lucy's voice woke her again. 'What a year.'

Kelsey pulled the loofah off the peg and rubbed it along her foot. 'I haven't worked in more than a year.'

'You work every day.'

'Work is cleaning up old people who torment their children.'

'That's harsh.'

'You never got old enough to see people become more themselves. Young assholes become old assholes. I never miss taking care of old men who grabbed my tits.'

The water was seriously cold by now. She opened the drain and refilled the tub. Now Lucy sat on the bench, flicking her finger back and forth across the flame. She always loved playing with fire.

'Lucy, did you say something?'

'Robin is dangerous.'

'Don't be absurd.' Lucy was dripping wax on the back of her hand, like she used to do. 'It's Gloria I don't trust. But being with Wren is mellowing her out. Maybe she's changed.'

'Robin has changed.'

'She has. I love her so much.'

'But what?'

'This next year. I'm sure we'll have lover drama. Someone will want her girlfriend to live here, or one of us will leave to be with a girlfriend.'

Lucy peeled the wax off her hand and fed it back into the candle. 'You're right. Ove won't last another year. Robin will take off in search of a better women's land. Then you'll need me.'

'I couldn't get rid of you if I tried.'

'Since you've been with Robin, you haven't been talking to me.' Lucy stood near the door. 'Last year's sun died in the ocean last night. You think it's time to leave me behind.'

'Lucy! No!'

The door opened. 'Who are you talking to?' Ginny and Pepper came in. Pepper sniffed the bench and Ginny undressed. 'Is there any hot water left? I didn't think you were asleep because I heard you talking.'

'I was talking to myself. Get in. There might be chai left.'

Her curiosity satisfied, Pepper curled in front of the door.

'Thanks. I won't stay long; the stars are fading.' Ginny slid her slight frame into the tub and adjusted her legs around

Kelsey's. 'That crown looks good on you.'

Kelsey had forgotten she was wearing it.

Ginny chattered away. 'Hand me the loofah, please. I can't wait until the sun comes up. Remember last year? Everyone's worn-out last-year face lights up golden and turns beautiful.'

Kelsey smiled at the memory. She took the crown and placed it on Ginny's head. 'This morning, you can be Sun Queen.'

'Thank you, Kelsey,' Ginny said in a queenly voice. 'And as your queen I'd like to know who you were talking to when I came in.'

Kelsey wanted to refuse, but as Ginny waited for her answer with her big warm eyes and gentle insistence, Kelsey knew a moment of transformation was upon her.

'I was talking to the ghost of my first lover.'

Ginny lunged forward, sloshing, trying to hug Kelsey. She gave up and held Kelsey's thighs instead. 'She died already?'

Kelsey reached over and straightened her crown. 'She was in a car with her parents when they were hit by some drunk guy. I went to sleep in one world and woke up in this one.'

'My mother said that's what it is like.'

Kelsey didn't know much about Ginny's family, but every family grieves. 'I talk to her sometimes, though she's gone.' She needed to not look at Ginny any more.

Ginny got her legs under herself so she could reach over and lift Kelsey's face with a dripping hand. 'She's not gone tonight. Yule is when ghosts come back to show us what can change before we die.'

'I don't want anything to change,' Kelsey said. 'But I'm ready to get out of this tub. I slept through the sunrise last year. I'm awake now.'

As they got dressed, Kelsey noticed wax all over the bench.

Was that there before? Must have been.

Kelsey's Yule Chai
1 tablespoon ginger
2 tablespoons cardamom
1 tablespoon cinnamon
1 teaspoon turmeric
¼ teaspoon cayenne
¼ teaspoon clove
½ teaspoon black pepper
No sugar or honey, just smoky black tea.

six

Long before becoming a priest of Athena, Wren loved Bridget, goddess of fire, oak and water. When she was fourteen, she devoted the last eighteen nights of January to tending Bridget's flame in a candle lantern unwisely hidden in her closet altar. The witches said whoever kept this annual vigil received Bridget's grace, as she was the benefactor of blacksmiths, poets and other creative people. On the nineteenth night, Wren left the flame to be tended by Bridget herself. The ritual left her feeling the presence of the goddess, and thousands of her flame-keepers, for thousands of years, keeping watch.

At the close of that first Bridget vigil, young Brenda renamed herself Wren Kildare. She never revealed her magical name to her mother, the first secret she kept.

Wren tended Bridget's flame for ten years, but this year she skipped it, spending every January night sensibly in Gloria's bed. On January's Dark Moon, the two of them together set their intentions for the month, and when Wren awoke the next morning, she felt she had set the direction of the rest of her life. Athenic wicca left little room for Brigidine improvisation.

She turned and buried her nose in Gloria's warm hair. She listened to Gloria's soft snores. She remembered the first months, when they made love every morning – 'glorious' mornings, Wren called them. Wren had asked her – just kidding, of course – for a glorious Yule, but Gloria said it was natural for passion to fade. They hadn't made love in weeks.

Wren had to pee, and heard voices downstairs. She slipped from under the quilt, pulled on socks, found her clogs and buttoned her coat. She carefully stepped around the icy veranda to her bedroom. The sky was turning pink. Woodpeckers chattered in the dark woods. How she loved this forest, in every season.

In her room, dirty clothes and an unmade bed greeted her. In the corner next to the window was her altar, stacked high with the sketchbooks she'd filled with ideas for the magical statue. She hadn't started a new one since she and Gloria became lovers. Athena wasn't the inspiration Gloria said she would be. No one else in the coven liked Athenic imagery anyway. Maybe the Ovem wouldn't need a Sacred Art Object to save them from internalised Patriarchy. They'd been together for more than a year without one.

Wren considered lighting a candle for Bridget, but the worldwide Brigidine vigil had started a week ago. Instead, she pulled on overalls and headed down the stairs. She opened the kitchen door to warmth and aromas and Ovem and their lovers.

'Wren! Bahdrina made scones!'

A shock of light and babble. The table, heaped with jams, butter, honey, cheese, sliced apples and cream.

Nikki was there with her friend Bahdrina, who was wearing purple like she always did. Lupe's girlfriend Letty wore Lupe's denim jacket, and the two of them were in animated conversation with Hazel's girlfriend. Wren first knew her as the Dyke at the Hardware Store, but her name was Sharon and everyone called her Ron. Hazel sat pensively, her hair flowing around her shoulders unbraided. Someone Wren didn't know was sitting next to Ginny.

Wren poured the last of the coffee and squeezed in next to Ginny's friend. She hadn't taken two sips of the lukewarm coffee before she learned the friend lived in Aptos and was a Reiki master.

Lupe turned around, curious. 'You're a master of mushrooms?'

'You mean *reishi* mushrooms,' Ginny's friend said with authority. 'Reiki is an energy massage technique.'

'Never mind.' Lupe turned back to Letty and finished her thought. 'But we're not separatists; we just like to live without male supervision.'

Wren asked the Reiki Master if she wanted coffee.

'I don't drink coffee. This is chicory.'

'I can make you more.'

'I'm fine.'

'How do you know Ginny?'

'We met at Community Foods. We started talking because she looks like my sister. We're both Armenian.'

Ginny leaned forward. 'Good morning, Wren. This is Cheryl.'

'My name is Cher,' Reiki Master said. Ginny looked confused and embarrassed.

'Cher? Like Sonny and Cher?' Wren loved Cher.

'No.' The woman looked annoyed. 'Just because we're both

Armenian doesn't mean I have the same name.'

Wren hoped this wasn't Ginny's first lover.

'I spell it s-h-a-r-e. Share. Because I'm a healer.'

'You're a healer?' This conversation required hotter coffee. 'The world needs more healers.' Wren waved her mug to Letty who was now at the sink; she filled the kettle.

Wren turned back to Share and looked for a bit of common ground. 'I changed my birth-name too, and I'm glad I did.' She noticed Nikki smirking across the table. 'Nikki! Good morning! What are you up to today?'

'Bahdrina and me are doing a lumber and materials inventory in the barn.' Wren knew that meant they would end up in bed most of the day.

Letty and Ron were recounting the demonstration at the town clock a few days ago, protesting Reagan's inauguration.

'The DC witches cast a spell and froze them out. They had to do the inauguration ritual inside. First time in history that's happened,' Ron said proudly.

'If we can control the weather, why can't we elect Sonia Johnson?' Lupe complained.

'Women's land is great,' Ron said diplomatically, 'but you can't hide on this mountain and expect anything to change for women.'

Letty agreed. 'We have to be politically active, too.'

'I say women doing whatever they please will destroy Patriarchy,' said Kelsey.

Wren noticed Robin wasn't there. The water boiled, so she got up. Ginny joined her at the stove as she filled the filter.

Wren kept her voice low and said, 'So about your friend, *Share*. She's intense.'

'She's straight.'

'That's...not what I meant.'

'She spent the night with me because she thought the road was too icy. Then she told me she's straight.'

'Maybe she's open?'

'I don't want to be someone's experiment.'

'Right on, sista-woman.' Wren slipped an arm loosely around Ginny's waist. 'What are you up today? Do you need help?'

'Hoof trims. Then cashmere spinning.'

'Let's spin by the fire. Maybe Robin will tell us Amazon stories.'

The back door opened and Gloria came in. 'Coffee's ready,' said Wren, knowing she would want it right away.

'Ovem!' Gloria commanded the room. 'I have an announcement. Tonight after dinner, we need a Magic Moot to talk about the coming year.'

There was a murmured consultation with the girlfriends, but eventually everyone agreed.

Wren handed Gloria the steaming cup and listened to the conversations. These women – with their motley clothes, chaotic menu and discursive conversation – were the sisterhood young Brenda the Bridget acolyte longed for. Thank the Goddess Gloria kept them organised.

⊙⊙

Before the Magic Moot, Wren sat at her altar and looked to the picture of Pallas Athene. 'Give me courage,' she implored. The proposals Gloria would bring to the Magic Moot worried her.

When she entered the living room, Robin was telling Nikki about her latest gadget. 'It's a computer, but you point at pictures instead of typing.' A computer with pictures sounded promising. Wren left the big chair for Gloria and sat down next to Hazel.

When everyone had settled in with mugs and blankets, Gloria started the Magic Moot. 'When I founded this coven, we focused on healing ourselves. We blossomed. We reclaimed women's spirituality to heal ourselves and our Mother, the planet. But now it's the Eighties. A new age. We've lived on our sacred land together for more than a year.'

Lupe raised her mug. 'To everything we've done so far!'

The coven toasted themselves.

Gloria brought their attention back to her agenda. 'As the Witches of Ove, we've twice welcomed the new light of Yule.'

The coven were amazed at the years flying by and toasted themselves again.

Gloria continued. 'Since last summer, some of us have formed closer relationships, and we rely on magic to heal from the unintentional hurts we do to each other.' Wren wondered if Gloria was referring to her Robin-drama, but realised she was talking about her own disappointment that Robin couldn't make her immortal.

'Through my work with Athena over the Yule season, I understand now that we must heal from our own Patriarchal damage.'

'If we're planning our magical year,' Hazel chimed in, 'each ritual should be inspired by the land herself.'

Ginny raised her hand. 'If we're picking holidays, I want summer solstice.'

'Yes, Haze, at this Moot we will assign Priestess duties. And I propose an Imbolc ritual next week to prepare us for those responsibilities. Even in a woman-only community like ours, we carry Patriarchal damage inside us.'

'Remember that Burning Up Patriarchy ritual last summer?' Nikki deadpanned. 'It didn't work.'

Lupe pretended to pass a joint to Nikki. 'You spent a lot of time working in the barn since Yule.'

'I wasn't born popular,' Nikki bragged. 'I had to work at it.'

'I've been working on myself too,' Gloria said. 'Athena has shown me I haven't been an effective coven leader.'

Lupe blinked in mock surprise. Wren hated it when Gloria implied she was in charge of the coven.

'Athena has made it known to me she is the true Goddess of California.'

'Come off it,' Kelsey sneered. 'Athena is Greek.'

'California is the Goddess of California,' Ginny asserted.

'Gloria has a point,' argued Robin. 'Athena appears on all government paperwork.'

'Robin is right,' Gloria said, and looked grateful for Robin's support. 'Men designated Her as the symbol of California. They acknowledge what she Herself made real. This she told me, Herself.'

Kelsey snorted.

'Please, listen.' Gloria was trying very hard. 'I think you will like what I'm about to propose.'

'Sorry. I'm ready to hear your stellar proposal.' Kelsey could try too.

'Thank you. The Dianic wicca we practise was informed by European teachers going back to ancient times. But we live in California, and it's the Eighties. Our coven includes women of *this* continent, and beyond.' She nodded to Hazel. Wren knew Hazel hated that, too. 'Our land is a unique ecosystem—'

'You're right!' Robin interrupted. 'I was drawn here because I had never lived in the redwoods. Old memories don't intrude as much.'

'Yes, Robin. Athenic wicca is rooted in our landscape. That's why this year, I want us to adopt a more Athenic practice.'

'Gloria, your Athenic wicca is fine for you, but I'm a Dianic,' asserted Kelsey. 'Dianic wicca is for all women. It doesn't matter where we come from.'

'I get your theory about Athena and California,' said Hazel, 'but she still feels European to me.'

'She's a Californian, like you,' Gloria said.

'Gloria, please don't question Hazel's feelings,' Lupe said. 'As for me, the Ove Goddess *I know* isn't anything like the stuff in Wren's octagon.'

'Let's learn from the Ove Goddess,' Robin suggested. 'The living symbols of our own land.'

'I already said that a minute ago,' Hazel complained.

Robin rubbed her fist on her chest in apology.

'Symbols like our secret handshake?' Lupe held up her fingers, and everyone interlocked their fingers and laughed at the absurd power of this gesture to build rapport.

Gloria looked a little deflated, but Wren had known the coven probably wouldn't go for it. Gloria moved on to the other proposal. 'Settle down everyone. Never mind.'

Wren tried to send admiration to Gloria with her eyes.

'I have another proposal for Imbolc – and Athena has nothing to do with it.'

Now that she wasn't imposing Athena on them, everyone was willing to listen. This felt good, and more like how they used to be.

'When we first created intense rituals like the Beltane massages, it brought up issues, but now we're better at it.'

'That's for sure,' said Lupe.

'We invented the Beltane ritual when we were in the *maiden* phase of life. Now we are entering the Saturn Return. We need to focus on *shadow work*.'

'What is Saturn reborn?' asked Robin.

'*Saturn return*. Yours was five years ago, Robin,' said Gloria. 'Wren and Ginny, who are the youngest, will go through it in a few years. I'm in mine now.'

'I studied astrology and all that almanac stuff,' Hazel offered, 'because I thought it would help in the garden. When I learned the Saturn return was the culmination of four seven-year periods, I wondered if it was related to the tradition of leaving land fallow every seven years.'

'Our lives seem to have seven-year cycles,' Robin mused.

'Maybe Gloria is proposing she lie fallow for a year,' Kelsey said, but only Wren heard.

'It takes Saturn twenty-eight years to go around the sun,' Gloria instructed them. 'So when you are twenty-eight, the planet has *returned* to the same place in the sky.'

'But you need an astrologer to tell you exactly when,' Wren said. 'Is that right, Gloria?'

'True. But you don't need an astrologer to prepare for your Saturn return. You need to get rid of anything from your childhood that you don't need as an adult.'

'Did you do it, Glow? Since you're in Saturn Return?' Kelsey asked.

'I left my old life behind when I moved to Ove.'

'We moved here too,' Kelsey said. 'But weren't in our Saturn Returns.'

'By the time I'm fifteen,' said Robin, 'I have remembered who I am, but in a Saturn Return, I need to figure how that unique childhood fits the rest of me.'

'That's how it would be for you,' Gloria said, 'but let's not get off track.'

Robin looked thoughtful, probably counting her memories by sevens.

'So that's what the *Saturn Return* is,' continued Gloria. 'Next, *Shadow Work* is bringing out our unconscious fears and unpleasant parts of ourselves. This is our internalised Patriarchy. It is impossible to name those things, because that's Younger Self stuff, and she doesn't have words. I propose we do a ritual that will help us uncover our shadows and get rid of them.'

'So, what's the ritual?' asked Kelsey. 'Does it let you see ghosts and get rid of them?'

'I don't want to tell you ahead of time.'

'We *always* know what the ritual is,' said Nikki.

'It will be better if you don't.'

'It would be better if we do,' Hazel countered.

'It's like an initiation. It's about trust.'

'We're not initiated and we trust each other,' said Ginny.

'Of course we trust each other. And you can trust me,' said Gloria. 'Just think of all the things that are wrong in Patriarchy, like "ecological destruction" and "war in Central America" and "women make less money than men".'

'I'm new at this,' Robin said. 'But Gloria comes up with a lot of good ideas. Like, I'm glad you came to the stone circle at Samhain, even if Gloria regrets it.'

There was some grumbling, and they decided to assign High Priestess for the other holidays at another Magic Moot. Gloria would lead Imbolc, the first ritual of the year. It was true she was excellent at ritual magic, and arguing with her was too hard.

Seven

Gloria didn't tell Wren what the ritual would be either, but the promise of ridding herself of unconscious internalised Patriarchy seemed a healthy way to start the magical year.

The witches cleared the centre of the living room and filled it with pillows and futons. Gloria and Wren covered an altar in the northeast corner with pine boughs. No goddesses. They lit black and brown candles and sprinkled incense on hot coals.

The coven filed in. Gloria blessed each woman with well water and anointed her with amber oil. They raised and grounded a cone of power. They didn't know any songs for this ritual, and Gloria didn't teach them new ones.

'We will now perform the spell together,' Gloria said. 'It's quite simple. We will state facts of our lives without comment. We will name the harms of Patriarchy for us personally, for us locally, and for us as women on Earth. We will name it like this: "men are destroying the planet" and when a woman says that thing – and keep it short – we all respond "Yes, it is so".'

'That's it?' The ritual did not impress Lupe.

Nor Hazel. 'Where's the magic in that?'

'You'll see. Just name bad things, and we will all acknowledge them.'

'How long does this go on?' asked Nikki. She looked uncharacteristically uneasy.

'Until we've said it all.'

Ginny raised her hand. 'Can't we say what is good, too?'

'No, Ginny. If you do that, the spell won't work. Just say things that are true, in the present tense.'

'And what do you think will happen?' asked Robin.

'We should just do it.'

Robin looked over at Kelsey, who asked sharply, 'Did you research this? Do you know what you're doing?'

Wren moved around the back of the circle and stood next to Kelsey. 'It will be fine,' she whispered.

'I know what I'm doing,' Gloria said adamantly. 'You have to trust me.'

No one said anything else, so the coven stood in a circle, and Gloria started the spell by saying, 'Our Mother Earth is dying,' and everyone together chanted, 'Yes, it is so.'

Robin said, 'Men hate women.'

Yes, it is so.

'Oil pollutes the earth,' said Hazel.

Yes, it is so.

The coven named everything wrong with politics, the environment, poverty, racism, war and…and…and…by stating the truths that women knew already, the reality and immediacy of the personal, political and detailed harms of Patriarchy rose around them like a mist, and then a choking poison. They stated every proof that the world was not what it should be.

The declarations of what was fucked-up grew more personal.

Robin said, 'The neighbours hate us.'

Yes, it is so.

Lupe said, 'Someone called my dad a wetback.'

Which inspired Ginny to remember, 'Someone called my mother a whore.'

The word shocked Wren, coming out of Ginny's mouth, but it must have been true.

Yes, it is so.

Hazel continued the theme and said, 'They sent my family to a camp and stole their farm.'

Yes, it is so. Yes, it is so. Yes, it is so.

It was horrible. Soon, the witches could no longer stand; Ginny and Robin fell to their knees, and the rest dropped to console them, their own sorrow flooding their faces.

Yes, it is so. Yes, it is so. Yes, it is so.

Despite the acute emotional pain, the rhythm of the ritual responses beat away everyday denial. Their declarations flooded out. 'They raped my grandmother.' *Yes, it is so.* 'They kept me away and Lucy died alone.' *Yes, it is so.* 'We couldn't afford the hospital.' *Yes, it is so.* 'He raped me.' *Yes, it is so.* 'She gave him my own money.' *Yes, it is so.* 'She told me not to say anything.' *Yes, it is so.*

On and on the witches continued the terrible call and response: one horrible, hurtful thing declared in detail, followed by the anodyne acknowledgement of its truth. The witches collapsed in a pile of tears and sorrow. They emptied themselves of every sad thing they could think of, and not once allowed themselves to mitigate the facts. Abuse at every scale, as intimate as the skin of their fingertips, as vast as the air they breathed; in and out, in and out, in sobs and cries.

Finally, no one could say anything else. They wiped each other's faces and blew their noses.

'Well, shit. Now what do we do?' Lupe looked around and found Gloria. 'You look pretty blown out.'

'I…I don't know.' Gloria looked disassociated.

Wren felt the intense magic of the undefined ritual destroying them. Gloria had lost control because she had no clear intention. She should have known better. Wren reached for her favourite prayer. 'We need to say *The Charge of the Goddess*,' said Wren. 'We need to picture her.'

The women stood up, hands lightly on each other's waists, and put their heads together in a circle. They felt their circle come together, as if assembling a dynamo, and heard it humming.

Many pagan traditions recite *The Charge of the Goddess*. The Ovem wrote their own version to suit themselves. First they recited the names of their goddesses:

Demeter, Persephone, Hecate, Isis.

Deborah, Innana, Al-Lat.

Artemis, Melusine, Cerridwen, Aphrodite.

Bridget, Arianrhod, Anna Marie.

Then they recited, not their creed or commandments, but Her Promise.

Keep my days holy; observe my nights. Convene in secret, and there I affirm my promise: thou art free.

All joy is my presence embodied. You may sing, you may eat, you may love. I abide with thee in these my rites, forever and for always.

I crave no burnt offering. I never demand blood. I am your Mother, my children drink from my ever-filling cup. Fear not the illusion of death; you need only listen to my voice at the end.

Hear me, hear me, hear me:

I counted you my own in the womb of your grandmother. Ever I am with thee. Thou art me.

The familiar images and comforting promise of the goddess restored them, and they looked around at reddened faces with relief.

'I need more hugs,' said Ginny, and Nikki pulled her close.

Kelsey got up and Wren followed. When they came back with a teapot and a tray of mugs, the Big Fight had begun.

'I want an answer. *What the fuck* was that?' Lupe had risen to her knees and was pointing a finger at Gloria.

Wren froze.

'I already said. It was a grief ritual to get in touch with our pain and uncover patriarchal fears that control us.'

Lupe sat back down and asked as calmly as she could, 'What is wrong with you?'

Gloria tried to explain. 'What we're feeling right now is the Patriarchy we hate in ourselves. We can't escape it. Athena helps me accept—'

'For fuck's sake, Gloria!' Kelsey said as she and Wren sat down at the edge of the circle, the baskets of the feast on their laps.

'My goddess helps me find my meaning,' Gloria said coolly. 'What meaning did you find?'

'What I found is anger,' said Hazel. Unlike everyone else, her eyes were dry.

'Exactly,' Gloria said, as if that was a good thing. 'That's Patriarchy for you.'

'Bullshit!' Nikki yelled. 'This isn't Patriarchy. It's poor planning.'

'I've been a witch for six years; longer than anyone here.'

Nikki threw up her hands. 'Are you pulling rank right now? Look what you did!'

'But it worked, didn't it? Everyone is getting angry. That's what should happen. Ask yourself, what are you angry at?'

Wren started to pass around the tea mugs, but Kelsey stopped her with a gentle gesture and said, 'I'll tell you what I'm angry at. I'm angry at you for manipulating us into a giant puddle of grief and sadness with a power trip.'

'But it's not about me. What's really making you angry?'

'How dare you,' Kelsey growled.

Wren put a hand on her shoulder.

Nikki tried again. 'We needed preparation, and an ending.'

Gloria sat up with her hands on her thighs in her teacher mode. 'Think about that ritual last summer. We all failed.' Her soft voice belied the lash of her words. 'Lupe smokes as much as she ever did. Hazel pretends she's not Japanese. It's a miracle that Nikki is with the same woman she met six weeks ago; Ginny, you're still the same bliss-ninny you always were.'

Ginny looked stricken for a second before she buried her face in Nikki's chest.

Wren's thoughts were racing. *Is this the ritual? Is she still priestessing?*

Gloria was goading each of them with what they hated most about themselves.

'Are you fucking kidding me?' said Nikki, no longer trying.

Wren's heart stopped. *Is this intentional? Why didn't she tell me?*

Gloria wouldn't stop. 'Look at you, Nikki, with all your little girlfriends. Where's the sacred in that?'

'I don't care if you call me a slut. I call myself that every day. Fuck you.' Nikki held Ginny tighter and her lips grew thinner.

Gloria turned on Ginny. 'Why don't you *grow up*? Do you wonder why you never found a girlfriend? Because women want *women*, and you're so childish.'

To Kelsey: 'Maybe if you ate less of your own cooking, you'd feel better about yourself and not take it out on us. And get some exercise. Laying in bed until ten every day can't be healthy.' She had straight up called her a fat bitch.

'Don't.' Lupe said.

But Gloria did. 'Lupe, you try to be all cool, but your jokes are lame, and you're always so fucking negative. The world isn't perfect; we're not perfect. Boo fucking hoo. We don't need your constant sarcastic commentary.

'And Hazel. I just want to slap you sometimes. Yes, your parents are second-generation and tried to assimilate. Get over it. All our parents have internalised racism.'

She turned on Robin, and the root cause of this tantrum. 'Robin, you have no *superpower*. You're not *immortal*. You just need an excuse to explain why you're rich.'

Robin barked a laugh.

Wren sat stunned, trying to work out Gloria's ritual intent. She didn't see that she was next, as Gloria said something only Gloria could.

'You abandoned your mother and you'll abandon me. You'd rather smoke pot with Robin and put patches on your handmade clothes than help me with my class. You aren't committed to Athenic wicca, and I wish I had never initiated you.'

Wren's eyes filled; she swallowed a gasp and choked. After months of devotion, Gloria wasn't satisfied? The walls tilted and tore. She clung to herself and searched for a compassionate connection to Gloria, her lover, her friend.

'Gloria, what are you saying? Is this like what happened last year when you dropped out of the astral? Are you disappointed?'

Wren should have known it was a mistake to remind Gloria of that failure.

'I'm not *disappointed*, Wren. I'm telling the truth for once.'

Even Robin lost her patience. 'This is so heartless,' she said. 'Why have you done this?'

Gloria didn't answer. She was finished.

Everyone felt a thick black tar welling up in a flood, filling their insides with an odious truth. They felt like monsters. Monsters made of shit.

Nikki announced she was going to the barn. The others retreated to the places at Ove they felt safest. They left the front room a mess, dishes in the sink, the circle broken.

Eight

Wren hid out in the octagon. She lit a fire. Held on to her pen without sketching. Heard only Gloria's voice: *Abandoned. Abandoned. Wish I had never, never, never.*

At the centre of Gloria's rant was a core of truth, and it hurt. Whatever this *shadow thing* was, Wren had to get rid of it before someone used it against her again. Gloria was right. Wren *had* cruelly abandoned her mother at a vulnerable time. For the first time since burning the portrait, Wren wanted to call her mom and apologise.

But yearnings like that touched a bottomless reservoir of fear. Something lived down there. She didn't want to be alone with it. She wanted to be with her coven. She wanted her tummy full of Kelsey's granola bars and Lupe's cider, laughing at the feast, and making love with Gloria afterward.

Instead of this Gloria-inflicted mind-fuck. Gloria had brought Patriarchy into their sacred living room and poisoned them. This was much worse than Robin bringing the tractor onto the land.

Only *The Charge of the Goddess* got them out of that shit-pit. The Ovem needed those symbols, that promise. Remembering *The Charge* succeeded like the magical statue Wren never made.

At two in the morning, her exhausted eyes crossed, and she knew she had to sleep. She couldn't sleep in the loft, which Gloria had filled with file boxes. She decided to check on Gloria and then sleep in her old room.

But Gloria had left the nightlight on, like an invitation. So Wren stripped off and crawled under the quilt. Before she knew what was happening, Gloria was sobbing into Wren's chest. She was sorry. She had said terrible things.

Wren could only say, 'You didn't mean them.'

'I knew shadow work was intense, but afterwards, all this dark stuff came out of my mouth. Maybe I'm not ready.'

'Maybe none of us are, honey.' As Wren tried to compose the polite words for 'Maybe your shadow makes you do stupid shit', Gloria got up and poured a glass of water from the crock.

Wren sat up and glimpsed Athena on Gloria's altar behind her. Athena gave her courage. She would risk it. 'Did you mean it? Will I abandon you?'

Gloria dissolved into a torrent of apologies again. 'Darling, no! I'm so sorry.' Her obvious sincerity made Wren forget her fears and focus on Gloria's regret. Then they both cried until the sadness of that horrible ritual came to the surface like a spasm, but then subsided.

Wren felt safe to ask again. 'You don't regret initiating me?'

'Not for a minute.'

'Because I was wondering – if you did regret it – maybe I could use the octagon for something else…'

Gloria pulled away, panicked. 'But I need it. Don't take it away from me. Please!'

'Okay, okay,' Wren soothed. 'I just wondered…'

'You're an Athenic initiate, forever. My first! – and you have your studio! You already have a studio for your stinky paints and stuff. I don't have my own space. I need a Sphere, just like you.'

Wren felt reassured and disappointed, a familiar combination in life with Gloria. 'Don't worry. I *want* you to have an Athenic temple. You know I'm committed to Athenic wicca. I just wondered.'

Gloria relaxed. She switched off the light. 'Turn around. Let me hold you.'

Wren pressed her head into Gloria's arm and remembered Gloria was in her Saturn Return. She was going through a lot right now, getting rid of what she didn't need for the next phase of life. Wren knew somewhere in her own art she would find how to help Gloria and the Ovem stay together as they got older. Shadow work clearly was the wrong direction. After tonight, she couldn't be complacent. Robin was right. They needed her art to help Gloria avoid mistakes like this. She pressed her backside into Gloria's warm body and fell asleep.

The next morning, her orgasm ended any reason to move to the octagon.

⚭

Wren may have felt better, but even *Breakfast in Bed* – the Sunday morning women's music program on KZSC – couldn't cheer the Ovem as they sullenly cleaned up, and then separated to do chores. They had to Juggle the Spheres like they did every Sunday afternoon, and all day they dreaded it. Robin asked Kelsey to make enchiladas and fresh tortilla chips, a meal which always comforted them. Then she drove an hour down to Watsonville to get the good peppers.

First, they had to get through the meeting. Gloria volunteered to facilitate, and Wren would take notes. The women gathered at the kitchen table, dirty from chores, and still sore inside from yesterday's fight.

Gloria shocked them all. 'Sisters, I apologise. I'm sorry for what happened yesterday.'

Everyone looked up from their mugs of tea.

Gloria continued. 'Magic is powerful. Sometimes when we go out there beyond what we know, we encounter forces we're not ready for. I thought I knew what I was doing, and we all paid a price.'

'We're still paying it,' said Lupe. 'I feel pretty *kah-pow*.' She made a gesture like explosions with her fingers.

'Me too,' said Hazel. 'But we learned something.'

'A reminder we're not perfect?' Lupe attempted.

Hazel wasn't ready for humour. 'You should have asked someone to help you, Gloria.'

'I know that now. I thought a journey to the unknown would be powerful.'

Kelsey shook her head. 'You have to set an intention.'

No one else wanted to comment on, or accept, Gloria's apology, so she moved the meeting along. 'Do you want to go first, Ginny?'

Wren wrote 'Ginny' on a fresh page in the notebook.

Ginny started tentatively, but her voice found confidence as she described her beloved goat herd. 'The ram and wethers are more sensitive to cold than the females, and produce more cashmere.'

'Is that a usual thing?' Gloria asked.

'I don't know. But I'll keep more of the wethers after they're born.'

'The males?' Gloria said significantly.

'The castrated males,' clarified Robin.

Everyone laughed for the first time that day.

'It's weird, but I do love them and their wool.' Ginny pulled a handful of fluff from her pocket. 'Check out how soft it is,' she said, and they passed it around the table.

Wren wrote the word 'cashmere' and drew a ball of yarn with goat's eyes.

'I'm bummed we don't have our own goat dairy,' said Kelsey. 'But there's plenty of cheese at Community Foods.'

'That should be a bumper sticker,' Lupe quipped.

'You always say that,' Gloria said, without humour. 'Anything else?'

Ginny shook her head.

Lupe opened her pocket notebook. 'I'm harvesting shiitake next week—'

Everyone cheered and Wren wrote 'Lupe shrooms'. The meeting was returning to normal. Gloria had apologised.

'After harvest, we'll have more mushroom compost for the garden.'

'That reminds me, I'm making goat-poop compost,' Ginny said.

'And to add to this mountain of rot,' Kelsey said, 'I figured out a better system for separating kitchen compost from chicken food.'

Wren wrote 'mushroom poop', and 'kitchen poop'.

'We'll need all of it,' said Hazel.

Lupe continued down her list. 'Letty told me about a fermented tea I want to try. She's going to give me a *scoby*. It's like sourdough starter.'

'You first.' Hazel commented dubiously. She turned to her notebook. 'We're done with winter vegetables. The seeds are here, so I will start sprouts in the greenhouse.'

Wren wrote 'Hazel'.

'We need to put more sunny land under cultivation. The biggest is the plaza, but it's a polluted parking lot. That chaparral hill on either side of the garden road gets good sun. I think we should cut terraces into it.'

Wren drew a sun with rays streaming on a row of women emerging from the soil.

'That sounds good, Haze,' Gloria said, with a careful warmth in her voice. Actually supportive.

'As you can imagine, cutting terraces will be hard to do with hand tools.' Hazel looked over at Nikki.

'I told you I can rent a bobcat, but it requires a trained operator.'

'If you're talking about a tractor again,' Hazel surmised, 'I'm still against it.'

'What about the mule?' asked Ginny.

'What mule?' everyone asked, all at once.

'After we sold Penny, Robin promised to buy us a mule.' Ginny looked at Robin. 'You did.'

Surprisingly, Robin agreed. 'Sort of. Wren, will you write down that Ginny and I will research getting a mule?'

Gloria couldn't help herself. 'But no one knows how to use a mule either.'

'I do,' Robin answered.

'How convenient,' said Gloria. She was really trying to be nice.

Wren wrote 'Robin Ginny mule'.

Hazel returned to her list. 'Ginny and I propose we learn

how to keep bees. It will improve yields and give us wax and honey.'

'I know a guy who keeps bees,' said Nikki. 'He's the guy loaning me a small saw mill so we can make our own lumber.'

'You always know a guy,' Gloria accused. 'Can he teach us without coming here? It's hard to get the training we need with our no-men rule.'

Lupe said she wanted to learn the saw mill and bees.

Wren wanted to join them. 'I'm not working on anything big right now.' She added a swarm of bees above the seedling women.

Gloria said softly, 'I thought you were helping me with the Athenic chakra project.'

'I am,' Wren said, writing *Robin* at the top of a fresh page. 'My art needs me to work in the garden too.'

Gloria glanced around the table. 'Thank you, Hazel. Is everyone looking forward to fresh tortillas tonight?' She didn't look at Robin, but Robin spoke anyway.

'I'd like to say something about my Sphere. Last night's ritual was a disaster—'

'This is Juggling the Spheres, not a Magic Moot,' said Gloria. 'I've apologised. Can't we put it behind us?'

'This is my Sphere,' insisted Robin. 'We need to talk.' Everyone knew what she meant. The enchiladas smelt delicious, but the meeting wasn't over.

'I was thinking about that moment when Wren reminded us of *Charge of the Goddess*. That is one of the most powerful prayers that your – our – tradition has.'

'It's not just ours, all pagans have some form of it,' said Gloria.

'I like your form of it. "Thou art me," she says. I think you know by now that I don't believe in the goddess as a female deity. To me, the goddess is us. You and me.'

Robin stood up, walked over to the stove, and leaned against it, like a dyke professor. 'We recite *The Charge of the Goddess* in her voice. That means we are *already* divine. Take a moment and feel her inside yourselves.'

'You think I'm a goddess,' said Wren. 'But I'm a work in progress.' She tried to say it like a joke, but it sounded apologetic. The other women muttered their agreement.

Robin said, 'That kind of talk is propaganda,' and sounded kind of mean about it. She shook her head as if to clear it and started again. 'I met those goddesses you name in that prayer. I prayed in their temples, attended by brown-skinned, blue-eyed acolytes wearing an acorn on a string. The temples are gone, but their truth remains. Know thyself, because you are already divine, perfect and whole.' As she said those three words, she ticked them off on calloused fingers. 'Each of us is born unique and treasured. Like we remember during our birthday back rubs.'

Robin turned and faced Gloria, who sat frozen, enduring her lecture. 'Gloria, forgive me, but you don't understand what the shadow is. She's not a broken thing we should get rid of. She is born from hurt – yes – but protects us from being hurt again. She hides beyond language because Patriarchy would find her and subvert her. When we are threatened, she stands behind us, whispering her wisdom. Patriarchy tells us we must hate her, but doesn't give her a name because doing so would reveal the secret of her power.'

Gloria snorted, opened her notebook and wrote something in it.

'Does that make sense to you, Gloria?'

Gloria looked up. 'That's what the ritual was about.'

Wren knew that was a straight-up lie.

'*Now* you tell us—' Kelsey began.

Robin gave Kelsey a look that interrupted the tirade, and continued, 'Last summer I wasn't sure about that burning-things-up ritual. I thought I didn't understand it. I was curious to see what happened. Looking back on it, you didn't get rid of your *shadows*, you named them. There is power in naming.'

'We all know that,' said Gloria, like a reprimand.

'Do we? Gloria, there is *no Patriarchy* inside us. We come with our perfect selves and our raw open hearts. The memories of hurts are not *damage* or *baggage* or *issues*. We each have a shadow, a true giant as a friend, but better than a tractor.'

Lupe and Ginny grinned at each other.

'This is an ancient teaching, and cultures teach it differently. The shadow is an evil twin, your demon lover, an unnatural monster. It is the Strength card of the tarot. The name of that card is not "taming the lion". It is about putting your tender, precious hand in her mouth, trusting she is actually your friend. Be brave, befriend the monster inside and meet your strength.'

Wren sent her attention inward, looking for a monster who might protect her. She sensed only a filthy residue of fear left by her mother's rages and manipulations.

'Gloria, you weren't wrong to do your ritual, but you didn't understand what would happen.'

'I know that. Don't make me apologise again. Anyway, *The Charge of the Goddess* was there for us, thanks to Wren. I'm *sorry*, Robin.' Gloria gathered herself, closing her notebook. 'Thank you for explaining it.' She stopped speaking and everyone waited. 'Will you forgive me for not being as perfect as Robin thinks we are?'

Everyone reassured her they knew she didn't mean the ritual to go that way. They just wanted this conversation to be over.

Everyone but Robin. Robin jerked herself off the stove.

Kelsey gently pushed her out of the way and opened the oven door. 'Are we done? I'm hungry.'

Gloria stepped out from the bench and approached Robin, while the women buzzed around preparing for dinner. Wren stood near Gloria.

'Robin, I am grateful to you for explaining my intention. You knew the least, but understood it the most.' She put her arm around Robin's shoulders. 'Look everybody,' Gloria said over the clatter. 'She's learning to be a real witch, isn't she?'

Robin tried to take the attention off herself and joined Ginny in setting the table. 'What's important is that while we're learning, we're alone together.'

'We know,' Gloria said, as if she were humouring her. She repeated Robin's only rule in a sing-song mockery, 'No men on the land.'

Wren wished she would stop, but Gloria continued, pretending she was teasing. 'You'd rather *die* than let a *man* on the *land*.' Now Gloria was picking a fight, and everyone tried very hard to ignore her.

But Robin couldn't. 'That's not what I'm saying, Gloria. It's about women alone together.'

'Without men. I know. What's the difference?'

'There's *no language* for how we live,' said Robin emphatically. 'No word for women alone together.'

'I don't get it,' said Gloria, turning to Wren. She really didn't.

'This coming year,' Robin said, attempting to wrap up the discussion, 'I don't expect to contribute much to…being a priestess. The real magic is women working side by side, alone together. I know it's hard to do things without men's help. I know there are good men who could help us. Lupe, Hazel, Nikki – you work with men on your projects off the land, and so do I. I'm not against working with men out there. But I promise you, if we work here alone together, we'll invent something.'

'I don't need to be lectured,' Gloria said. 'Separatism was necessary, but it's not needed.'

'It is the only way.'

'Is that a rule you have?'

'I guess it is.'

'But isn't it a feminist thing to break the rules?'

'Sometimes.'

Kelsey poured oil into her biggest pan. Everyone washed their hands and started patting masa dough into tortillas. Everyone wished Gloria and Robin would shut up.

'Men can do things that women can't,' Gloria said. 'Like when we need a "man's hand",' like the song goes.'

'I always sing "need a friend's hand",' said Robin.

'But that changes the song,' said Gloria.

'We must change the songs,' said Robin.

Wren desperately wanted Gloria and Robin to stop bickering. She rummaged through the tape box for the cassette of *Breakfast in Bed*. She turned up the stereo. She knew words couldn't save them, but she had to do something. Singing those songs felt good, and they didn't need to change the words.

Nine

Heavy rainstorms arrived with February, as is common on the redwood coast. The creek under their bridge roared and shouldered her way to the sea. By mid-month, the forest had shaken off the sleep of winter and chased every ray of sun. Wren liked to stay next to Gloria's warm body. But on this morning, when she heard Robin's engine turn over out front, she left their bed and met Ginny in the plaza.

'I got a mule, her name is Sal,' sang Ginny, and embraced Wren in a long hug. She was wearing her horns again. Robin was already behind the wheel.

'I'm so happy for you.'

Wren waved at Robin, who was staring into her coffee. 'Drive safe!'

Ginny lifted Pepper on to the seat and pulled herself in after. Wren reached in and held Ginny's hand.

'When are you getting back?'

'Tonight. It's three hours to Paso Robles.'

Wren kept waving until she saw their tail lights disappear. Nikki came out of the barn. 'They're off to get the mule?'

'Ginny looked like a bride.'

'I've never met a mule.'

'Robin says she has, in a past life.'

'Then I suppose she has. Let's make coffee.' Nikki turned and walked toward the house. 'What are you doing today?'

'I'm doing Ginny's chores.'

'Would you be my apprentice carpenter and help me with the stable?' Nikki stopped under the porch light and pulled out her notebook. 'Take a look.'

Wren turned the pages and admired Nikki's careful sketches of a lean-to stable attached to the shroom shed. Front and side elevations, dimensions and a materials list in Nikki's square printing.

'I would love to.'

They brewed coffee and started a pot of oatmeal. Wren got out honey, dried fruit and yogurt. Nikki made more notes in her book.

Wren realised how little time she and Nikki spent alone together these days. 'Can I talk to you about something? It's intimate, but I need help.'

'Sure.' Nikki meticulously layered fruit at the bottom of her bowl. 'You know how much I love intimacy.'

'Gloria used to bring us tea every morning, and then we'd make love, but she doesn't any more.' Wren stirred her oatmeal.

'Hard to keep that up.'

'True, but when I invite her to…make love, she never wants to any more.'

'We've all noticed you aren't as happy with Gloria.'

Wren hadn't noticed anyone noticing.

'But I'm not the expert in long-term things,' added Nikki.

'You're not with Bahdrina any more?'

'Probably not. And she went back to April.'

'She went…back in time?'

'She changed her *name* back to April after we broke up.'

Wren didn't laugh until Nikki did.

Nikki added tiny squares of butter on top of the fruit and sprinkled in brown sugar like grout between them. 'So you and Gloria are just housemates again?'

'Not just housemates.'

'What's the difference?'

'We sleep together.'

'Without having sex. Like friends. Like you and Robin used to.'

'We're friends, but you and I don't sleep together.'

'But would you? What if I needed you and asked?'

'Of course.'

Nikki sighed. 'Again, not my area. Is the oatmeal ready?'

Wren poured oatmeal over Nikki's concoction. If she spent the day with Nikki, she might ask her about what the Ovem noticed. But she couldn't. 'I said I would build the stable with you, but I forgot Gloria needs me to distribute flyers.'

'Wouldn't you rather wield power tools?' Nikki bounced her eyebrows.

Wren returned a weak smile. She stirred a lot of butter into her oatmeal.

'Are you doing art for Gloria instead of having sex?'

Before she could deny it, Gloria appeared through the back door. Wren jumped up and reached for her. 'Happy Valentine's Day.'

'You know I don't recognise Patriarchal holidays,' Gloria said sharply. She turned away and poured the last of the coffee.

Wren sat back down. 'Somebody's grumpy.' She chuckled, but no one joined her.

Nikki was shovelling in her breakfast. 'I'm driving the lumber up to the garden. Want a ride?'

'Sure.' And for Gloria's benefit, Wren added, 'I need to do the chickens and goats while Ginny is away getting the mule.'

Gloria only stared at the blue flames.

Wren grabbed the chicken scraps, leaving her oatmeal behind.

∞

Wren wasn't sure if she had Nikki's sympathy or judgement. She held the bowl of scraps steady on her lap and stared out of the passenger window at those tiny white flowers greeting the slanting sun. She wished she knew their names.

When they got to the garden, Wren thanked Nikki for the lift. She gave the chickens their breakfast and listened to them gossip about the good bits. Their conversation comforted her, and she tried to speak to them in their own language, like she knew Ginny would. She heard a woodpecker ak-ak-ak across the sky, and another answered it from inside the forest.

'Good morning, Wren.'

Wren turned and saw Gloria jogging up the road, carrying a thermos and greasy brown bag.

'I'm sorry.' Gloria held the bag out to Wren. 'Granola bar?'

Wren bit into the buttery crunch, suddenly hungry.

'I woke up on the wrong side of the bed. Happy Valentine's Day.'

'But it's Patriarchal!'

'I love you. Be mine.' She opened her arms. Gloria smelled like amber. 'Can I help you with Ginny's chores?'

Wren's spirits lifted. 'I'm done here. Let's take the goats to the pasture.'

Gloria followed Wren to the goat shed.

'Why can't they stay in the pasture all the time?'

'Ginny says the mountain lions would get them.' Wren's breath came out in clouds, but she could feel the delicate warmth of the weak sun. 'What a beautiful morning, Gloria. I need to get outside more. I'm off-balance – Hup! Hup!' Wren opened the goat pens and shook a pail of kibble, luring them toward the road.

'Why leave that one behind?'

Wren didn't tease Gloria about her cluelessness. 'That's Artemis. He only gets to be with them during Yule.'

'Because it's a holiday?'

'That's when they are in season.'

Gloria nodded and lost interest. She walked at the rear of the flock and chivvied them toward the pasture. 'You think I get mad when you do your own things, but I don't.'

'You might feel abandoned when I work in other spheres?'

'Of course not – hey!' Gloria tugged Amalthea away from a clump of berries. 'I just hope you aren't regretting your initiation into Athenic wicca. I need you. For *our* projects.'

'Sometimes it seems your projects are *our projects*; but everything else are *my projects*. Are my projects *our projects* too?'

'I'm with you right now! How can you ask that?'

Wren felt mortified. 'I'm so sorry. What are you doing today?'

'I told you. The flyers are done and I need to take them to

the bus stops.'

'I can help with that.'

'See? We are working on *our things*.'

Wren closed the gate after the last goat. As she did so, something caught her eye on the other side of the meadow. 'Is that a person?'

A man held down the barbed wire and two women stepped over it, followed by another man.

'Shit – men on the land! Are they Robin's uncles?'

'Let's go talk to them.' Gloria stepped toward the group, trying to look friendly.

Wren was seething.

'Hi. This is private property.' She knew she sounded like a redneck.

The taller man said, 'Sorry to intrude. We were foraging mushrooms and got lost.'

'Pretty early in the morning to get lost.' *Not the uncles.*

A woman with two blonde braids held open her basket. 'You have to wake up early to find these.' The basket was full of yellow chanterelles. *From Lupe's spot?*

'Does this road go back to Empire Grade?' Taller Man asked.

'You have to go back the way you came.'

'We saw a road on the map that goes through here,' said Shorter Man.

'It's a private road now.' Wren kept her voice steady.

Gloria spoke for the first time. 'Can't we let them through?'

The four people looked bedraggled and cold. It would be an act of kindness to let them walk through.

Wren imagined Nikki by herself at the shed. Lupe and Hazel might be working by now, too. She didn't want these strangers to surprise them. 'Sorry. No. This is private.'

Gloria turned to Wren and said conversationally, 'I've been saying men on the land is inevitable, and this is a perfect example of it.'

'Gloria, please don't.' Gloria wanted to argue in front of these people.

'You can't keep men out any more than you can keep out a mountain lion,' she said. 'It's their world too. We should prepare for it. They're part of life.' She turned to the mushroom hunters. 'I don't mind if you come through here – but I'm not in charge.'

Wren took a step toward the strangers. She held out her arms as if herding them back into the forest. 'I'm sorry. She doesn't speak for all of us, and this is our rule.'

Behind her, Wren heard Gloria walking away. Leaving her alone with these people.

Wren tried to sound helpful, but her voice shook a little. 'If you go up the hill behind you, you'll find the road again.'

The two men looked at each other as if they knew that.

'The other girl said we could,' said Taller Man.

Wren noticed the mushroom knife in his belt. She let her fear make her voice sound angry. 'It's private. Your detour isn't far.'

'Come on,' said Braids, and she held the barbed wire down as the other woman re-entered the woods. 'Come *on*, Mark.'

Mark did what she asked, and after a pause, Taller did too. Wren stayed at the edge of the pasture until she couldn't hear them crashing through the forest any more. She would paint a huge 'No Trespassing' sign and they would cover it in magical wards. She knew picture-magic couldn't stop Gloria from letting men in next time.

Wren walked back to the garden. Gloria wasn't there, but she heard Nikki's saw on the other side of the greenhouse.

Nikki switched off the saw and removed her goggles. 'Are you coming to help me?'

She wanted to stay, but she had promised Gloria. 'Gloria needs me. Something just happened, and I need to make sure she's okay.'

'I know. She's pissed you said no to men.'

'How did you know?'

'She told me – not in so many words.'

'Maybe we should decide to let lost mushroom hunters through sometimes.'

'Maybe we should. But it should be something we decide together. Go get your tool belt, lady.'

Wren was tempted. She wanted to finish the breakfast conversation. 'Can I do it later? Gloria helped me, so now I'm helping her.'

Nikki put her goggles on. 'Sure.'

'Thanks for your advice this morning. Gloria and I had a good talk about supporting each other. Later this afternoon I'll help you.'

'I'll be here.'

Nikki set the teeth of the blade to the board and built the stable for Ginny's mule all by herself.

Ten

They didn't say it, but despite Gloria's apology and the passing of time since the disaster in February, when it came time to celebrate Spring Equinox in March, no one was ready for 'perfect love and perfect trust'.

So they decided they would create a different kind of ritual, with the intention of adding arable land to both sides of the sunny road between the plaza and garden.

Hazel presided as high priestess in new overalls and a purple bandana. The witches greeted the dawn with a song about chaparral, a biome of manzanita, madrone, buckbrush, mountain lilac and insignificant but profuse flowers on gray-green stalks. The enormous circle they cast ran from the plaza at the bottom of the hill, up through the chaparral on the west side, across the road at the garden, and down through chaparral on the east. As they pushed their way through under the scrub, they found the blackened roots of a forest that had burned away long ago. Some made nitrogen offerings.

Then they got to work. Robin explained to Ginny how to handle Sal, how to stand close to her haltered head and bark commands. But Ginny leaped onto her back instead and guided her with thighs and whispers. Robin protested, but Kelsey squeezed her arm and convinced Robin to let her be. Sal knew where to put her feet.

Wren noticed how Kelsey stopped Robin from doing something stupid. *Why can't I put my hand on Gloria's arm and tell her she's her own worst enemy?*

A dozen young women in overalls swung pickaxes and jumped on shovels, filling the air with billows of dirt incense. Robin and Hazel wrapped chains around scrubby trees, while Ginny sat on Sal's withers, encouraging the mule to pull when needed, and delicately easing back while Robin and Hazel furiously chopped out roots with hand axes. They cheered as each tough little shrub pulled free.

With this ritual, the witches intended to transform the sunny chaparral hill into a terraced garden. By mid-morning, the mule crew had already cleared the brush from the east side of the road. Lupe and her girlfriend Letty, Nikki and her construction pals Alix and Julz attacked the denuded hillside with pickaxes.

Great clods and spills of dirt fell down to the road, where Wren, Kelsey and Ronnie – Hazel's girlfriend – shovelled it into a low wagon that Sal would later haul up to the garden. There the dirt would undergo a magical process, where composts transmogrified it into soil.

Since Gloria wore a yellow sundress instead of work clothes, Hazel asked her to sing while they worked, which she did with grace, and everyone appreciated it. Gloria had a much-admired ability to improvise sacred songs for each holiday. While the witches grunted, Gloria sang of the rains that fell and the high mountains they moistened. She sang of life pressing up from the darkness, yearning for union with light, birthing tender leaves.

Wren loved listening to Gloria sing as she jumped on the shovel and tossed the clods exactly where she wanted. It felt good to sweat alongside other labouring women, breathing heavily. She missed having sex.

She looked up to see Gloria sitting in the shade of a manzanita, too big to cut down. Gloria finished singing her invocation with the line 'and the maiden returns to the meadow' and everyone paused their work, murmuring praise.

Hazel suggested she sing 'She's Been Waiting'.

Gloria agreed. 'Does anyone need water?'

She stood up and Wren admired her figure in that pretty sundress as she passed the canteen.

'You know,' Gloria cajoled, 'this is what men are good at. This kind of hard labour. We shouldn't have to do work that gives us blisters.'

Wren felt her fingers in her gloves. No blisters yet.

Kelsey tossed another shovelful into the wagon, nearly hitting Wren. Hazel noticed the near-accident. She left Ginny and Robin at one end of the hillside and approached Wren.

'It's too crowded around the wagon,' she told her, but Wren said it wasn't Kelsey's fault. 'I have another job for you. Make some of those drawings like you did when we first arrived.'

'I'm needed for real work.'

'Four women wielding shovels is too dangerous. Your part of the ritual is to record it.'

Wren pulled off her gloves and ran to her studio. When she got back, Gloria was singing the final chorus of 'Heretic

Heart'. Wren sat next to her under the manzanita. She watched one crew chopping away at the hill, while the other women methodically tore brush off the other side. She didn't open her notebook yet.

'What did Hazel tell you?' Gloria asked Wren when she had finished the song.

'She wants drawings of the ritual, like I used to do.'

'Can you include how the owl, mountain lion and snake are present?'

'But this isn't one of our Athenic rituals.'

'But she's here, she's always here. Can't you feel her?'

Wren looked around and saw women working below her, sweating and dusty, muscles shifting under brown skin. She watched them rip a mountain lilac to death – a sacrifice to agriculture. Not a hint of Athena.

'This is a project we can do together. You're drawing. Don't leave me out of it.'

Wren observed the myrmidian activity below her. Sal strained against her harness. Ginny urged her on until everyone cheered as the roots gave way.

'I'll do my best.'

'That's all I ever ask.'

Wren opened her sketchbook and drew Sal, with soft hairy lips and black eyes looking out from under her forelock like a shy teen. She drew Ginny, somehow secure on Sal's back, whispering into her ears. She drew Hazel holding one end of a string, while Nikki held the other. They pulled the string across the hillside, assessing their progress against the plan. She drew Alix in her cowboy hat, sharing a cigarette with Julz. She drew Nikki's biceps in three aspects. She caught the moment when Lupe and Letty passed the canteen, then kissed. She drew Robin's hands gathering the chains. The coven's kinetic energy sent her pen across the paper. Shoulders, calves, grim mouths, sweaty armpits, gloved fingers. She sketched fast, riding an urge to capture how they transformed chaparral to garden. She filled the page, wrote 'The Strength of Women's Land' at the bottom, and turned to a fresh one.

Gloria finished another spring song with: 'Rejoice! Rejoice! Persephone returns, and Demeter dances in bliss.'

Wren remembered the revelation about Demeter from last Halloween. Why wasn't she the symbol of terrible mothers?

Out of the blue, Gloria shouted, 'We could do this so much better if we hired men to do this hard work.'

Wren groaned.

Ginny and Robin hitched Sal to the front of the wagon and hauled it up the road to the garden. Hazel got the second wagon into position, and Lupe and Letty filled it. Nikki, Alix and Julz hacked brush from the hillside.

Gloria tried again. 'Hey everyone, did Wren tell you about the mushroom hunters we saw a few weeks ago?'

'She did,' answered Nikki. 'Wren is right. We need better barbed wire.'

Once she had Nikki's attention, Gloria returned to her real topic. 'Nikki, don't you agree we'd finish faster if we hired men to do it? With a machine or something?'

'Please stop,' Wren whispered. 'Work is fun. It's women alone together, like Robin says. Men would ruin it.'

'I hear what you're saying, Gloria, but I hate supervising men.' Nikki swung her pickaxe and loosened another cascade of dirt.

'We should be building wildflower altars instead of grunting on a hot hillside,' Gloria grumbled to Wren.

Wren stopped sketching and noticed Gloria wasn't

sweating.

'Look, I'm lesbian,' Gloria went on. 'I *love* women. But men are good at some things. Even that song says we need them when we have to move the piano.' She shouted down to Nikki: 'We don't need to be afraid of men!'

'I'm not afraid of any man,' Nikki boasted.

Julz laughed, like she remembered how true that was.

'But you need their help more than any of us. Why not hire them?'

Nikki thwacked a root and freed it. 'I didn't want to, and neither did anyone else. Except you. Not your Sphere, as you might say.'

Gloria tried to rally support. 'Hazel can't have her Farmer's Co-op friends come visit her own garden.'

Hazel wrapped chains around another shrub. 'I don't need your help to make friends, Gloria.'

Wren put her hand on Gloria's arm. 'Please stop talking about it. No one wants men on the land.'

Gloria gave her a sharp look and asserted icily, 'I don't *want* men on the land either. If you need them, that's different. Robin's no-men rule is ridiculous. It almost killed her.'

Sal and Ginny began another descent from the garden, and as they walked down, Robin forgot to hold back the wagon. It rumbled forward too fast, fouling the harness and nearly hitting Sal's legs. Sal gave it a solid kick, and Ginny could only cling to her neck. Sal kicked again. Robin – too late – grabbed the back of the wagon. Ginny settled the mule. Robin untangled the harness and apologised.

When work started up again, Gloria took Wren's hand in her own, and tried to sound concerned and loving. 'What just happened was a perfect example of how dangerous separatism is. Sal could have bucked Ginny off and killed her.'

Gloria exaggerates, thought Wren. 'All farm work is dangerous,' she couldn't stop herself from saying, knowing she'd never win. 'Nikki makes sure we take precautions now, since Lupe's explosion.'

'Doesn't anyone see how dangerous Robin's separatism is?'

'It's not Robin's separatism.'

'Then why is she so rigid about this ridiculous no-men rule?'

Wren drew a spiral, which is what she drew when she couldn't draw.

'I'm concerned Ove will fail if we do it her way. You can't separate from something that you want to change. You need to change it from the inside. That's why Athenic wicca is so revolutionary.'

'I know,' said Wren. 'You're right; it makes sense. But let's not talk about men for a while. How about another Demeter song?'

Gloria sighed. 'You're right, my dear. I should be focusing on Equinox and the joyful reunion of Demeter and Persephone, instead of this – this destruction.'

'Demeter and Persephone aren't...' Wren decided not to share her new interpretation of Demeter and Persephone's unhealthy relationship. She started a second spiral.

'But that one rule ruins everything. Nobody but me sees it. I don't even know if Robin is a feminist. Feminism is about respecting women – all women. Robin doesn't respect me.'

'She respects your priestessing. Will you sing something?' Wren knew Gloria wouldn't sing again. Hazel and Robin wrapped the chain around the last mountain lilac. They had been at this for hours. This ritual wasn't fun any more.

Hazel must have sensed it, too. 'Time for lunch!'

◯◯

The Ovem walked back to the house to wash up. Kelsey and Wren spread out cheese, tuna, lettuce and bread. Everyone made her own sandwich and poured pitchers of water and buttermilk. They carried lunch upstairs to eat together on the veranda.

Hazel asked Robin to tell a story.

Robin put down her sandwich, leaned back, and closed her eyes to remember. 'When Gloria suggested we invite men on the land to help us, she reminded me of when I first came to live in America. She's right. I've met men and women who lived together well. When Europeans arrived on this continent, I had money by then, but even wealthy women had little freedom. Then I heard about a colony founded by a woman in New England.'

'Rhode Island?' suggested Ginny. 'Armenians settled there too.'

Robin nodded. 'But I didn't stay with them for long. My friends and I met Native Americans living nearby, and we ran away to live with them. Remember that story I told about how I became a Sage?'

Gloria rolled her eyes.

'I met Indian people on this continent who reminded me of my first family. Many of us settlers ran away to live with the neighbours. Living with Indians, we gained freedom. Those notions of liberty and freedom that founded the United States came from the people already here. They governed themselves differently than the immigrants. We shared power, food, land. We had sexual freedom. But these new people kept moving inland, and we became a continent of refugees.'

'I didn't know white people moved in with Indians,' said Lupe. 'What tribe?'

'No matter who I lived with, we called ourselves "people" just like everyone else. People had always shared and traded with others, and they assumed the Europeans would be the same. When we learned how miserable they were, we tried to teach them how to be free. We could have shared these continents, but they took it all, and taught the Native American men Patriarchy.' Robin held out her cup with her melancholy expression. 'I'll have more buttermilk.'

Wren poured it for her.

'I was way out in Santa Fe when the Americans took it over. I walked to California because I heard the Spanish were only on the coast. I didn't expect another disaster.'

'You mean the Gold Rush,' said Lupe.

Robin nodded. 'Centuries of Spanish soldiers lost in the desert, searching for cities of gold, and the Yankees pick it out of the dirt with a spoon.'

'They get all the luck,' Lupe quipped, but it wasn't funny.

'I was living in a town again when I heard about women back east, inspired by their Native American neighbours, talking about freeing themselves from men.

'You mean Seneca Falls,' said Gloria.

'The early feminists – Gage, Stanton, Anthony – they all knew Indian women who led their communities. When women see other women living free, they break free too. That's why lesbians are dangerous.' Robin put her head into Kelsey's chest. 'We're free now to live like this, but we might not always be.'

'I never heard of suffragettes talking to Indians,' Gloria said snidely. 'I don't believe these *stories*.'

Wren took her pen from her overall pocket, pulled off the

cap, then clicked it closed again. She wanted to capture that tender scene of Robin and Kelsey, but couldn't.

'I don't know if I do either, Gloria,' said Kelsey, but without the same sarcasm. She rubbed Robin's back. 'But her stories help us make sense of the trauma of the unrelenting carnage that is history. If Robin needs to tell stories as if she lived them, where's the harm?'

Robin sat up. 'What's important is that women can heal from horrible things, if they understand the past, but act for the future. Look how I've changed just in the last year.'

'A story isn't a history book,' said Ginny. 'It's a striped blanket that warms up the loneliness.'

Contemplating that bit of wisdom, the coven put aside the remains of lunch and Hazel said it was time to go back to work. Nothing of note happened the rest of the afternoon, until the end of the day, when Robin and Ronnie uncovered a hibernating rubber boa.

'Don't kill it,' Hazel cried.

Robin tenderly lifted the snake, still stiff with cold. It was shorter than her arm, thin as a garden hose, the same reddish-brown as the forest floor.

The women passed the snake from hand to hand, examining her smooth coolness and curious face.

Wren took her turn holding the snake, running her fingers along its body, feeling a gentle energy under the scales. 'Remember the snakes when we moved in?'

'Those were rattlesnakes,' said Robin. 'This one is harmless.'

'Unless you're a gopher.' Hazel pantomimed a snake biting at its dinner.

Wren handed the snake to Ginny. 'Where should she live now?'

Hazel said she knew a place in the garden where the snake

could warm up.

'I think I know what this snake means,' said Gloria.

'Does it mean we have to let men on the land?' Kelsey scoffed.

'In a way. The snake is an Athenic symbol. The Medusa was an evil witch who lived on an island. Athena sent Perseus to kill her and bring back her power to the world. That is why Athena wears the Medusa's head on her chest armour. Her snake hair symbolises women's power, benefitting everyone.'

'That's not how I remember the story,' said Kelsey.

'That's because you've only read the Patriarchal version. In Athenic wicca, we have a feminist version. Finding the snake means that the world needs powerful women to heal the world, not to hide ourselves away like separatists.'

'Gloria, the snake represents our life force connecting us to the web of life waking up on Spring Equinox,' said Hazel. 'That's the ritual we're doing now.'

Gloria glared at Hazel. 'I don't want to be here.' She spun around and stalked away toward the house. Wren followed her. Nikki ran up and touched Wren's back.

'Stay here,' Nikki whispered.

'I can't abandon her.'

'Didn't she leave you with the mushroom hunters? Don't leave the ritual.' Nikki pulled the pen from Wren's overall pocket and handed it to her like a magic wand. 'Get back to work,' she told Wren, in her ritual voice.

Wren thought she was joking, but they stood within the sacred circle of their Spring Equinox observance. Wren remembered her Sphere.

The Ovem shovelled dirt and filled the wagons. Wren filled up her sketchbook like she used to. In late afternoon, two long bare slopes stood ready to be stabilised into terraces.

Sal hauled the last wagon of dirt to the garden.

'Merry meet, and merry part, and merry meet again,' the witches sang. They ended their ritual and went swimming in their pond for the first time that summer. Wren slept in her own room that night.

Eleven

Just like at Beltane the previous year, at the end of April Gloria walked Ove with her little leather bag containing the Elemental Rune Stones. Everyone chose her stone, and Wren and Gloria had the luck to be this year's Fire Women. Wren hoped Gloria would want to have sex afterwards.

The witches cleared the front room and put cushions and pillows in the middle. They built an altar of summer flowers and early strawberries in the southeast corner. This year, Robin picked Earth and so did Lupe. Lupe explained their black masks were 'for Mnemosyne'. Kelsey and Nikki wore the mermaid belts with green robes for Water; Ginny and Hazel wore blue for Air with thin grey shawls Ginny said represented summer fog. Gloria and Wren lit sage. They blessed each other's lips, hearts and vulvas with well water, and traced a pentangle on their foreheads with sweet holy oil. Then the witches raised their cone of power. By the time Lupe dropped the needle on *A Rainbow Path* – no more copied cassette – it was already hot outside, while the house remained deliciously cool.

As the music began, Wren relaxed into the delicious sensation of her coven sisters' hands on her bare skin. She imagined flickering lights along her spine. The brightest one glowed in brilliant crimson just beneath her clitoris.

The music changed the energy of the room, plugged her into the earth and focused on the Elements, urging her to open her spine – not her actual spine, but an energy thing glowing around her backbone. The Water, Earth and Air Women covered her with oil, imagining a bright ruby-red light, deep inside her pelvis.

Wren felt someone press her hand firmly along her right thigh, opening her leg and massaging the crease near her vulva with her thumb. She released a tension she didn't know she had been holding. Someone else swirled across her belly and then pressed over her vulva. Wren's clitoris leaped up, but those fingers swiftly squeezed over her left thigh instead. As the Elements stroked, they listened to her body, drawing up Wren's sexual yearning over and over, offering pleasure and then enticing her desire again. The witches were experts in the rhythm of in and out, touch and no-touch, yes and no. The witches saw reality as an unchanging oneness of delight in the illusion of separation.

During the first movement, they raised the life energy of the Fire Women and prepared everyone for travel. The Fire Women became a channel, connecting the triad of earth and sky and the life between them. In other words, the witches got the Fire Women excited. The Fire Women flooded their vaginas, reaching and yearning, then relaxing into the satisfaction of firm hands. Wren loved the sensation of her body charging up.

The sexual energy of the first movement set her on her way, travelling a road, her body the landscape. She began the ecstatic breathing with the second movement, feeling the contrast between the parched sexual life Gloria no longer shared with her, and this torrent of touch.

She searched for and found Gloria's fingers with her own. Gloria was already deep in her breath-trance. Wren brought her hands to her own breasts, oily and scented of almond. She felt her lungs filling and exhaling and she drew up life force from between her legs, swirling into her womb, and continuing up, spiralling around her spine and out of the top of her head. Breath after breath, rung by rung, she rode the rising.

The third movement was the hardest. In her imagination she squeezed out a drop of yellow light behind her belly button, yellow-gold like a poppy, and with her breath she spread it, curling around her spine, out of her head and through her feet. She never could figure out why she felt resistance here, because this chakra was about connection with others. But she concentrated on her skin, pressing back against the fingers of Water, Earth and Air, a Fire licking and lapping, pulling in their life force too, and joining it to her own. She tried to listen to three sounds at once. The Elements focused on her belly, swirling and pushing upward like pushing a brush up the canvas.

The fourth moment was easier, a relief to let the rocking rhythm beat along with her heart until it filled with big, big love, like elephants. Then it was time to take a break.

The Elements rested their hands on Wren's body. Wren heard Lupe get up and turn the record over. She drank from the chalice Kelsey held to her lips – the new one. She looked over at Gloria, drinking from the chalice Nikki held. It was good to see her vulnerable. How lucky they were both Fire Women this year.

She couldn't wait to restart the magical breath. She loved the fifth movement, which she imagined as a blue glow in her throat. She heard herself making a sound as she breathed out long, long breaths, it seemed like she would never need to inhale again, and the Water, Earth and Air sang with her, ever spiralling, pulling up from the ground, pulling down from the sky, swirling inside her body; an alchemy, forming an alloy, glowing, connecting. She felt she could sing like a bird.

The music changed. Her attention left her throat and moved to a place in her head, that place of imagination where art lives.

With the next movement, she was so high her body undulated. The Elements pulled at her limbs and tugged her hair. Each inhale seemed it would never end, each exhale, long, long, long. Her women's noises joined her to the Elements, creating spirit between them.

Near the end of the final movement, her blood full of oxygen and roaring, she heard Gloria breathing in a similar state. Her last thought, before the Bearing In: *I am divine, perfect and whole*. Who had said that? Robin. Last winter after the horrible shadow ritual. She filled her lungs and held it. *You have a giant as a friend.*

She released her breath and received a prophecy.

For a long while Wren and Gloria lay side by side, wrapped in sheets. Wren knew what she would reveal to the coven, but first she needed to consider that other, private message. She had always thought a shadow was something to get rid of, like mother damage. But what if, now that she had escaped her mother's control, a secret strength remained? Just like

Robin had said back in February.

Wren spun these thoughts through her fingers and rolled them into a ball. She knitted the thoughts into a picture: the closet door of her childhood bedroom, closed, leaking the light of an illicit candle. She would not forget and was ready to speak.

'I heard the owl,' Wren said in her ritual voice. 'The owl of our forest told me to tell our stories, share our knowledge, and become a college of wise women. Women alone, without men.'

Gloria described her revelation. 'Aphrodite-Hermes spoke to me. I saw a world without sexism, a world of power for women, and a world of loving people.'

The witches contemplated these prophecies and lay together until they got hungry. Robin and Lupe untangled themselves and went to the kitchen. When the feast arrived, Wren stayed in Kelsey and Ginny's embrace, but sat up when she saw the fruit tart.

The coven had been eating and chatting for a while when Wren thought she'd try to help Gloria. 'Let's talk about the prophecies.'

'You first.'

'Gloria, you're going to love this. It came from the grove. I heard the owl say we need to share Ove with women at the university.'

'University women are so critical of everything.'

That wasn't the reaction Wren had expected; she thought Gloria would love this. 'The entire women's community needs our women-only space,' she said, trying not to sound hurt. 'When we do the While the Days Are Still Getting Longer party, let's invite women from the university too.'

Nikki made a disgusted sound.

'I know what you mean, Nikki,' Robin said. 'I don't like them either.'

Wren poured Gloria more wine and then asked if anyone was actually against inviting women from the university.

Robin came to her side. 'Speaking as Mnemosyne, I do like some of the books they write.'

'Maybe the university women will work in the garden,' said Hazel. 'Sweaty work would do them some good.'

'As long as you tell them what to do,' said Lupe.

'I'm willing.'

Wren tapped Gloria's arm. 'Listen to the best part. I *know* university women will like Athenic wicca.'

'You don't know.'

'Think about it. These women come to Santa Cruz from far away and go to school in a redwood forest they know nothing about. They need a feminist spiritual practice that reflects their new home.'

Gloria softened. 'You might have a good idea there, Wren.' She sat up on her knees and held one hand resting in the palm of the other like a priestess. 'Let me explain my prophecy. It is a vision for everyone – even university women.' She closed her eyes and used her ritual voice. 'I saw a world without sexism. I saw a world where women were no different from men, and men were no different from women. I saw we defeated Patriarchy, and we did it by living as if we had already defeated it.'

She opened her eyes. 'The prophecy I brought back suggests that once a year we can act like men are no different from us.'

Wren wished very much that Gloria wasn't picking this fight. 'You mean inviting men to Ove for the party?'

'Yes.'

'Glow,' needled Kelsey, 'the point of women's land is that we're women.'

'A vision is not a ball of wool,' offered Ginny. Wren's mouth dropped open, but she closed it before anyone noticed. Had Ginny seen the ball of yarn in her vision? Ginny was tuned to a different wavelength most of the time.

Nobody understood what Ginny meant, but everyone wanted to stop talking about men on the land.

Gloria found a way to lose the argument and save her pride. 'I am honour-bound to pass on what Aphrodite revealed. We have the no-men rule. Don't blame me if something bad happens because we don't honour *both* prophecies.'

'No men on the land,' Hazel declared. Gloria made a face but didn't argue. Hazel continued. 'Let's focus on what we agree on. I assume we like Wren's idea of another party.'

'If we open up the land to the university women, why not our families too?' asked Gloria, with imitation innocence.

'Our families are always welcome,' said Nikki. 'Even Wren's mom.'

Wren threw her napkin at Nikki, then watched Gloria's face, now focused on some goal.

The Ovem opened the circle, and everyone left the house to do their afternoon chores. Gloria followed Lupe, Hazel and Ginny up to the garden. Wren stayed behind to clean up. As she did, she imagined a design that would signify to young women the power of women living alone together. She found all eight Beltane stones on the altar where the witches had offered them. As she slipped them into the leather bag so they would be ready for next year, she found a curious thing. The bag contained a thin leather partition. Wren realised if she wanted to put orange stones into one side, separate from the rest, she could. Like a magic trick.

Twelve

The Ovem worked hard to get ready for While the Days Are Still Getting Longer. Kelsey filled the pantry with vegetables and sauces, flours and grains, spices and sugar. Nikki and Robin built another composting privy. Lupe thinned the apples and weeded the chamomile circle, now thick in its second season of growth. Hazel never stopped weeding and mulching. Ginny raked goat shit from the pasture for the campers.

Gloria and Wren freshened the altars in the redwood grove, making it a sanctuary from the party's pandemonium. As they trimmed flowers and hung banners, Wren pondered, as she had for weeks since Beltane, how to break up with Gloria but still live with her.

Nikki, Alix and Julz built a second gate on the near side of the bridge and an arch above it. At the top of the arch, they affixed the sign of Ove: two interlocked circles, enclosed by an equilateral triangle, point downwards. This reminder of the gate toward a new life in Robin's vision had become the

Ove logo – they painted it on their tools and potluck dishes. They taught the Ove secret handshake to their friends, and some women might have gotten Ove tattoos in tender places.

A few days before the party, Wren overheard Gloria talking about her brother with Kelsey and Nikki. She later heard Hazel complaining about Gloria to Ginny, worried Robin could be persuaded. Lupe said she heard Kelsey was giving in.

So, the day before the party, Wren joined Robin and Kelsey for breakfast. She sat at the foot of their bed, drinking tea and eating granola bars.

Sketching would be too intrusive, but she wished she could take a picture of them, sitting in bed together, familiar and family. 'Robin, did you cut your hair?'

'Kelsey gave haircuts the other day. Where were you?'

'I'm not sure.' She must have been with Gloria. She waited until the tea was cold to start the hard part. 'I think Gloria invited her brother to the party.'

'I know,' Robin said. 'She wants the same exception women always want for their favourite men.'

'We don't know why Gloria is insisting on bringing her brother here,' Kelsey said. 'I'm against it, but you can't forbid it, Robin.'

'I'm not forbidding. We agreed.'

Wren marvelled at how easily Robin and Kelsey argued.

'That was a long time ago. Women change. Something might have changed in Gloria. We need to figure out another way of dealing with her need to bring her brother home.'

'Kelsey's right, Robin.' Wren could argue with Robin too. 'It's not like he will hurt anyone.'

Robin put her mug in the basket and got out of bed with a groan. 'This is one tiny place in one little forest. Men have the entire planet. Ove is for *women alone together.*'

Wren met Kelsey's eyes. Neither of them wanted men on the land either.

Robin pulled on her jeans. 'This was what we all wanted.'

'It was,' Wren said. 'It is. It just seems so mean.'

Kelsey got out of bed too. 'We'll figure something out, Wren. We can be kind to each other and still stay true to ourselves.'

⦾

Wren woke early to thumps and women's laughter above. UCSC students didn't mind sleeping in the big open attic. Wren smelled fried onions from downstairs. 'Are you awake?' she whispered.

'You were talking in your sleep.'

'Not telling secrets, I hope.' Wren moved her hand to Gloria's breast and gave it a squeeze.

Gloria ignored her invitation. 'I'm so excited. Grace – my niece – and her mother and my brother are coming to the land today.'

Wren froze. She couldn't argue, so she tried a joke. 'Maybe I should invite my mother.'

Gloria didn't get it. 'You should. It would be good for both of you,' she said, with a hurtful righteousness.

'I wouldn't inflict that woman on us, and you shouldn't do this either. You're stirring up shit.'

'It's no big deal – you'll see.'

'Why can't you meet him on the bridge, under the Ove arch?' Wren wished she had built a giant statue of Diana on the near side of the bridge, fierce, with a drawn arrow and her hunting dogs. She could drag Gloria to the foot of Her pediment and indict her for sacrilege.

'Trust me, it will work out. Robin needs to weather a little rebellion now and then, if she's really a feminist.'

'I really wish you wouldn't do this until we find a compromise.'

'Women will *never* all agree. That's the weakness of the women's movement: insisting on consensus.'

'I wish you would choose us.'

'I wish I could count on you, Wren. I've been supporting your Ove projects for months, but you won't help me now.'

'I can't help you if—'

'Don't fight me on this. No one can stop me from inviting my family to my home. Robin and Kelsey – they don't have families and don't understand La Familia.'

Wren couldn't resist. 'Lupe knows what La Familia is.'

'Nobody will care. He's bringing Grace – she's just a baby. Everyone will love her. I know what I'm doing.'

'I hope you do.'

'It is not the end of the world, or Ove. You'll see.'

'It's not how to end Patriarchy either.'

'It might be.'

Wren threw open the quilt.

'Don't go away mad.'

'I'm not mad,' Wren lied. 'I need to get my room ready for Scout. See you later.'

Robin was wrong. No big-art-thing-magical-statue could sway women like Gloria. As Wren walked around to the front veranda, anger felt red and roaring inside; good and powerful, like Athena. She savoured this, relieved she had lifelong practice in hiding it.

∞

Wren calmed when she got to her own room. She pulled the dark blue dress from her wardrobe, the one with the embroidered peasant bodice and full skirt. She wished it smelled like cedar. Last summer Gloria had filled the octagon's cedar closets with incense, polished stones, crystal pendants, holy oils, candles and figurines. Back then, Wren thought losing her new closets was a kindness.

She slipped the dress on. She hadn't had time to make herself a new one for this party. This was fine. She liked the fabric and colour. She wrapped the labrys belt around her waist.

Wren had promised her room to Scout and her new girlfriend. She wanted to make it ready for anything lubricious. She stripped the bed, threw the sheets in the corner and found another set of linens in the bottom of her wardrobe.

She plucked dead flowers from their vase on the altar and poured the rank water into her chamber pot. She abruptly stopped cleaning and sat at her altar. She loved her altar. She hadn't been here all year. All her magic now happened in the octagon with Gloria. She loved this big wooden chair that had held her spine upright on her many vigils over the years. There was the picture of Athena as she appeared in the Parthenon: the owl on her shoulder, a leopard sitting beside her like a giant house cat, and Medusa's eyes staring at her from Athena's breastplate. *What would Athena say?*

She lit a candle and settled into meditation. After a few minutes of focused breathing, she connected with the oneness and the endless reality of this present moment. It was always there for her, waiting for her to return. She relied on it. Then she remembered Gloria was bringing her brother to the land. She stood up and blew the candle out.

The sketchbook containing her ideas for *The Athenic Tarot*

was on the shelf next to all the others. At one time, Athenic wicca was the Important Sacred Art project that would keep them together. How ironic.

Gloria had kept the finished deck, so Wren consulted the coloured pencil drawings instead. What would Athena say about Gloria and her brother? She sat on the bare mattress and held the sketchbook to her chest.

To enter the divination trance, she sang, *One with the redwood, one with the shroom, one with the pasture, one with the dune.* Concentrating on her question, she waited for an image to advise her on what she should do about GLORIA BRINGING HER BROTHER TO THE LAND. She didn't mean to get angry all over again. *Breathe. Connect with oneness.*

She pressed her finger to the edge of the pages until one gave way, and she opened to: The Mushroom.

She knew what that meant. *Wait for enlightenment.* Sometimes the right action is to take no action at all. It meant she could join the party.

Wren made the bed and ate breakfast with two dykes who lived in a Kresge College collective. Then she thought she'd tidy the studio. Two girls were sitting at Robin's computer playing with MacPaint. But Gloria was in there talking on the phone, so Wren went out front. A van pulled up and women fell out of it, carrying tall drums and black instrument cases. Pepper, wearing her best purple bandana, jumped on everybody. The party had arrived.

Thirteen

'Athena ordered Perseus to retrieve the hidden power from Medusa.'

Wren had heard Gloria's version of How Perseus Slew the Medusa before. Her mind drifted. Until now, she'd loved every minute of the second annual While the Days Are Still Getting Longer Party. She met up with old friends and their new lovers. She helped women pitch tents in the pasture. She carried drums up to the chamomile circle, where the view made her happy to be alive. She danced on the veranda, stereo thumping. They served everyone barbecue chicken, three kinds of salad and chocolate strawberries. But then it was time for Gloria's Athenic wicca workshop.

Women sat on the floor of the octagon, *aka* Parthenon. Wren critiqued her wall hangings. The snakes, owls and mountain lion looked mis-proportioned. The women seemed not to notice, because Gloria was a captivating storyteller, and she looked especially classical in that gown – except for the tacky gilt owl pinned to her shoulder.

These women were younger; most of them from the university – Wren's Beltane prophecy manifested. They sat enraptured, except for an older woman who told too many of her own stories. Wren knew Gloria wouldn't invite her to the class. She wondered which women would become initiated and get their own ancient silver coins.

After the workshop, Wren stood on the porch and collected names and phone numbers on a clipboard. She hugged the last woman goodbye and turned to Gloria. 'If you don't need me any more, I'm going to the garden – you look exhausted.'

Gloria checked her watch. 'I'm fine. Don't fuss.'

'You did a great job.'

Gloria kissed her distractedly and rushed off, leaving the octagon a mess of handouts and dirty cups. Wren swore to herself this was the last time Gloria was leaving her with the scut work, and then realised this was the last time she would do anything Athenic.

⚭

Wren dumped the trash in the recycling and walked up the road past the terraces they had built at Spring Equinox. Hazel had already planted them with something bright green but inedible – to build up the soil, she had said. She ran into Lupe outside the shroom shed, and they greeted each other with the Ove handshake.

'You should go to the meadow,' said Lupe. 'Ginny is giving mule rides. It's like a million Lady Godivas up there.'

But before Wren could relish that spectacle, they heard someone shout, 'Man on the Land! Man on the Land!' Wren and Lupe looked at each other with resignation. They ran to the plaza and saw Gloria holding a baby, standing next to a man and woman Wren didn't know. Robin was with them, as were Nikki, Alix and Julz.

'What's going on?' asked Wren, her heart thumping.

'Wren! Meet my brother Jorge. This is Liana, and this is their little girl, Grace.'

Nikki asked Liana if she could hold the baby, and Gloria handed her over. Nikki and her friends cooed and patted her, praising her beauty and intelligence.

Wren shook hands with Jorge and gave Liana a hug.

'Hey buddy.' Lupe punched Jorge in the shoulder.

'How do you know Gloria's brother?' Wren asked.

'We've known each other for a while, since he and Liana moved to Seaside.'

Wren turned to Gloria. 'I thought we agreed Jorge would only come to the bridge.' She turned to Nikki. 'Isn't that what we agreed?'

'We did,' Nikki said, bewitched by the baby.

Jorge looked uncomfortable. 'Listen you guys…'

'Wren, I'm just showing my family around,' Gloria said, her tone unnecessarily nasty, as if she were speaking to Robin. 'They will leave soon. Don't be rude. It's only a few minutes.' Robin was right there and didn't say anything.

Lupe tried. 'Jorge, I don't want you to feel unwelcome, but we agreed that—'

Gloria interrupted. 'I didn't agree, and now you're embarrassing me. Ove is my home, and I can bring my brother to my home. I want to show him the grove. He's family.'

Wren imagined their party guests alone together in the grove.

'I'm fine here.' Jorge looked like this wasn't the first time Gloria had embarrassed him. 'Gloria, your house looks great.'

'You just got here, Jorge,' said Lupe. 'But would you like to go with me to the Seabright?'

'Seabright?' He said the name of that neighbourhood like it was code for something. 'Yeah, sure.' Jorge must have known what Lupe implied, but it was a mystery to everyone else.

'Gloria, don't worry about it,' said Jorge. 'Liana will want to stay.'

'I'd like to see the grove Gloria told me about,' Liana said.

Nikki handed the baby back and led them into the trees, trailed by Alix and Julz.

Gloria returned to berating Jorge. 'You'd rather do something with Lupe?'

Jorge had joined Lupe in her van. 'It's business,' he shouted from the window as they drove off.

Problem solved, Robin – who hadn't said a word – turned away from the group and walked toward the parked cars.

It was over, and nothing happened. Wren had to say something. 'You did it anyway.'

Gloria looked triumphant. 'We can have one day for family visitors. Ove is not a prison.'

Wren heard Robin's truck banging over the bridge.

'Don't put yourself in the middle, Wren.' Gloria spoke gently and confidently. 'Robin and I will work it out. She has abuse issues. She doesn't understand people who get along with men, especially the men in their family.'

'Is that it?' Gloria could be right.

'Isn't it obvious?' Gloria put her arm around Wren's shoulders. 'Did you hold the baby yet?'

Wren didn't want to hold the baby. 'I want to watch the mule rides.'

'Have fun. Don't let Robin ruin this day for you.'

Wren remembered the tarot card. Wait for enlightenment. Well, Lupe took care of Jorge. Gloria was right. Nothing bad happened. Everyone got what she wanted. Maybe men on the land didn't matter.

∞

Everyone partied and no one else noticed the Brother Drama. Wren took her turn riding Sal, smoked too much, and danced until they shut the stereo off. Eventually, groups settled into soft conversations with intermittent laughter. New and old friends bedded down. Wren didn't run into Gloria. Women from the Athenic workshop kept asking her questions. She told them to find Gloria.

She made herself a cup of hot chocolate and started upstairs. She ran into Kelsey and Ginny on the veranda coming down from the attic. The three of them saw Robin standing outside Gloria's bedroom. Gloria was shouting from inside.

'Is she okay?' Wren pushed past Robin, but Robin held her arm.

'I asked Gloria to leave.'

Kelsey inhaled slowly before saying, 'We live here as a collective.' She spoke to Robin, but looked to Wren and Ginny for confirmation.

Robin answered. 'She can visit, but can't live here.'

'You are fucking kidding me,' Kelsey said, in rage and disbelief.

'I'm doing it.'

'Can Robin do that to us?' Ginny's voice quavered.

Kelsey kept crossing and uncrossing her arms, ready for anything. 'Obviously, she thinks she can. Just like she thought she could bring a tractor here.'

Wren's mind roared in a bewildering pandemonium of threatened assumptions about the nature of reality. She finally said something inadequate. 'Kicking someone out by yourself is power-over.'

Robin had predicted this. 'Yes.' She glanced at Kelsey. 'I'm claiming it.' Her voice was shaking. Wren had never heard Robin's voice shake. 'Too many times, I've seen women tolerate women who do what Gloria did. You don't see the danger like I do.'

'*You* fail to see the danger. We could have kicked Gloria out, even before we met you, Robin. But power-over actions cause power problems.'

'Ove is my responsibility. In the end, I will be its shepherd.'

'I thought I was the shepherd,' Ginny said. 'Robin, you're the lunatic.'

Robin nearly smiled and then shouted into Gloria's closed door. 'Gloria, pack a bag and leave. We'll get the rest of your stuff to you later.'

Gloria opened the window next to her door and took in the half-circle of women standing shocked and scared. 'Look at this. Robin's audience for her little show.' She didn't seem to notice Wren was there because she spoke only to Robin. 'I didn't do anything wrong.'

'There's only one rule here.'

'Just because men abused you doesn't mean they abuse everyone. I'm not a separatist like you. It's unhealthy. Men exist in the world. We need them.'

'Pack a bag and leave. You don't have a choice.'

'Fuck you, Robin. I can stay if I want. I made a sacred vow to this land.'

Robin asked if she could come in.

'Not alone,' insisted Kelsey. 'Everyone needs to talk this through.'

'I'm the shepherd. I'll get everyone,' said Ginny. She and Pepper started for the stairs.

'Give us a minute,' Robin said. 'Trust me. I think Gloria and I can work this out.' She was mostly talking to Kelsey, who looked actually mad, not ornery. 'If we can't, I'll come get you and we can try something else.'

'Do it your way. But I'm still pissed.'

'I'm here if you need—' Wren said.

Gloria waved her off.

Wren, Kelsey and Ginny retreated to Kelsey's room. Wren sat next to Kelsey on her bed, while Ginny sat in the chair by the window. Wren sketched; Ginny knitted. Kelsey didn't move or speak, but Wren got the feeling she was having an argument with herself.

Gloria's room was just on the other side of Kelsey's headboard, but they heard no more yelling.

Murmuring.

Silence.

Movement in Gloria's room.

Gloria's door opened, and they heard a thumping down the stairs. Wren, Kelsey and Ginny ran out to the front veranda. In the plaza, Gloria flung open her car door and threw in a suitcase and the leather satchel Wren recognised as the one containing her most precious magical tools.

'Where are you going?' Wren called down.

'I'll be at the Dream Inn. Come with me.'

Wren ran toward her room.

Kelsey stopped her. 'Stay,' she pleaded.

Wren pushed her aside. 'This is fucked up, Kelsey.'

'Stay and support me.'

'Wren, are you coming?' Gloria shouted. She had backed the car out.

'Just a minute,' Wren yelled down, and reached for her doorknob. Gloria yelled back that she was leaving now, with or without Wren.

Wren turned, slid down her closed door, and sat down with a bump. Something knotted came undone inside herself.

Robin's face appeared close to Wren's own, intense and alarming. 'Wren, please stay. You don't like what I did, but I need you.' She squatted in front of her, her hand on Wren's thigh.

She didn't want Robin's impetuous behaviour to solve her lover-or-housemate dilemma. She pushed Robin's hand away and stood up.

'Hey, Robin!' Gloria shouted from her car window. 'Guess what my shadow told me?'

Wren joined Kelsey, Ginny and Pepper at the railing.

'Rich people always win,' Gloria shouted out of the window, punched the accelerator, and tore furrows in the plaza.

Wren felt something attached to her belly break and sting like a broken rubber band.

'Gloria is a lion, with the heart of a goat,' Ginny said as Gloria's car banged over the bridge.

Kelsey turned around. 'What the fuck does that mean?'

'Her heart is clever, but selfish.'

Kelsey gave up on Ginny and tore into Robin. 'How DARE you?!'

Wren felt exactly the same, but made herself as small and quiet as she could.

Robin stood placidly, ready for anything. Kelsey's anger didn't scare Robin. She just looked immensely sad, like an

Immortal Being the moment she throws away the best thing to happen to her in a thousand years.

'I won't stay here if you can kick women out when they disobey.'

'But we agreed...' Robin didn't try to explain again.

'Do you have any idea what you've done? Evicting Gloria is far worse than letting her brother hold his baby in the front yard.'

'But we have the power to say no to men.'

'I get it. I really do. I'm not arguing about men on the land right now. You *can't kick women out* just because you own it.'

'That's not what I did.'

'How can you say that? What did I just see with my own eyes? You will destroy your own utopia. This is so much worse than the tractor.'

'I had to make a decision.'

Kelsey scoffed. 'A one-sided decision. You're stupid and short-sighted, just like my idiot parents.'

'I will risk everything for this place.'

'Even us? Even me?'

'Let's talk about it.'

'Let's sleep on it,' Ginny offered, sensibly.

'I *will* defend this place from women like Gloria.'

'What about us defending it from you?'

Robin didn't reply.

Kelsey checked her watch. 'Shit. Fuck. It's already tomorrow. Ginny is right. I'm too tired and stoned to deal with this.'

Scout appeared on the veranda. She perceived some Land Dyke Drama was going on. 'Can we still sleep in your room?' she whispered to Wren.

What a relief. Wren wasn't sure if she was eavesdropping

on a break-up or watching her world fall apart. 'I got it ready for you.' She settled Scout and her friend in her room.

Five minutes later, as she shut her bedroom door on two women crawling under her favourite quilt, she saw Robin and Kelsey talking together softly outside Kelsey's room. Ginny was gone.

'I get it,' Robin was saying. 'I feel like sleeping in the grove anyway.'

'Good. Hope you find some wisdom there, because you ran out of whatever you had here.'

Wren walked around the other way and downstairs. She'd definitely been eavesdropping.

Fourteen

Kelsey shut her door behind her, closing away the scene of Gloria's tantrum, Wren's dilemma and… whatever the fuck Robin thought she was doing with that stunt. Her mouth was dry, and she wished she had a water crock in her room like Gloria did. She found Robin's cognac, but didn't pour any. She saw Robin's clogs under the end of the bed, and her bathrobe. She plucked at the fresh flowers on her altar. She wiped dust from the photo of her and Lucy, at that last birthday picnic.

She laid the picture on her bedside table and dug into the drawer for a candle. She lit it, climbed onto her bed, sat against the wall, put one hand into the other.

'Light of my life.'

'That was intense. She finally showed her true nature.' Lucy wore the same purple high-school sweatshirt she wore in the photo and sat where Robin used to. Did. Would. 'Why did she do that?'

'She's daring Robin to fight her.'

'I mean, why did *Robin* do that?'

'She was sick of Gloria's shit too. But we wouldn't kick Gloria out. We'd deal.'

'Gloria's been off on her own trip for months now.'

'She wasn't hurting anybody.'

'She only works for herself. Athenic wicca is *awful*.'

Kelsey chuckled and had to refocus herself into trance. 'Some women like it.' Lucy's head appeared in her lap and she put her hand on her hair. 'It's hard loving someone so much when she does something so wrong.'

'Why haven't you said anything about Gloria?'

'I left it between Rob and Gloria to work it out.'

'They worked it out,' Lucy said with a sneer. 'I bet you're glad you didn't get rid of me now. You need me more than ever if you're breaking up with Robin.'

Without a doubt, Lucy wanted them to break up.

Kelsey imagined her bed without Robin in it, without Robin's stacks of lesbian mysteries under it. She imagined a future without Robin's money, without a brimming pantry and cords of firewood stacked in the yard. She liked this life of no landlord, no banks, no bosses. She could never again eat twenty-five-cent ramen noodles. If Robin loved her, why did she risk all of it?

Kelsey got mad all over again, and nearly opened her eyes to fling open the door, go find Robin and yell at her some more. 'I thought Robin was the woman I could be with for a long time. If she can kick any of us out, I will never be safe.'

'It pisses you off.'

'There are other ways to deal with assholes.'

'Robin took everyone's power away. Because she could.'

'She did. What can I do?'

'I don't know.'

Lucy got up and went over to Kelsey's altar. She fiddled with the statues, pinecones and feathers.

'You don't have any spooky revelation from beyond the grave, some glimpse of the future, a prophecy?'

'I can't help you, because I'm not alive. You'll have to ask the living. Don't look to your memories of me. Look to what you have right now.'

'The power of the moment?'

'It's pretty much all the dead will ever tell you; it is our only regret.'

'That's all you can say?'

But Lucy didn't reply. Kelsey was asleep with the light on.

⚭

Downstairs, the lights were on too but the party was over. Wren quietly stepped between sleeping dykes, blew out candles, emptied ashtrays and salvaged the better leftovers.

As she left the kitchen, she saw lights in Lupe and Hazel's cabins. Someone was singing in the bathhouse. She stood in the quiet dark, trying to make sense of what Robin had done. She wanted to break up with Gloria but still live together. Robin had just erased that possible future.

Robin clumped downstairs with an awkward armful of blankets.

'Don't you have a sleeping bag?'

'I don't like that rustling sound.' Robin dropped a pillow.

'Do you need help?'

'Yeah.' Robin strode across the yard and pushed into the trees concealing the path to the grove. Wren picked up the pillow and followed. The white stones lining the path brought her safely through the dark trees. Wren heard someone playing a guitar in there. She caught up with Robin at the stump.

Robin gestured to the redwood circle. 'I'm going to sleep here. Join me?'

Wren pictured the alternative, sleeping next to Gloria's cold pillow. She'd try one more time to change Robin's mind. 'I'll lie with you for a while.' She felt brave and not reckless.

It was Julz at the campfire, playing a Ferron song on guitar for a woman Wren didn't know. Julz nodded, but kept singing. The other woman looked significantly at Wren, as if she expected Kelsey to be the one holding Robin's pillow.

'Don't stop,' Robin told Julz. 'We'll just lie down up there. We won't be going to sleep soon.'

Robin led Wren to the foot of the northern altar where the duff was thick and soft. They spread out the blankets and removed their shoes. Robin took off her boots and jeans. Wren only kicked off her sandals and got in with her dress on. She lay next to Robin, not touching, not talking. The blankets were freezing; the fog must be in.

Julz sang earnestly to the woman sitting across from her about how you can always feel alone when your lover is your home. Robin felt like home. Always did. Wren remembered when they first met, almost two years ago now. Since then, they had slept in the grove many times, before Kelsey, before Gloria. Tonight, Robin needed to sleep with her.

Robin kicked Gloria off the land, and could do it to any Ovem. Wren shivered, not just from the cold, and squeezed her eyes shut. She felt something old and familiar tugging at her, pulling her from under this blanket, this woman, these trees. She opened her eyes and watched the fire shadows rippling on limbs reaching across the circle, illuminating the mist. She remembered the owl the day she met Robin. *Who* will liberate women? We will liberate ourselves.

'Do you like Ferron?' Robin asked, and Wren jolted as if she had fallen asleep. Robin apologised.

Wren pulled the blanket closer to her throat. She felt warmer. 'I love her. I hope she finds a decent girlfriend someday, but her breakup songs helped me get over Nikki.'

'Ferron's songs give me courage,' Robin replied, and then confessed. 'I've been thinking of telling Gloria to leave since she tried to convince us at Beltane to invite men to the land.'

Wren had never told anyone how Gloria manipulated the runes so she controlled the Beltane prophecies. 'It's the kind of thing that causes women's lands to fall apart.' She left it ambiguous whether 'it' meant what Gloria wanted, or what Robin had done in response. Because it was both.

'Did I make a mistake?'

Was she looking for a reason to let Gloria stay? 'Not a mistake like the tractor was.'

Wren felt Robin chuckle. She didn't mind being reminded of her fuck-ups. The blankets had warmed. Wren turned on her side. In the fire light she admired Robin's strong profile. Robin's mouth wasn't turned-down, but tight and tense.

'Would the magical statue have stopped you?'

'Not a chance. It might have reminded me to tell Gloria to leave sooner.'

Wren hadn't thought of that, and felt less like a failure. From the campfire, she heard Julz singing about points and lines and staying free. They listened until she got to 'Testimony'. All four women joined in on the chorus, singing that they were women, open and whole. The encircling trees above the fire's glow absorbed their voices, the forest snug and dark around them.

When they had finished the song, Robin asked, in a voice

thick and wet, 'What will you do about me?'

Wren stretched her arm out across Robin's chest. Robin twisted under it and spooned up close to Wren, like she had been waiting for the invitation. Wren pulled up her skirt and pressed her warm legs under Robin's. Robin shuddered against her. Robin was *crying*.

Wren wondered if they could do a reconciliation ritual with Gloria, but remembered reconciliation magic only works when everyone desires a future together. Gloria didn't want the same future any more.

Wren swallowed. She'd known this for a while. Gloria had to leave, but Kelsey was right: Robin fucked up.

Julz was singing another break-up song. Robin pulled away to search her pants' pockets and found a bandana. She blew her nose. 'Turn over,' she whispered, pulling the blanket back over herself. They spooned the other way.

'Wren, I am afraid.'

'You're never afraid.'

'I'm afraid tonight. I don't know what will happen.'

'But you know everything.'

'Not any more. Not since Kelsey showed me how to live as if this is my only life. I can't lose Ove.'

Without thinking of the implications, Wren wiggled her butt. 'How could you do something so stupid?'

'Maybe my shadow made me do it.'

Wren felt Robin pressing herself against her, and her tummy did a quickstep. She remembered Robin lecturing them after Gloria's awful ritual, something about how your shadow is a friend.

'I wonder what everyone will do. Everyone saw what Gloria was doing. So I did something. You need to figure out what to do next.'

Wren knew what she wanted to do next. 'You own the place.'

'Ove isn't what I own.' Robin might have been smelling Wren's hair. 'Kelsey is right. She can't tolerate what I did.'

'Is that why you were crying?'

'I remember every time I failed a woman I loved.'

'If you love us so much, why do something so cruel to us, not just Gloria?'

Robin shuddered. She might be crying again. When she spoke, her voice was thick and croaky. 'I'm out of memories. You'll have to invent on your own.'

Wren heard Julz's friend laugh when they sang the one where Ferron says her own name. Of course Ferron is pretty.

Robin lay quiet behind her and not asleep. Wren imagined repositioning Robin's hand to hold her breast. But instead, she simply savoured the possibility.

Julz and her friend were singing the song about how life comes together and comes apart. When they finished, the women at the fire laughed at their own profundity and then started shuffling around.

Julz called over. 'Should we put the fire out?'

Robin sat up and blinked in the firelight. She had been asleep too. 'Don't worry, we'll take care of it.'

She lay down beside Wren and pulled the blankets up around them. 'We can't fall asleep again without taking care of the fire.'

'Did Julz just sing the entire *Testimony* album?'

'She did. That girl knows what she's getting into.'

After banking the fire, they slept spooned. Wren forgot Ove politics and tomorrow. Tonight, her lust was her own. Her love for Robin was her own. She could sleep beside her all night and desire nothing more.

Fifteen

'There you are!'

Kelsey was shouting.

Wren reached out her arm and touched someone. Robin. Why is Kelsey yelling? Wren opened her eyes and saw the silent trees in the morning fog, red and gray, like slender old ladies in dressing gowns.

'I've been looking for you two.' Kelsey's broad face suddenly blocked Wren's contemplation of trees.

'Here!' Wren said, like a roll call.

'We're getting everyone off the land sooner than planned. We have to deal with last night.'

'N-nothing happened last night, I swear. Robin, tell her!' Wren shoved Robin's back.

Robin rolled over. 'Good morning, sweetheart,' she said to Kelsey.

'For pity's sake. I don't mean you two. I mean Robin evicting Gloria.'

Robin held her wrist over her face and checked her watch.

'We slept in.'

'Wren, get up. Help get the university pookies on the road. We need to have an Ovem meeting. Robin, will you feed the chickens?' Kelsey held out the bucket of kitchen scraps.

Robin pulled on her jeans. 'Gladly. If you're still speaking to me.'

'Not yet.'

Robin reached for the bucket and tried a joke. 'Is this my breakfast?' She searched Kelsey's expression for a sign of warmth. She didn't find it.

'Hazel asks if you'll water before the sun gets too high.'

'I know what morning chores are. Does that mean I can skip the meeting?'

'We were thinking it's better without you.'

Wren looked at the two friends standing over her. She wished this was a dream – or an astral conversation where she could turn herself into dust and float away in a sunbeam.

Robin slipped on her boots and loped through the forest toward the garden.

Kelsey called after her. 'We'll come get you when we're… done.' She choked on something.

Wren expected her to say, 'I still love you,' but she did not.

⚭

When Wren got to the plaza, women were packing their cars. Scout from Oregon was warming up her van. Wren jogged over.

'Sorry about this. How did you sleep?'

'Not much sleeping. We found your massage oil.'

'Come back another time, when we've figured this out. I'm sorry for the drama.'

'Don't apologise. Robin had to do what she did. I get it.'

'We make mistakes sometimes. No one knows how to do this.'

'Wren, the Ovem are my sheroes. Vegetarianism, jealousy, chores… You solved it all. But intentionally bringing men on the land… I guess if you don't screw up now and then, there'd be no story to tell.' Scout shook her head and fiddled with the rear-view mirror. 'Every women's group has a Gloria in it. That's why they never last more than a year or two.'

'That doesn't make Gloria evil.'

'I didn't say she was evil. Don't get defensive, sister.'

Wren reached in her hand to touch Scout's shoulder. Scout glanced up at the mirror and smiled. 'Here comes trouble.'

Wren turned and saw Scout's girlfriend approaching. 'Gloria's not evil,' she repeated.

'Whatever she is, if you figure this out, let us all know how you did it.'

'I'll draw you a picture.'

Scout's girlfriend got in, Scout put the van in gear, and Wren stepped backward. Scout was right. If they couldn't figure this out, no one could.

⚭

She found the Ovem in the kitchen cleaning up after the party and swirling around to one of Hazel's albums of instrumental piano. Solving big problems required the maximum amount of coffee, so Wren got both kettles going. Lupe made a huge pan of scrambled eggs and onions.

They ate with enthusiasm, and no one mentioned Gloria and Robin's absence. Lupe and Hazel said someone at the party invited them to talk on KZSC about organic farming.

Nikki told a funny story about two vegetarians the previous day arguing about leather jackets. Ginny had met a woman who said she was Natalie Barney reincarnated. Kelsey kept her thoughts to herself.

They reminisced about the party – every detail, except the last hour. After the first round of coffee disappeared, Hazel got up to boil more water. Kelsey and Nikki stacked plates. Wren got the Ovem Book from the pantry. She brought it back to the table and sat next to Ginny, who was knitting a fluffy sock with tiny needles.

'Let's get started,' Kelsey said. The energy shifted. 'Let's make sure we all understand what happened.'

'I heard it from you, Kelsey,' said Lupe. 'But I'd like the less grouchy version.'

Ginny raised her hand from the needles and told the whole story. 'Gloria got mad at Robin and brought a man on the land. Robin got mad at Gloria and evicted her from Ove. Kelsey got mad at Robin and evicted her from her bed.' Ginny's tiny needles returned to clicking around the sock.

'Thank you for that,' said Hazel. 'I missed everything because Sharon and I ended it. She's moving to Israel.'

'Israel?' Lupe said, surprised. 'I didn't even know she was Jewish.'

'Neither did she,' Hazel said, and didn't explain. 'What about Gloria's brother?'

'What about him?' Lupe challenged. 'He didn't do anything wrong!'

'Was he aware of Gloria's plan?'

'He guessed she was up to something, but he didn't know what,' said Lupe. 'He feels used, and not for the first time.'

With a green pen, Wren drew a vertical line and crossed it with a horizontal one. She would draw a labyrinth.

'Nothing to be learned there.' Hazel moved on. 'Does anyone support Gloria's idea about inviting men once a year?'

Everyone shook their heads.

'I liked the baby,' Nikki said. 'She can come back.'

Wren drew four small dots to define the quadrants. 'She warned us. Athena told her to do it.'

'True,' said Nikki. 'You can trust Gloria to follow through.'

'I haven't trusted her since that awful ritual,' said Kelsey. 'I wish we had never messed with those shadowy things.'

'I was never the same,' said Lupe. 'No one but her likes Athenic wicca.'

Wren put her pen down carefully. 'Lupe, some women feel connected to a Californian goddess.'

'But she's doing it wrong,' said Hazel.

'Can we do this without saying terrible things about Gloria?' Wren wiped her eyes with the hem of her skirt.

Kelsey slapped her hand on the table and everyone jumped. 'Hey! Life is short. Why are we talking about Glow? She has nothing to do with what Robin did.'

Wren didn't want to talk about Gloria either. 'Robin told me last night she's afraid of what we're going to do to her now.' She couldn't handle everyone looking at her, so she returned to the labyrinth.

'Kelsey's right,' said Hazel. 'Let's focus. Robin fucked up.'

'She did,' said Kelsey. 'Robin did this alone. Just like Gloria and that shadowy ritual, and Robin buying the tractor. When you live together, you make decisions together so we can stop each other from Patriarchal habits. I don't want men on the land either. Now I don't know if I can stay.'

Wren drew arcs between the dots and the line-ends.

'I don't know if I can stay either,' said Nikki. 'Robin will fuck up again.'

'But none of us want men on the land,' Wren pleaded. 'Robin promised me she won't do this again.'

Kelsey snorted. 'If Robin can kick any one of us out, she's already destroyed Ove. I can't live here.'

Wren felt Ginny's leg spasm, and a ball of yarn rolled under the table. Wren bent down to fetch it as Ginny said, 'You two can leave, but I can't. I won't work in an old people's home again.'

Wren had nowhere to go either. 'Please don't leave just because you can.'

Nikki looked guilty. Kelsey looked cornered.

Hazel leaned forward. 'I get what you're saying, Kelsey, but I'm not ready to give up.'

'I won't give you up,' Kelsey promised. 'Even if I have to give up Robin.'

Wren finished her labyrinth. With a red pen she traced its path inward, and outward, trying to find what they needed.

Lupe said 'Robin wants us to just…' – she affected a bliss-ninny accent – *'live here and be free! Find out what happens!'* She returned to her own voice. 'Then she pulls this power-over shit.'

Wren remembered Robin's tears the night before. 'Robin did something wrong, but with the right intention. How she did it – maybe that was her mistake. Last night she said her shadow made her do it, and I thought she was joking.'

'The less we talk about shadows, the better,' Kelsey said.

But Wren wanted to talk about shadows. 'I hated Gloria's shadow ritual too, but—'

The Ovem interrupted like a chorus: 'She meant well.'

'That's not what I was going to say.' Wren curled her fists and held them tight against her chest. She pressed her lips to her knuckles, trying to squeeze out the words for what she saw in her mind, like in a mushroom trip.

'Our shadows help,' was all she could say at first. Then she had to sneak up on the idea from her memories. 'Since we moved here, I did a lot of dumb things. I thought Robin would be my lover if I did art for her, I ignored what a real lover like Willow offered, and I never noticed that Gloria stole my creative life.'

It hurt to say the words out loud. Maybe that's why she preferred painting pictures. Her eyes welled, and her sister witches leaned toward her. She patted their hands, then pushed them away. 'It wasn't Gloria's fault that I hurt myself. Gloria wanted us to fix our shit, and maybe the way to do that is to understand our shadow selves.' She wiped her eyes and took in the concerned faces of her friends. 'Does that make sense?'

It did not. Their faces showed pity, not comprehension.

Kelsey's dependable practicality put an end to Wren's esoteric explorations. 'Magic and metaphors only go so far,' she said.

Everyone's attention returned to Robin's control of their lives. That was the real problem they had to solve, not Wren's romances. Wren picked up her pen and turned to a new page.

'Robin *owns the land*,' said Hazel. 'Nothing magical about that.'

'She doesn't own *us*.' Ginny picked up her knitting again. 'If we didn't live here, she'd be sitting in a big old house alone, telling herself lies.'

Nikki let out a long sigh. 'Robin has all the power here.'

'She has power in Patriarchy,' Ginny said. 'Not in Ove.'

'She's right. We live in the *real world*,' Lupe said. 'Patriarchy is the false world.'

Kelsey brightened. 'If that's true, Robin lives in Ove, not

the Patriarchy. She didn't evict Gloria with her Patriarchal power, she did it because she has power in Ove. We gave her that power.'

'We did,' said Wren. 'Beginning with me.'

'We need the power to tell someone they need to leave,' said Lupe.

Nikki shook her head. 'I couldn't tell a woman to leave.'

'We need to tell *ourselves* when it is time to go,' said Ginny. She paused, then continued, needles clicking. 'You know how when we ask, *how do you enter the circle?* and the answer is, *with perfect love and perfect trust*? Sometimes, when we haven't dealt with something, I don't want to say *perfect love and trust*.'

'I know what you mean, Ginny,' said Wren. 'Like when I couldn't say *perfect love and trust* at the reconciliation ritual. You know it when you're saying ritual words and lying to yourself. We need a ritual.'

With that, they converged on a shared vision.

'We need a thing that tells us we're lying to ourselves.'

'We need to take a vow.'

'We need to make a wish.'

'If you can't say the magic words, you know they aren't true.'

'We need a manifesto.'

'We need a *lan*-di-festo.'

'Landifesto!' They raised their coffee cups, and Kelsey got more water boiling.

They spent the rest of the morning writing the Landifesto. It was the most elaborate ceremony they'd created since their early rituals, full of original poetry and long quotations from feminist books. Wren wrote detailed notes in the book of Ove.

'If we do it every year, we will change it as we change.'
'Robin will still own the land. She still has power over us.'
'The Landifesto takes away her power to kick us out.'
'It will change her.'
'It will change all of us.'
'We might die.'
'Isn't that the point?'

Twenty-minutes later, Wren recorded how the ritual would end. 'Let's ask Robin if she wants to do this.'

'No,' said Kelsey.

'But Robin must go first,' Ginny said. 'She's the oldest.'

'I mean,' Kelsey said resolutely, 'we're going to *tell* Robin. No asking.'

Wren walked with everyone up to the garden. She hadn't felt this happy in months. Gloria had brought a man to the land. She was right: nothing bad happened. In fact, the Landifesto would be the best ritual ever.

Sixteen

They found Robin in the pasture, searching the sky with binoculars. She met the coven at the gate. Ginny took the lead, explaining the Landifesto.

Robin listened, rubbing Pepper's ears.

'This ritual is just for us, not part of anyone else's magic,' said Lupe. 'It's homegrown.'

'I get it, Lupe,' Robin said, trying to smile.

Hazel said that they had invented a ritual perfectly timed for where they were in their growth as Ovem.

Nikki thought it would help resolve minor disagreements. 'All the little things that push us apart.'

'I think I'll finally find your magical statue,' Wren said.

'The Landifesto is real and imaginary,' Ginny said, in some sort of conclusion.

Kelsey asked, 'Do you understand what the ritual is, Robin?' Her voice was harsher than Wren had ever heard.

Robin nodded.

'And you will go along with it? Once we do this, you can't

kick anyone out.'

Robin looked relieved. 'You know I will do anything to protect Ove.'

'You should have considered that when you kicked Gloria out.'

'I did.'

Kelsey stared at Robin. 'Are you hungry?'

Robin nodded.

Kelsey turned and walked toward the house.

'Kelsey!' Wren called out. 'Don't leave mad!'

But Kelsey only waved her hand and kept walking.

'She's just getting Robin something to eat,' Ginny concluded. 'They didn't break up.'

When Wren realised Robin and Kelsey were back together, inspiration seized her. 'Let's invite Gloria to swear the Landifesto.'

Lupe, Hazel and Nikki hated that idea. The arguments ensued: 'Better without her – her own way – brother on the land – you're too good for – obsessed with money – using you –'

And then Ginny started muttering something that sounded like 'chickens, chickens, chickens'.

Wren foundered in the wave of criticism, every word true but unhelpful. 'If she's so terrible, why didn't anyone tell me until now?'

'Chickens, chickens, chickens,' Ginny suggested.

'I bet you feel good about finally telling me this,' she accused. 'You're saying to my face what's been gossip for months.'

'We did try to tell you,' said Hazel. 'But you seemed happy with Gloria and never complained to us.'

'Maybe that's true.' Wren knew she'd later berate herself

for denying reality. 'But we need to invite her to the ritual. If the Landifesto shows her that it is time for her to leave, then we can separate without hurting each other.' Wren didn't say there was a place in her heart where Gloria understood, and returned to Ove.

Lupe huffed. Hazel needed some time to think. Ginny gave Wren a hug. Wren recognised a familiar emotion on Nikki's face.

She turned and asked the one who hadn't spoken. 'Robin, what do you say?'

'No woman is my enemy,' Robin declared. 'I'll trust your lesbian ethics.'

⚭

As Gloria left Ove that terrible night, she said she'd be at the Dream Inn, the most expensive hotel in town. As improbable as that was, Wren left a message for her there. Gloria called back to leave a message on the machine, saying she would meet Wren at the Saturn at five o'clock the next day.

Wren borrowed Robin's truck and drove alone to the Saturn Cafe. She hadn't been back to the Saturn since that awful Christmas day, almost two years ago.

Gloria needed the Landifesto. Robin was right, Gloria wasn't their enemy, and Wren didn't want her to be left behind in the new way of living together after the Landifesto. A lightness rose in her heart as she pulled into the crowded parking lot.

Wren was surprised to see her old friend Cayenne at the register. They shared a long hug.

'Are you here for Congabelle? Four women drummers!' Cayenne pointed to the tiny stage near the back door. Then she felt Wren's anxiety and broke off the chit chat. 'She's sitting back there.'

'Thanks. Will you bring me brown rice with sesame sauce when you have a chance?'

'Sure.' Cayenne wrote up a ticket.

'And I might need a Chocolate Madness when this is over.'

She made a note. 'To celebrate?'

'I hope so.'

Wren made her way through the noisy café and slid into Gloria's favourite booth. 'You're staying at the Dream Inn? How can you afford it?'

Gloria had finished a big salad. She'd be irritated if Wren had kept her waiting long.

Gloria lifted a tooled leather purse from the bench beside her. It looked so soft that Wren couldn't resist putting her hand out to touch it.

'Robin gave me this that night.' Gloria opened the flap with a flourish. Wren looked inside. Index cards? She reached her hand in.

'Don't take any out. Be cool.'

Wren jerked her hand back. 'I *am* cool.'

Gloria closed the flap. 'It's cash. Robin gave me five stacks of a hundred hundreds. She told me not to take it to the bank all at once. So I keep it with me for now.'

Wren tried to calculate a hundred hundreds times five.

Gloria knew she sucked at arithmetic. 'Fifty thousand dollars. I can buy my own land.'

Wren fell back against the booth. Robin had given Gloria what she wanted, but she still needed the Landifesto.

'Robin didn't tell you?' Gloria hid the purse on her lap under the table. 'Typical. That woman is an expert on everything but her own problems. She divides us with her secrets.'

Wren tried to keep her face still. 'I'm not here to listen to you bash Robin. I'm here to invite you back to Ove.'

Gloria responded with a nasty laugh. 'I'm inviting *you* to live on my own land. Is Robin sorry?'

'I don't think so—'

Gloria shook her head. 'No surprise.'

Wren tried anyway. 'We have something better than apologies. We call it Swearing the Landifesto. I brought the ritual we wrote.' Wren pulled the book of Ove from her backpack and read:

This land is my land.
I belong to it, and it belongs to me.
I belong to this land as a child to her mother
As a shoot to a seed
As a spore to a gill
As wool to a goat
As light to dark
As smoke to fire
As fire to wood
As wood to water
As water to clouds
As clouds to air
As air to fire.
I belong to this land, and the land belongs to me.

'You think reading bad poetry is going to stop her?'

'Not stop her, but—'

'You Ovem are so impractical. If you don't own your land, she will always have power over you.'

'That's not what we think.'

'Who wrote it?'

'We all did. Look, there's this. *I swear to do what I promise and not promise what I cannot do. I swear to agree, to stand aside, and offer my judgment according to my own wisdom.'*

Wren looked proudly up from her notebook. 'After we swear the Landifesto, no one can kick anyone else out, as long as they are keeping their Landifesto vow. We will do it every summer, because we will change, and we will renew our vow to the land, and to each other.'

Gloria scoffed. 'Let's see how that works out. I already looked at properties in Boulder Creek.'

Wren's heart sank. 'But you can come back if you swear the Landifesto.'

'Wren.' Gloria held Wren's hands across the table. 'I don't want to.' She was wearing a silver ring set with a big black obsidian oval. 'Come live with me and be an Athenic priestess.'

Wren laid her cheek on that new ring. This wasn't going well.

Gloria leaned over. She smelled of cedar oil. She whispered in Wren's ear. 'Athena told me to find the *other one* who remembers, like Robin.' She sat back in the booth. 'Remember how you heard an owl in the grove the first time you went there?'

Wren sat up. Gloria's eyes had that inspired shimmer. 'I remember.'

'In the entire time I lived at Ove, everyone heard owls, but not me; not once. When I went to a property – there's a house on it and acres of redwoods – I heard an owl. It was Athena.'

'Does that mean you won't live with us…because you heard an owl?'

'Robin did me a favour. I think she actually wants me to create my own women's community. She knows Ove will fail.'

'Ove will *not* fail. We have the Landifesto. Let me…'

Wren opened the Ove book again, but Gloria closed it.

Wren looked at Gloria's hand on the book and saw another new ring there, a copper serpent.

'Robin's land never belonged to Athena!' Gloria said, as if that was a good thing. 'Athena will bring women to her *own* land. They will learn how to wield power in the real world.'

Wren hated how her eyes filled up.

'We will live on our *own* land.'

'But our coven, the redwood grove—'

'I don't want to be harsh, but if you stay at Ove, you're never going to get over Robin – or your mother, speaking of controlling bitches. Athena wants nothing to do with that land. She doesn't share with other goddesses.'

Wren remembered Athena and Gloria agreed on everything. She dried her eyes with a brown paper napkin.

'And I have good news. Now I can afford to publish the Athenic tarot.'

'My deck? I never wanted—'

'We intended the deck to be in my lineage. That's why I put so much work into it.'

'I don't want to say no, but—'

'Admit it; it's mine as much as yours. I incorporated Athenic motifs. You were stuck on the Fives, remember? You're more of an illustrator than an artist.'

Gloria looked away from Wren and fiddled with her rings, found an uneaten bit of cheese in the salad bowl and waited, daring Wren to contradict her.

But Wren didn't need to. She knew who she was, and in that moment, she realised who Gloria was too. 'Why did you pick us to be the Fire Women at the Beltane ritual?'

'*I* didn't pick us.'

Wren wanted Gloria to say it. 'It seems like a coincidence.'

'*The goddess* chooses the Elements of that ritual.'

Wren stared at Gloria, stunned by the giant lie. 'I'm staying at Ove.'

'Hope you don't regret it.' Gloria got up from the booth and stood at the side of the table, holding the leather purse to her chest. 'I still love you.'

'I love you. But I can't live with you.'

'Robin thinks she won. You know in your heart she will always be in control.'

Wren had some feelings in her heart but couldn't express them. She looked down at her own ringless fingers until she knew Gloria was gone.

Cayenne skipped the rice and brought over the Chocolate Madness. Another lesbian break-up at the Saturn Cafe.

Seventeen

The lesbian witches intended to fix their own shit, not the whole wide world and everybody in it.

On the summer solstice evening they walked to their sacred redwood grove, with their blankets and lanterns, thermoses and granola bars, and passed the night in a slumber party around the fire, telling stories under towering trees.

The next morning, the witches woke without speaking. They tended the animals, watered the garden and wandered their wild wood to the secret spots on secret footpaths.

The sun crowned the high limbs and streamed to the dank duff, warming the earth and painting the forest in light and shadow. Just before noon, the witches built their altars in the grove. At the east, they arranged three feathers found under their own trees. At the south, coals from their fires, candles from their bees. At the west, water from their well, the snake skin discarded in their meadow. At the north, white quartz in a pot of compost.

They wore astral travelling cloaks. Bare feet drew power from the duff. They painted their lips black and called each other by their real names. At the stump, they pressed their fingers to its charred skin – a living scar, ancient and strong.

With their knives, they cast the circle, and entered it in perfect love and perfect trust. They blessed each other with salted water, and anointed their brows with a pentacle drawn with bitter oil. They sang the names of their goddesses:

Demeter, Persephone, Hecate, Isis.

Deborah, Innana, Al-Lat, Artemis.

Melusine, Cerridwen, Aphrodite.

Bridget, Arianrhod, Anna Marie.

They passed a chalice filled with Lupe's tea. With voice and drum, wailing and song, the witches raised their cone of power, then bent and grounded. They now possessed the intent, force and vessel for the journey.

The witches lay in a circle of their blankets and quilts. With tea in their bellies, they put their heads together in the centre, listened to their breath, and held their fingers entwined.

On their breath alone, they urged each other on. Inhale and exhale, like bellows under a grate. They brought up fire from the earth, harnessing the vigour that sent them travelling.

Leaving their bodies secure, they rose through the centre of their grove, the long redwood limbs and needles passing through their spirit selves. They floated up and away from their mountain, into the lightless void. A coven of witches, flying through a dark sky. Seconds, minutes. Minutes, hours. They soared. Time flowed differently.

The black thinned, and the witches descended to a circle of trees crowning a peak on a long ridge, the sea on the west, a valley to the east. The encircling trees stretched into a blue cloudless sky, much higher than their own grove. The witches occupied a mushroom's view. In this sacred place, they would swear the Landifesto.

Wren waited for Robin to begin it. Robin would swear by the land of Ove and the women who lived there. She wouldn't have power over them. The vow would bind her, and every year they would return here and renew their vow. Anyone who couldn't swear would know it was time to leave. And so they would live together for the rest of their lives. A ritual simple and sincere.

Robin stepped forward in her travelling robe. Wren expected her to recite, 'This land is my land. I belong to it, and it belongs to me,' but instead, she felt distracted by a wave of lust for Robin, like nothing else since that first day in the grove. It felt weird and inappropriate.

Heat penetrated Wren's skin. She shifted her feet and felt wet already. She shook her left hand to free it from the cloak's long cuff and reached out for Nikki. Nik looked back at her in that way she did when they first got together, when they were new witches in a women's spirituality class, learning how to say 'bless your breasts, formed in strength and beauty'.

Nikki wanted her. Wren could smell it. And she wanted Nikki. Here, in the astral.

Not taking her eyes away from Nikki's dear face, she reached behind for Hazel, but Hazel wasn't there. Nikki was watching something over Wren's shoulder. The air thickened. Wren slowly turned her head and saw Hazel and Lupe standing embraced. They were already breathing hard.

It took forever for Wren to bring her head slowly back around toward Nikki, who quickly pulled her close. Wren wrapped her fingers around Nikki's upper arms, so strong. Nikki pressed Wren tight against her. So unexpected. She heard noises.

They conjured quilts. Nikki rolled Wren on her back, their robes melting. And Ginny. *Come here.* Wise Ginny. Ginny with horns. Here is Ginny's hand, so nimble in another world, and now here pressing against Wren in perfect rhythm. Here are Nikki's breasts. Wren rose toward an orgasm, all booming and sparkles. She floated downward. Where was Nikki? Nikki was kissing Ginny.

Wren rolled onto her back, becoming a unique knot of atoms, a woman who would never live again, who would someday die and alloy her atoms with the duff of a redwood circle. She sat up and beheld other unique knots of atoms ablaze. She watched them in a synaesthesia, desire yearning toward pleasure, pleasure toward desire.

Couples, trios, more. They made love, and it piled around them in drifts, like sugar. The witches' circle became what every lesbian longs for: creation and communion.

Wren considered the unique collection of atoms known as Robin who assembled herself again and again, immortal and forever. Wren moved through the liquid bodies of her coven sisters like a ladle through soup. Her palms found Robin's shoulder blades, and Robin curled in pleasure as Wren pressed the edge of her backbone. Without hesitation, Robin slid her fingers into Wren. Wren pushed back into Robin's palm, and then giggled at the ridiculousness of it, and the rightness. Beautiful as a pounding waterfall.

Dancing extraordinary.

Idiosyncratic. Peculiar.

Wren couldn't stop laughing.

She turned herself inside out and delighted in her pussy,

wet and well used. Her clit soft now, and her limbs vibrating in a euphony of orgasms. Of course, they made love first. It is what lesbians do.

Wren was choking. Dust – no; ashes. Cold, bitter ashes, gritty and dirty, everywhere. Robin and Kelsey were breaking up.

Robin stood, a tentative flame in a bed of ash and coal.

'This is not the ritual we planned,' she said, unnecessarily.

Everyone untangled from inside each other, their channels polluted by something stinking and rough.

Kelsey stood, ashes falling from her body in clouds. 'You planned this.' Her confrontation pushed Robin backward.

'No, I didn't. Not really.'

'Not *really*?' Kelsey's sarcasm bit the air, and Robin flinched.

'I didn't know what would happen. My memories are useless for what we do together.'

'I'm not talking about your magical memory banks, Robin. I mean, you forced us to defy you.'

Robin's head snapped like she was caught. 'There was no other way.' She didn't look magic or cute. She looked confused, caught between what is and what isn't. No different from any dyke Wren had ever met. Ordinary.

'This is why you kicked Gloria out, alone.'

'I alone.'

'Someone else might have stood up to Gloria.'

'Maybe they would have. I chose the moment to take action.' Robin pointed a finger toward something behind Kelsey. 'Look who's here.'

Someone Wren didn't know waved shyly at Robin. A teenager with long straight dark hair and high cheekbones, her too-big-for-her jeans held up with a thick belt. She wore one of Kelsey's plaid shirts.

Kelsey turned. She fell backwards, but Robin caught and held her. The young woman lifted Kelsey's hands to her own breastbone, and…aged. Her hips swelled, her face matured. Her hair was now short and spiky on top. Then she took one step in her big boots and disappeared into Kelsey's body.

Wren recognised that this was Kelsey's shadow, a part of herself who protected her when she was younger. Wren felt herself and her friends leaving girlhood. Someday we will be mothers, even grandmothers. We allow our childhood protectors to mature with us.

Kelsey coughed and shook herself. She straightened her spine and restarted the fight. 'You forced us to act together, as if you didn't have power over us. You acted as-if.'

'Yes, and now I don't have power over you for real.'

'And that's why you did it.'

'That's what I did, and why.'

'You didn't need to trick us.'

'It wasn't a trick. It was magic. You had to live it.'

Kelsey edges softened. 'I don't want to fight any more.' The lovers stood above the reclining coven, silent. The wind changed and blew clean the ashes. Warmth rekindled.

Robin was speaking. 'I don't know what to do. The ritual… If you want me to swear the Landifesto, I pledge myself to the Ovem, alone together. My memories will serve the present, not preserve the past.'

'*So Mote It Be*,' the witches sang.

Robin lay down between Wren and Nikki. Kelsey remained standing. Like all of them, she appeared naked. Her long hair was loose and wild. Her breasts hung down and touched the top of her big belly. Her arms were like strong, deadly redwood spears, her legs like trunks.

Kelsey got mad. 'Why do we have to leave reality to experience the love we make? Why don't we live in perfect love and trust? Who stole this from us?' Her ritual voice blared hot. 'I know, because of *Patriarchy*. Because men hurt women. They fuck up sex and love, and fuck up everything good and decent. Women fight each other for the scraps men leave them. It's not enough that we love one another. Love alone doesn't heal us. We can't love away those things we named in Gloria's horrible shadow ritual. You can't visualise them gone. I have every right to be pissed off.'

Energised by her anger, the coven rose and stood in a circle with their backs to Kelsey, facing a dark forest. Inside their protection, Kelsey confessed, 'I never let go of Lucy because I didn't fight for her. After the accident, the parents kept me away, like I wasn't her real family. I thought my anger couldn't help. I was too young. But I'm a woman. And my anger will change the world.'

And so Kelsey swore the Landifesto in her own way.

The circle turned to the centre and sang, *So Mote It Be*.

Lupe switched places with Kelsey and spoke from the centre. 'Kelsey, you are so right.' She delicately touched each of their bellies, pulling out a thread. Everyone's skin shimmered gold.

Wren tasted Lupe's tea tingling inside her. She felt the same hope and dread she always felt when she drank Lupe's tea. She wouldn't be poisoned, but she wouldn't be the same.

'Sex between women brings both love and righteous anger,' said Lupe. 'These feelings connect us. We will never have memories like Robin, but we won't have her sorrow, either.' As she spoke, she unfurled a net of golden light above them, knotting it in the limbs of the breathing trees. 'This is how I see the world. I may seem like I'm stoned every day. I will know the world in its perfection, and won't apologise.'

And so Lupe swore the Landifesto in her own way. *So Mote It Be.*

Hazel stepped to the centre. Light from Lupe's golden net threw Hazel's shadow across their bodies. Hazel touched each witch; their skin thickened and darkened, drinking in the light. She sang the song of the sun on the leaves, a wave made firm. Under the network that Lupe had woven, Hazel heaved soil and filled the air with the taste of a flower's eagerness and the perfume of decay.

'I will husband this land, as it is the inheritance of all women, and share the generosity of this fecund chaos.'

And so Hazel swore the Landifesto in her own way. *So Mote It Be.*

Wren knew what to do. She stood in the centre of her sisters to make her vow. So simple and obvious. Her purpose here: to make imagined impossibilities real. She opened her throat and sang in her unpleasant voice, painting the air in story, image and pattern. She clothed her coven in spectacular garments. Eight colours flew from her fingertips and combined into every hue, recording and consigning to some future time: we loved, and lived alone together.

And so Wren swore the Landifesto in her own way. *So Mote It Be.*

Wren stepped back. That was beautiful. But her vow had left her disappointed. Robin and Kelsey, Lupe and Hazel – they had done exactly what they needed to do, and their part of the ritual was perfect. She had thought she might finally see the magical statue that would represent the Ovem's desires and possibilities. But her moment passed, and Nikki stepped forward.

Nikki, the centre of attention like she always avoided. 'My

favourite thing is making love for the first time. And once. That's what I like. I'm not sorry. I love this land, and I love what we're building. Living at Ove and keeping it liveable is my purpose.'

Wren loved Nikki's alchemy, transforming trees into houses, sand into stone, women into lesbians.

Nikki made one quick nod of her head and stepped back.

And so Nikki swore the Landifesto in her own way. *So Mote It Be.*

Ginny, wearing dilating arabesques and paramecium paisley. Ginny, shape-shifting to a psychedelic rhythm, soaring like an owl, gliding like a snake, and emerging from the trees a tawny cougar. Gloria was wrong about so much, but Athena's emblems *were* their animal neighbours. Ginny evolved her transformations: a grey fox, a blue jay, a quail hen, an orange butterfly, a redwood newt. All the animals of their forest, shifting faster and faster, until no one could name one before she became the next. Ginny ended as herself, slightly built and uneven legs and skilled fingers, a young woman with exuberant brown curls that could not hide her tiny horns. She declared something nobody understood.

And so Ginny swore the Landifesto in her own way. *So Mote It Be.*

Far away, in the warmth of a summer sun, the witches draw up their legs, open their vulvas, hold their fists to their chests, and Bear In. Without breath, their bodies lie as seeds, entire, like the instant of death.

When the moment arrived, they laboured, opened their lungs, and roared. Light sprayed from the tops of their heads and the bottoms of their wombs, bright and strong, a trick of light and fluid.

The Landifesto is sworn.

Far away, in the warmth of a summer sun, the witches lie in a circle, head to head, hearts beating red and doughty. A nameless goddess witnesses their intent. Dust motes drift. Woodpeckers chatter.

Kelsey started the song that carried them home. *The Earth, the Water, the Fire, the Air, return, return, return, return.* Each woman sang her part, in a fugue tugging their bodies upward and toward. *Return, return, return, return.*

The witches flew through the astral sky, through the black, then floated, rushing to their robed bodies in a redwood circle in the middle of summer, the land of Ove, their home forever.

The witches sat up and embraced each other, laughing.

'What a trip!'

'That was amazing.'

'Magic is afoot!'

'I love you all so much.'

'Where's Wren?' Robin screamed.

Wren lay inanimate between Nikki and Hazel; her skin cold, and yet she breathed. In. Out.

∞

'*The Earth, the Water, the Fire, the Air, return, return, return, return,*' Kelsey sang. The coven joined in, each of them singing her part.

Wren opened her voice to sing herself home, but it went all wrong. Above her they flew, dark specks in the sky like crows. That was weird. Why did they abandon her? She clenched a scrim of fear, then tore it back and exposed the anger. Anger boiled up from deep below, filling her from root to crown, alone where she never should be alone. They didn't care about her.

Her mother strode out from the forest, incandescent.

'Mom?'

They had left her alone with her *mother*. Mom with hair sprayed solid, a cigarette ablaze, the purse on her elbow, heavy with money and makeup.

Wren turned to face her mother, anger meeting anger, and she understood. This was how she should swear the Landifesto. She needed to get rid of her inner mother, once and for all. She had her home, a sisterhood of love and trust, with the Landifesto to guide them. She was going to fix her shit.

Wren filled with compassion, lifted her hand, and beckoned.

The voice sliced her cheek. 'You think you can run away from me?'

She wrapped arms about her head and waited for it.

'You little crybaby. You were always so sensitive. You think that makes you an artist, with your homemade clothes and your knick-knacks?'

Wren tried to find the solidity of the revelation, about fixing her shit, about getting rid of her mother damage once and forever, but an old theme shrieked in her head like scary music. She sang along perfectly. 'I'm sorry I burned your portrait. I'll make you another one. That was so juvenile.'

'You'd rather see me old and alone.'

'I'll live with you again and take care of you.' She melted into familiar dissociation.

'You'll only run away. You never cared about me!'

'I will now. I'm sorry.'

'You've never really loved me. So ungrateful. I rescued you from the orphanage and raised you *alone*. Do you know how hard that was?'

But when Wren heard the word 'alone', she located a core of herself. She remembered Robin saying 'women alone together' like she always did. She pulled those words around herself like a cloak. 'Mom, I have a life now. I want to share it with you.'

Wren remembered the Landifesto and her sisters. She summoned their love, remembering how anger was righteous and righteous anger brought connection, growth, expression, transformation and union.

She painted it. She showed her mother the truth.

'Will you look at that mess?' came the reply. 'I swear, you were a better artist when you were a child.'

Wren clutched her heart, and a scab between her breasts fell off. 'I hate you.' That felt great. She said it again. '*I hate you.*' The hole behind the scab became a scar.

'Hate me? I *am* you. If it weren't for me, you would never have survived your mother. You *need* me. You'll die if you get rid of me. I saved your life a thousand times.'

'You're *my shadow?*'

'I protected you. I taught you to survive that monster.'

Wren recognised this creature, cultivated in her childhood. Not a monster. 'You need a new job.'

'You'll die without me!'

'I'm no longer that child.' The horrific thing that looked like her mother froze, flattened, tilted, fell to the ground and shrank to the size of a wallet photo. Wren picked it up and secreted it in her robe, for when she might need it again.

And so Wren swore the Landifesto in her own way. *So Mote It Be.*

She found herself at the stump, about to enter the redwood grove. She touched the stump like she always did when she entered the grove, enjoying its surface softness and firmness beneath. She stepped in and saw the four altars. She peeked around at the triangular black opening of the stump.

A voice that came from every direction said, 'Sit down and listen.'

Suddenly Wren was sitting inside the ancient tree, no longer a stump, but alive, rising into the fog.

California approached her. Gloria was right, she did resemble Pallas Athene. She strode toward Wren, majestic, attended by birds and cats, golden with rejuvenation and recreation.

'If you would live on my land, you must tell my story, use your arts to celebrate me. Forget the old goddesses and serve me.'

California personified stood before her, wild and magnificent.

The monster that had protected Wren through her childhood now gave her the strength and courage of an adult woman. 'I won't.'

Wren saw something on California's chest, an emblem with a woman's face. Her hair a nest of snakes. Her eyes bulging. Her teeth bared in labour or orgasm. Scary. Wren wanted that emblem for Ove. She threaded her fingers through the waving snakes. She tugged.

'You don't even know what that symbol means,' California snarled.

'Not yet. I only know someone who called herself Athena stole it from an island of women and kept it for three thousand years. We can live three thousand more and figure it out.'

Wren tore the Medusa free and pressed it to her breasts, *formed of strength and beauty*. The snakes spiralled up and down her backbone, shooting through her mind and into the trees; taking root in her womb, and further, into the duff.

She sang *return, return, return, return* to herself. She sang *the Earth, the Fire, the Water, the Air.* She floated effortlessly through the black and then descended. She released one last long breath.

She sensed she was propped up in someone's lap. She opened her eyes to the anxious faces of Robin, Lupe, Hazel, Nikki and Ginny. She shivered, and Kelsey's arms tightened. 'Why are you looking at me?' she murmured.

'We thought you died out there, sweetheart,' Robin said, putting a calloused palm on Wren's cheek.

Wren lifted her hand and put her thumb against Robin's sad mouth. Robin kissed it.

'Bring her some water,' said Kelsey.

Wren sipped from the chalice Lupe held. She drank it all and was still thirsty.

Ginny tugged at her hair above her ear. 'Are you really back?'

Lupe brought another full chalice to Wren's mouth and before Wren could sip, flicked water in her eyes.

'Quit it!'

'She's back.'

They were the Women of Ove, in a circle outside. And it was time to eat.

Eighteen

A hand-fasting is not a wedding, although Robin and Kelsey publicly declared their intention to be more than lovers. They wanted to show their gratitude for their new lives together, and they wanted an Autumnal Equinox Witches' Thanksgiving that no one could forget. A hand-fasting traditionally lasts a year and a day, which is a magical formula that might mean a year and a day, and it might mean forever.

On a warm afternoon, their friends and lovers, mothers and sisters, gathered in the sacred grove. They sang that Kate Wolf song about giving yourself to love, if love is what you're after. Robin and Kelsey invoked the Elements of the Four Directions, and their love formed a circle that held everyone inside.

They lit matches from a glowing coal, and then their own candles. From the two, they lit everyone's, and the grove blazed with the circle of their sisterhood.

When the ritual ended, Robin and Kelsey left on a road

trip. They would get as far as the Russian River that night, and then head north, visiting Women's Lands.

A hand-fasting is not a wedding.

But the party is the same.

'Hi Wren! I want you to meet someone!'

Gloria. If Wren had wanted to be alone, she wouldn't have been sitting on the octagon porch, in her new blue dress, in full view of guests streaming between the garden and the dance party.

Wren waved, set aside her sketchbook and stood at the railing.

Gloria introduced her guest. 'This is my girlfriend, Lila.'

'Lila, nice to meet you. Thanks for coming.'

Lila had a wide face, big boobs, feathered blonde hair, and wore a coordinated pink and teal short set.

'We met at my new property.' Gloria gave her girlfriend a side hug. Lila looked pleased and awkward. 'She was my real estate agent.'

'That's great! Gloria only told me she met an owl.'

Lila said she loved the ceremony and 'how their love flowed into everyone else's candles'.

Gloria had to ask what she really wanted to know. 'I heard you did that Landifesto ritual.' She even remembered their made-up word for it.

Before Wren could answer, Lila interrupted. 'Gloria, I want to dance. You two catch up.' She gave Gloria an air kiss.

'Enjoy yourself, Lila.' Wren didn't invite Gloria to sit on the porch with her. She wished she could, but she wasn't that healthy yet.

Gloria admitted that she and Lila weren't out as a couple. 'She's afraid her husband will take the kids. This is her first lesbian party.'

'She's straight?'

'Not any more.' Gloria tried to appear salacious but only sounded pathetic.

Wren decided she could answer Gloria's question. 'We swore the Landifesto, like I told you we would.'

'You swore to dedicate yourselves to the land.'

'More like a reconciliation. We know what we do and why.'

'You know how well women keep their promises to each other.'

Wren laughed, as if Gloria knew what she was talking about. The Landifesto was a secret to be experienced, never revealed.

Gloria looked across the plaza toward the party, then turned back and extended her arms in a kind of blessing. 'Wren, you look better than ever. I'll leave you alone to your cartoons.'

Wren watched her borrow a drum and fall instantly into the rhythm. She was so good at that. Gloria would remain part of their community. Despite their differences, they wouldn't exclude her.

Wren sat back down, and listened to the women's voices, women's music. While Robin and Kelsey were gone, she'd fill Kelsey's Sphere. She'd never be the chatelaine, but she looked forward to digging through Kelsey's recipe box and coordinating meals with the harvest.

She took a sip of mead and finished a piece of cake, utterly satisfied. Because she was happy, she thought about death and how someday she would be an old woman, maybe dying at Ove. She felt grown-up, feeling like an older sister to those younger women dancing in the plaza. They needed her art.

She began sketching on a new page. Since her vision in the Landifesto, she had explored the Medusa: snakes, eros, attraction of women for women, the lesbian power to create and transform and – in a way – live forever. The magical statue she had long sought was the mask of the shadow. Like in a sacred play, the mask got a body when a living woman wore it. She could then learn who she was, and why. Wren looked forward to future revelations, though they already frightened her a little.

Lupe, Hazel and Ginny appeared on the road in front of her with a woman Wren didn't recognise. She was a little older than they were. Her wavy black hair was grey at the temples. She wore a faded embroidered Indian tunic like an old hippie and was thin like a life-long vegetarian. Her eyes were sad.

'Wren! We found you!' Lupe called up.

'This is Abby!' Hazel said the name as if Wren had been looking for her.

Ginny skipped forward, tugging the visitor by her hand. 'Abby is like Robin. She remembers all her past lives.'

Acknowledgements

In writing this psychedelic lesbian feminist pagan utopia novel, I drew on a lifetime of reading other authors' scholarship and visions, too many to list. So there's a bibliography at lindarosewood.com. For key notions in the story, I must mention three influences. I was inspired by the discoveries found in Vicki Noble's *The Double Goddess: Women Sharing Power*. For forty years I have enjoyed Sarah Schulman's novels and essays, but her *Conflict is Not Abuse: Overstating Harm, Community Responsibility and the Duty of Repair* clarified my understanding of conflict resolution and why everyone must practise it. Finally, Clark Heinrich gave us *Magic Mushrooms in Religion and Alchemy* and now every religion makes sense to atheist me.

The dozen or so readers who gave early feedback include two women who pointed out that one of my neologisms was already in use on the internet in a disgusting context, thus saving me much embarrassment. I'm thankful for the encouragement of my discord writing group, especially our beloved founder, whom I can't name because we are all anonymous.

My friends Irene Reti, Hilary Hamm, Helen Simmons McCleary, Jessica Bernstein, Richard von Busack, Andrea Hesse, Lori Klein, Ellen Farmer, Roger Swain, Sally North, Joan McCarthy, T.D. Mehlman and Michelle Erickson read drafts and offered feedback with skill and honesty. They never said they were tired of me talking about my imaginary world.

Some people may wonder why two men (publisher Dan Hiscocks and editor Simon Edge) published a novel about lesbian separatists. If you look at the Eye/Lightning catalogue, you'll see it's full of humorous books about interesting communities with serious themes. I'm grateful and proud to be among the authors they believe in.

Writing a novel is lonesome work, but I wrote *A Circle Outside* in the delightful and constant company of my wife, Artemis Crow. I owe her everything.